# Promise of the Betrayer's Dagger

JAY TALLSQUALL

# Dedication

*To my Dad.*

*His example built the foundation of the man I am today and continues to be my inspiration for who I hope to become.*

# Table of Contents

## LOSS AND FOUND

# Author's Note

The relationships between fathers and sons are never straightforward or easy, and it often is too late when they discover just how simple it all could have been.

At the core, there is always love if they both are just willing to see it.

****Content Warning: Mild Gore and Body Horror, Eye Injury, Ritualistic Self Harm****

# Map of the Rhymera

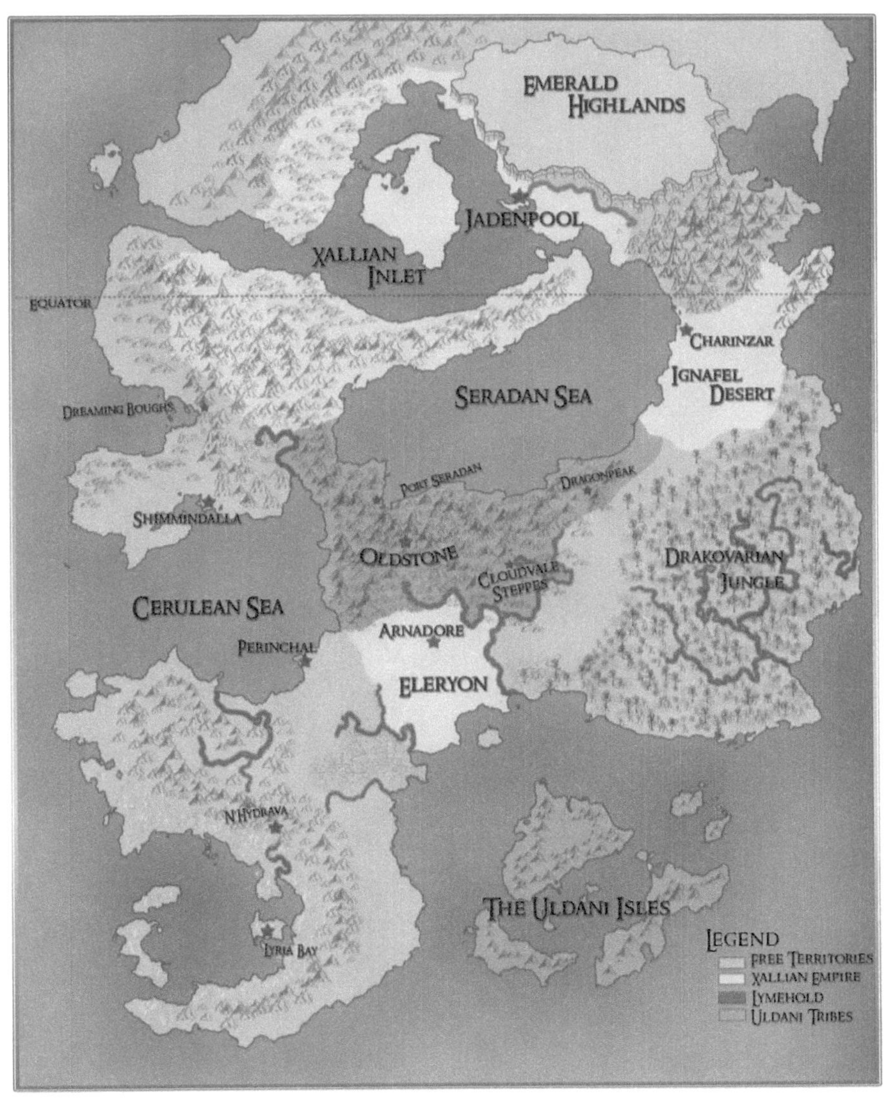

# Detail of the Uldani Isles



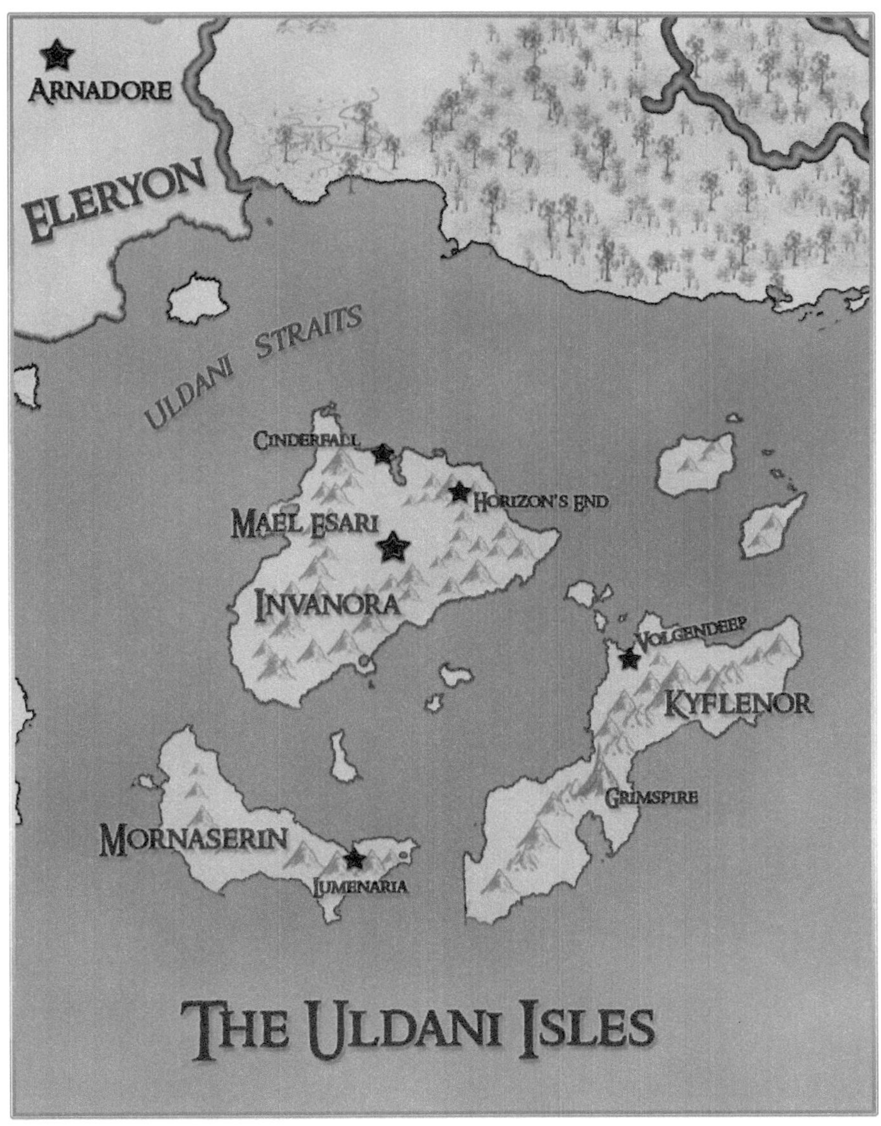

# PROLOGUE

*Year 874 PXF (Post Xallia Founding) ~ Late Spring*

The last traitor of Arnadore Keep sat in the Hall of Judgement awaiting his rendering. The weeks prior had seen two dozen executions of the seditionists who conspired against the Emperor, and as intended, the populace of Jadenpool had now wearied of the spectacle. Even the unique circumstance of this last conspirator failed to reignite the interest of the noble factions of the capital.

Veronic Cour-Vermane entered the circular chamber deep within the black marble walls of the Hall of Judgement as her station dictated was her right. The raised gallery where she sat overlooked the accused. He was in chains, seated in a severe, low-backed stone chair perched on the small dais at the center of the room. Surrounding the accused were the seven Speakers. Each sat at a point of the Star of Fate, dressed in white robes with tight-fitting elbow-length gloves.

Brushed platinum masks devoid of expression covered their faces, each enameled with the mark of their station: War's red sword, Prosperity's silver coin, Diplomacy's crossed olive leaf and dagger, Divine's golden ring of light, Arcana's blue flames, Labor's black silhouetted worker, and Peace's white dove. The speakers all wore a blood-red mantle, symbolizing the seriousness of the crime they judged and the verdict they would render. The accused, positioned in the star's center, was faced so only two of the seven figures deciding their fate flanked their eyeline. In this judgment, their gaze fell between War and Diplomacy.

Osman sat slouched with head lolling slightly to one side, blank eyes facing forward, a limp corpse with no more life than a doll made of flesh.

Veronic's face, as still as ice in midwinter, gave no hint of her approval at seeing his catatonic state. She had visited his cell two nights earlier.

The Emperor had placed Osman in the deepest, most dilapidated portion of the dungeons below the Hall, but that hadn't deterred Veronic from her visit. She had been in far worse places. Veronic knew that when she spoke to Osman, her words would need to be more than just a slap in the face to reach him; they would need to jar him with the force of a knee to the groin. She had discovered over her life most assumed her delicacy as a noblewoman was unimpeachable, but they had not endured the life she had lived.

The guard opened the door to Osman's cell for Veronic as though he was opening the door of the Imperial Palace. She had purchased his compliance and discretion with a laughably small number of enchanted platinum coins that would magically hold the guard's tongue if it began to wag about her visit. The esteemed lady of House Cour-Vermane strode into the cell without pause. Excrement and filth covered every surface, and there in the corner, huddled in abject misery, was Osman.

"Do not speak. They monitor your every word," Veronic warned as she stepped into the center of the cell. "Mine, however, are undetectable." Her hands smoothed the angled hem of her midnight-green fitted duster coat, and she paid no mind to her long, narrow-cut gray walking skirt dragging in the muck. "We've never spoken, but I would hope you know who I am as you were bedding my whore of a niece under the roof of my estate." Veronic's words were flatly stated as fact, reserving any accusation and judgment for Cerena alone, which made them hit Osman all the harder.

Osman's gaze lifted and met hers, the slightest ember of Uldani rage bringing clarity to his thoughts momentarily. His chapped lips opened in an attempt to form words, but Veronic held a finger of her black-gloved hand to her lips for silence. *Good,* she thought to herself, she had his attention. "You have been used. Cruelly, maliciously, and with exacting premeditation. Cerena executed her seduction of you for one reason and one reason only: because my husband ordered it. You were a pawn my husband needed to fulfill his aspirations and to enact his manipulation of my son."

Veronic studied Osman's reaction to see if her words were sinking in; seeing his eyes narrow, she continued. "Perhaps you were contemplating confessing your actions to the Speakers to fulfill some code of honor and die with the rest of Duke Issul's guard. Or perhaps give your life out of loyalty or love for Cerena to show your faithfulness to her cause?" Veronic examined the dried blood surrounding his eyes and trails leaking from his ears. "Or maybe even out of pure cowardice, realizing that your actions brought death and misery to so many innocent lives. A truth that has undoubtedly drifted to your ears even down here."

Osman lowered his eyes from hers. The Lady Cour-Vermane stepped forward and bent at the waist to bring her face to Osman's, lifting his chin with her gloved hand. "Tying one's honor and loyalty to those with neither is to play into their game. My husband will pay no price for what he has done. Cerena held no love for you. Not when she left you weeping on your knees in my courtyard nor when she reached out for you to be her courier through the Winter. You were nothing more than a tool my husband commanded her to use."

Osman wanted to turn his head away, but Lady Cour-Vermane's delicate fingers held his chin like iron. Veronic knew she could now make her proposal.

"If you owe anyone your loyalty and honor, it is your Krolh'dran." Osman's eyes widened and locked onto hers. She raised a knowing eyebrow as she spoke. "Oh yes, I know the meaning of those braids you put into Talon's hair the night of my Gala."

Veronic paused to hammer home her accusation. "You abandoned your soul brother when he needed you most. Yet even after betraying your bond to him, my son still saved your life." Her gaze bored into Osman like a knife. "You may have run away from the Isles, but you can't escape the blood that flows in your veins and the bonds your people made to the elements when they split from the elves. You owe my son a Qat'malorn, and I expect you to pay your debt as a betrayer of his love for you by choosing to live."

Veronic stood back up. "You need not lie. Just say nothing at all. Sink back into the madness the Emperor ensured would visit you by placing you here. I will take care of the rest." She straightened her gloves. "Then do whatever is necessary to redeem yourself in my son's eyes." Veronic left the cell without another word.

To influence the outcome of a rendering would require leverage over all forty-nine potential Speakers who could have ascended to each of the seven stations of Judgement. Coordinating four dozen pieces on a bureaucratic chessboard muddied with intrigue and fraught with peril would be considered political suicide for any of the nobility, but not Veronic Cour-Vermane. She had spent decades of her extended life honing her ability to move mountains by displacing pebbles, and as such, she had been gifted many favors through the years, one of which was about to come due.

Veronic rose from the deep curtsey she had assumed to show proper deference to Emperor Brinton Aurorus while his staff remained in his private spell-warded chamber.

"Veronic, I cannot allow your husband's involvement in this treachery to go unanswered," the Emperor spoke with candor once they were alone.

Lady Cour-Vermane looked the Emperor directly in the eyes, "Brinton, I am not here for my husband." His visage rankled from the use of his first name so casually, but curiosity held his tongue from any rebuke. He instead raised a manicured dark eyebrow at his guest.

"The Uldani guard. He is not to be executed. Exile shall be his sentence." Veronic's request continued in a measured, weighted cadence. "You know the facts of his involvement. He lifted no weapon against the Empire, and therefore, no harm shall come to him." She crossed to the crowned ruler of the Xallian Empire's desk, where he sat blinking in disbelief.

The Emperor's face flushed further at the demand. "He is a traitor to my throne!" the Emperor bit back his words through clenched teeth—a caged outburst atypical of the Emperor's usual measured demeanor.

Veronic placed a book upon his desk, sliding it under the Emperor's gaze. She added in clipped cadence, never breaking eye contact, "I think I must *insist* on this matter." The color that had risen drained from Brinton Aurorus' face as he glanced down and recognized the book before him. Veronic turned and left without waiting on an answer but added as she exited, "I expect that returned to me after the Uldani's rendering."

Staring up at the Emperor like a scorpion poised to strike was the book Lady Cour-Vermane had left: *200 Years of Blood: A History of the Xallian -Uldani War.*

Back in the sterile marble chamber of the Hall of Judgment where Osman awaited his fate, no words were spoken, as was the custom. Veronic looked on as the Bell of Fate rang seven times; on each tolling, one Speaker raised a white-gloved hand which then turned black—the vote of exile. Lady Cour-Vermane did not linger; she had heard Blossom Festival in Jadenpool was quite a sight to behold, and her dear friend Kristoff Callesen had five ships in port for the celebration.

# Part I

## Wounds of the Soul

### CHAPTER ONE



The abusive guards who had watched over Osman in the dungeon had 'helpfully' encased him within a complete set of guard's half-plate armor after enjoying a final beating of their favorite prisoner. They also loaded him with a pack of heavy provisions and equipment to ensure their plan succeeded. With much grumbling at their slow progress, the two guards escorted their stumbling, catatonic charge through the passageways until they finally reached their destination. Having taken far longer than their attention span could be asked to endure and eager to be away from the fussy condescension of the mages who ordered them about, the dungeon guards considered their duties fulfilled as soon as they released Osman's manacles and placed his rigid form on the transit platform.

Standing on the teleportation circle, Osman watched from under languid eyelids as the guards who escorted him abandoned him to his fate. As soon as they exited the room and closed the heavy iron door, his hands sprang into action.

Osman yanked open buckles and unfastened straps as he stripped off the heavy armor and poured out the pack's contents, letting it all drop to the floor around his feet. The flurry of his movement and the muffled commotion he was creating worked exactly as he hoped and prevented the mages from beginning their incantation. As he dumped the equipment onto the transit platform, including an iron ingot, Osman was surprised to feel the weight of something remaining within the upended pack. Reaching inside, his fingers encountered a false bottom and felt the familiar flow of healing energy course up his arm and through his body—a restoration rune.

Osman did not react to his discovery of the hidden compartment and the new vitality he felt in front of the mages and startled squire assigned as their security. He returned a wadded-up light tunic, tinderbox, flint, and a single length of rope to the emptied pack, leaving whatever lay under the false bottom undisturbed for investigation later.

The doffing of the armor had only taken a moment, and Osman knew if he attempted to delay any longer, the mages would call back the surly guards who escorted him here. If they returned, he would get no second chances. Strapping the nearly empty satchel tightly to his torso and standing barefoot and shirtless on the magical transit runes, Osman raised his hands in acquiescence to his fate, allowing the mages to cast their spell in peace. Osman took a deep breath and braced himself as the arcane energies gathered around him; he knew what was coming.

The spell completed with the familiar rush of translocation, and Osman materialized twenty feet beneath the ocean's surface in the frigid and deadly currents of the Uldani Straits. The shimmering sunlight that penetrated into the depths revealed dozens upon dozens of suits of heavy armor and a field of sunken cargo. The armor and items he had rid himself of on the transit platform had accompanied him and fell to the graveyard that covered the ocean floor. They joined the remains of those who had tried to circumvent the protective magical wards around the Uldani Isles and had their transit intercepted, depositing them here.

Osman was familiar with this place. All children who lived on Invanora, the largest isle of the Uldani nation, were. As a boy, he often braved these currents and dark waters to pluck some piece of treasure from the outside world for his collection. Letting his memory of those times guide him, he relaxed his body and let the current sweep him westward. Osman didn't spend energy on swimming, only a scant few strokes to get his head to the surface for air. He would need all his strength for what was to come.

Osman was just over a hundred yards offshore but knew the folly of being lured to swim toward the beach. A reef of volcanic glass strong enough to slice open the hull of even the stoutest ships lay just below the surface, whose razor edges would rend through flesh and bone as easily as any chef's blade.

Just as he began to worry he had misjudged his location, Osman spotted the familiar break in the reef from his childhood. Powerful strokes learned here on his native shores drove him through the freezing waters and treacherous currents. Timing his approach with the breaking surf rolling over the reef, Osman threw his arms over his head and let the wave thrust him through the gap in the Isle's deadly natural bulwark. Once deposited in the relatively calm shallows on the other side, Osman began to swim toward shore before the frigid waters sapped away what little strength he had left.

Gasping for breath and near exhaustion, Osman staggered ashore. Adrenaline and a primal instinct to put as much distance between him and the cell that had entombed him under the Hall of Judgement pushed his body further up the beach. He finally collapsed on a tide-worn craggy rock that punched through the sand like an old tooth. Numb fingers struggled to pull the pack he had strapped tightly to his torso off his back, letting it fall to the rocky sand. Osman's muscles spasmed as the emotion driving his flight from his captors faded. Its *qil*, the tactile sensation that accompanied a corresponding emotion in the Uldan people—in this case, the feeling of hundreds of tiny points of sparking lightning across his skin that, for Osman, was always paired to his flight response– also began to lessen.

Somehow, after everything he had endured, he still lived.

When his breath finally slowed and he had flexed some feeling back into his fingers, curiosity spurred Osman into action. He sat up and pulled the satchel he had sloughed off his back to his side. Digging past the tunic and rope, Osman fumbled with the concealed closures of the hidden compartment and opened it, anxious to see what lay within. His unexpected patron had gifted him a pair of well-crafted leather boots and, shockingly, the iron dagger Talon had stabbed him with to save his life.

Examining the boots, Osman found a small, embroidered outline of a magnolia blossom inside the folded-over cuff at the calf. Trusting he knew who they had been gifted by, Osman slipped them on and found an enchantment perfectly resized them to his wide feet, accommodating even his long toes. Any other secrets the boots held were not immediately evident, but his Krolh'dran's dagger being present in the bag left no further doubt about his patron's identity and Lady Cour-Vermane's message: a gift and an obligation.

A cold gust of wind raised goosebumps on Osman's wet skin. Even at the height of Summer, the coasts of the Isles were chilly as the currents that swirled around their coastlines welled up from the depths under the frozen expanse of Icefel to the South. However, Osman couldn't attribute his pimpled flesh only to the breeze and damp clothes.

He was home.

When he closed his eyes, he could feel the elemental pulse of the Isles pressing against his skin. The rainbow geysers and fog-shrouded titan forests of Mornaserin, the Invanorian lava fields and bustling covered thoroughfares of Mael Esari, and even the howling winds of the lonely tundra and glacial falls of Kyflenor seemed to thrum in welcome to one of their own returning to its shores.

No qil leaped to the fore to guide Osman in deciphering his emotional state. Being back home - exhausted, cold, and alone - he closed his eyes, turned his head skyward, and did something he had not done in over two decades. He let out a *sha'feruat*, the primal scream all children of the Isles were taught as an outlet when they could not find a direction for their emotions.

Osman intended it to be no more than a quick yelp, but once the scream began, his emotions flooded into it, and it thundered out of his lungs like an avalanche. He screamed until he was out of breath and then gulped down more air and screamed some more. Qil raced through his body in a tangled cacophony. His hands tore at his hair and raked across his tear-stained face as he fell to his knees on the rocky beach, but none of the qil compared to the pain in his heart. The roar of the surf and relentless gusts of wind seemed to join him in vocalizing his torment. As his anguish continued pouring out of him, his mind pulled forth all it had shrouded from him to survive the dungeons.

He had betrayed the only true family he had. The brother who had tried to save him with his words, and when Osman had failed to listen, he had saved him with his dagger. Out of honor and obligation, Osman would have fought alongside the Arnadore Watch against the Jadenarme had he been able. Hearing how the battle mages slaughtered the guards he trained and how his comrades on Duke Issul's guard were captured and executed, Osman knew his life would have been forfeit had he raised arms against the Empire. Despite having that knowledge, what had followed in many ways made him wish he had died in Arnadore Keep or been given the immediate mercy of the guillotine.

Caging a person of Uldani heritage for even a matter of days, more often than not, is a death sentence. Once despair sets in, an Uldani's instinctive embrace of experiences magnifies it, and there is little that can stop the emotional cascade of qil that eventually snuffs out their will to live. Osman had been buried alive in a magically-warded cell for over a month. Every day, more details from the trials above trickled down to his ears, confirming everything his Krolh'dran had told him, deepening the depth of his betrayal. He could not say what kept him alive past the first week of revelations. Every time his heart began to slow, life blissfully leaving his body, he was yanked back to his misery by what felt like a ring of thorns digging into his heart, not a qil but something else entirely.

The following weeks were a walk through the darkest of the hells. Every breath was like drowning in mud, every forced heartbeat a biting agony. Osman had tried to dig his eardrums out with his fingernails to stop hearing the painful recounting of the atrocities his actions had contributed to. Qil turned his tears to blood that flowed down his face as he begged every element to grant him a release from his torment. When the stately woman walked into his cell, there was so little left of Osman he did not recognize her until her words slapped him awake.

Osman had lied to himself that perhaps Cerena had actually loved him, that she was an unwitting participant, and maybe she would find it in her heart to come and save him from this torture. Talon's mother destroyed that fantasy. Her words had cut so profoundly because if he was truthful, Osman had known that throughout the previous Winter he had allowed himself to be guided by misplaced hope. A hope that Cerena's renewed affections were confirmation that he was somehow rekindling their love by committing the treasons she requested of him. Lady Cour-Vermane had rendered that to no more than a childish daydream. However, he still could not dispel his belief that Cerena may have felt something for him back in Arnadore when they first met, and she had been his first true love.

Staying quiet during the interrogation prior to his rendering had not been hard. The questioners seemed shocked he was alive, and his condition alone spoke volumes. He needed only to sink back into the place his mind had inhabited for the weeks of eternity he had spent in the cell. The mage who probed his thoughts ran from the room, retching after brushing against his mind and sharing his emotional state. Even his unresponsiveness under spells of truth-telling was attributed to madness and despair. He remained an impassive zombie until the last moments in the teleportation chamber when he prepared for the transit here.

As his mind returned to the present, reinhabiting his body lying prone on the beach, Osman found he was still screaming. His vocal cords long since strained beyond the ability to continue making sound, his scream no more than a croaking burble. Osman fell to his side on the cold, rocky sand and curled into himself. Eyes barely above the pebbles that made up the shore, he stared at the bruised surf, catching his breath with wracking sighs, qil slowly fading from him. Twenty years of exile. With so much time and distance separating them, how could he ever earn the forgiveness of his Krolh'dran and fulfill the Qat'malorn Lady Cour-Vermane had invoked?

Nearly an hour passed as Osman lay motionless on the beach until the chills shaking his body demanded that he move, and the debt he carried insisted that he survive. He gathered pieces of driftwood and flotsam that littered the beach and coaxed a spark out of his tinderbox to make a fire in the lee of a grouping of the toothy rocks that punctured the shore. Osman retrieved the tunic from his pack, spreading it out to dry. He then settled into the small sanctuary of stones to think. Talon's iron dagger had found its way into his hands, and he contemplated it as he rotated it over and over again, the point digging into the callouses marring his fingers.

He knew the course he must follow, but he had yet to be able to force the voicing of it in his mind. He needed to go to his father's home. Being back on the Isles was not enough. He needed to go to Horizon's End, where he grew up—the place Osman had banished from his life nearly a decade ago.

Returning home would not be joyous nor provide a place to live out his exile. His only reason to venture there was because that was where he could perhaps find answers—clues to what had happened with his father and Richen.

The dagger's point bit into Osman's hand as it slipped off the callous on which he had been spinning it. He stared at the single drop of blood that welled up. It was a full day's journey up the mountains to his old home, and while Summer's daylight lingered far later in these southern reaches of the world, it was folly to begin the trek at this late hour. Shrugging on his mostly dry tunic, Osman collected enough wood to feed the fire through the night, along with some surf plums for sustenance.

Settling into his makeshift hovel and savoring the comforting flavor of roasted plums, Osman looked out over the sea at the breathtaking sunset. As the waves pounded the rocky shore, the elemental energies that bound all Uldani to these isles flowed through him like a cleansing tide. While so many parts of him reveled in the familiarity and reconnection to his homeland, the jagged stone of his memories remained unmoved.

# CHAPTER TWO

*Year 874 PXF ~ Early Summer*

Dawn broke across the rocks and surf of the Uldani Isles, the Summer sun having barely skirted below the horizon for a scant six hours. The shining glow of morning lightened Osman's eyelids, pulling him out of a sleep that had swung like a pendulum from deep restoration to restless torment as his time in captivity below the Halls of Judgement refused to be exorcised from his subconscious. Even after Osman had gathered his things and tarried among the tidepools, the hour at which he set out for Horizon's End was still painfully early by any standard other than that of bakers and the most diligent farmers.

Heading along the shore sorely tempted Osman, where he would eventually come to the fortified port city of Cinderfall. Even though diplomats ended the war with the Empire a century and a half ago, the port still proudly displayed its battle scars. It bustled with the many Uldani who were unable or unwilling to leave the war behind them and craved the emotional addictions that were Cinderfall's hallmark at the height of the Xallian conflict. Osman knew months or years could slip by, perhaps even his whole exile if he dived deep into the qil provided there. While tempted by the excuse it offered to change his destination, Cinderfall's siren call did not sway Osman from his path. As much as he dreaded it, he turned inland toward the cliffs and mountains where Horizon's End lay.

Most who walked the panoramic trail leading to Horizon's End would spend hours engulfed by the qil of the sheer thrilling wonder it presented around every twist and turn. They would amble awestruck by the towering cliffs bisected by arrays of waterfalls, high verdant meadows filled with carpets of shimmering wildflowers, tranquil grottos with secret burbling brooks, and valleys as still as a cathedral made silent by towering sentinel evergreens. The journey could take days for some, unable to keep from stopping and gorging themselves on the tactile cornucopia their qil distilled from the majesty surrounding them.

These same vistas had called his father here over three and a half centuries ago, each scene along the meandering path washing away the emotional onslaught of the war that harrowed his every moment within the sprawl, heat, and ash of Mael Esari. Architavia Therandus, Farseer of the Argutheris, Holy Champion, and Shaman of Tamul Vigos the Living Breeze, built his sanctuary and home high atop the cliffs that marked the eastern ridge of the isle of Invanora. While the proper name of his refuge was *Sorna'toc* or 'where the sky dies' when accurately translated from the old tongue, modern romantics and admirers of Osman's father had softened the name into Horizon's End.

Long before Osman's father became known as the Farseer, a shaman, or holy in any sense of the word, he was simply Architavia, and most just called him Tavi. At that time, predating everything his future held for him, Tavi, a child of the war, had been an artist. When the rest of Uldani society had embraced the tumultuous flood of righteous anger, patriotism, and sacrifice that accompanied the war, Tavi had fled to the wondrous beauty of the mountains to try and capture their timeless hope and a dream of peace.

For Osman, any qil from the spectacle of the familiar vistas that so inspired his father did not exist. He might as well have been walking through a barren landscape without features or interest. It wasn't that he had grown bored of it from dozens of times traversing this path or had never felt its soaring joy in his heart. He once had.

Osman had done the unthinkable, a sin and transgression of the highest order to all Uldani. Eight years ago, when he left his father and Sorna'toc behind him, he severed all his emotions tied to this place in a ritual most Uldani considered akin to self-mutilation.

Osman had no idea what kind of reception he might encounter at Horizon's End. Only three months had passed since word of his father's death had reached him, and as such, it was well within the mourning period observed by many, but also enough time had transpired that the *Allinari*, a ritual celebration of an Uldani's life, could be in full swing. If the denizens of Horizon's End were true to form, both could be happening simultaneously.

In the century following the Xallian war's end, a revolving cavalcade of artists and visitors passed through Horizon's End. By Osman's birth, their encampments had littered the property with dozens of newer structures spread around the cliffside thermal pools, towering evergreens, and glacial streams. The commune's population could swell to over fifty residents in the Spring and Summer months and dwindle to less than a dozen during the dark, frigid Winters. The ever-changing cast of inhabitants created both a wonderland and a warped dystopia for a young child. With his birth parents absent throughout his childhood and early adolescence, Osman had a rotating gallery of caregivers who raised him, none of whom seemed to linger more than a season or two.

The likelihood of finding a familiar face, much less someone he trusted enough to try and begin untangling the last decades of his father's life, was slim. Even during the eighteen years he had lived at Horizon's End, there were less than a handful of guests that returned regularly and those that did flit through the enclave like an errant breeze.

When Osman reached the outskirts of his father's home, the sun was low in the sky, its ruddy orb threatening to present yet another 'once-in-a-lifetime' sunset of stunning vibrancy and magnificence. The current residents of Horizon's End had all gathered outside as always. They filled the common areas around the main lodge and outbuildings to feast on the qil inspired by the spectacle nature would serve up for the evening.

Osman spotted many still wearing ice blue, the color of mourning inherited from the time before the Uldani split from their elven cousins, but others had already donned the blazing scarlet, orange, and yellows of the Allinari. To Osman, the jumbled dichotomy of the rituals was a disappointing reminder of his rudderless childhood subjected to the fickle whims of any caregiver who decided to take him on as a project and drift into his life for a time.

Obscured by the dark silhouette he presented against the bright western sky, Osman examined the crowd and saw only strangers. As his identity resolved, a wave of discomfort rippled across the gathering as qil manifested in those who had spotted him. Some wrapped their cloaks more tightly around their shoulders. Others fidgeted as though their clothes were suddenly made from crawling ants. A few shifted their feet as though needing to catch their balance on a swaying ship. At least two gifted with empathic resonance turned and retched, unable to hold back their nausea at sensing the aftereffects of the ritual he had performed upon himself.

For those who did not already know of him, Osman's identity spread quickly among those gathered. There were any number of reasons for him not to be welcome here at his father's home. Whether it be judgment, pity, disgust, empathy, hatred, dismissal, or even a thirst for the drama he might cause, every eye and posture held a message for Osman. Even so, no one approached or stopped him as he crossed the courtyard.

The sea of unmasked emotions and whispers of derision parted to allow him to pass. Osman traversed the bald stone of the compound and entered the main lodge. None followed. For the gathered crowd, a more critical experience was at hand; the sun had started its show, and a wayward son's return could be confronted later.

Osman was not surprised that the lodge's main room had been rearranged again, the same as it had always done every season when he was a boy. A few pieces of décor and furniture were familiar, but most were new and unmatched, all individually added without concern or care to the overall aesthetic. Osman crossed the great room to the hallway that led to a single destination: his father's chambers.

As was the custom, the lintel above the door had been marked with ice-blue ink, effectively sealing the room from prying eyes or sticky fingers until the period of grief and mourning was complete. Having little reverence for the tradition of his people or his father, Osman did not let the mark stop him. He opened the unlocked door without hesitation or emotion and stepped across the threshold. Breaking mourning protocol, he locked the door behind him.

Architavia Therandus' suite of rooms was a residence unto itself within the larger main lodge, much of it comprised of the original abode his father had built before additions and expansion had created the main building of Horizon's End as it now existed. These rooms had been Osman's one constant in his childhood, including their current state of housing only echoes of his father and not the man himself.

Osman was ecstatic. Perched on his knees, looking over the back of the couch at the door, his small form vibrated with anticipation as he waited. His father, the man he only knew from the stories he diligently read, then had fought and struggled to remember, even though every adult said it was folly even to try, was coming home. Osman knew his dad had left less than a year after his birth on an *Omenara*, a fated journey. Now, six years later, he was returning.

Osman never knew his mother and had no memory of her. Adults at Horizon's End whimsically teased him that at every introduction from as soon as he learned the word, he had asked each person he met, male or female, if they were his mother. For reasons Osman never understood, the storyteller would add with a ruffle of his hair as though it was some excellent jest, "Well, and of course, none of them were."

Osman's current caretaker was a genial and ruggedly handsome sculptor named Anson. He had been looking after Osman for the last two years while he painstakingly worked on a towering sculpture carved out of a single ironwood log as tall as the grand hall of the lodge. He even showed Osman how to use a wood chisel and gifted him a small one with a dulled edge to practice with. When Osman asked Anson why he sculpted instead of painting like everyone else at Horizon's End, the sculptor stopped his work and squatted down in front of Osman.

"A painting is an experience for your eyes where the artist guides you into seeing only what they saw and how they saw it." Looking up at his massive project, he continued reverently. "A sculpture is the sharing of a memory, real or imagined, for each person to view from their own perspective. You can change your experience with light and angle and even time." Anson lifted Osman with his strong arms to reach and touch the area he had been sanding, "Or decide to see it without using your eyes at all."

Anson's words ignited Osman's creativity, especially after his precocious struggle with committing the stories in the Xallian books about his father to memory over the past year. Osman wanted to create a sculpture of something unique like Anson was doing with the ironwood tree out behind the lodge. However, being just shy of seven years old, he couldn't think of anything special he had experienced personally. Two days later, an idea came to him, but he didn't know where to start. That morning at breakfast, as Anson pulled roasted mushrooms out of the oven, Osman asked, "How do you sculpt an idea?"

"Well, ideas can be the easiest and hardest," Anson mused. "The slightest impression or infinite details can represent them. Often, what matters is context."

"What's context?" Osman asked innocently.

"Context is what's not necessarily in the sculpture, but what's around it or the experiences that inform or created it," Anson explained in a knowing, patient tone that Osman recognized as him preparing for all his further questions.

"Oh," Osman replied sagely.

Osman always liked that Anson patiently waited for him to think and ask his questions before returning to his adult things. But this time, Osman had heard all he needed to hear, so he finished his breakfast and headed to his room with determination. He could feel Anson's eyes following him, but his caretaker did not call him back suspiciously like most adults when he set his mind to something. Anson just remained sitting at the table, sipping his coffee.

Once in his room, Osman retrieved the wood chisel gifted to him by his current guardian and prepared to begin his first sculpture, which he might never finish, but he hoped he would not have to continue to work on beyond today. There was one thing Osman knew was unique about him from his books. He didn't have his father or mother raising him.

He lifted his chisel to the log that ran over the head of his bed and made a single deep vertical mark. That was Anson. Biting his tongue and squinching up his face, he put two more slashes to the left of Anson's – they were 'context': the two caretakers that had come before Anson that he had fleeting memories of. He knew there were probably more prior to that but including them felt like a lie since he couldn't remember them at all.

The gouges in the wood were just to the left of the bed. That way, Osman would see them as he went to sleep each night and again when he woke up each morning, the light catching them differently and the angle changing as he moved from standing to sitting to prone. Almost-seven-year-old Osman smiled at his first sculpture, not realizing the pain it would indelibly capture over the next decade.

*Present Year 874* PXF ~ *Early Summer*

The central room of Tavi's residence seemed to have been locked in amber for the eight years he had been away. Osman spotted the same tattered knit blanket he grew up with haphazardly thrown over the back of the ancient broken-in couch that faced away from the door. Heavy curtains covered the curved bay of windows across from it, hiding the most envied view in all of Horizon's End. The same unfinished painting, a representation of dawn breaking upon the cliffs beyond the covered window, sat on an easel adjacent to the closed curtains. It had remained frozen in the identical position and state of completion as it was from Osman's earliest memory.

It was the only painting, finished or otherwise, in the abode outside his father's studio, whose door stood unlatched beyond the easel.

The collected mementos from Architavia Therandus' life before Osman still perched on every surface and clung to every nook. They were as unchanged as the hand-laid stacked stone walls that transitioned to rough-hewn logs as they climbed toward the open rafters of the ceiling. Each room differed as to where that boundary between stone and tree lay based on his father's aesthetic or whim as he built Horizon's End. If there was some secret behind its meaning, Osman had never been able to decipher it.

Osman drifted around the rooms, disconnected from the nostalgia or sentiment any living being would have in the same circumstance. In the small kitchen, he recognized the iron kettle from his childhood hanging near the hearth, and the memory of smokey Mael Esari spices haunted the air. His father's bedchamber was still dominated by the deep feather bed Osman had crawled into alone many times as a child to pretend his father was home.

Across the living space and down an awkward hallway lay the one addition to Architavia Therandus' rooms since its original construction. The door was closed, and the hinges creaked deeply as though they had not once been exercised in the time he had been away. Unlike the rest of his father's residence, within Osman's bedroom dust lay deeply over his belongings. Where time had seemed to have stopped elsewhere in his former home, here it seemed to have raced forward in a sprint.

His once cherished books were scattered across the floor. The quickly constructed shelves on which he had meticulously stored them as a child had finally buckled like a ship's keel broken on the rocks, its cargo spilling across a foreign shore. The bed seemed laughably small after the relative luxury of his bed and the beds he had shared in Arnadore. The bedclothes and quilt that laid upon it sagged from time and weight. The stitching and fabric stretched like weary flesh too long of this world. To the left of the bed, just above the height of the headboard, was his first and last sculpture, the log with twenty-one crudely carved hash marks Osman had made there.

The light that weakly penetrated through the threadbare curtains was fading, and the weariness of the long trek from the shore hit Osman. Combined with his time in captivity and the fully healed but still aching wound from Talon's dagger, exhaustion landed on him heavily, almost making him swoon. For every other of his kin, this room would have been filled with a banquet of qil. For Osman, it had no more sustenance than a rented room that an innkeeper had over-decorated with personal items. Dropping his pack to the floor, Osman lay down with the corpse of his childhood on the too-small bed and slept.

# CHAPTER THREE

*19 Years Earlier ~ Year 855* PXF *~ Late Winter*

As Anson instructed, Osman waited patiently on the couch for his father's long overdue arrival. For months, he had been 'waiting patiently,' but today, Anson assured him, was finally the day. His excitement had nearly resulted in him bouncing the couch off its legs, toppling it and himself a half-dozen times in his enthusiastic anticipation. Osman heard the approach of people coming down the hall. Anson calmed him with a gesture and a smile, mouthing the word *wait* through his warm grin.

The door opened, and Osman stood on the couch cushions, ready to greet his renowned father home from his Omenara. His exuberance drained when an old man leaning heavily on a tall, thickly muscled woman was half-carried, half-dragged over the threshold. Not understanding, Osman looked to Anson, whose face had drained of color as concern and worry replaced any sense of frivolity that was once there. Osman's caregiver rushed to the door to help carry the broken man into the residence.

"Tavi, what has happened?" Anson asked.

There was no response from the man as he lifted his eyes to the question. The tired, haunted orbs scanned the room and alighted on Osman, filling with resentment.

"Don't make me see him. I can't," dribbled out of the old man's slack lips. In that same instant, Osman registered what Anson had said. He had called this shell of a man Tavi. They were carrying his father.

Anson and the woman moved his father quickly into his bed chambers and closed the door, leaving Osman shocked and uncomprehending on the couch. How could that man be his father? He had worked so hard and memorized all the stories of the heroic shaman whose voice commanded the elements. A holy healer of all wounds. The Farseer who, without any aid of magic, imagined a better world when all that surrounded him was war. That person was none of those things. And the way he looked at Osman. That was not how fathers looked at sons. That was how one looked upon finding that worms had spoiled a barrel of apples.

*Present Year 874* PXF *~ Early Summer*

Osman awoke to the qil of a rancid worm crawling across his tongue. His body reflexively gagged and attempted to spit the invader out of his mouth, but the phantom emotion and sickly sensation it evoked quickly dissolved into memory. Moonlight streamed across his face through the gap in the curtains as Osman drifted out of the liminal space between dream and reality, his back nagging at him for the folly of sleeping in his childhood bed.

The moon had stripped all color from his room just as thoroughly as his actions had stripped the emotion out of them eight years before, but apparently, the same could not be said for his dreams. He attempted to adjust his position and rediscover sleep, but his mind betrayed his effort, deciding instead to stay fully awake without even a hint of drowsiness.

Osman sat up and couldn't help but look at the twenty-one marks in the log running over his bed. Eighteen more faces and names had stepped into his life after he had made the first three marks. All had been 'concerned for his well-being,' but they had never been concerned enough to stay. At fifteen, he had emancipated himself from the constant carousel of caregivers, having grown tired of their platitudes. For his last three years at Horizon's End, Osman had lived alone in his father's rooms until, after another five-year absence, Tavi had darkened its door once again. That was the last of his father's homecomings Osman endured. He didn't share his father's home with him for long, and when he left, he ensured by his final act on the shores of Invanora that any emotional longing would never draw him back.

Leaving his room, Osman drifted barefoot through the gray landscape of chambers that, after Anson, never again felt like home. He tried to ignore the gravitational pull of his father's studio, but on his fourth orbit around the colorless rooms with no anchor holding him elsewhere, Osman discovered he was standing outside the studio's unlatched door. It was barely pushed into the frame, allowing a crack of blazing moonlight to cut the darkness like a razor blade. He leaned into the door, letting it swing open, and peered inside.

Osman had been in his father's studio dozens of times while living at Horizon's End. It was in no way forbidden from him. What had kept him away was its transformation from a place of color and light before his father's first homecoming to the dark, tormented place it was now. Tavi the Farseer, an artist of peace and a future without war, could never again capture beauty on canvas after that day. When he did lift pigment-laden brushes to paint, only despair and darkness flowed from them. The studio walls, which had once displayed the exuberant splattered colors of artistic joy, were now a showcase of grey and black, thrown at their surface in desperation and pain. The hope that gave Tavi the moniker 'Farseer' in his youth eluded him throughout Osman's memory of the rest of his life and presumably to the end of his days.

A lone easel holding a large black canvas stood in the center of the studio. Shadows thrown by the moonlight darkened its surface and confirmed

Osman's assumption. Even though Osman could only vaguely see the details, it was evident that the image was of a shattered pane of clear glass frozen in time. The shapes of the flying shards and their razor-sharp crystalline edges were rendered three-dimensional by reflected streaks of stark white highlighting them. Against the dark studio walls and beams of moonlight pouring through the wide bay window, the image seemed to bleed off the canvas into every corner of the room.

Osman approached the canvas not only to turn it into the moonlight and examine it further but to break the disconcerting illusion that enveloped the room. As the moonlight hit the canvas, its glow transformed the painting. What had been a flat black field showcasing a shattered transparent window burst into vivid life.

The clear glass exploded with color, the pane now revealing itself as a stained-glass mosaic in the moonlight. A warped red crescent moon loomed at the center, where there had been only darkness previously. Osman involuntarily took a step back out of surprise and the unnerving feeling of familiarity radiating from the scarlet moon. Only then, from a distance, could he perceive what was right before him.

The highlighted crescent masquerading as a moon was light reflecting off one of the razor-sharp curved edges of the Vermillion Blade. Talon's glaive was unmistakable in its shape and contour, dominating the center of the painting. Once recognized, Osman could see the remainder of the blade cloaked in shadow stealthily disappearing behind the brilliant shower of shattering stained glass.

Eyes now drawn to the broken window, Osman saw it was not depicting a pantheon of deities or a mosaic of scripture as most stained-glass windows he had encountered in Arnadore did; it represented the seasons. The specific Uldani motifs used were unmistakable as he examined the cascading shards. They were identical to the patterns and designs Osman had used for his outfit at the Gala. Hypnotized by the imagery before him, his gaze scanned for more hidden details, and there, centered below the false moon, was another. He recognized the dark silhouette of a featureless person with curves he knew as well as his Krolh'dran's blade—the voluptuous figure of Cerena.

Osman's knees buckled, and he fell hard on his backside, scrambling away from the painting until his back bumped against the short wall under the window. How had his father painted this? Farseer was a romantic name for a young artist who dreamed of a world without war, not for some gift or magic sight he inherently possessed. He could not possibly know all these details about that night at the Gala, the naming of his Krolh'dran, or how the blade and Cerena would shatter the joy he had found only months after that pinnacle moment.

Osman stood and cautiously approached the painting as though it was some venomous creature ready to strike. He tentatively ran his fingers over the broken stained glass, feeling the ridges of paint that created the image. The whole story of the Gala was there in the shattered panes, from him standing on the tailor's dais to him unbraiding Talon's hair in the baths below the Sojourn's Rest.

While the scenes were not exacting replications of the actual moments, they were unmistakable to Osman's eyes in their content. As his brain tried to comprehend what his eyes were seeing, the brushstrokes of paint under his fingertips began to feel like the broken glass they represented. The qil of crystalline razor edges slicing into his fingers spread to his palms, and a familiar presence laid their hand on his shoulder. Osman could not repress the shudder of fear that skittered down his spine, for who would not have a moment of trepidation when the Last Friend paid them an unexpected visit?

The God of Death was not here to take him on his last journey; at least, Osman didn't feel that was their intent. This was not the first time he had felt the presence of the Last Friend. They had wistfully lingered nearby during Osman's incarceration as he lay buried alive in his cell beneath the Hall of Judgement. A palpable mournfulness filled their vigil over Osman through those many days and long nights. During their time together in that place of despair, Osman could sense the Last Friend's grief was not due to Osman's impending demise. It was due to The Last Friend being powerless to rescue him from his suffering even though their duty had repeatedly called them to this place.

Through those endless days and nights, Osman's initial sharp fury at the God of Death eventually faded to dull resentment. He realized whatever covenants that existed between gods and fate had bound the Last Friend's hand from taking him. In Osman's darkest hours, the qil of death's proximity became a comfort, reminding him that he was not alone.

The shattered glass in his father's painting was now even more profound. Osman's insight expanded through the Last Friend's touch, and he understood that Architavia Therandus must have known he was dying as he painted the scene before him. Death had lingered over Tavi's shoulder with every stroke. Was it the God of Death who gave his father this insight into Osman's life?

Osman could feel the Last Friend's presence retreating from the room as the sharp sting of glass biting into his flesh faded entirely from his palms and fingers. He turned around to face the window, bathing his countenance in moonlight, his spirit subconsciously craving light after being in the presence of Death. Osman's eyes remained unfocused, lost in the revelations that had flooded his mind until movement outside the window caught his attention. Beyond the small seating area behind his father's residence was a familiar form from his youth among the flowers: Alerese the Bloomsage.

The Bloomsage was one of the rare timeless Uldani elders who carried with them a pearl of enlightened wisdom that negated all constructs such as clocks, calendars, social niceties, age, and gender. Even the Last Friend seemed to defer to their sage understanding of the greater world. Instead, visiting them not as an undeniable caller but as a familiar guest who patiently sits for shared tea, awaiting their host's cue for when it is time for both to leave the table.

Osman balked at the idea that his recent visitation by the Last Friend was just an errand Alerese had sent them on, but he also couldn't completely dismiss it. Regardless of the answer, Osman felt it unwise to tarry and not greet the unexpected visitor. He left the studio, stepping out into the night through the narrow access door onto the patio, and crossed the stony ground to the figure crouched over a patch of blooming midnight jasmine.

Whenever Alerese made one of their few fleeting appearances through Horizon's End, Osman had gathered new tales of their travels from the artists in residence. From every shore to every peak of the Uldani Isles, wherever flowers bloomed, people had spotted Alerese and, if lucky, were gifted one of their tiny palm-sized canvases. Many would lurk near their presence, hoping to receive one of their treasured paintings, but most knew such actions were the surest way never to be gifted one.

Their title of Bloomsage was in reference to Alerese's uncanny knack of appearing just as a region's treasured native wildflowers were at their peak bloom. Never gardens or cultivated varieties, only flowers that could roam the land as they did, free and untethered. Many romanticized that the Bloomsage did not chase the blooms at all but that it was the wildflowers who greeted Alerese wherever they wandered.

Osman approached the hunched form, their feet planted wide and squatting so deeply Alerese's knees were level with their ears. Gnarled dexterous fingers danced a sharpened porcupine quill across the tiny canvas palmed in their other hand, capturing the luminescent jasmine before them. Osman waited patiently just behind them, beyond their peripheral vision, to avoid any interruption of their work. After a few moments, the quill stopped and disappeared into the folds of a simple set of infinitely patched and pocketed cinched robes.

Alerese slowly stood and turned to Osman. Their timeworn face was as unique as the secrets it kept: a turnip-shaped nose framed by deep golden eyes that held the same promise and danger of well-guarded beehives laden with honey, rosebud lips made crooked by a knowing smile, skin the texture of a beloved satchel that dutifully carried a lifetime of treasures great and small. Their visage was a mélange of nature's shapes and textures as welcoming as Spring and stern as the depths of Winter.

Alerese's sturdy form crossed to Osman and, without hesitation, laid their weathered hands on his face in the traditional greeting Uldani used between beloved friends and family. A shocked, sharp intake of breath crossed Osman's lips uninvited. It had been nearly a decade since another Uldani had overcome the revulsion he induced in them and read his face. Tears welled in his eyes, and he melted into Alerese's gentle touch as they explored his emotions etched there. Osman had never interacted with Alerese directly before this moment but knew through their touch that they invited him to return the gesture. He gently placed his hands upon their face.

Osman could read the tiny micro-expressions that flowed across Alerese's features as their fingers explored his life as written upon his own. Loneliness, abandonment, resignation, resolve, new joys, family, heartbreak, betrayal, torture, obligation, and now a swirling maelstrom of questions. He felt through his fingers upon their face that Alerese lived it all with him. With a strength Osman did not expect, the Bloomsage pulled his head to their own. As their foreheads touched, Osman, for perhaps the first time since his childhood, felt someone truly saw him. There was no need for explanation, apology, or excuse. Such things were meaningless in light of Alerese's understanding of his life. After a moment's pause and a slight loving squeeze, the Bloomsage released his face.

Osman slowly opened his eyes to find Alerese peering into his own. "Your father carried a burden as well. One that damaged him as profoundly as you have damaged yourself and your memories of this place." Alerese said the words without accusation or judgment. "I was here the morning he received his Omenara, the same day you received your name, Osman." Alerese gave a slight nod to Osman to confirm what they had just conveyed and paused to let it sink in: "A fated son tied to a fated journey."

Alerese then continued their statements becoming a story in their delivery. "The Dawn Flower vines had painted the cliffs violet, orange, and gold as they caught and magnified the first lightening of the sky as it heralded the coming of the sun." Alerese's eyes brightened, their voice adopting meter and melody as their body began to sway with the cadence of their tale. Osman's numbness to emotion in this place slipped away as Alerese wove their hypnotic account. More than words, or chanting song, or dance, Alerese slipped into the Uldani language of emotion and qil as one might slip into a warm bath. It was a language Osman had eschewed as a youth. Indeed, he had only attempted it once. Not with his own body but with the outfit he wore just over a year ago in a land he was now exiled from, standing within the courtyard of the brother he had betrayed.

"Tavi's Omenara was not the product of meditation or late-night wanderlust placing one's feet on the road. The Fatesinger, enigmatic fourth sister of destiny, visited Tavi herself to bind his life to her design." Alerese's arms twisted above their head into the air, creating intricate patterns as though conducting an orchestra and weaving a tapestry simultaneously. "I did not see the Fatesinger, the Maiden of Destinies Reborn, but knew her voice and heard the echoes of her workings. On this morning, she played no mere grouping of simple chords but a symphony resonating through the fabric of reality itself." The Bloomsage twirled around then bent at the waist, hands touching the stone beneath their feet as they continued their intricate motions. Their feet stomped the ground as they rose, making the very stone of Horizon's End resonate with their story, arms weaving, and voice crescendoing. "A song like none other. Everything touched by even its echo was forever changed by hearing it." Alerese threw their hands wide, their body and face frozen in awe and terror. "And your father, poor doomed and blessed Tavi, was the focus of all its terrible beauty and power."

Alerese dropped to the ground in a squatting stance, not unlike the one Osman had found them in this night, except looking over their shoulder like a timid, frightened songbird hiding in the brush from raptors in the skies above. "The world held its breath, enraptured and fearful. All were desperate to hear the melody she sang more clearly, but none willing to face its terrible power." Barely above a whisper, the Bloomsage intoned, "Held frozen, strangled by fate's will, every grain of sand and every mountain alike prayed for the song to stop but also for it never to end."

Silence filled the night around them, and Osman, frozen by cascades of qil invoked by Alerese's telling, found he too was holding his breath. When his lungs began to burn and beg for air, Alerese spoke again.

"After an eternity of mere seconds, dawn broke, and destiny's song faded with it." A tentative, relieved smile began to turn their lips as the Bloomsage looked back to Osman. "The morning music of nature began to overtake the crashing power of the Fatesinger's symphony." Alerese stood, arms open at their sides, turning in wonderment like seeing the dawn for the first time. Their arms dropped to their sides, abruptly ending their reenactment of the memory. Voice, posture, and expression becoming bland by comparison, "And that is when I saw Tavi stumble toward me."

The change to the simple statement left Osman's soul hungry for the sharing Alerese had gifted him with. But as the void within him swallowed his emotions once more, even that slipped away. In his youth, Osman had prided himself on reading facts and histories of his father in the Xallian style, unencumbered by qil and the oral traditions of Uldani teachings.

Now, by his own doing, when it came to his father and this place, that would be all he would ever have.

The calloused hand of the Bloomsage alighted on his shoulder and pulled Osman's attention back to their words. "Tavi's body shook, and all color had drained from his sun-kissed skin. In a glazed-eyed daze, he said, 'I must leave and await a call for aid from an old friend in the North. A blacksmith I once knew.'" Alerese looked deep into Osman's eyes. "Your father, mind seemingly still overwhelmed by the song, stood silent then finally continued, 'I will then find the burden that I must carry for him.'"

After a moment of silence, Alerese answered the question in Osman's eyes. "No, I did not know then where the Omenara took him or who this blacksmith was, but perhaps you now do?" They let the question hang in the air for a moment. "It wasn't until much later that I understood the burden he had taken up." The elder Uldani gathered their breath. "More than half a decade later, not long after his return to the Isles and word of his broken condition had reached my ears, your father and I crossed paths for the last time. He was a broken man, struggling to cross the frozen high plains of Kyflenor, and he was not alone. A boy was with him."

Osman reeled from the statement. A boy? Osman tried to calculate the years in his head. He had just turned seven when the crumpled form of his father returned home. That was nineteen years ago. In the brief mentions of Richen, Talon had said he had been looking for him for nearly two decades. The boy must have been Richen. But how? Osman certainly would have seen a human boy at Horizon's End when his father was recuperating before he disappeared again, crossing paths with Alerese.

Did his father hide Richen from him? And why had the Singer of Fate tasked his father to take this human boy, his future Krolh'dran's first love, to Kyflenor? Had his father abandoned him for a new son fate had burdened him with? One he'd never even known he had?

Osman's confusion turned to an outrage devoid of qil fueled by what he saw as justification for every ember of disdain he held for his father. Jealousy planted its insidious seed in Osman's heart, for Richen especially, but also for Talon. The love and obligation he held for his Krolh'dran began to sour and numb. The parent Osman had so desperately needed in his life had chosen to carry this burden for Talon over being a father to him.

Alerese's words continued without pause, paying no heed to Osman's darkening countenance. "The boy was dead. Only his spirit remained, but the boy traveled with Tavi nonetheless. His corrupted soul bound to a shard of crystal your father had driven into his chest."

The revelations were coming too quickly, and Osman's thoughts couldn't change tracks. Had his father chosen a dead son over a live one? Was Richen the cause of the 'soul wound' that had so damaged his father?

As a child, Osman had never understood how a soul could be wounded. It wasn't until much later that he realized how grievously one could injure that incorporeal part of oneself. A moment of reflection stilled Osman's anger. The injury that had so changed Tavi and stolen the father he dreamed of having—the man in all the stories from the books he memorized—had been self-inflicted upon his soul much like his own had been. The moment of empathy for his father turned numb, pulled into the ragged void within him where all emotions toward his father flowed. Osman's anger reasserted itself as he painted a path like a trail of falling dominos from his father's self-mutilation to his own, all for a dead human boy.

Like an unbreaking tide, the Bloomsage's onslaught of revelations pummeled Osman. "Your father was on a pilgrimage, I suspect, taking the soul to the Argestian Inception, the nexus of the elements of air and water. Tavi had prepared himself in such a way that I believe he was going to petition the guardian of the inception to begin cleansing the boy's soul for reincarnation."

Betrayal manifested in Osman's senses. Its qil swept over him, twisting the world sideways as a profound vertigo buckled his knees and yanked his legs out from under him. A reincarnation? Not only had Richen stolen his father and his childhood, but even in death, his father fought to give Richen a second chance rather than attempting to provide Osman with a first one. The world tilted precariously under Osman. Spinning stars filled his vision, and nausea wracked his body as he hit the hard ground.

Osman, head on the cold stone beneath him and eyes unfocused, felt Alerese press a small square canvas into the palm of his hand as they said their last words to him, "The guardian of the Argestian Inception will know what happened from there, but be warned, for the ancient primordial ones, knowledge always has a price."

Osman croaked a single word toward Alerese's retreating form, "Why?" His voice was still raw from screaming on the beach the day before and weak from months left unused in the cells below the Halls of Judgement.

Prone on the bare rock outside his father's lodge, Osman realized the last meaningful words he had spoken to anyone were to Talon on the day of the revolt. Dagger plunged into his chest and locked in place between his ribs, Osman, lying on the stone floor of the keep, had asked himself the same question he now posed to the Bloomsage. A question he had screamed at the sunrise through tears and sobs when he found his father, broken and wounded as he was, had left again in the dark of night without saying goodbye.

*"Why didn't he choose me?"*

Alerese paused, turning to Osman's still prone form. Returning to him, they squatted down like a sage and wizened toad perched upon a lily pad and patted his cheek. "Only you can answer that, broken one."

# CHAPTER FOUR



*Two Months Later ~ Year 874* PXF *~ Late Summer*

Osman nibbled on dried fish and traveler's bread as he surveyed the deep fjord below him flowing out to the sea. His legs dangled over the edge of the rock shelf where he sat, and the wind buffeted the loose curls of his unkempt, overgrown hair. The rocky cliff faces still wore their lush carpet of greenery that had encroached on every nook and roothold under the near endless sunlight of the Summer months this far south. Twenty-two hours of daylight lent a frenetic energy to the flora and fauna of Kyflenor, and the people who called this land home also seemed to be infected by it.

Even though distance and the towering cliff faces hid it from view, Osman could visualize where the small fishing village of Volgendeep lay near the coast at the mouth of the fjord. He had arrived at the tiny port of Kyflenor a week ago via a fishing vessel on which he had traded his labor for a small wage and passage to the southeasternmost isle of the Uldani nation.

An unsleeping bustle filled Summers in Volgendeep. Seasonal commerce and temporary residents had swollen its facilities and borders to bursting. Sprawling districts of tents and tanned skin pavilions surrounded the town's less than two dozen permanent structures. Many housed the hundreds of fishermen flocking to the southern sea to ply the bountiful waters free from ice for a scant two months out of the year. But there were also visitors from the interior of Kyflenor who had arrived to trade with the influx of outsiders visiting their island.

Kyflenor had no permanent settlements across its vast landscape other than Volgendeep, the land remaining locked in ice and snow for seven months of the year only to thaw completely in the height of Summer. The few Uldani tribes that lived in the high tundra and boreal forests year-round walked the way of the elders, living off what the land provided and migrating with the herds of giant elk and caribou that roamed the vast landscape.

Kyflenor was a lonely yet sacred place. Many Uldani approaching the end of their days traveled to these shores to walk the paths of the Solenfel, whose trails of iridescent light flowed through the sky even in the daylight of Summer. The solemn guides of the Yuelan tribe, known as the Solenrone, in their black furs made of elk and wolfskin, came to Volgendeep in the Summer to assist these elders on their last journey, and it was them whom Osman sought out when he arrived.

The low, wide tents of the Yuelan tribe were easily spotted due to their whipping pennants of tattered ribbon and the painted trails of the Solenfel that decorated them. However, Osman was barred from entry as the fierce guardians of the Solenrone shunned him from even approaching. After three days of attempting bribes, subterfuge, and stealth, Osman found himself face-to-face with those he sought.

He had been turning the corner at the intersection of two narrow corridors between the pavilions that made up the makeshift temporary tavern district of Summertime Volgendeep when a hand the size of a bear's paw slammed into his chest. A man that eclipsed even Talon's stature and breadth knocked him to the ground and pinned him firmly there. His deep-set eyes shone like a feral beast from beneath a fur hood made of hide white as snow. From his shoulder, a feline head with long white saber-like teeth, a saldrig, the legendary predator that prowled the highlands of

Kyflenor, looking as lifelike as the day it took its last breath, grinned at Osman menacingly. The voice that emerged from cracked lips was one of barely tempered bestial challenge and rage.

"Your soul has no path here," the massive beast of a man growled. "Take your scarred and festering spirit back to the Northlands and the new gods who flood your soul with their stench."

The man, not just any Solenrone but a chieftain of their order, as marked by the saldrig hide he wore, pulled a horrifying bladed hook no longer than a finger out of his belt and brought it to Osman's left eye. Osman had heard the tales. The price for those who sought out the Solenfel heedless of the Yuelan tribe's tradition and proper reverence was to lose an eye for their transgression. Osman feared that debt was now his to pay.

"I am not seeking the Solenfel!" Osman stammered. "I seek the Argestian Inception and follow the path of my father who sought it before me." Osman tried to dig into his pouch, but the massive Yuelan slammed his knee onto Osman's wrist, stopping him. "Alerese the Bloomsage sent me." Seeing only a tiny pause in the chieftain's intent, Osman pleaded in a panicked voice. "I owe the Qat'malorn to my Krolh'dran."

Whether it was the mention of Alerese or his debt to his soul brother, the massive chieftain of the soul walkers narrowed his eyes and probed Osman's face for deception. The hooked knife disappeared into his belt, and his enormous hand dug into Osman's pouch, its size rupturing the leather stitching along the seams. He examined the contents and turned back to Osman.

The Solenrone chief barked at him. "Gather your supplies, Betrayer. Do not let another twilight's gloaming find you in Volgendeep." The Yuelan chieftain stood, leaving Osman in the dirt with his belongings strewn around him. Heart racing, Osman sat up, drew a deep breath, and gathered what his attacker had spilled across the ground. While far less than he had hoped for, the encounter had not been fruitless. Osman had spotted recognition in the chieftain's eyes as he looked at the tiny painting Alerese had gifted him, which was more insight into his destination than when he arrived.

No path or map marked the way or exact location of the Argestian Inception. Osman had only heard snippets of tales about the four elemental inceptions during childhood. The inceptions were often the subject of abstract and esoteric paintings by artists at Horizon's End attempting to impress other artists or gain favor. The two inceptions of creation—Argestian, the inception of water and air, and Eurucian, the inception of earth and fire—were most often the subject of painters visiting Tavi's sanctuary. However, those with a darker aesthetic would visualize the fetid swamps of the Caecatian Inception of earth and water or ancient Mael Esari sitting upon the untamed Helsparian Inception of fire and air.

Other than the Helsparian Inception, the exact location of the other two was hidden or, in the case of the Caecatian, a guarded secret. Pilgrimages to the Argestian and Eurucian inceptions were not unheard of; however, those who had made those journeys believed the search and discovery of them was a critical part of actually finding them. The only guide Osman had was the tiny painting Alerese had gifted him.

Back at Horizon's End, once the vertigo induced by his feelings of betrayal had faded and the Bloomsage had long since disappeared into the night, Osman had examined the canvas Alerese had pressed into his hand. It was not a painting of the midnight jasmine as he expected but instead an image of Grimspire, the strange leaning mountain of Kyflenor whose peak soared above all others in the Isles.

Scholars taught that Grimspire was the only remaining part of the massive ancient volcano that once encompassed the entirety of the Uldani Isles. Eons ago, in the age of the primordial dragons, long before any other sentient creature walked the land, its cataclysmic eruption ripped the mountain asunder. What didn't collapse into the sea became the Uldani Isles and the sloping peak of Grimspire, the only remnant of its existence.

The painting Alerese had gifted Osman of Grimspire was not from the usual vantage point that most artists captured the unique majesty of its peak, the northern face as seen from Volgendeep. Their painting was from the south and in a towering up-close perspective instead of seen from leagues away.

Osman knew better than to test the patience of the Yuelan tribe and the grace they had gifted him, so he gathered his few belongings and rations, shouldered the short hunting bow he had purchased, and made haste to be on his way. It had taken him two long days to arrive at the inland extent of the fjord. There, a massive glacier halted further progress near the water's edge. However, Osman spotted the pathway of a natural switchback trail that painted its way across the eastern wall of the fjord, easily discernable by its telltale stairstep distribution of greenery and stunted trees. The course was treacherous and little used, other than by the goats that made their vertical home among the rocks, but Osman, breathless and aching, had finally reached the ridgeline above.

Osman finished his midday meal and took a deep breath to clear his head. The steep climb was behind him, but now the daunting expanse of Kyflenor's high tundra lay before him in all its vast and harsh beauty. Grimspire loomed far to the south, easily visible though it was still hundreds of leagues away. Osman could also make out the craggy broken ridges known as the Shieldwall Spine that flanked Grimspire, peaking over the horizon as often as they hid behind it.

Osman had no clear indication of where he might find a passage to the other side of the mountains and the location of Alerese's painting. With neither path nor plan, he placed one foot in front of the other and set course for a low rise pockmarked with a sparse scattering of trees that he saw within reasonable walking distance. He would need shelter when he camped later, and even though true darkness did not fall on Kyflenor during the summer months, Osman would try to find rest during the few hours of twilight when it fell across the land.

Osman had considered following the coast or even hiring a boat to transport him to the far side of Kyflenor, but neither were viable options. Time was not on his side for a coastal route circumnavigating the central spine of mountains instead of his current course, which relied on finding a pass through them. The nightless days of Summer would soon turn to the frozen darkness of Winter in just over a handful of weeks, and that time would dwindle even more quickly the further south he traveled.

While a boat would be the quickest, there were no sheltered coves or even beaches on the southern coast of Kyflenor. Towering cliffs of ice and granite dropped thousands of feet into the sea and created currents where even the most experienced sailors could find their ship smashed against their impenetrable walls. Even if a fisherman or guide knew of a landing, finding one with that knowledge would have taken time in Volgendeep, which was a luxury Osman did not have after he wore out his welcome. The only path open to him was the one he was on.

Osman arrived at the stand of trees and rocky knoll just as the sun's low trajectory began to kiss the horizon. He nestled his canvas tarp into the dense branches on the leeward side of a tight grouping of bushy firs to help blunt the ever-present wind that whipped through Kyflenor's forests and scoured the tundra. Osman laid the makings for a fire in a protected ring of gathered stones, but before lighting it, he lifted his eyes to the sky to witness its beauty before the fire blinded his sight.

Above him, the Solenfel danced its fanciful ribbons of color across the firmament. Time and distance away from Horizon's End had unmuffled his emotions, and as he looked up, Osman embraced the feeling of wonder that filled him. He felt the tickle of its qil dance between his toes and over the arches of his feet and couldn't help but smile.

Osman sat and pulled off the soft leather boots that Lady Cour-Vermane had gifted him. He scrunched and stretched his toes after their day in captivity, relieving the fatigue that even the enchanted footwear could not completely stave off. Leaning back on his elbows, late Summer's fragrant moss filled Osman's nostrils with its earthy aroma, and long grasses formed a bed for his aching muscles. Placing one calf on the other knee, he looked to the mystical display unfolding in the twilight above him.

The Solenfel swirled and flowed across the sky's vast canvas over the plains of Kyflenor. The looping currents of green and purple looked to be both a gateway and a river, a procession of a thousand souls and the painted brushstrokes of a single master artist. At times overwhelming the whole sky, and at others merely the whisper of a forgotten dream, Osman understood why so many of his ancestors came to this place as their last journey. A single soul could feel tiny, but to join the procession and currents of the Solenfel was to become a part of an eternal dance and silent song with one's brethren.

Osman couldn't keep his eyes from drifting to his foot silhouetted against the breathtaking display in the sky and the tickle of qil fluttering there. He quashed down but couldn't ultimately stifle the rising giggle induced by the interplay of the overwhelming wonderment infecting his feet and the breeze that swirled across them.

Osman flexed his long toes and pretended to catch one of the dancing ribbons of the Solenfel like a magic lasso. A memory rose to the surface of his mind like a trout to a lure cast in a stream. A vision of sitting looking at the constellations on the patio of Horizon's End with Anson, his tiny six-year-old form engulfed by the reclining wooden chairs, flooded his mind. Raising his feet to the night sky to catch stars had been a silly game they would play together. Osman would stretch his feet into the darkness and pretend to grab the twinkling fairies of the firmament between his tingling toes. Then Anson would wrestle them away and pop them in his mouth like a tasty treat, stealing whatever wish they might have granted. It never bothered Osman that Anson ate the wishes he captured because even six-year-old Osman knew fairy gifts were not to be trusted. But how they would laugh and giggle through the summer nights while sharing fizzy birch brew.

The wonder dancing through Osman's senses turned to a wistful ache as the memory of his happy childhood with Anson solidified in his mind—the time before his father's homecoming. Osman focused his eyes on the sky as his foot drifted off his knee and back to the ground. He tried to regain his hold on the present in this place and time, but fighting the rushing flow of the memory and where it was inevitably leading was as useless as fighting the tide. The current of recollection brought him to the day his father sent Anson away, and Osman's emotions fell into the abyss he carved out of his soul to swallow all memory of his father. All that remained as the memory unspooled was a child's confused recollection of the shouts, pleas, and questions emerging from behind closed doors, and then Anson was just gone.

Osman felt the qil of wonder drain from his senses as the majesty of the Solenfel above him became flat and lifeless in his eyes. An excised memory of his father was now indelibly connected to the skies above Kyflenor, infecting it with their emotional sterility. Osman had felt a numbness creeping into his feelings for Talon after Alerese had imparted all the revelations about his father's connection to Richen, but nothing like the immediate and definitive shutdown of them he was experiencing now.

Osman had thought the wound he had inflicted upon himself was clean and contained. It had never spread during his time in Arnadore, but that was no longer true. Visiting Horizon's End and the journey he now undertook had somehow disturbed the scars of that rite. It was not the clean and surgical separation it had been when he had performed the ritual eight years ago. It was metastasizing and infecting every thought it touched.

Osman looked back to the Solenfel, trying to feel anything, but what moments before had held him in wonderment was now barren to his senses. He would have plunged into the sorrow of losing the sky, but even that consolation was denied him. He felt nothing. Osman sighed and stood up in a single motion from his reclined position to fully upright. In that burst of movement, he realized he wasn't alone.

Sitting next to the unlit firepit was a wilicho. Osman stood perfectly still, waiting to see if the phantasm would fade or move on, but it seemed perfectly content to remain where it had settled. Osman knew of wilicho and had even had fleeting encounters with a few in the forests around Horizon's End, but never one that persisted like this. Wilicho were not ghosts, spirits, or undead per se, but more the echoes of an Uldani's emotions and personality manifested through the active elemental nature of the Isles. There were dozens of Uldani bedtime stories featuring wilicho and their antics ranging from whimsical and benevolent to malicious and harmful. However, one rule was always the same: do not disturb or interfere with a wilicho's set routine and treat them respectfully.

The wilicho seated at Osman's campfire was an older gentleman of diminutive stature with features that belied a hint of dwarven ancestry mixed with his Uldani heritage. Osman's first guess that he was a fisherman was confirmed when the wilicho assembled an intricate rod and cast his line into the unlit fire pit, leaving a shimmering float on the surface of the gathered wood as though it was the surface of a pond. Other wilicho Osman had encountered earlier in his life had been nothing more than a glimpse of shape and light out the corner of his eye. This one, however, was nearly indistinguishable from a living person other than its slight translucence and a shimmering glow surrounding it that mirrored the colors and wavering intensity of the Solenfel above.

The casual nature of the wilicho lessened the tension that had filled Osman's body at the discovery of his surprise visitor, but he remained frozen in place, not knowing how to proceed. He would need the fire for its warmth and the protection its light would provide from creatures that stalked the gloaming of Kyflenor, but he didn't know what actions, if any, might provoke the wilicho. Locked in indecision, Osman got his direction from the fisherman himself.

"Well, c'mon, light that fire, lad, or are ye just gonna leave me here to freeze my bobbers off!" The wilicho chided in a thick dwarven accent with a heavy Uldani cadence and inflection.

Osman was so startled by the demand cutting through the silence of the forest he had to take a step to keep from losing his balance. In so doing, his bare foot found a thorny pinecone that bit deep into the center of his arch. With a yelp, Osman reflexively yanked his foot back, cradling it in his two hands, setting himself further off balance. Like a tree felled by an axe, Osman fell to the ground, foot still in hand, leaving his nose brushing against the small firepit and eyes looking up at the wilicho.

"Oh, for Phara's sake, you have the grace of a skate on a sandbar." The wilicho proclaimed with a tone that magnified his exasperated expression and the roll of his eyes.

Osman finally found his voice and, spitting out a leaf that had stuck to his lips after the fall, asked rhetorically, "You talk?!"

The fisherman sighed, "And the wits of a walleyed wellfin to boot. You're quite the catch, arn'tcha?"

Osman scrambled across the ground back to his boots and pulled them onto his feet, never taking his gaze off the wilicho. Collecting his tinderbox, Osman, as requested, put a spark to kindling and coaxed the fire he had laid to life. The wilicho's fishing bobber bounced merrily in the flames, and the wilicho supporting his rod on one knee produced a pipe and began to smoke contentedly.

"So, um, I'm going to heat some broth and jerky now. Is that okay?" Osman stammered out cautiously. Then, quickly remembering the part of the tales about respect, he added, "Would you like some?"

The wilicho, with a lifted eyebrow, leveled a gaze at Osman that, with little subtly, questioned Osman's intelligence once again.

"Yeah, right," Osman said sheepishly while scratching the back of his neck. "I'm just going to do my thing over here while you do your fishing, okay?"

The wilicho answered, but his words and delivery made it obvious he was answering a different question that had been asked under other circumstances. "Fix your grub, hang the hammocks, swab the deck. Routine is what makes a ship sail."

It occurred to Osman that even though their first interaction seemed like a normal conversation, it just as easily could have been the wilicho echoing back something he often said in his life. Osman pondered on that as he boiled water and added a dried ball of spices to make broth, sprinkling in some hard jerky and half a turnip for extra flavor and bulk. The wilicho watched approvingly at the process and laughed heartily when Osman reflexively jumped back as he yanked his ghostly bobber out of the fire through the stew he was preparing.

"Ha," Osman stated with very little humor in his voice, having almost dumped his dinner in the fire over the jest. "Very funny." He was, however, becoming increasingly intrigued by his visitor, so Osman asked respectfully, "May I know your name, honored elder?"

The wilicho opened his mouth as if to answer, then closed it, seemingly frustrated. He opened it again, then closed it, looking to his side, now seeming puzzled. He finally answered, "I seem to have lost my hat on the east coast of Lyria Bay." The fisherman looked to Osman hopefully, "Perhaps you can lend an old man a hat?"

Osman took a beat to comprehend the request but caught on. The wilicho would like him to provide a name. Like all Uldani, Osman felt deeply about names but knew they could, in fact, be changed as easily as a hat, so he blurted out his first thought without much consideration other than it felt right and was fun to say. "How about Wilfred? Wilfred the wilicho." Osman added the last part without taking into account it might be offensive. Maybe he should have gone with Farnsbury the Fisherman.

"That smells mighty tasty," the wilicho said in reply.

Osman wasn't sure if he was now talking about the name or dinner as the fisherman's eyes were looking to the fire as he spoke. "Are we talking about your name?" Osman asked.

"I done told you it smelled good. Now serve it up." The wilicho snapped back.

"Okay, Wilfred, it is nice to meet you." Osman continued, "I'm Osman. It's an honor to have you at my fire."

Wilfred smiled and, with a hint of kindness and emotion, replied, "The honor is mine."

# CHAPTER FIVE



The rest of the night had consisted of Wilfred telling several long and very dull stories about fishing as Osman ate his evening meal and then settled in to sleep. The even cadence and distant quality of Wilfred's voice transported Osman back to the Sojourn's Rest. The muffled din of the common room had become like a lullaby to him when returning to his own or Talon's rooms to find sleep after a long day at the keep or longer nights in taverns. And now, in the wilderness of Kyflenor, Wilfred's voice did the same. For the first time since the siege of Arnadore, nightmares did not plague Osman's sleep, and he found the peaceful respite that had so long been denied him, calming his churning thoughts.

Osman awoke not at the first light of dawn after a scant few hours but to the bright daylight of the risen sun long above the horizon. Osman immediately felt the restorative effects of his night of uninterrupted peace. A clarity of thought and a feeling of being present in his own body filled him as he stood with a smile to greet the day. From the small knoll he had camped on, the vast plains of Kyflenor spread for leagues in all directions. The sprawling tundra felt full of possibility and promise in the golden morning light instead of seeming like an insurmountable obstacle. He could even imagine that something better lay beyond this trial.

For a moment, Osman's life felt as complete as it had been two years earlier as Spring painted the fields of Eleryon. A daydream overtook his vision as he imagined that his Krolh'dran would soon arrive after a morning hunt with some small game to roast on the fire. Osman would greet Talon by reading his face with his hands, and Talon would read his own. They would sit and laugh and share their morning meal as brothers.

Osman would have a family again.

A gust of wind rustling the firtrees around Osman blew the fantasy away and brought him back to reality. He and Talon had never camped or even journeyed together outside Arnadore. He had never taught his Krolh'dran about the reading of faces but now wanted nothing more than to share his with his big brother.

Even with the turmoil in his head about how he should feel about Talon, Richen, and his father, his heart longed for connection in this moment. Letting only a single lonely, shaky sigh escape his lips as loneliness's familiar qil sent a tingle through his back teeth, Osman took one last look out across the landscape. With the cool winds of Kyflenor tussling the curls in his hair and blowing them across his eyes, he turned back to his small camp to prepare for the day's travel.

Wilfred sat stoically, glowering by the firepit, the wood and embers long since turned to ash with just a thread of smoke still hinting at any remaining warmth. Fishing rod and pipe were nowhere to be seen as he sat with crossed arms and feet firmly planted on the ground. The wilicho's stern expression softened as their eyes met, reading the complex emotions playing across Osman's face. The fisherman abandoned whatever barbed remark he had planned and instead said enthusiastically, "Ah, there he is! Nothing like a good snoozle to clear the nets." Wilfred continued in a grandfatherly fashion, "Now stow all that extra tackle for another time and get your hooks baited for the day at hand."

Wilfred's advice and demeanor swept Osman's flash of loneliness and longing away, allowing him to tap back into the revitalized energy he had felt upon awakening. Not bothering to relight the fire, Osman broke his fast with some travel loaf filled with dried fruits and grains he had bought in Volgendeep. He washed it down with a long draw from his waterskin and tossed a few berries foraged along his trek the day before into his mouth as he stowed his tarp and readied his pack.

From every story Osman knew of wilicho, their existence was tied to a specific place, always encountered in the same way at some particular interval. They were resigned to repeating forever the same short excerpt of their lives and emotions that had become imprinted on the elemental forces at work in a specific location. Osman had just been lucky enough to stumble upon this one when he needed reminding of why he was on this journey. Once prepared to leave, Osman turned to Wilfred seated by the fire, dropping to one knee with bowed head in reverence. "Thank you, Wilfred, for sharing my fire and bringing me company. May you find the same peace you brought me."

Wilfred reached out an incorporeal hand and laid it on Osman's shoulder. Osman felt no weight or sensation from the gesture, but it comforted him. The wilicho gave a slight nod and gruffly stated, "Now, if that isn't the chef's portion of your meal, I don't know what is, but enough of that." Wilfred reclaimed his hand and tapped his index finger on his nose. "I can smell when someone is casting for a rare catch, and I'm not gonna have you fishin' in my waters without at least giving me a shot of landing that lunker myself." An oversized ghostly pack appeared out of thin air with Wilfred's stowed rod and an assortment of pots, pans, and lures decorating the outside of it. The wilicho slung it over his shoulders and marched out of camp.

Osman remained on one knee momentarily, assuming that this was just the end of the wilicho's looping existence, the opposite bookend to his arrival and demanding a fire be lit. The hollow qil of being alone once again manifested as a tingling in his molars, not unlike hitting an elbow at the wrong angle. As Osman had done hundreds of times before when loneliness struck him, he set his jaw, took a deep breath, and steeled himself to carry on.

"Stone Father, give me strength! I swear you are slower than a snail swimming upstream in a river of molasses," Wilfred barked from the tree line. Osman remained momentarily stunned, still down on one knee, and unsure if Wilfred was now acting independently or within the normal confines of its existence. None of the tales Osman knew spoke of wilicho traveling far from where someone had encountered it. Not wanting to risk another admonishment, he scrambled to his feet to follow the enigmatic spirit. Wilfred did not bother to wait for him to catch up or lead the way. Osman just heard Wilfred's voice calling back from up the trail, "There's a stream up ahead. I suggest you take advantage of it. You smell worse than a basket of dead crabs left in the sun."

*Year 874* PXF *~ Early Autumn*

Nearly three weeks had passed since Wilfred had come into Osman's life. The wilicho had never faded or reached some endpoint on its existence that reset it back to the campfire where they met, even though Osman had begun to wish it would. While Wilfred was an excellent guide, knowing all the best places to camp, find water, and shelter when needed, he was not the easiest of travel companions. Long, tedious, and repetitive stories of catching or chasing some fish peppered with questionable generalizations and statements about other tribes of the Isles and peoples of Valknor streamed endlessly from the wilicho day and night.

In addition, Wilfred seemed to have a bottomless well of barbed remarks for Osman. The browbeatings came not only when chance or folly would delay their journey but also for any regular tasks Osman performed around camp or along their path. The kindness and sincerity Wilfred exhibited at the camp the day of their first meeting had been non-existent over their time traveling together since then. Any hint of sentience beyond the repetition of phrases and stories had disappeared entirely. The immediate and unnecessarily hurtful rebukes of his every action and his unkind words about others in his stories made Osman wonder what kind of person Wilfred might have been in life.

Osman's frustration with the wilicho's insults had finally come to a head two nights earlier. After a day hiking to the same tiresome stories and then a string of complaints about Osman's every action at camp—berating Osman for being the dullest knife in the block, the slowest minnow in the school, and as graceful as a squid soaked in sangria— Osman snapped. The skin of his scalp behind his ears felt like someone had lit his hair on fire with a torch as anger's qil overtook him.

"Then why don't you go bake your bobbers on someone else's campfire and leave me the hells alone?" Osman roared. Any concern with being respectful of wilicho had long since faded. "All you do is complain and nitpick every last thing I do. Were you this hateful when you were alive? Cause you sure are a pain in the arse and unbearable to be around now that you're dead."

If Wilfred had been corporeal, Osman would have punched him, but all he had were his words, so he maliciously added, "No wonder you're a wilicho. Even the Solenfel got sick of you."

A torrent of dwarven curses flowed out of Wilfred that Osman could neither translate nor care to understand. As he prepared for his next verbal attack, constructing the cruelest sentiment he could conceive, Osman got in Wilfred's face, practically nose to nose with the wilicho. That's when Osman saw the utter shame and remorsefulness in Wilfred's eyes. The juxtaposition to the wilicho's words surprised him, but he would not let it stop him from having his say. Then, in a flash, Osman realized what was happening. Everything after that first night *was* the cycle that trapped Wilfred—the echo of his life he was doomed to repeat. The flames of rage burning at Osman's temples extinguished as quickly as if he had plunged his head into one of the pools Wilfred had constantly insisted he bathe in.

The stream of epitaphs and curses continued to flow out of Wilfred, but his eyes seemed to notice the change in Osman. Hope filled them as a ghostly tear pooled in the corner of one eye.

Osman sat back on his heels and asked gently, "What can I do?" The words somehow cut through the barrage of insults, and Wilfred shook his head, not having an answer. Even if he did, Osman knew he could not communicate it through the ongoing tirade. Osman closed his eyes and opened his senses, letting his body act instinctively. His arms raised of their own accord, and his hands reached out to Wilfred's face. Eyes still closed, what Osman's fingers encountered was not incorporeal air. They found the exhausted face of an old fisherman who had lost more than he could bear in life and was terrified that he was on the verge of losing all over again.

Wilfred's curses ended abruptly. Silence engulfed camp, leaving the two lone figures silhouetted under the shifting luminescence of the Solenfel and the endless sky of Kyflenor. Osman slowly opened his eyes. He saw his fingers gently laid on the surface of Wilfred's incorporeal face, creating tiny ripples at the contact, but his senses read the emotions etched there as though they were living skin.

Osman reverently stated what he saw there. "You had a son. A son that you drove away." Wilfred gave a slight nod of affirmation. His gaze pulled Osman in as the story unfolded under Osman's touch. "Your son longed for adventure, but not at sea. He wanted to explore the land." Osman saw in his mind's eye a lean, gangly young man so different from Wilfred but with features that left no doubt that he was of the same blood. Osman watched the young man as he coiled a rope awkwardly, not just due to an inherent lack of coordination but also his distracted glances across the docks, past the small fishing port, and to the mountains beyond.

"You…" Osman began to speak again and then was interrupted by a wince that passed through himself and the wilicho. Through Osman's fingers, the story in his mind had continued to unfold. The living fisherman Wilfred had once been had entered the scene and struck the young man. It was not a playful jab but a brutal clap to the ear done with anger and hostility.

Within the vision, Osman heard the echo of the familiar insult that followed, "*You have all the skill of a squid soaked in sangria.*" The fisherman then ripped the rope from his son's hands, throwing it to the ground. "*Do it again, you witless sea slug. Mollusks are mages compared to you.*" Osman almost pulled away from the wilicho, so vile was the tone and intent of the living man in the vision. He had suspected that Wilfred might not have been a good man in life, but the man he had just witnessed wasn't just bad; he was cruel and malicious.

Osman would have broken contact with the wilicho and walked away, no longer interested in being of help to *it* in any way if it hadn't been for the absolute shock and horror written on Wilfred's face that he felt through his fingers. It was as if the wilicho was also seeing this memory fully for the first time. The wilicho certainly knew the insult and had thrown the exact phrase at Osman many times, but he did not seem to have known the context. Wilfred's pleading eyes convinced Osman to reluctantly leave his fingers in place on the wilicho's face so together they might learn more.

Wilfred's son slowly and carefully recoiled the rope as the side of his face swelled into an angry red bruise. A familiar crossed-arm glowering stare followed every movement of the young man as he timidly completed the task. There was not a hint of remorse in the fisherman, just indignation and disapproving judgment of his offspring. Wilfred was mortified by the actions of the man who shared his face. Osman pondered to himself, isn't a wilicho just a remnant of the person they were? How could the fisherman in his vision and the echo of him have such different reactions to the same event?

Osman wondered how long Wilfred had wandered Kyflenor as a wilicho. Turning his mind back to the vision, Osman searched for clues as to when this event he was reading on Wilfred's face might have occurred. He focused on the port, which he did not recognize, and looked to the mountains Wilfred's son had so longed for. Osman pushed his mind deeper into the memory.

He spoke out loud as he had done previously. "Not mountains but a plateau." Osman pulled more details from Wilfred. "The Emerald Highlands. By the gods, that's Jadenpool!" Osman now recognized the single low building that still existed in the Xallian Capitol, the old counting house. He and Cerena had visited 'the oldest structure in Jadenpool' on one of their weekends together before the events that relocated their rendezvouses to the South. "You lived centuries before the Xallian Empire was even founded."

Wilfred pondered for a moment, then nodded. Osman continued, "That is over twenty-five hundred years ago. You've been wandering here for all that time?" Wilfred nodded again. "That's half a dozen lifetimes." Osman then added introspectively, "You aren't him anymore, are you? If you ever really were, other than at your creation."

Wilfred sighed and smiled as ghostly tears welled up further in his eyes. Through his fingers, Osman could feel and read Wilfred's deep relief in finally being understood and seen. It echoed the same emotion Osman had felt with Alerese. The overwhelming feeling of acceptance and understanding that comes from someone recognizing the totality of your story, even if they don't approve of all the twists and turns it might have taken along the way.

Wilfred finally spoke. He seemed to struggle painfully to find the words and break free of the repeated phrases from his living self. "Thank... you, Osman. I'm... sorry."

It was the first time Wilfred had used his name. In answer, Osman, as though a wilicho himself, repeated the gesture the Bloomsage had gifted him. He placed their foreheads together reverently. After a moment, Osman sat back on his heels, placed his hands in his lap, and said directly and earnestly, "I forgive you, Wilfred."

Wilfred leaned forward and said slowly, "You stink."

Osman couldn't help but chuckle. "I know, Wilfred. I will wash again in the next stream."

"No!" Wilfred said frustratingly. "The last person who smelled as bad had a dead fish in their net."

"So you've told me a dozen times." Getting to his feet, Osman replied with a gentle dismissiveness reflective of all they had been through in the last hour, as opposed to the defensiveness he typically snapped back with.

Wilfred blocked his path. "A dead fish full o' worms." Wilfred was getting more frustrated and snapped at Osman in a tone akin to the fisherman he had been when he was alive. "Listen, ya chowda head!" Catching himself with an exasperated sigh and struggle akin to his apology.

"Ye stink... like... the last person. He had a dead fish... full o' worms." Wilfred's eyes pleaded with Osman to understand.

Osman now gave more thought to Wilfred's words, repeating them back. "I smell the same as the last person. A person who had a dead fish full of worms." Understanding hit Osman like an avalanche cascading down his spine, sending chills from his scalp to his toes.

"Dear gods. My father carrying the corrupted soul of Richen. You saw my father!" Osman looked to Wilfred, who was signaling with his hands to keep going. Osman continued, having to sit on a log as his knees became far too wobbly to support him. "Not just saw, *traveled with*, yes?"

With a pointed look at Osman, Wilfred nodded and added, "You stink."

His speech, still encumbered by phrases he had said in life, was limiting what he could say, but Osman was convinced that there was more Wilfred needed to convey. Taking this perceived cue, Osman dug deeper and asked, "I stink because I am my father's son? Because we are related?"

Osman could see answering a direct question was a struggle for Wilfred, but the wilicho finally replied, "Aye, but more. The dead fish. The worms."

Osman thought back to the Solenrone chieftain, who also said he had a stench about him. The smell of the new gods and the Northlands flooded his soul. "I smell like Richen and the corruption?" Osman asked, almost afraid of the answer.

"Aye!" Wilfred stated with a mournful excitement at Osman's understanding. "The same, but different." Wilfred struggled and seemed unhappy with the words that he found, saying with a grimace of frustration. "A salmon returning to spawn in the river where it was born."

Osman didn't know how to interpret that, and no matter the question he asked, Wilfred seemed unable to articulate anything that would provide more clarity. Did it mean the corruption had infected Richen, had left, and was now returning? Or that he was returning to the Argestian Inception following his father's path? Or that, just like his father, he was burdened with Richen's future? There were too many possibilities, and every course led to more confusion and further questions.

The night was quickly growing cold. In the three weeks of travel with Wilfred and their path ever Southward, the two hours of twilight gloaming that previously passed as night were now four of true darkness. The low angle of the sun's daytime warmth no longer held back Autumn's early advance as it encroached on Kyflenor. If Osman didn't find the elemental inception soon, he would have to find a place to shelter for the darkest months of Winter, but that was all worries for tomorrow. Now, he needed a fire for warmth and shelter from the wind.

The rest of the night in camp was as peaceful as the first had been. Whatever compulsion that had driven Wilfred to his combative attitude no longer pressed him to berate Osman. Osman watched the Solenfel ripple overhead as he ate while Wilfred smoked his pipe and 'fished' in the fire. While the wonder of the Solenfel's majesty was still locked away from Osman, he no longer felt alone.

# CHAPTER SIX



*19 Years Earlier ~ Year 855* PXF *~ Autumn*

The storm had been raging outside for three days. Freezing rain and sleet had made the trails treacherous and darkened the skies day and night, making travel impossible. However, the cold and darkness that plagued Tavi's ruined body were not just from the weather. The corrupted shard wedged between his ribs that contained the boy's cursed soul was feeding his despair, pushing his mind into dark corners better left unvisited. Alone and shivering in the night, Tavi had little strength or hope left to call upon the elements to aid him.

Months before, Tavi, in his hubris, had not returned to the Isles with the afflicted boy to fulfill his Omenara. He was confident he could banish the infernal infection at a nearby minor upwelling of elemental power. Wrongly surmising what had taken root in the boy's body would weaken if removed from the dark forces permeating the Cour-Vermane estate and perhaps even be destroyed just from exposure to the site he had chosen, Tavi traveled north into the dwarven mountains. Taking the boy deep into the crystal caves there, Tavi naively thought his only task would be to watch over this boy Richen and cast minor healing magics as the elements did their work, but he had woefully underestimated the forces working against him.

The parasitic conjuring had not weakened. If anything, it had been fortified by the elemental forces rising from deep under the mountains. Tavi did not recognize the extent of the cursed disease's power until it thwarted his considerable elemental gifts and most potent rituals. When Tavi finally thought he had the upper hand and was on the verge of banishing the corruption, he realized too late that the conjured parasite had one final avenue of escape. It ripped the boy's weakened body apart to avoid being dispelled, the malignant curse just as content to feed on Richen's soul as it had been feeding on his life. That was when despair first planted its seeds in Tavi's mind.

The Fatesinger had told him the importance of this boy, how critical he was to everything to come, so he took the only option left to him. He captured the boy's soul in one of the cave's crystals and, to keep the soul intact, fed his own life force into the shard to sustain the boy's spirit contained within. The failed ritual to save Richen's life had taken every bit of strength Tavi had, and the added burden of the shard and its precious cargo ravaged his physical form as he traveled home. He was very nearly dead when he reached Horizon's End with only enough will remaining to draw on the restorative energies he had stockpiled and bound there.

He had not stayed long at his home, just over a fortnight. Richen's soul was too fragile, and it would be too easy to ignore destiny's call if he remained. The warring temptation to release the human boy's soul to the fates and never leave again versus the need to fulfill his Omenara and his destiny was too close at hand at Horizon's End. It threatened to tear Tavi apart as thoroughly as the spell had ripped apart Richen. As soon as he had gathered enough energy and hardened himself for the journey he knew he must now take, Tavi left under the dark of night, hoping he might return one day.

The trip across Kyflenor was arduous. His magic barely sustained his failing body and dwindling spirit. Tavi's only companion was a silent wilicho of a fisherman that appeared to him every day or so. Always ahead on the trail disappearing over the next rise, behind a stand of trees or rockfall. Six weeks of travel had brought him this far, but there was part of him that believed with each passing day, he might not make it any further.

With Winter approaching and no insight from the elements if the storm would last another hour or another week, Tavi was losing hope. He could feel the Argestian Inception in the distance, but it was still leagues away. Tavi knew if he did not stave off the despair growing in his soul, he would not survive. It was just a matter of what would kill him first.

Tavi didn't remember packing his paints. Perhaps they had already been in the pack as he filled it full of supplies when he absconded off on this current journey in the middle of the night. It didn't matter how. All that mattered was they were here and perhaps the only thing that could save him. With the wind whipping outside the cave and fire banked to give even light, Tavi lifted his brush to paint the image he had kept locked in his mind along every step of this never-ending Omenara—the vision the Fatesinger had gifted him on the cliffs outside Horizon's End and that now was his everything.

Present Day ~ Year 874 PXF ~ Autumn

With complete trust and faith, Osman allowed Wilfred to guide them forward. Grimspire loomed large to their west, dominating nearly a quarter of the horizon as they climbed the slopes of the Shieldwall Spine, hopefully toward a pass that would get them to the southern coast of Kyflenor and the Argestian Inception. The marching progression of the seasons now had daylight and darkness splitting the day evenly, with the winds of Autumn carrying the bite of the coming Winter. Osman had resigned himself that whether the inception was found or not, he would be spending the Winter on the tundra of southern Kyflenor.

Since the breaking of Wilfred's cyclical existence, Osman began to fill the hours of their trekking with talk and musings in place of Wilfred's fish tales. He told stories of his Hearth's Rest duels through the Trellis Market of Arnadore, tavern crawls with Talon, and barracks follies with his fellow guards. Wilfred listened attentively as far as Osman could surmise and even threw in some relevant sailor's musing and commentary when appropriate. Still, even the most lively stories could not banish away the trudging enormity of the obstacles in their path. As they, inch by inch, made their way up the steep slopes of the Shieldwall Spine to the invisible path that Wilfred could only indicate with a pointed finger and repeated phrase, "Follow the current," Osman put words to the insecurities gnawing at his mind.

Calling to the stout figure ahead of him who, even with his incorporeal nature, inexplicably seemed to be putting in as much effort in the climb as he was, Osman confessed, "Wilfred, I'm not sure if I know why I am even doing this anymore." Wilfred stopped his ascent and waited for Osman to elaborate, giving him his full attention. "Leaving the Hall of Judgement, it was a debt to Lady Cour-Vermane. Then arriving here on the Isles, I confronted how completely I had betrayed my Krolh'dran in his hour of most need, and my Qat'malorn debt to him eclipsed all else." Osman paused and sighed, then continued with a melancholy lament, "But with everything I have learned about my father, Richen, and even the Fatesinger's hand, I just feel used. Like a baited bear that doesn't know when to fall down and instead keeps getting cut to ribbons by his tormentors."

Wilfred seemed to be searching for something to say, some comfort or wisdom, but Osman filled the silence himself. "It's okay. I know you don't have the words, and they aren't necessary. There is only one path to choose now. I only hope my misgivings aren't the stone that eventually blocks our way forward."

Wilfred laid a ghostly hand on Osman's shoulder and repeated, "Follow the current," pointing up the slope. Osman's eyes followed his guide's outstretched finger and finally saw what Wilfred was referring to. Two swirling eddies broke the line of clouds above, not unlike how sea foam swirls through a broken sandbar.

Osman excitedly repeated back, "Follow the current! Of course! The wind through the pass breaks the clouds showing its location!" Osman surged past Wilfred with a smile and charged up the dwindling trail shouting, "Well, come on, you old salty sack! Don't just sit there like a beached tidehopper. Let's go!"

The words he had shared with Wilfred about his misgivings and reasons for being here rattled around Osman's mind for the rest of the day and through the next. They had found the pass below the break in the clouds just as Wilfred had predicted and crested the ridge of the Shieldwall Spine before making camp. Suddenly the next step of their journey seemed very close. Looking up at the angled peak of Grimspire, Osman's mind told him there must be leagues still to travel before Alerese's painting would match the looming landmark overhead. Nevertheless, his whole body felt like it was experiencing the last moments before being carried by a rushing current over a waterfall.

"I think I hate Richen," Osman blurted out as he stirred a pot of hot broth as it simmered on their small campfire banked against the howling wind. No qil accompanied his assertion, but Osman couldn't be sure if its absence was because of Richen's connection to his father or if the feeling wasn't a true one.

They had made camp in a protected alcove made by boulders that had fallen as part of a large rockslide into the mountain pass. The swirling wind through the flickering campfire made every shadow cast on the sheltering rocks writhe in a frenetic dance. Wilfred furrowed his brow with concern and disappointment. Osman reconsidered his admission and tried to put into words what he was feeling.

"Maybe not *hate* him, but everything that has happened because of him." The volume of Osman's voice drifted louder as he continued. "I want to hit him or shake him and ask if he knows all he has taken from me." Osman's diatribe picked up pace as he continued. "He stole my father from me, my childhood, my home, my Krolh'dran... my *life!*" His words echoed through the pass as the wind stilled between gusts.

The silence surrounding the camp stretched out to what seemed like days. Even the wind seemed to be stilled by Osman's outburst. Finally, Wilfred spoke. "Have you heard of the Fisherman's Folly?" Osman couldn't tell if Wilfred's words were a spark of sentience or a so often repeated story that it seemed conversational. Wilfred continued as his form shimmered in the firelight, "Many a young angler will chase angrily after a single fish that got away as they let the catch in their boat spoil." The old fisherman's eyes landed pointedly on Osman. "They never appreciate the bounty of all the fish they've landed along the way because they can't see past the spite for that one fish they feel is eluding them." Wilfred looked pointedly at Osman and said sagely. "Look to the bounty in your own boat and not to the sea for what might have been."

Hearing the words but not wanting to accept them, Osman mindlessly tried to explain why his situation was different. "But look at what he's done to me. I grew up without parents because of the Omenara my father took for him. When he did make appearances at Horizon's End, my father had been ravaged by the actions he had to take for Richen." Seeing no change in Wilfred's expression, Osman pressed on in a pleading voice,

"What he did made me maim my soul and sever the emotions I had for my father and my home."

Wilfred's eyebrow now rose, and in the tell-tale halting cadence that signified these were his words and not repeated phrases, he asked leadingly, "So, Richen made ye do that now, did he?" Wilfred continued logically, "Richen, the dead human lad who knows nothing of Uldani customs or rituals, forced ye to commit the atrocity ye inflicted on yerself?"

Osman dropped his eyes but then raised them again, unwilling to acknowledge his culpability for his actions, "And when I had finally found a family, a Krolh'dran, he was ripped away from me – again because of damned Richen!"

Wilfred kept his steady stare leveled at Osman. His questioning eyebrow lowered, and his expression fell into one of sadness and disappointment. He said no further words. Gave no comfort or additional wisdom. The wind returned, gusting around the boulders and through the pass. The Solenfel, which had seemed frozen in the sky above them, began to flow along its winding path once again. Wilfred's fishing pole appeared in the wilicho's hands, and he cast his line into the fire, float bobbing among the flames.

Osman pulled his simmering broth off the fire and stood up abruptly, frustrated that Wilfred refused to see his side of the story. He assured himself that Richen was the cause of all of this. Growing up unloved and unwanted, the numbness now infecting his emotions, him abandoning his homeland, losing the one bit of happiness and family he had with Talon, and now even being here on the edge of the world, most likely to die frozen and alone. The logical parts of Osman's mind tried to break through his self-pity, using Wilfred's words as a chisel, but they could find no purchase in the wall of moral certitude Osman had erected around his current emotional state.

He chugged his broth, the hot liquid burning his tongue and throat, adding to his foul mood. Despite the howling wind and cold, Osman abandoned the camp and walked into the night, letting his legs decide which direction to take. He did not venture further through the pass or back the way they came but instead retreated further into the narrow canyon and stacked boulders sheltering their camp. Osman walked for longer than he thought possible down the winding canyon, squeezing around boulders and climbing over treefalls. When he had finally walked off his frustration and decided to return to camp and face Wilfred, he determinedly snapped his body around in his tracks, surprising the beast that had silently stalked him. Deftly perched on one of the small ledges that ran just above head height along the length of the canyon, white fur and saber fangs glowing in the moonlight, was a crouching saldrig.

The predatory cat looked down on Osman with its ice-blue eyes cold as the glaciers they mimicked. The saldrig was easily three times Osman's weight, with claws and teeth far more effective than the iron dagger in his belt. Even if he had his twin swords and armor from the Arnadore Watch, Osman was unsure if he could survive a fight against the great cat. Osman could only hope the deadly predator above him was only curious and not hungry, but with Winter approaching, he thought it unlikely. Slowly taking steps backward, one behind the other, Osman inched deeper into the canyon. The saldrig, having been discovered, no longer stalked from above but leaped to the canyon floor and paced forward as Osman retreated.

The canyon grew even more narrow, and Osman could now easily place his outstretched hands on opposite walls as they closed in on him. His fear that the saldrig was pushing him toward its den or an ambush by its cubs or mate was soon realized as his back hit solid rock and the canyon's end. There was no escape. The saldrig continued to advance, and Osman instinctively drew Talon's iron dagger from his belt. The beast's deep growl seemed to vibrate the very foundations of the canyon as it saw the weapon in Osman's hand. He wondered if he even wanted to defend himself. His shoulders dropped as he contemplated if having his story end here might not be easier. The saldrig scented the air around Osman, took a deep breath, and roared through its saber fangs into his face. Its hot breath billowed across Osman's cold skin. An almost human look of disdain crossed the mighty cat's expression, and a single unspoken thought entered Osman's mind.

*Unworthy*

The saldrig turned in its path and walked back up the canyon without even a single glance back. Had it spit on the ground before leaving, it wouldn't have added any more contempt to its utter dismissal of Osman and his worth.

Osman slid down the canyon's wall and dared to look over his shoulder to examine the wall at his back. It was, in fact, not the end of the canyon but a giant boulder wedged between the walls of the ravine, a small gap opening into deeper darkness underneath it. Not wanting to wander again through the moonlight with the saldrig lurking nearby, Osman scrambled under the suspended rock. Winding under the boulder and then around and through the rockfall beyond, he found a small nook not much larger than himself that not even a breath of wind touched and still held the warmth of the day. Pulling his hood up and wrapping his cloak around him, Osman released a shaking sigh of relief as his racing heart began to settle.

He had left the camp in a sulky huff leaning into the sensation of his torso being bloated like after taking too large a breath and holding it. It was one of the few qil left to Osman that he could still feel, so he dove into it and made a great show of his *bad mood* by going off into the darkness to brood and think. It easily could have cost him his life. Still immersed in the mindset of his adolescent angst and stark lesson, Osman had no intention of braving the night again to attempt a return to the fire. He only hoped the shelter of the nook he huddled in could ward off the deep chill of night. Osman closed his eyes and tried to find sleep.

Osman awoke to sunlight penetrating through his eyelids. His body ached from sleeping upright in a sitting position, knees to chest and head leaning on a large stone wedged between the rocks cradling him. Osman flexed his aching limbs, stiff from cold and confinement, and crawled on all fours toward the sunlight, pins and needles plaguing his every extremity.

After several minutes Osman realized the path he followed was unfamiliar and did not seem to be the one he had used to get to this place. With no room to turn around, Osman continued crawling forward, hoping the light leading his way would circle back to the camp or at least the pass through the mountains so he could find it again. The path ahead opened up, and Osman scurried forward, anxious to escape the claustrophobic space he traversed and put the night behind him.

Osman stood up and immediately stretched his arms to the sky, lifting his heels off the ground to make himself as big as possible after feeling so cramped and confined. He had assumed he was back in the pass in one of the cliffs' switchback alcoves, but that was not the case. Before he could even assess his surroundings, he saw the man staring at him from across the chamber.

Osman, startled and instantly wary, dropped into a defensive stance. Out of habit, the iron dagger leaped to his hand, and through instinct and Talon's training, Osman scanned for cover or anything he could use to his advantage, but there were scant options anywhere near. The man did not move a muscle, and as Osman's mind slowed out of survival mode assessing his rival, he processed who the man was.

Osman stood frozen in place as a shaft of sunlight breaking free from the clouds illuminated the face of the man across from him. His face.

"It's me." Osman spoke the words out loud to solidify what he saw as reality and not some dream or vision. Looking around, Osman realized he was not in another canyon or the mountain pass but a cave with a large opening high in the eastern wall through which the morning sun poured in. Across from him was not a man. It was a painting, practically a mirror image of himself in the dueling armor he used to wear on Hearth's Rest in Arnadore.

The image of himself was happy, swords drawn in a relaxed cocky stance and a smile that looked as if it barely contained an outburst of laughter. As Osman approached, he could see every stroke and detail was perfection in its line and care. This was a masterpiece—a work of love. Osman reached out and touched the hard stone the miracle before him had been painted on. He examined it through his eyes and fingers, every stitch of cloth, rivet of armor, and nick in his swords recreated in paint. There was no question as to who had painted such a tribute, and when Osman looked into the joy mirrored on his own face, the force of the emotion behind the masterpiece dropped him to his knees.

There on the creases he never saw or knew in life were the fingerprints of his father reading the face of his son, too impatient to wait for the paint to fully dry.

# CHAPTER SEVEN



*Year 874* PXF *~ Autumn*

Osman's body was overwhelmed with so many qil and emotions he barely had time to process them. Then, one by one, they faded into numbness.

"No!" Osman wailed in a cry of anguish as the familiar hollow gray void in his soul swallowed every bit of emotion the painting had revealed. Even his tormented plea lost all meaning, the only evidence of it ever causing him pain receding as its echo faded in the cave's depths.

Osman wept tears of frustration and a loss he could no longer feel.

Wracked by sobs, Osman curled in on himself into a kneeling fetal position before the painting, unable to lift his eyes. His mind's eye, having nothing to feel emotionally, logically analyzed the realities of his father's work. This was nothing like the image of the shattered stained-glass window Osman had found in Tavi's studio. While still being expertly realized by his father's talents, the painting in the studio was more a dream captured in pigment, impressionistic, leaving many details to be interpreted by the viewer. The image on the cave wall was akin to the result a wealthy patron would expect from standing for a portrait for weeks on end. The painting before Osman was the meticulous recreation of something his father had seen or, perhaps, been shown.

Osman lifted his eyes and raised on his knees to examine the painting further. It was easily a decade or more older than the few years earlier when he had been the man in the image. Tavi had to have painted it near the same time he and Alerese had crossed paths nearly twenty years ago. When Osman was just a child.

A shimmering glow washed over the image before him, interrupting Osman's thoughts. He turned his head, and there was Wilfred with his weightless incorporeal hand laid on Osman's shoulder, his form casting the undulating light of the Solenfel across the cave's wall.

"He knew," Osman said through choked breath. "Somehow, he knew the man I would become. Not the man he wanted me to be or the man with the life I wished for, the man I am now." Osman paused in self-reflection, "He saw the broken man I became and still wanted to know me."

Osman miraculously felt Wilfred squeeze his shoulder comfortingly as he said, "Osman, now you are ready."

Osman got to his feet shakily and had to ask, "Did you know? Were you here?"

"Nay, 'twas different. His net 'twas already full while yers is empty." Wilfred replied cryptically, having exhausted his ability to converse further without using the repeated phrases from his life.

Osman rose to his feet and gingerly placed the tips of his fingers on the fingerprints his father had left in the paint. He hoped for some magic or emotional connection that could pierce the damage he had wrought upon himself to let him feel anything for the man who created this, but there was nothing. The injury Osman had done to himself was too grievous.

Osman slowly pulled his hands away and looked at Wilfred. "I know why I am here," Osman stated with a wistful smile. "I am here to know my father for the man he was, not how I wanted him to be." He continued with conviction, "I will finish what he started, not for him, or Talon, or Lady Cour-Vermane, or even the Fatesinger, but for *me*." Osman turned and strode from the cave with purpose, "This is my journey now."

Osman and Wilfred broke camp and proceeded through the pass across the Shieldwall Spine. Before midday, they found the far side of the cut between the ridge of mountains and looked down upon the southern coast of Kyflenor. The swath of land between the mountains and sea looked laughably narrow from this height, even though it was undoubtedly several miles wide. Coastal glaciers marked the boundary between sea and land, their jagged icy forms locked in the deep crevices they had carved out of the towering cliffs that fell to the sea. In the narrower parts of the landscape below, the glaciers completely filled the land from the Shieldwall Spine to the crashing surf. In the wider areas, evergreen forests created pools of deep green nestled between the stark grey and white of the mountains formed from either ice or stone.

Wilfred raised his finger and pointed to the southwest. Opposite Grimspire was a large teardrop-shaped plateau of land covered in birch trees shining like molten gold, their leaves having already turned with Autumn's arrival. With a twinkle in his eye, Wilfred called out, "Thar she blows!"

Osman couldn't help but laugh. In his worst dwarven pirate accent, he replied, "C'mon, you scurvy dog! Bait your hooks and cast your lines. We've got a whale to catch!"

The trip down the southern side of the Shieldwall Spine was far easier than the climb up it had been. The ebb and flow of the glaciers had ground many of the cliffs and crevasses of the ridge into smooth albeit steep slopes. When they were able, and with Wilfred's guidance, they slid down the permafrost on a makeshift toboggan made from bark and spruce branches. What had taken nearly a month to climb, the two were able to descend in less than a week.

They reached a narrow open vale at the base of the Shieldwall Spine that would lead them to the grove of golden birch trees, still several leagues away. A palpable silence permeated the liminal space the vale occupied between glacier and granite—a cathedral-like atmosphere, not due to any deity but a reverence of nature itself. There were several hours of daylight left in which to travel but without a word of direction uttered by either, Wilfred and Osman began to make camp.

The sense of purpose that filled Osman energized him, but he couldn't help but feel the weight of the coming end of his travels with Wilfred. He looked across the fire at his enigmatic, extraordinary guide and friend who had become so much more to him on this journey. Osman didn't know if the rules that bound the wilicho's existence could steal him away as early as tomorrow with their arrival at the Argestian Inception. He hoped Wilfred could stay with him and wait out the Winter before he continued the journey before him.

Osman pulled the tiny painting Alerese gave him out of his pocket and looked up at Grimspire, its peak still bright with sunlight even though the shadows in the vale had grown long. The imposing mountain looked nearly identical to the tiny painting resting in his hand. Even the quality of the light was the same as though the Bloomsage had painted it this very evening. The few leagues of travel to the grove should make the two a perfect match.

Osman felt he had come so far since crawling out of the surf months before, but also like he had just scratched the surface of all that he needed to do. He tried to reach out with his emotions to feel something, but they were all muted or already numb. Even simple pleasures and pains were fading from his ability to experience. All his thoughts inexorably led to his father and his need to uncover who he was. With every connection, he further blunted his emotions and qil. They all had dwindled to no more than poor reflections trapped in a milky mirror.

Osman had started this journey looking for knowledge, but now he wondered if the guardian of the inception could undo the numbness that had engulfed his soul. If it had cured Richen of the corruption that had infected his spirit, perhaps the guardian could also help Osman. Would he need to choose? Alerese had said the guardian would exact a price. A month ago, Osman would have said he had very little to lose, and now it seemed like he could be gambling everything.

Looking up, the Solenfel flowing above them was as spectacular as it was hypnotic. Although the gaping void in Osman's spirit had stripped it of all its wonder and majesty, he could still admire its aesthetic beauty. "Is this where my father camped as well, Wilfred?" Osman asked, not turning his eyes from the dazzling display in the sky.

"Aye, he dropped anchor hereabouts," Wilfred answered, then paused. Osman looked at his friend and found he was also looking at the sky. He had never seen Wilfred turn his eyes up to the Solenfel in all their time traveling together. The fisherman sighed and repeated the same cryptic phrase from days before, "His net was already full, so the currents pulled us each on our separate course."

"I don't understand, Wilfred. Is this where we part ways? What do you mean by 'his net was full?'" Osman's head filled with questions, scenarios, and thoughts of how to coax the answer out of the wilicho, even with his limited ability to communicate.

Wilfred raised a calming hand. "Tomorrow."

It was a resigned request not to spoil this night with worries that would come with the morning. Osman held his tongue, turned his back on their small campfire, and sat next to his friend to spend the night looking at the eternal dance of souls across the sky of Kyflenor.

Osman and Wilfred broke camp at first light, and well before midday, they arrived at the forest of golden birches. Less than fifty yards within the tree line was a large standing stone easily visible between the slender silver-barked trunks of the trees. Wilfred nodded, and they proceeded into the forest to stand before the granite monolith. Primitive carvings covered the stone, their imagery timeless and ancient. At its pinnacle, a winged serpent wrapped its sinuous form around the combined elemental symbols for air and water. Below was a procession of countless figures, some in pairs and others walking alone.

Wilfred pointed to a pair depicted on the boulder. "A full net." He then pointed to a figure standing alone, "An empty net." As Osman pondered the meaning of Wilfred's words, the wilicho's expression dropped as he sighed and added, "A full net catches no additional fish."

Osman looked to the stone, then back to Wilfred, and questioned, "A choice then? To continue alone or together?" Osman looked to the stone and wondered, "To go together with a 'full net' could mean I gain nothing from the guardian, and all of this has been meaningless." Osman contemplated his need not only for knowledge but also a cure for his condition and whispered aloud, "To go alone could allow my 'empty net' to gather everything I want." Osman looked to Wilfred and then to the forest ahead of him, bracing himself to say goodbye.

Osman turned to Wilfred's shimmering form, so like the Solenfel above them. He wanted to remember every detail of his friend and guide: his sun and salt wrinkled face, his scraggly beard, his ridiculous pack covered in lures, and his fishing pole waving like a flagpole above his head.

"Wilfred…" Osman started apologetically, then the words caught in his throat. It wasn't emotion that choked off Osman's words but the fishing pole. The story of the Fisherman's Folly rushed into his head. Osman realized he was about to not just let his catch rot but toss it overboard entirely to chase something that might not even be real.

Osman began again, "Wilfred, will you come with me?" Osman asked the question with a spreading smile and confidence in his voice.

Wilfred's expression lifted, hope filling his eyes as he said, "Yes."

Osman led the way around the rock and looked back, waiting for Wilfred to join him. The wilicho hesitated nervously, not yet breaking the imaginary barrier created by the standing stone. He looked into Osman's eyes, and Osman reassured him, "Wilfred, I don't just want you to come with me. I need you. I need your guidance and wisdom, of course, but what I need most right now is a friend."

Wilfred took a confident step forward and another one until he was fully past the stone. Osman smiled and was about to quip with one of Wilfred's maritime sayings to get them underway when he noticed the shocked expression on Wilfred's face.

"Wilfred, what is it?" Osman asked, trying to read the cause for the wilicho's distress. That is when Osman noticed the undulating illumination that normally emanated from Wilfred had become stable. It was no longer the shifting colors of the Solenfel but a light green constant glow the color of sunlight through new leaves in the early Spring. "Wilfred?" Osman questioned, concern entering his voice.

Wilfred opened his mouth to speak, then closed it again. He wet his lips with the tip of his tongue, then whispered tentatively, "My mind is clear." He continued gently as though coaxing a wild hare that would spook if startled, "My thoughts are my own, not just the repeated statements of my living self." Wilfred looked up to Osman, a cryptic expression spreading across his face.

"I don't think I'm a wilicho anymore."

# CHAPTER EIGHT

*Year 874* PXF *~ Autumn*

Osman was stunned. He slowly reached out a hand and passed it through Wilfred's incorporeal form.

"Whatd'ya think ye're doing?" Wilfred chided. "Do I look like flesh and bone to ye?"

"Well, no, but you said…" Osman began before Wilfred interrupted.

"I said I'm not a wilicho. That doesn't mean I'm gonna start juggling jellyfish anytime soon." He added, "And yes, I said that intentionally. I'm not gonna be tickling trout or slapping salmon, either." Wilfred began to chuckle at the last alliteration. As Osman started to guffaw at the testy fisherman, Wilfred added with mirth, "Give me some slack in my lines. Twenty-five hundred years having only a few dozen phrases worth of vocabulary will take some time to break out of."

Osman caught his breath and asked with a genuine curiosity, "But how?"

"I've never been able to get past the stones before," Wilfred explained. "The few times I tried, the stone sent me back ta the coast where it all started." Looking back at the stone and then at Osman, his voice trailing off, "No one's ever wanted me before."

"So, my father? He had Richen?" Osman asked.

"I din't see him cross. All I know is people may only enter alone or with one other, never more." Wilfred explained. "I've seen hundreds of pilgrims try an' reach the inception. Only a few dozen have made it here. Twice I've seen a group of three attempt ta cross." Wilfred looked down at his feet and continued with a voice barely above a whisper, "The stones din't grant them passage together."

"What happened?" Osman asked gently.

"Selfishness. Pride. Doubt." Wilfred became lost in the recollection for a moment. "Friends, lovers, family. They tore each other apart."

Osman felt guilty that he had dampened the mood of Wilfred's newfound freedom with such a grizzly memory, but it also made him wonder what trial might lie ahead for them at the inception. Osman said the thought aloud as it crossed his mind, "Whatever lies ahead, perhaps it will be easier together." Wilfred nodded. With Osman holding Alerese's painting like a compass and marking their direction from Grimspire's peak looming overhead, the two walked deeper into the grove toward the Argestian Inception and its guardian.

Just over an hour later, Osman and Wilfred came to a clearing in the forest of birches. The glade was utterly empty. Neither rock nor vegetation broke the flat expanse of ground, its only covering a carpet of fallen golden birch leaves. Osman looked to the sky and the peak of Grimspire. Holding the tiny painting that had guided him all this way at arm's length so its image was side by side with the landscape before him, he saw they were now a perfect match. With a nod, he looked to Wilfred and stepped carefully out of the tree line onto the carpet of leaves.

The leaves crunching under his footsteps seemed louder than thunder rolling across the mountains as Osman crossed the clearing. Trying to make each step more gentle than the last, he finally reached the center with Wilfred at his side.

"Hello?" Osman hailed to whoever or whatever might be listening. He did not draw Talon's dagger, but it was close at hand on his belt. He knew even a weapon like the Vermillion Blade would be of little use against an ancient guardian of the elements, much less an iron dagger, but he also was not willing to have it entirely out of reach.

Wilfred then raised his voice and spoke, "We seek the guardian of wind and tide, the keeper of the frozen inception of primal air and water."

Osman looked to Wilfred and whispered out of the side of his mouth, "How did you know that?"

"I've kept my ears open around many a campfire through the years," Wilfred whispered back.

The first few moments of silence drew out into a minute and then a minute more and another after that. Osman shifted his weight from one foot to the other and back again. Slowly turning in a circle, he spoke again, "I seek knowledge of my father, who came here to cleanse a human boy's soul nearly twenty years ago. I am..."

## I Know Who You Are

The voice came from all around them, howling like the wind but also no more than a whisper in their ears.

A swirling wind surrounded Osman and Wilfred. The carpet of leaves rose from the ground in a flurry, creating a golden curtain blinding them even from each other standing side by side. The air grew chill and then colder still. The golden leaves bleached white with frost and began to shatter into a maelstrom of snow and ice. The force of the blizzard was impossible to stand against, and Osman fell to his knees and huddled over his core to try and retain warmth. The darkness and frozen fury of the storm was all-encompassing. Osman's only comfort was the soft green glow of Wilfred's form standing over him.

Osman could barely discern over the howling gale that words were being spoken. Wilfred was saying something, but the wind drowned out their meaning from his ears. A deep instinctual need to survive filled Osman's mind, and he curled deeper into himself, cowering from the forces at play around him, trying to conserve what little heat his body produced as it shivered violently under his cloak. The voice then focused on him.

*What Do You Truly Seek?*

Osman, his body chilled beyond being able to shiver any longer, knew he did not have time to say anything but his truth. "My father. A family. To be whole again."

*Then Leave that Shell Behind and Stand to See
What It is You Ask*

Osman stood without thinking, but only his spirit was now on its feet. His body remained on the ground, frozen in a huddled ball. Incorporeal as Wilfred, his ghostly eyes looked around the clearing, seemingly free of the storm. Beyond the glade was not a forest of birch trees but one made of ice-covered Uldani bodies frozen in every conceivable pose possible. Some were peaceful, some in a rictus of terror, but all were statues frozen in time. Osman looked around for Wilfred.

The voice, no longer all-encompassing, came from beside him. "He is not with you in this place but also not far away." Osman turned his head to the voice and found himself face to face with a shimmering white serpent head as large as his torso. The serpent's frosted-crystalline body was continually in motion behind the head, held aloft by a half-dozen wings as they slid past each other in a writhing dance of reflected light.

"To be whole is to be healed. To be healed, one must first be cleansed. And you are the opposite of cleansed. Stolen power flows into you like a tide returning to the shore." The serpent slithered through the air around Osman's back to whisper in his other ear. "You want to know your father? It is his life your flesh now consumes." The serpent's maw loomed over his corporeal flesh as it spasmed on the ground from the cold.

"I don't understand what you mean. I hardly knew my father. I only recently discovered he might have even wanted to know me." Osman confessed.

The serpent's voice softened, "Let me show you what he did for his son."

Osman saw before him two figures carved of crystal-clear ice. One he immediately recognized as his father, the other a young, strongly-built human nearly his father's height with cropped hair in the style of blacksmiths—Richen. Within the young blacksmith was a shadow given form, an abomination of darkness and ruin with a wavering spider-like shape that shifted and writhed as though not fully corporeal. Its circular mouth, full of needle-like teeth, dripped with ichor and undulated unnervingly as it feasted on Richen's young and vibrant soul. Its body was bloated like a tick too long on a hound's ear. The wraith spider's hind legs were in constant motion. They meticulously wove an intricate blood-red silken chain from the golden energy it consumed from Richen's soul, digested, and then excreted for its purpose out of spinnerets on the nightmare creature's abdomen.

Osman felt bile rise in his incorporeal throat despite his physical body being on the ground at his feet. The serpent guided Osman's ghostly eyes to follow the winding filament of the vile chain as it flowed into the sky northward.

"See the truth," the serpent hissed into Osman's ear.

Above him, at the point where the silken chain passed through its dancing ribbons of light, the Solenfel opened the sky to Osman's eyes. The Solenfel was no longer just an awe-inspiring display of color and motion. It was a mosaic of pictures and forms as though painted by his father's hand. He saw a young Talon nearly unrecognizable but for his wild mane of hair. Grief had twisted him into a pitiful wretch as it wracked his slight frame and lean physique, so different from the towering powerful man he knew. Osman saw the spider's corrupt gossamer chain snaking toward his Krolh'dran. Osman watched as it struck like a scorpion's tail and pierced the large artery in Talon's neck. Bloated with energy pulled from Richen's soul, each link wormed into Talon's flesh and began to flow through his veins.

The image in the Solenfel shifted. Osman saw Talon older, now near the end of his teenage years, his form looking more like the man he recognized but still not yet fully formed. He was training in the familiar Cour-Vermane courtyard with a silver-haired warrior in black armor. Now dozens of the spider's ethereal chains flowed into Talon, undulating with their harvested energy. Where the filaments of crimson chain pierced his flesh, his veins seemed to devour them link by tiny link, swallowing their power, leaving Talon utterly unaware of their presence.

Osman saw other chains bound Talon as well. A shifting web of arcane links seemed to surround his Krolh'dran, guiding his glaive as he trained, but Osman could see what Talon could not, their addictive nature trying to bend him to their will. Finally, there was a black chain forged of hate and spite large enough to anchor an Uldani battle galleon. It stretched out of Talon's abdomen through the cobblestones toward the bowels of the Cour-Vermane estate like a desiccated iron umbilical cord.

As Osman tracked the chain of darkness toward its source, he lifted his eyes to the study window he and Talon had magically passed through at the Gala. There, like a malevolent conductor, Toman Cour-Vermane loomed over the courtyard, weaving fiendish and arcane runes, shaping and augmenting his son like he was no more than a necromancer's construct built of stolen corpses. Not an ounce of care or remorse marred Toman's face, just a malevolent zeal as he watched the ripening fruit of his labor.

The serpent's voice slithered into Osman's ears, "The servant of darkness poured the energy his abomination stole into your Krolh'dran's flesh, flooding it with the things he coveted and valued most: size, power, and strength." The serpent continued with an undertone of malice for Toman's actions, "His son, no more than a weapon of muscle and bone in his eyes, became a transgression against nature itself and all its designs for Talon. An aberration formed in response to Talon's broken heart and fueled by the lifeforce being pumped through his veins by Toman's parasitic minion the hellhound infected his lost love with."

The Solenfel advanced through time. Osman now saw himself painted in the sky fighting Talon at the base of the stairs of Arnadore Keep the day of the failed coup. The spider's silken chains no longer flowed into Talon, but at the hundreds of sites where they once entered his body, his skin had grown translucent and revealed thousands upon thousands of their tiny links pulsing through his veins and flesh. The other chains were still evident as well. The arcane links that had been his ally in training now swarmed around him like vicious snakes flowing out of the Vermillion Blade, trying to move his limbs against his will, screaming for him to draw the glaive and strike Osman down.

The black chain at his abdomen pulled and yanked at Talon's mind and soul, adding its dark energy to all the other forces at work on him in this final effort to bend him to his father's will. With the Solenfel's added perspective, Osman realized how dire Talon's struggle had been. Osman watched Talon plunge the dagger into the image of himself painted across the night. He recognized the depth of the miracle his Krolh'dran's love had achieved. Talon had been more chains than man—the totality of the forces controlling him all but unimaginable. Yet, he still saved Osman even after

Osman had refused to stand by his side, betraying his Krolh'dran for the lies of Cerena. He turned his head away and averted his eyes in shame.

The serpent grabbed his head roughly in its coils and snapped it back to the sky. It hissed angrily in his mind, "You do not get the luxury of denying what you have done and was done for you."

An image of Talon floating lifelessly in space filled the entire sky. His face was peaceful and almost angelic, with his hair spread around him like a halo. But, where his hands should be, his forearms ended in blackened stumps, and his body hung obscenely from the black chain welded to his abdomen. The sound of a fading heartbeat, echoing off the impossible heights of Grimspire in the distance, filled the night around Osman's ghostly form. He became dimly aware of his own body's dwindling heartbeat, but he no longer cared. All that mattered was his Krolh'dran.

Ghostly tears spilled out of Osman's eyes as Talon's heartbeats grew further apart and finally stopped, one final beat echoing across the plains of Kyflenor. Osman wailed into the night, unable to move, still immobilized by the serpent's coils around his head and body, forced to stare at his brother's corpse hanging in the sky. Sobs wracked his spirit so violently that his uninhabited corporeal body lying on the ground shook from their intensity.

## CRACK!

The sound rang out at a volume that would turn a thunderclap to little more than a kitten's purr by comparison. The foundation of Grimspire seemed to shudder at its power as Osman watched the image of Talon above him flash bright gold, the black chain holding him shattering as though it was no more than an icicle under a blacksmith's maul. It evaporated into the ether. From Talon's body, as though being shed like pollen from a summer flower, Osman watched as thousands of the now broken tiny crimson links woven by the spider spilled across the sky.

The painting flashed backward in time, and the scene of teenaged Talon training in the courtyard hung in the sky as the serpent forced Osman's eyes back to the figures carved in ice of his father and Richen. "The whole story is not yet told, Son of Tavi. Your father was not one to underestimate a rival twice."

Under the sky filled with the image of Talon training with the warrior in black, Osman watched on the ground before him as the icy form of his father reached into Richen's chest and pulled the bloated spider out of the boy. The vile creature struggled and screeched in his father's grasp, the woven chain of energy unraveling in the sky as it did so. Osman thought his father would surely crush the parasite in his hands or immolate it in a blaze of fiery magic, but he did not.

Tavi looked up at the silken chain of energy as it frayed, lowered his gaze to look directly into Osman's eyes as though he was there, and said, "For you and to keep him safe." His father then pushed his hand holding the bloated spider into his chest. Like a tick, it burrowed deep into his body and latched onto its new host's life force and soul. Clenched agony contorted his father's face, but the parasite, feasting and content, began to weave its chain once more. Tavi's life force, flowing freely through the abomination, was incorporated into the crimson chain and rose into the sky uninterrupted to its destination: the Cour-Vermane estate for Toman to empower the thrall he was creating out of his son.

Both admiration and kindness filled the serpent's voice as it spoke again, "Your father deceived the dark weaver right in front of his own eyes. By substituting his life force for Richen's soul, he not only freed Richen to be reincarnated, but Tavi's considerable will and connection to nature and the elements were embedded into Talon's flesh by Toman himself." The serpent's voice held amusement and almost a sense of pride as he finished and directed Osman's eyes back to the crystal figures before them.

In the scene before Osman, Richen's form coalesced into a shining white crystal shard that his father placed in a small box. With a sigh, Tavi staggered westward as the spider in his chest continued its grim work.

A heartbeat broke the trembling and stunned silence consuming Osman. The Solenfel image in the sky was once again the ruined body of Talon surrounded by a growing cloud of broken crimson links leaking out of him. Another heartbeat echoed through the night, and the image of Talon moved of its own volition. Some links swarmed to Talon's hands, regenerating the flesh at an astonishing rate, but others began aligning themselves in an array, like metal filings around a magnet. The tiny links started to flow along whatever invisible currents of force guided them. One of the larger groupings began to wind out of the Solenfel and down from the sky. Osman followed their path like he used to follow lines of ants as a child and discovered their destination. They flowed into the body at his feet. They were merging with him.

"What was sacrificed by the father returns to the son." The serpent's head slid into Osman's line of sight. "But are you willing to accept all the gift carries with it? What your father freely gave has been shaped by demons and gods alike. Even one such as I cannot predict all it brings with its return."

Osman's mind was reeling. He thought of how the Yuelan chieftain in the saldrig pelt had said he stank of the new gods. Wilfred had said nearly the same. Before he could fully process the implications and how long he had been on the receiving end of energy stolen by the parasite, first from Richen and then his father, the serpent offered a choice.

"There is also the easier path. Deny the gift and become part of my forest. Let your father's energy find other paths and disperse into the world as fate sees fit." The serpent looked out at the forest of frozen bodies. "What you see are not corpses of the dead. When joined, the domains of air and water are of cleansing and protection, not healing, but a person within my care can draw upon the healing forces of the world and repair itself if given time and if the body and spirit are willing."

The serpent circled Osman, all the while looking at the frozen figures almost lovingly. "Many among my grove bear the same scars and wounds as yourself. Some take years to heal, others decades." The serpent returned its gaze to Osman. "Those unwilling to face their trauma can spend centuries mending their soul. Time is meaningless for those among my grove. It passes only as quickly or slowly as one desires. When their work on themselves is complete, the ice melts, and they leave."

The serpent's offer to be whole again sorely tempted Osman. To regain his emotions so he could grow to know who his father genuinely was once he had healed. So he would be able to experience everything he lost once more. Osman was but a youth by Uldani standards, with centuries still to live in front of him. Some peace from all the turmoil in his mind and heart would be a welcome respite after the chaos of the last few years. He could spend his exile here in the grove and be free to roam whole again wherever he wanted when he emerged from the serpent's garden.

But then he thought of the look on his father's face, his words, and his painting on the cave wall. Tavi might not have known all of what would return when his sacrificed life force flowed back to Osman, but he had meant for his son to have it. Osman looked to the serpent, "I will receive my father's gift even if it means you cannot cleanse me, and my soul will not heal."

"I did not say I would not cleanse you. I said it would not be the gentle respite of my grove." The serpent continued in a terrifyingly curious, almost scholarly tone, "Perhaps this power touched by gods and demons and tempered by your father's sacrifice will even allow you to survive it." The serpent offered consolingly, "At least you will not be alone." Suddenly, Wilfred appeared at his side.

"Wilfred, I'm not sure what will come of this, but I think it's what I must do." Osman hurriedly sputtered out, not sure how much time he had.

"Whatever it is, I won't leave ye," Wilfred stated without hesitation.

The serpent opened its maw, and an icy cone of ethereal frost and ice spewed forth, enveloping Osman's spirit and driving it back into his body, still huddled against the cold at his feet. Osman could feel all the damage the cold had wrought upon his flesh during his spiritual encounter with the serpent. Even through that searing pain, though, he felt the serpent's breath scour clean the wounds that had banished his emotions for his father, Horizon's End, and all the things now infected by the spreading void he created years ago. The debrided wounds in Osman's soul screamed out with the return of each and every emotion banished from his childhood and denied them for the last eight years.

An onslaught of qil slammed into Osman's flesh. Every muscle tensed in a rictus of pain, his body stretched spreadeagle in the snow carpeting the clearing. Osman felt his skin melt in the flames of rage, flowing off his limbs only to reform under the petal-soft touch of kindness. His joints dislocated and his bones broke under the torsion of his muscles as they reacted to guilt and malice. His jaw clenched so violently from reliving decades of loneliness it cracked his teeth in their sockets. Even smiles from pent-up joy and gratefulness took their toll on his body as the magnified strength of the emotion ripped his facial muscles off his cheekbones. For every injury his unleashed qil inflicted on his physical body, the crimson energy returning to his flesh healed it. Each respite the qil of love, kindness, or comfort gave only heightened the following sensations and injuries caused by hate, abandonment, and loss. How many times Osman's body contorted, twisted, and ripped itself apart, only to be remade by the crimson energy, was impossible to tell.

Osman fell into an abyss of unending pain. His mind, lost in anguish as his emotions and waves of qil tore his body to shreds once again, grasped for anything to hold onto. The last thing he heard as he took his final breath was Wilfred's voice yelling, "Stop! I agreed to yer terms. Now, stand by yers, snake! He is my charge now, and ye shall harm him no further."

Darkness.

# CHAPTER NINE



*Year 874* PXF *~ Last Friend's Remembrance*

Darkness.

Osman's consciousness floated weightless in a void without light, sound, dimension, or time—a faint spark of awareness, little more than a glimmer of stardust against the vastness of an empty night sky. The spark arced deep within his mind trying to connect with anything familiar, but there was nothing. It dimmed and went dark again, perhaps for no more than a blink of an eye or perhaps for an eon.

A gentle muffled sound ignited activity in the darkness once again. A grumbling hum that resolved into a purring melody permeated the black nothingness that enveloped Osman like a heavy blanket. There was scant tinder upon which the spark could catch hold to bring full wakefulness, but it found a single thought upon which to light a flame—a name: Wilfred.

"That's it, Osman. Find yer way. Let me guide ye." Wilfred's voice was gentle as a Summer breeze across a meadow. Osman didn't so much follow Wilfred's whisper as he let it carry him like a dandelion seed drifting upon a dream. Across the void, the mote of sentience that was Osman floated indiscriminately. As it traveled, more pieces of himself ignited across the landscape of his mind and joined him until he began to think and to remember.

Pain. Unbearable, inconceivable agony. The spark hesitated, cowering. Osman wanted to retreat back into the blissful nothingness of the dark, but Wilfred's voice intervened. "'Tis just a memory. S'not real. Ye're safe." There was a pause in the assurances Wilfred's voice offered, then it continued, "Yer body is free from that now."

The spark voicelessly queried as to what that meant.

"There's much to explain, but first, ye must recover the rest of who ye are," Wilfred's voice expounded comfortingly. The spark surrendered to Wilfred's presence and allowed him to carry it further across the mindscape that seemed to extend infinitely in all directions. Memory by memory, experience by experience, the spark absorbed its life back into itself until it became Osman once again. Still without form, it now could sense weight and dimension and time. Osman's consciousness drifted before the presence of Wilfred.

"Osman? Can ye speak?" Wilfred asked.

Osman tried to articulate all the questions he had but failed. His consciousness had neither lungs to provide breath nor lips to form words.

Wilfred clarified, "No, not speak. *Communicate*. Forget about speech 'n forming words with yer mouth. Just project what ye want t'say."

"Wilfred?" Osman's voice echoed within his consciousness.

"There ye go. It'll be tiring at first. Ye're very weak, but ye *are* healing." Wilfred spoke like the cleric who removed Talon's dagger from his lungs.

"Am I dead? Am I in the grove? What happened?" Osman's rapid-fire questions left his consciousness weak, and he felt himself fading.

Wilfred's presence reached out and somehow infused Osman's consciousness with energy stabilizing him. "I'll explain all I can, but we're both recovering, and I have little energy t'spare, so let's not squander it."

Wilfred's presence took what amounted to a breath in this place and began to explain.

"We're alive, but we're different," Wilfred stated without preamble. "In cleansing ye, the serpent's breath destroyed yer body a dozen times over. No amount o' healing energy flowing into ye could keep up." Wilfred paused, seemingly reluctant to revisit the memory of all he had witnessed. With a haunted voice, he said, "T'was like a stream trying to quell a volcano. The unleashed power of all the emotion ye had locked away overwhelmed yer father's sacrifice returning to ye."

Osman shied away from the memory as the torture he had endured flashed across his mind. Even Osman, as just an incorporeal spark of consciousness, perceived the outflowing of care and empathy from Wilfred's presence as he spoke.

"I couldn't bear it any longer. So I stepped into the serpent's breath to shield ye from it. And that's when whatever the designs that deities, fiends, and fate had imprinted on yer father's sacrifice began their work." In a questioning tone as though he was still trying to make sense of everything that happened, Wilfred surmised, "Even the serpent guardian of the inception seemed overpowered by the forces at work, its breath no longer fully under its control."

Wilfred addressed Osman directly, "The guardian's breath redoubled in force, an yer Uldani body distended and contorted beyond anything that had come before. Yer tormented screams became tortured, inhuman howls punctuated by roars of anguish. The serpent's power, yer father's sacrifice, and the forces imprinted on that parasitic chain ignited around ye in an arcane tempest. It swept me along like a raindrop in a hurricane. Whether I was accidentally entangled in their purpose or the catalyst for it, I cannot fathom," Wilfred paused, "but everything in that storm of fate, magic, elements, and the gods flooded into yer tortured form and merged with it."

"Including me," Wilfred added after a pause.

Osman could not comprehend what Wilfred was telling him. It made even less sense than his current predicament as a formless spark of consciousness hovering near the presence of Wilfred in this infinite space. "Where are we then?" Osman asked. Trying to fit the pieces together, he intuited, "Wilfred, are you in my mind? In my body?"

"It's a tad more complicated than that, lad. It's better to show ye bit by bit than to try to explain the little I know." Wilfred confessed. "I need ye ta reach out and connect with yer body. Not yer physical body, but yer body here in this place with us."

Osman tried to do what Wilfred asked, confused about how to differentiate. He reached with his consciousness attempting to feel the weight of his limbs or the residual pain and ache from the serpent's breath. What he sensed was unfamiliar, misshapen, and distorted. Osman instinctively recoiled from it.

"Not there, Osman. That's the real world, and what lies there will come soon enough," Wilfred gently guided. "Look for *yer* body as ye knew it, as it once was."

Osman was shaken by Wilfred's words. What was waiting for him in the real world? What did this mean for the life ahead of him? Wilfred's gentle push on Osman's consciousness redirected his scattered focus. Osman tried to reach out again, but every attempt drew him back to the deformed flesh Wilfred had steered him away from. How could Osman find the body he once had while he was filled with dread and suffocated by what he might now be? He felt like he was drowning just below the surface of the truth but unable to break through.

The effort he was using and the rising panic in his mind began to drain his strength. As his consciousness faded, one sentence cut through to his dimming awareness, "Look to yer own boat, Osman."

The painting.

His father's masterpiece, hidden on a cave wall high in the mountains of the Shieldwall Spine, became Osman's lighthouse. He turned away from the imagined water's surface that trapped him and followed the beacon of Tavi's love for the son he never knew. As Osman remembered each line and stroke of the image, it was as though he was painting his flesh into existence in this place. However, to his surprise, his mental brushstrokes were not painting a body around his consciousness as intended but off in the distance. Somewhere up ahead.

Osman's consciousness drifted toward where he knew his rediscovered body lay. As the last details of the flesh he painted fell into place on the body ahead of him, he felt a tingling around his consciousness. An ethereal version of his imagined body shimmered into existence around his naked mind, finally giving him form and dimension in this place.

"Ah, there ye are." Osman heard Wilfred's voice come from beside him. Heard with ears from a point in space outside himself instead of just sensing it in his mind. "Ye can open yer eyes now."

Osman opened his newfound eyes, having not realized they were closed. His ghostly form actually *seeing* the surroundings for the first time. As his eyes swept across the blank mindscape before him, his sight acted like a giant paintbrush leaving behind a mélange of color, shape, and motion without reason or proper form. The swaths of jumbled reality his gaze created faded just as quickly from his peripheral vision once his attention moved beyond his eye's focus. The only constants were himself, Wilfred standing beside him, and a humanoid-sized crystalline chrysalis floating within arm's reach before him.

"You'll get used to it, lad." Wilfred intoned. "Reality is a bit what ye make of it here. But some things are persistent regardless of what ye wrap around them." Wilfred's shimmering wilicho-like form motioned to the chrysalis before them.

Through its semi-opaque surface, Osman saw his body. Not as he imagined it in the painting, smiling in his dueling armor, but broken and battered, the clothes he had been wearing in the clearing shredded to less than rags. Every instinct yelled in Osman's mind to look away, but his ruined flesh held him transfixed. He remembered the time he had found a mauled elk while exploring the woods around Horizon's End. Antlers torn off, legs broken, neck snapped, and bleeding out. Somehow still alive, drawing in ragged breaths, eyes wild with fear. Osman had been eleven years old, overwhelmed with pity for the massive creature enduring so much pain and filled with anxiety before him. He knew quickly ending the elk's misery would be a kindness, but he stood frozen, joints and limbs petrified by the qil of his pity and indecision.

Osman's body in the chrysalis was in a similar condition as the elk's. Breath shallow and face in a rictus of pain, gaping wounds showing bone, sinew, and the organs beneath. Limbs broken and brutally twisted out of their sockets. Somehow still living but a vessel incapable of life.

Osman's ghostly form stood before the chrysalis that encased his physical body, frozen just as he had been all those years ago in front of the elk. At that moment, he realized he *felt* the petrification of pity's qil weighing on his incorporeal limbs as he looked down at his broken flesh. The qil and emotion of that memory from his childhood and Horizon's End was no longer numb to him.

Osman lifted the arms of his spirit form to feel the reawakened dusty grinding of his joints afflicted by qil. As his forearms came into view, he recognized the wounds upon them and realized what encased his consciousness in this place was his soul. Written upon his shimmering arms were the open wounds of the ritual Osman had inflicted upon himself to excise his father and home a decade ago—now cleansed and no longer festering. The harm he inflicted upon himself then was not a mirror of the overwhelming trauma imparted on his physical flesh resting in the chrysalis before him; however, it was the cause of all his corporeal self had endured.

Osman examined his soul-self as easily as one might assess the fit of a new tunic, he saw carved into his forearms the eighteen slashes mirroring the marks on the log above his bed at Horizon's End that he had added after Anson's departure. Looking down past his forearms, Osman saw his feet. Where wonder had once danced, his toes were blackened and desiccated as though from frostbite. Channels etched the surface of his legs and arms like rivers cutting through a desert. They ran from his extremities to the heart of the injury he had inflicted upon his soul—the gaping hole in his chest. In that central place was where Horizon's End and his father's memory had lived before the ritual he undertook cut them out.

Osman could imagine the nightmare the wound must have been when it was festering and swallowing his every emotion. Its ichor oozing across his soul, carving channels in his soul's flesh as it spread to consume him. The crater in his torso was no longer empty, however. His fingers encountered shimmering spiderweb-like filaments of his healing soul that stretched across the wound's cavernous void that he dared not disturb. Osman might be beginning to be able to feel again, but he was far from being whole.

His hand drifted to his soul's face, knowing the number of emotions he had lost that manifested their sensations there. He looked to Wilfred. "How bad is it?" Osman asked tentatively.

"I won't lie ta ye. Ye might want to hold off on taking a look until ye have healed more." Wilfred stated as neutrally as possible, but Osman could see the pain behind his eyes. To his credit, Wilfred had never averted his gaze or turned away, always looking him straight in the eyes as they spoke.

"The serpent said those in his grove must face their trauma to heal," Osman stated introspectively. "I did this to myself, and I need to see it. Can you show me?"

"Aye, I can show ye," Wilfred confirmed.

Osman felt his consciousness separate from his soul and move across the space between himself and Wilfred, merging with the wilicho. Osman then found himself seeing through Wilfred's eyes, looking up at his soul from the wilicho's slightly lower perspective. From this vantage point outside himself, Osman saw that the wound in his torso was far more grievous than he perceived with his own eyes. It encompassed nearly the entirety of his soul's core. Had there been daylight in this place, he was sure it would have been visible through what little substance remained at the far side of the gruesome tunnel through his chest.

The channels Osman had noticed carved into his arms and legs were more profound and numerous across his chest and running up his neck, finally reaching his head. Osman's face, the visage of his soul, was a horror dreamed up from the nightmares of the Night of the Drowned Moon. Barely recognizable even to himself, the smiling countenance of his father's painting was reduced to a withered wraith split by gaping wounds and splintered bone. Osman's gaze traveled from feature to feature, taking in every horrifying detail, cataloging the damage he saw with its corresponding lost emotion.

"Will I heal?" Osman asked Wilfred tentatively.

"The guardian of the inception promised that all flesh and souls heal with time and rest, which brings us to our situation," Wilfred explained.

In a blink, Osman was back in his own form, seeing with his eyes and looking down at Wilfred. A profound gratitude overcame Osman seeing only loving concern in Wilfred's eyes, knowing full well the horror his friend confronted with an unflinching expression. Without Wilfred, he would be going through this alone or not at all. His cresting emotions and all else he had experienced since awakening sent a wave of exhaustion over Osman, almost making him swoon.

"That's probably enough for today. Yer healing has just begun, and as ye saw, there is still a long way to go for both yer soul and flesh." Wilfred's voice took on a gentle but firm bedside manner, "Let's get ye comfortable."

Osman suddenly found himself in his room at the Sojourn's Rest, his freshly made bed calling out to him. The din of the tavern below vibrated through the walls, and if he concentrated, he could hear Talon's rumbling snores echoing from his adjacent suite of rooms. As he curled into the familiar bed and consciousness left him, Osman heard Wilfred say, "I'll wake ye again soon to give ye the rest of the tale."

Osman dreamed of a lone saldrig sitting on a snow-covered ridge with eyes to the sky; the Solenfel's secrets and truths open before its glowing eyes.

# CHAPTER TEN



Osman awoke to a gentle shake of his shoulder. He was in his room at the Sojourn's Rest, and as he rolled over, expecting to see Lolly or Talon, he instead saw Wilfred's face. A wave of disorientation rolled over him as his mind couldn't rectify the juxtaposition of his surroundings with the wilicho.

Then he remembered.

As he looked down at his forearms, the illusion of unblemished skin faded, revealing the scarred soul beneath. Osman tried to reconjure the illusion of his healed body to cover the injuries he had inflicted on himself but was unable to. His initial disappointment at his failure transitioned to resigned acceptance as he recognized that denying the parts of his life he didn't like was what led to his current situation.

Osman's sleep had not been entirely peaceful. His mind could not help but fret over all that was still unknown to him. He trusted Wilfred implicitly, but the growing uncertainty over what "the real world" held for him and his future made his sleep broken and fitful. Osman had felt the unfamiliar and distorted flesh that awaited him "out there" when searching for his body that lay in the chrysalis. And while Osman dreaded what kind of existence awaited him outside this mindscape, darker shadows lurked behind that fear that unnerved him even more.

"I wanted to let ye rest and heal longer to gain more strength, but yer growing distress has begun to affect us both." Wilfred's voice held the gentle tone of a parent waking a child from a nightmare in the early darkness of morning. "It's time for ye to face what the future holds for ye."

"I'm sorry, Wilfred," Osman apologized, "I never intended for you to have to endure all this as well."

"Nonsense," Wilfred chided gently. "We're a part of something much larger now. And I have been facing my own unmapped shoals and shark-filled reefs while ye slept. We both have plenty o' wounds to heal and scars to accept before moving forward."

Osman swung his legs over the edge of the bed and stood up. He found he was wearing his favorite pair of cotton calf-length cutoff sleeping breeches that he used to wear when lounging around his or Talon's room. However, once Cerena began staying overnight, she had thrown the breeches in the hearth and insisted he wear a silk robe she had purchased for him and nothing else. At the thought of Cerena, a shadow fell across the room, and a chill filled the air. Even Wilfred glanced around, noticing the change.

"That's for another day," Wilfred said cryptically. "Today, we need ye to open yer eyes."

Osman's room at the Sojourn's Rest dissolved around him, and he was once again standing in the vast empty mindscape alone except for himself, Wilfred, and the chrysalis containing his physical form. Osman stepped forward, gently laying a hand on the translucent container, and looked down on his ruined flesh. While by no means whole or remotely viable, it did seem somewhat healed since he last saw it.

"How long has it been? How long have I slept?" Osman asked.

"Another five months. Spring has already prepared the land for Summer, and the days have grown long, and the night will soon leave us altogether," Wilfred answered. Osman sighed. Wilfred, picking up on the resignation he was feeling, offered, "Perhaps things will speed up as we both become more comfortable with our new lot in life."

Osman took a deep breath and squared his shoulders. He looked over to Wilfred confidently, "I'm ready." And then added a little more tentatively, "Will it hurt?"

Wilfred's smile beamed from his wrinkled continence, "Trust me, and just follow the current." Wilfred reached out his hands and waited for Osman to take them. "Let yer mind connect with the outside world," he intoned somewhat hypnotically.

Osman closed his eyes as their hands made contact and felt a rush of motion, although he sensed he was not moving. No, not motion—wind. The familiar sensation from his childhood of standing on the high bald meadows near the cliffs of Horizon's End, arms raised out to his sides with the sky flowing around him. Osman leaned into the sensation, but as he did, he felt a torsion on his soul, pulling on it unnaturally and uncomfortably.

"Wilfred?" Osman cried out nervously. He tried to open his eyes but found he couldn't, now helplessly caught in the current that pulled his soul and consciousness forward. The torquing of Osman's spiritual body worsened, reminiscent of the serpent's breath that had torn his flesh apart, leaving it the ruin resting in the chrysalis behind him. Panic began to fill Osman, and he lashed out wildly, trying to fight the forces acting on him.

Wilfred's calm voice cut through Osman's growing anxiety. "It won't hurt, I promise. We just aren't the same anymore. Accept the vessel. Flow into it like the tide."

Osman tried to calm himself as he let the current thrust him forward but could not quell his racing heart and his breaths rushing in and out like bellows. Osman felt his spine extend while his hands and feet painfully distorted and stretched like overcooked caramel. A feeling of heaviness and mass settled on his shoulders, thighs, and haunches. Osman gritted his teeth at the unnatural sense of *otherness* that washed over him, only to find his teeth similarly were no longer his. Before he could contemplate the change, with a twang akin to a plucked lute string vibrating through his being, Osman found he inhabited his new flesh.

The sounds and scents of life filled his nose. The smell of new growth and retreating winter mixed with the sounds of animals scurrying through the last snow drifts assaulted Osman's senses in a way he had never experienced.

"Open yer eyes, Osman." Wilfred's voice, no longer heard with ears spiritual or otherwise, was once again only an echo in his mind with no specific direction or source.

Osman's physical eyes opened on a nighttime landscape, yet the darkness did not cloak it in shadow. His vision could drink in the details of every movement and texture. Osman's mouth opened in wonder, and he again encountered the teeth that were not his. His lower lip scraped down the length of two saber-like fangs that extended past his jaw. Osman looked down at himself, discovering two powerful paws covered in iridescent white fur that unsheathed wicked claws with a flex of his fingers.

"Uh... Wilfred?" Osman asked internally with astonishment and trepidation. "Am I a saldrig?"

"Aye. We are," Wilfred replied. "The tempest of forces unleashed at the elemental inception when I stepped into the guardian's breath empowered yer human flesh. It soaked up the storm of magical energies like a sponge. Best I can figure is as ye teetered on the brink of death, yer body, harnessing that power in an instinctive reaction to keep ye alive, transformed into the strongest thing ye could think of to survive the serpent's power." Wilfred's voice continued explaining to the best of his ability, "You were unconscious, but I remained lucid as the guardian suspiciously cast its serpentine eyes on us, wary of how it too was used by the forces surrounding us." Wilfred intoned, "It spoke to me."

In a flash of insight, Osman was transported to the memory as if it was his own.

*Ten Months Earlier ~ 874*PXF *~ Autumn*

### *Treachery! What Trickery Have You Wrought, Spirit?*

The giant guardian of the Argestian Inception coiled menacingly, ready to strike. Osman felt Wilfred's panic as he tried to speak, but the only sound that passed the prone saldrig's toothy maw was a pitiful confused mewling whimper. Osman watched the tension in the serpent's expression lessen and then become quizzical.

### *No, Not Your Doing–The Games of Fate and the Gods.*

The serpent's writhing coils calmed into the hypnotic undulations of its guardian aspect and spoke to Wilfred directly. "Are you in control of this form, Spirit? Can you stand?"

Still submerged in the wilicho's memory, Osman felt Wilfred test his control of the corporeal saldrig body he now inhabited along with him. There was a strange parallel between the fisherman Wilfred had been learning a new vessel and him familiarizing himself with the feline predator. Whether it was from his centuries as a sailor or millennia as a wilicho that eased the process, Osman could not tell, but Wilfred seemed to have a much easier time adjusting to the saldrig's shape than he had had. In short order, Wilfred got up off the ground, sat regally with tail wrapped around his haunches before the serpentine guardian, and gave an honor-filled nod to the serpent before him.

"It is no common beast the two of you have inhabited. A saldrig can see the material world *and* what lies beyond the veil. From within its flesh, the currents and truths of the Solenfel are open to you, as are the deepest wells of nature's healing energies," the serpent explained. Its eyes then glowed with an icy blue light as its voice took on a tone of conjecture. "But, Spirit, this form is not your final fate. The body you now cohabitate with your Uldani charge is malleable—that of a soulchanneler."

Wilfred pulled up a distant memory from his living life and projected a question toward the guardian serpent. "I thought the legends of humans who could change into beasts were just tales told by drunken sailors and defeated warriors. Was Osman always the same as the human druids of the North? Is that how this happened?"

"Your flesh is now similar to them but unique." The serpent confirmed. "Your companion did not enter this grove as a soulchanneler, but it is what he is now. However, this power was infused upon one of elven lineage no matter how far removed the Uldani have become. Their nature is rooted in a resistance to change, practically immune even to the onslaught of time. That which is instinctual to the druids of the North could be a challenge for him, if possible at all."

The serpent peered deep into Wilfred's eyes and continued, "I can sense your companion's human body still exists within the beast's shape you now wear, but to manifest it at this moment would mean death to you both." The serpent looked out to its grove. "Much as I tend to those frozen here, you will tend to this boy. Guide his healing, both soul and body. Listen to the flesh of the beast you wear to help you survive and the knowledge of the Solenfel to guide your healing."

Present ~ 875PXF ~ Late Spring

The memory faded from Osman's mind, and he found himself again looking out into the night through the eyes of the saldrig. He asked internally, "A soulchanneler? Druids? Wilfred, what does that all mean? What have I become? What have *we* become?"

"I don't rightly know," Wilfred answered. "But until ye heal, none of that matters. For now, we're a saldrig. We're safe, and ye're cared for." Wilfred said the last with a certainty that harbored no doubt.

Osman could feel Wilfred's command of the saldrig form they inhabited step aside as he used his flexible tongue to test the sharpness of his elongated teeth and unsheathe his formidable claws.

"Take it slow," Wilfred instructed, "but 'tis time for yer mind an' body to remember what it's like to be alive."

Osman smiled inwardly as he shifted the new saldrig body slightly, feeling its muscles terrifying strength and lightning-quick reflexes. He felt his mind connect with the instincts of the predatory beast he now inhabited and, with a roar of delight, leapt forward into the night. Off to his left, Osman's pounce startled a grazing hare that darted away fast as lightning. Without hesitation, he twisted in midair, landing his huge saldrig body on all fours, already crouched for action, and the hunt was on.

The hare zig-zagged across the still-thawing open ground as Osman barreled forward in a straight line after it, quickly closing the distance between his razor-sharp front claws and the hare's flashing tail. With a burst of speed, his prey juked right and then dove under the low-hanging snow-covered boughs of a fir tree. Osman twisted awkwardly to make the sharp turn, his back legs scrambling on an icy patch of ground to find purchase before leaping blindly into the fir tree where the hare had disappeared. While Osman had considered the branches he would crash through, correctly assuming the mass of the saldrig would have no issue pushing them out of the way or breaking through them, he did not anticipate the steep drop-off just beyond.

Osman tumbled snout-over-tail down the snow-covered embankment. Even the natural grace of the saldrig could not lessen the ridiculous spectacle of churning paws, spinning tail, and surprised yowls as eight hundred pounds of mighty snow-covered apex predator finally plopped into a snowbank and came to rest. Osman heard Wilfred's chuckling sigh as he directed Osman's gaze to the hare sitting atop the low ridge above them, casually grooming its face before hopping off.

From the trees on the ridge, a flock of birds took to the sky, startled by the terrifying sound emanating from the grotto below them. They had never heard a saldrig laugh before.

Wilfred chimed in once Osman regained his composure and pulled them out of the snowbank, checking for any wounds. "Crafty little buggers, but they're tasty."

"Wha…?" Osman exclaimed before understanding hit him. "Oh," he added guiltily, "so, you have had to hunt to keep us alive."

"'Twas a bit of a hurdle to get over mentally, but when ye're starving, ye sail over it quickly." Wilfred continued sardonically, "Not to mention, when ye haven't tasted food in twenty-five centuries, everything tastes brand new. Our beastie has quite the appetite, and we're still getting our weight back after the winter."

Osman felt Wilfred gently nudge his consciousness, and he contentedly slipped into observing as Wilfred took control of the saldrig. A satisfying weariness settled into Osman's muscles once he relinquished the adrenaline and amped-up senses of the saldrig to the wilicho's more experienced hands. It reminded him of the beautiful exhaustion that would overcome him after day-long duels with Talon in Elery Square. This wasn't the mental exhaustion of his last awakening but a physical one, which in Osman's experience, was always the best way to rehabilitate after a wound. Perhaps being active in the saldrig would speed the healing of his body in the chrysalis.

Osman turned his attention back to Wilfred. Even though he wasn't in direct control of the saldrig body he and Wilfred shared, he still saw through its eyes and felt all it sensed. While Osman had only steered the saldrig's actions, Wilfred had become one with it. A whole array of sensory inputs that Osman didn't even realize were available to him flooded into his senses.

Wilfred prowled silently and invisibly through the newly sprouted underbrush, low to the ground and with the breeze in his face keeping him downwind of any prey ahead. Osman could feel the tiny vibrations made by the movements of creatures around him through the sensitive hand-sized pads on his massive paws. Whiskers tickled under his nose as they brushed against leaf and limb and judged the exact amount of noise they would make with his passing. Ears twitched and swiveled directionally to pick up any errant sound within his vicinity. Nose and tongue worked in tandem to taste the air for scents of easy prey or formidable predators alike. The saldrig's instincts and senses embodied the culmination of nature's evolutionary apex, but when paired with Wilfred's intelligence and insight, they became something genuinely terrifying.

Osman became acutely aware of the mercy gifted him by the saldrig that had stalked him back in the Shieldwall Spine the night before he found his father's painting. He pondered if it had sensed the parasitic chain made from his father's sacrifice returning to him, saving him from being devoured. At the thought of the chain, the world around Osman changed. He was no longer seeing the world as he knew it, albeit with far better vision, but into the world beyond the veil. He saw the aura of life around every tree and bush. Beneath his paws, he saw the thrum of roots pulsing with energy, and on the snow superimposed upon a faint set of tracks Wilfred was following, the stain of age marring the glow of life nearing its end. Wilfred had stopped his hunt when the change overcame their vision.

"Aye, it's still there," Wilfred stated. "The chain wasn't exhausted by the events at the inception, just overwhelmed. I suspect, along with the saldrig's innate abilities, it's why ye're healing at all and haven't died from yer wounds." Wilfred looked back over the saldrig's shoulder, and from the sky beyond the veil, snaking one by one into the side of their ribcage, flowed the links of the parasite's broken chain.

Osman looked around further with the saldrig's veilsight. A glow of familiarity cloaked the land around them. This was their territory, their home. Vast acres claimed and borders marked. Osman even keyed into multiple dens and warrens known to them for shelter, safety, and rest. Wilfred waited patiently, gently guiding Osman's eyes to the tracks they were following. Understanding dawned on him.

"This beast knew where it was venturing. It sought us out as it knew its last journey was upon it." Osman stated reverently.

"Aye, it did," Wilfred confirmed. "A caribou stag, prince of its herd, ready to set down his heavy crown here on his terms instead of waiting for the humiliation of age to steal it from him."

Osman lifted his eyes from the caribou tracks to the sky. Overhead the Solenfel was not the river of light he saw with his human eyes but an infinite mosaic of pictures painted across the night akin to what he witnessed with the serpent at the inception. He began to pose a question to Wilfred regarding the guardian's comment in their shared memory about the truths revealed in the Solenfel, but Wilfred interrupted.

"Tonight, we hunt. We all need nourishment and have a duty to the beast that has sought us out." Wilfred's tone brooked no room for argument. With a blink of the saldrig's heavy-lidded eyes, its veilsight reverted to taking in the light of the material world around them. In less than a quarter of an hour, Wilfred tracked the caribou to a clearing where it absently grazed while patiently waiting for their arrival.

The majestic stag was far larger than Osman had expected. It was easily a match in mass for the draft horses he remembered from Arnadore, but the caribou's longer legs would have it standing taller at the shoulder. Not only did their prey carry more mass than the saldrig flesh he and Wilfred inhabited, but a pair of branching antlers the size of broadswords stood atop the stag's head, held aloft by its powerful neck. As they prowled forward, the regal stag's gaze bore unflinchingly into the feline eyes that stalked him. While this prince of the tundra might be resigned to its fate, it would not go quietly into the Solenfel.

Wilfred crept forward, closing the distance between predator and prey with a silent skill that left Osman holding his metaphysical breath. The eyes of the two beasts, locked together in nature's final dance, never faltered or darted away from one another's gaze. The stag snorted with confident derision, its hot breath fogging powerfully out of its nostrils in the chill of the early springtime air. The moonlight and rippling Solenfel above transformed its exhalation into a cloud of ghosts and specters that swirled menacingly around its mighty antlers. Osman fretted that perhaps they were the beast facing their final journey this night.

Without warning, Wilfred's slow creep forward became a rapid scurry, body low to the ground, large muscles still coiled and ready to pounce. The stag defensively lowered his antlers, head tilting slightly to the side with eyes forward, judging the distance between it and Wilfred versus the length of its deadly branching antlers. Just outside the reach of the caribou's bony armaments, Wilfred feinted that he was about to pounce with all the saldrig's fearsome strength. The full length and eighteen points of the stag's antlers, each the size of a short sword, swung through the space the saldrig would have occupied had Wilfred followed through with his attack. Instead, he crouched underneath them as they passed harmlessly overhead.

The caribou trumpeted in defiance, but its eyes opened wide, the whites shining in instinctual terror with recognition of its error. The mighty swing, making contact with nothing but air, left the entirety of its muscular neck exposed to the saldrig poised to spring just below it.

Wilfred did not hesitate.

Osman, pulled into the adrenaline of the hunt, leapt with Wilfred at the exposed flesh, claws raking across the stag's neck as their momentum swung them around to the caribou's side and nearly on its back. Once in position, Wilfred dug their claws into the stag's bulging shoulders, locking them in a deadly embrace. Wilfred reared the saldrig's head back and drove their saber-like fangs into the caribou's neck with instinctual accuracy.

Their teeth severed the pulsing arteries flowing with the stag's lifeblood, releasing it in a hot torrent and staining their iridescent white fur. The caribou stag, prince of the tundra, fell like a stone with hardly a twitch as Wilfred snapped their powerful jaws shut, crushing the caribou's spine. The two majestic beasts ended their dance lying on the ground like lovers. One calmly catching their breath as the other's life bled away.

Osman's consciousness reflexively recoiled as Wilfred swallowed the large chunk of flesh in their jaws as they disengaged from the corpse of the caribou.

"This is who and what we are for the time being," Wilfred stated without consolation or apology. "We cull the herds and balance the scales so all may thrive." He paused, his voice and presence laying a phantom hand on Osman's shoulder, "Including yer human body healing within us."

Osman turned his consciousness back on the scene before them, letting himself flow back into the senses of the saldrig. While he was not ready to be the one actively feeding on the still-warm flesh of the caribou, he would not shy away, either.

As they fed, Osman could feel the vitality and strength of the stag flowing not just into the saldrig's flesh but his own body and spirit as well. A deep hunger filled him as though he had been starving through months of sickness and finally had regained his appetite. He could not be sure, but in his need, Osman might have been the one to take a bite when Wilfred paused past the extent of his patience.

As his initial ravenous appetite became satiated, Osman blinked their vision over to veilsight in a stupor, curious about what it would reveal. He was shocked to see the spirit of the caribou stag watching over them as they feasted on his corpse. The prince of the tundra gave a slight bow of acknowledgment to Osman, its spirit recognizing it was now visible to his eyes. With a shake akin to a hound ridding its coat of water, the elder stag shook its form, sloughing off its age and afflictions, becoming once again a young buck in his prime.

The giant antlers seemed to fall in slow motion from their great height where they once perched upon the stag's head. Osman's saldrig eyes drank in every detail, reading in them the entirety of the great stag's life. Decades of scarce Winters and bountiful Summers, migrations crisscrossing the length and breadth of Kyflenor punctuated by Autumn's rut and the new foals of Spring. A princely life well lived guiding a herd of his mates and progeny, living in balance with the beasts and tribes who shared the island with him.

The ghostly antlers never hit the ground but instead dissolved into motes of starlight and flowed into Osman's soul through the saldrig's eyes. Osman felt the caribou prince's memory and form take its place within his own, as though waiting to be called upon when needed.

In the snow next to its corpse, the spirit of the young caribou buck who had been prince pranced in a small circle before giving a last look over its shoulder and a slight nod to Osman. With a flash of its tail, the caribou's spirit scampered not into the forest but up into the sky, its story joining the infinite mosaic of souls painted there.

# CHAPTER ELEVEN



A weariness of both body and spirit engulfed Osman. Not the exhaustion of a troubled mind but the satisfying need for rest well-earned. Osman let his consciousness briefly check on Wilfred. He was using the saldrig's powerful jaws to worry at a femur, cracking it open and enjoying the tender marrow within. With little more than the thought of letting go, the sensation of gently falling floated over Osman, and he found himself back in his room at the Sojourn's Rest sitting on the edge of his bed.

The memory of the hunt remained fresh in Osman's mind but also seemed dreamlike. Even knowing he was no more than a sentient idea within his and Wilfred's shared mind, he could still feel an ache in his muscles, a fullness in his stomach, and a renewed energy in his soul. At the thought of such corporeal things, Osman longed to see his Uldani body.

He had never manipulated the environment of the mindscape before. It had always been Wilfred. Osman concentrated on his body and willed the chrysalis to become visible. It appeared with nothing more than the need he felt to see it. The chrysalis situated itself at the foot of his bed. Standing, he circled the bedpost to look down through the semi-translucent shell at what lay within. No miracles of healing had occurred from the single hunt, but where before his body's lips had been pursed together in a tight line biting back pain, the tension now seemed somewhat eased.

Osman patted the chrysalis comfortingly, catching the deep scars on his forearms from the corner of his eye. Both flesh and spirit still had much healing to do, but Osman now understood there was a path forward. With Wilfred's help, he could be whole again.

Osman made one last addition to the room in his mind. A small mirror appeared on the wall, and he faced the wraith-like visage of his soul. The deep pits of his eyes that once had been empty of light reflected a tiny spark of joy in the shape of a hare bounding across the snow.

With an inward smile that, with his unique perspective, he could genuinely say touched his soul, Osman put himself to bed. Osman's consciousness slipped into a peaceful meditative healing sleep. He awoke of his own accord nearly eight months later, hungry for another taste of life and external activity to stimulate his muscles and senses.

Wilfred taught Osman all he had learned about hunting, and after many unsuccessful attempts, Osman finally did catch his first elusive hare. The seasons and years slipped by in the surrounding plains of Kyflenor. It seemed to be less than a handful of weeks for Osman as each awakening filled him with the vitality needed to retire to his room and heal his broken soul.

*5 Years Later ~ 880* PXF *~ Autumn*

Osman awoke invigorated and starving. Sitting up in his familiar bed, he stretched his arms wide and let out an exuberant vocal yawn to shake off the last of his weariness. Osman brought his bare arms down in front of him, laying them parallel to each other above the light quilt covering his legs. Upon waking, he performed a similar ritual to the one he had adopted as a child. He examined the hashmark scars etched across his forearms that marked his soul.

Unlike the marks in the log above his childhood bed, these hashes were changing. While the centers were still not fully closed, their far lengths had become no more than raised silvery scars. Waking up to the marks carved into the log above his bed at Horizon End had always brought resignation, but these on his forearms now brought him hope. They were healing. *He* was healing, and he had survived.

Osman's hand absently went to his chest, gingerly examining the hole that was still present. Where once there had been only the thinnest filaments of 'soul flesh,' wide bridges now spanned the gaping wound. He could feel the tension in them pulling his soul back together where he had sliced it apart. Osman smiled at the progress he felt under his fingertips and leapt from his bed.

His room had changed from the exacting memory of what it had been when Osman lived at the Sojourn's Rest, and while it was still recognizable as that space, Osman had made a few changes. Most noticeably, it was bigger, nearly the size of the main room in Talon's suite. The chrysalis remained at the foot of the now larger bed in the same spot he had summoned it after his first hunt. No longer cramped into the space between the end of the bed and the opposite wall, it now anchored one side of a large sitting area with a comfortable couch and a small carved table in front of it. The table was a twin to what Anson had intricately carved for Tavi's living rooms at Horizon's End.

Overlooking the sitting area on what should be the inn's outside wall, the structure's timbers transitioned to the cave wall upon which Tavi had painted the portrait of Osman. Opposite the image, tucked in the corner but proudly displayed, was a mannequin dressed in Osman's Gala outfit cycling through its full retune of the seasons and tricks. Other memories adorned the room across the walls and tucked into corners: his matching swords from Arnadore, Alerese's painting of Grimspire, and near the hearth, the boots gifted him by Lady Cour-Vermane. In an honored position on the mantle, Osman had placed Talon's iron dagger—a reminder of his Qat'malorn.

Osman padded over to the couch on bare feet. His favorite cotton sleeping britches' hem catching on fuller calves whose skin was no longer etched with deep channels and were slowly returning from their desiccated state. A glass of chilled apple juice appeared on Anson's table with a mere thought. While it had no sustenance, it gave Osman comfort—another ritual he had adopted akin to Talon and his morning tea.

Osman could sense Wilfred was awake and prowling. With a quick close of his eyes and a deep inhale, Osman could recognize the smells of approaching Winter. He did not pick up a sense of urgency from Wilfred, but there was a purpose behind his movements, and that purpose required him. He finished the apple juice in three large gulps while simultaneously standing up. The motion did not culminate in his soul standing in front of the couch in his room but instead with him looking out of saldrig eyes on the world as he strode along a high snow-covered ledge.

"There ye are." Wilfred's welcoming voice echoed in Osman's mind. "Four months. Ye missed a lovely changing of the leaves. How does boar sound for breakfast?" Wilfred recited how long he had slept, any news, and what they were hunting without Osman needing to ask.

Osman slid easily into control of the saldrig body he and Wilfred shared and, looking around at the altitude and rocky terrain, stated jokingly, "You're casting your net in the wrong place for boar, old man."

"We're hunting boar in the morning. Tonight there is other business for ye to attend to." Wilfred's tone sounded like Talon's when assigning latrine duty. Directing their eyes to the Solenfel and shifting them to veilsight, he continued, "It's been stuck like that for days."

The scene painted across the sky was immediately familiar—the dining hall of the barracks at Arnadore Keep. Osman could almost smell the miasma of sweat-stained leather armor, weeks-old leftovers, and bodies too long unwashed. Judging by the scant number of guards present at mealtime, the scene was from a time before Talon became Knight Captain. Osman's eyes slid to a familiar corner, and reaffirming his suspicion, he spotted his younger self.

Osman ate alone at the end of one of the tables as far from the doors as possible. He sat as an island of one with the next nearest person nearly half the room away. Upon recognizing himself, the frozen image painted in the sky began to flow forward through time. As he watched, Osman recalled the din of knives on cheap tin plates playing amongst the ebb and flow of conversations that moved from raucous empty braggadocio to grumbles of discontent.

Caught in his memory as much as he was watching the scene unfold, Osman saw nothing amiss. However, being tapped into the saldrig's senses, Osman became wary as his hackles rose and nerves jangled, registering nearby danger. He scanned the ledge they were on for anything approaching but quickly ascertained the threat was not to their saldrig body but to himself in the image playing across the Solenfel.

With eyes locked on the sky, Osman's bewilderment at what he sensed roused Wilfred. "The image has always remained frozen before, lad. This is new," Wilfred responded in his head.

Osman examined the scene more closely and finally recognized what he was seeing. The guards were eating summer pies overflowing with ripe fruits of the season. This could only be the night before his promotion and Talon's accepting the role of Knight Captain. Rank and file guards never had something so fine as fruit pies, but with the bountiful harvest that year, some local wives brought dozens of them to the keep.

As the local women distributed thick slices of pie to the guards, including himself, Osman spotted what was amiss and had triggered the saldrig's warning. Watching him out of the corner of her eye from across the mess hall, dressed inconspicuously as a simple laborer, was Cerena. Osman's heart and throat clenched tight as a growling voice, the impression of which he had only once before experienced but never heard, entered his mind.

> *She eyes you like an ice serpent secreted beneath the snow*
> *waiting to strike.*

The voice of the saldrig.

Osman mentally checked in with Wilfred, but he seemed just as shocked. Osman returned their gaze to the Solenfel. What he was seeing happened nearly a year before Osman had met Cerena at the Gala. It was apparent, however, that she knew who he was and had ill intent laid out for him. Osman continued to watch as Cerena pulled a pie out of a box separate from the others.

> *Poison. Disease. Corruption.*

The saldrig's nostrils flared wide by instinct with neither Osman's nor Wilfred's volition.

Cerena followed another pie-carrying local out of the mess hall. They exited through the door leading to the officer's dining room, where Knight Captain LeSalle, Duke's Guard Holden, and the rest of Duke Issul's private regiment were dining. By morning, LeSalle and Holden would be dead, and Talon and Osman thrust together as Knight Captain and newest member of the Duke's private regiment.

The scene within the Solenfel faded, and it returned to its usual ebb and flow across the sky. The implications of all he had seen hit Osman like a physical blow, and he retreated into his mind. His knees buckled, and he fell heavily back onto the couch as though he had not entirely made it to standing.

Osman sat dumbfounded. A few moments later, Wilfred appeared and sat on the carved table across from him.

"It was all a lie—every moment. From even before I knew she existed, I was just a part of her plan." Osman recited the words emotionlessly.

Wilfred placed a comforting hand on Osman's knee, both fully solid to each other in this place. "I'm sorry, lad. I didn't know what the sky held for ye. If I did, I would've waited to show ye."

Osman laid his hand on Wilfred's. "It's okay. I needed to see. My heart still held a bit of hope that some of what we had was real. I could never fully accept everything my head knew to be true." Osman paused, then continued, almost struggling to say the words, "Now I know."

Osman doubled over as pain wracked his chest. His shoulders heaved as the muscles in his torso clenched. He felt like he was retching, but the spasms weren't coming from his abdomen. They were coming from the wound in his chest. Again and again, his chest muscles cramped and released, threatening to tear open the delicate, still-healing tear in his soul.

In a panic, Osman covered the hollow void in his chest with his hands, trying to protect the delicate soul flesh that had taken so long to heal even partially. A horrifying full-body convulsion lurched him forward, chest over knees, pinning his hands between the two. Wilfred flew off the table and knelt at Osman's side, arm over his shoulders, trying to steady him. Osman felt something cold and sharp drop into his palm, expelled from his chest. Gasping for breath, he sat back up and looked down at his hands. In his grasp was a shard of black glass, and encased within its crystalline facets was a mortifying lidless eye—the iris an exact match for Cerena's.

Startled by the gruesome sight and the manner in which it had arrived in his hand, Osman reflexively threw the shard to the floor as though it were a scorpion.

"What in the Nine Hells was that?" Wilfred exclaimed as he jumped to his feet. Osman's arm shot out, grabbing Wilfred before he could approach the black glass, slowly spinning to a stop on the floor.

"How is it even real? How is that thing in here?" Osman wondered aloud. Everything in here was in his mind or a part of his soul. A wave of revulsion roiled in Osman's throat as the image of the parasite attached to Richen entered his mind. Had Cerena put something inside him? She had ample opportunity during all the nights they spent together. This didn't seem as sentient or virulent as the parasite conjured by her uncle; it seemed more like a piece of shrapnel lodged in his soul. Cerena even took advantage of the perfect spot and placed it deep within the void where he had carved out the memories of Horizon's End and his father.

Osman slowly rose from the couch and circled to the mantle, giving the black shard lying on the floor a wide berth. There, he firmly grabbed the hilt of Talon's dagger and warily approached the roughly triangular-shaped medallion of black glass.

As he got closer, Osman realized he was mistaken. It was not glass but a stone similar to the obsidian found in Mael Esari. The object on the floor looked like it had been fractured off a larger piece and then crudely shaped into its current form like one would sharpen flint. The result was a polished central face surrounded by dozens of irregular facets.

Dropping to one knee and leaning over the jagged crystal, Osman shuddered, reliving his initial confusion and revulsion. The stone was not translucent, with Cerena's eye encased within it. The smooth surface of the main face reflected her lidless eye peering into it from somewhere else, with the irregular facets creating half a dozen smaller eyes circling the prominent central one.

Osman bit back the bile rising in his throat as his mind recoiled from the thought of Cerena secreting that aberrant *thing* within his soul. He raised the dagger and brought it down on the dark talisman staring up at him. He struck not just with his weapon but with the force of his will that shaped this place. His intent not only to shatter the vile crystal but to banish it as well. Osman struck true with Talon's dagger, shattering the stone. The fragments skittered across the floor before quickly dissolving into a fine mist that ignited in white fire from the force of Osman's will.

Osman hadn't realized he was holding his breath. His eyes rose to Wilfred, who stood slack-jawed beside the couch.

"Whale humping whirlpools... Who would create such a thing?" Wilfred whispered earnestly, still frozen in shock.

"What?" Osman asked, baffled by Wilfred's expletive and failing at holding back the chuckle that rose from his belly. "Really, Wilfred? Whale humping whirlpools?"

Wilfred, trying to remain serious, explained, "They are quite dangerous, actually. Ye see the whales..." Wilfred failed to finish his thought, unable to hold his stoic demeanor any longer.

Osman raised up off his one knee and crossed to Wilfred, where they both flopped down on the couch side-by-side, chuckling. Simultaneously, their stomachs growled, and both felt a deep hunger in their bones.

"That's not just us," Osman stated matter-of-factly. "And what was that with the saldrig's voice? I thought the saldrig body was just a manifestation of my body protecting itself." Osman looked to the chrysalis across from him at the foot of the bed.

"I've no idea. Perhaps it was due to the message from the Solenfel. Or something else entirely," Wilfred conjectured. "Once we get ye healed up, we can explore more of what it means to channel the souls of beasts."

"But first, breakfast." They said in unison, and in a blink, they both were looking out the eyes of the saldrig still standing stoically on the high ledge looking out at Solenfel, which was becoming washed out in the light of sunrise.

"Boar, you say?" Osman asked Wilfred internally as they leapt down from the ledge descending to the boreal forest below. "Gods, I miss bacon."

With the expulsion of Cerena's talisman from his soul, Osman's recovery quickened, but even with the accelerated rate, souls do not mend themselves overnight. With each awakening, Osman grew stronger, and soon he was spending whole days in control of the saldrig instead of just having the stamina for one hunt and then returning to unconsciousness within his mindscape. Wilfred's presence was always near when Osman needed him, whether for rest or company. As Osman became more self-sufficient, though, he could tell Wilfred was finally taking the time to do some healing of his own and address the demons he carried with him from his living life.

Time winked by, coalescing quickly into years. Likewise, Osman's days as the saldrig turned to weeks, then months, his recovery becoming a more active endeavor instead of passive bedrest. The voice of the saldrig never spoke again, but as Osman's time immersed in the beast's form grew longer, he found rest in letting his mind fade into the saldrig's primal thoughts and instincts, recognizing him as an individual and not just a form Osman wore. During those times, he would become fully one with the predator, nearly forgetting an Uldani named Osman ever existed.

Osman's body in the chrysalis was healing but was also going through a metamorphosis of its own, the full extent of which Osman could only vaguely identify. Looking down through the translucent surface, Osman could see his body was whole again. If anything, it looked more hale and hearty than it had ever been. Still barely covered in the scant strips of remaining clothing that survived after facing the serpent's breath, his body was thicker with muscle than ever before, and when comparing it to the painting of himself on the cave wall in his room, it seemed more than a few inches taller as well. The strangest part, however, was when he reached out his consciousness to what should be its rightful place, a slight pressure always pushed him away. It almost seemed to say, "Not yet."

Headstrong as Osman was, he had once tried to force his way through the barrier, curiosity and longing pushing him forward. As he did, his mind brushed against his body's senses. Instantly, it felt like a thousand acid-covered briars raked across every inch of his soul. Osman yanked himself back from the shock and pain of it, but in that instant of contact, he recognized the senses in his body were not the same as the person he once was.

*Four Years Later ~ 884 PXF ~ Spring*

The saldrig prowled through dawn's early hours, the cacophony of emerging life filling his senses. The unending darkness of Winter had broken, and the pent-up energy of the long night had burst forth with unbridled exuberance for the season of rebirth. The saldrig had kept himself well-fed through the winter on the old and infirm, culling the weak, but Spring held the promise of the succulent flesh of youth and easy kills.

The predator was not tracking his next kill this morning, however. He had had his fill on a flick of three dozen hares, halving their number, the evening before. The saldrig was following curiosity through the early morning light. Curiosity was a strange concept for the saldrig. He had no need to care about things that entered his territory that were not for sustenance or challenged his dominance. However, the scent he followed was important and familiar even though the saldrig knew he had never encountered prey of its like before.

The saldrig slowed his pace and crouched low to the ground, creeping forward, ears resting flat against his head. His quarry was just ahead. This creature was wily. It had masked its scent within a field of bright yellow, newly bloomed daisies where it now squatted low to the ground, back turned to the saldrig's approach. The strange creature's slow, steady heartbeat began to thrum through the saldrig, eliciting a flow of saliva into his mouth. Perhaps a morning meal would be nice after all.

Jaws open, ready to lunge forward to make a quick kill and a tasty morsel of the plump creature, the saldrig crept closer. Quick as a viper, the creature spun and swatted the saldrig across his tender nose with a willow switch.

"Stop being ridiculous." Alerese the Bloomsage chided.

The saldrig leapt back like a kitten encountering its first cricket instead of the over eight hundred pounds of muscle, fangs, and claws he truly was. The startled shock of the saldrig brought Osman's mind to the foreground, no longer submerged in the instincts of the beast he wore.

"Oh!" Alerese exclaimed. "It's you, Osman. And look, you have a new costume to wear, just like the ones you made as a child to play pretend. How nice." Alerese's demeanor was almost giddy, unlike the sage and timeless mystery they had radiated in late Summer at Horizon's End. It was as though the energy of emerging Spring had infected them as much as it had all of nature around them.

Alerese continued, paying no mind that they spoke to a saldrig that loomed before them and could strike them down instantly. "Now take that off and come greet me properly." They waved their tiny hands, summoning Osman closer. "Don't be shy now. Come along."

Osman didn't know how to react. While his body in the chrysalis appeared healed, he had not attempted to reenter it after encountering the excruciating pain of his still-developing nervous system. Wilfred was suddenly with him sharing his consciousness but not assuming control. They both hesitated, flabbergasted.

"That's okay. You can bring your friend too." Alerese invited genially. Osman, not knowing how to proceed, hesitated. The Bloomsage's voice snapped out like a whip, patience having faded. "Osman. Come *here*." It was not a request or even a command but a tectonic imperative that moved Osman to obey without thought.

The giant saldrig padded forward and bowed his head. The Bloomsage reached out their hands and brought the beast's head, nearly as large as their whole body, to their own. Atop a slight rise in a field of dark-eyed golden-petalled daisies, the sun rising behind them, where once there was the silhouette of a mighty predator bowed over a tiny figure before it, now stood Osman, an Uldani man once again, forehead pressed together with Alerese.

"Ah, there you are," said Alerese as they stepped back and looked over Osman from head to toe. "With all the holes mended back as they should be." They absentmindedly added with a hint of an unsettling cackle, "I never did like cheese with holes."

Osman held his hands before him rotating them in dawn's light, examining his true flesh that now seemed so unfamiliar. He felt vulnerable and exposed, experiencing the material world in his Uldani form without the claws and fangs he had grown accustomed to. Osman flexed fleshy, clawless fingers and ran his tongue across teeth that were mere nubs. His senses were muffled whispers compared to the saldrig. Simultaneously, he felt his soul expanding and flowing into the extents of a body not entirely the same as when he last inhabited it.

Confirming his observations from outside the chrysalis, his lithe, flexible muscles so suited for his acrobatic prowess now bulged with a thickness and strength they never previously possessed. From the perspective change he was experiencing, Osman also estimated he was at least four or more inches taller than he had been. He felt like he was standing on the dais where the tailors had fitted his Blossom Gala outfit even though his boots were firmly on the ground.

At the fleeting thought of his Gala attire and wondering if it would still fit, or any of his clothes for that matter, Osman recognized his current state. He wore his enchanted boots that were none the worse for the wear; however, the same could not be said for the rest of his clothing. The guardian of the inception's breath had ravaged them. Tattered breeches barely covered his thighs, the remains held up by his belt, which miraculously remained serviceable, unlike the remainder of his tunic and jerkin, which fell to the ground as a pile of rags upon his inspection. The bare blade of Talon's iron dagger was shoved into his belt. However, Osman could feel an unnatural chill flowing off it through his ragged breeches as it pressed against his hip.

As he became reacquainted with his Uldani body, Osman began to notice the most significant change. The loss of the saldrig's superior senses had masked the difference from him initially, but he now recognized that every one of his Uldani senses was more acute than what they had been or naturally should be.

Osman could feel the vibrations of a mole burrowing through the rich soil under his feet, even through the soles of his boots. On the wind, he detected whispers of musk off a young male fox looking for a mate in the trees to the north. His eyes spotted details of bumblebums half an acre away sipping nectar in the field of black-eyed daisies. As Osman drank in the world, emotions flooded out of his soul bringing with them all the qil his Uldani heritage gifted him. Wonder tickled between his toes. Relief kissed his fingertips as gently as butterfly wings. Joy bounced in his stomach, and the dozens of little emotions that expressed themselves across his face danced there once again.

"You cared for him well, Guide of the Guardian," Alerese stated, eyes shifting off Osman for the first time.

In the overwhelming distraction of returning to his proper form, Osman's mind had yet to consider Wilfred. His incorporeal form stood just behind and to the side of Osman, his springtime-green aura still shining brightly.

"Wilfred!" Osman exclaimed, the name tumbling awkwardly out of his mouth as he reacquainted himself with an unfamiliar tongue and lips. Unable to find all the words he wanted to say, Osman spread his arms wide and presented himself like a child showing a new toy to a doting elder and repeated, "Wilfred." He filled the name with all the gratitude, excitement, and uncertainty-filled wonder he felt.

"Aye, ye pulled yerself back together quite nicely," Wilfred observed proudly. "Looks like a bit of our saldrig friend rubbed off on ye in the process."

Osman went to hug Wilfred, and his friend's arms even came up to meet him, but a pained look crossed Willfred's face, matching the disappointing ache Osman felt in his heart as they both realized they were no longer in the mindscape and could no longer touch.

"So what happens now? Will we ever be," Osman waved his hand vaguely at his head, continuing, "like that again? Together?"

"I don't rightly know, lad," Wilfred confessed. "But I know I won't be going with ye any further on this journey," he continued looking abashedly. "I also had an arrangement with the guardian."

"Guide of the Guardian," Osman intuited Wilfred's words in the familiar way their conversations had gone for over a decade. "What's it mean?"

"To remain this," Wilfred motioned to himself, "'Not-a-wilicho' outside of the stones, I bound myself to the guardian and the land. To guide others in need as they traverse Kyflenor. My sole condition was that I would not agree unless my first duty was to see ye whole again."

Osman smiled a huge toothy grin, eyes damp with emotion, now wanting to embrace his friend more than ever. "Wilfred, I am so grateful and so happy for you. I can think of no one better for the job."

Wilfred scratched the back of his neck as he said, "Well, it's a pretty sure bet there will never be someone quite like you again, *Soulchanneler*." Osman spotted Wilfred's desire to elbow him in the side as they used to when sitting side-by-side on the couch in his mind. "Speaking of which, I have a gift for ye."

Wilfred motioned for Osman to bend down and bring his face closer to his own, no longer able to simply reach up to it with Osman's now taller form. Osman dropped to one knee instead, reminiscent of the first morning in the camp when he thought he was saying goodbye. Osman felt the slightest tingle where their foreheads touched, and the door to shared memory opened between them.

In the memory, the saldrig's veilsight revealed the spirit of a huge mist owl, its silver-grey feathers rippling in the moonlight. The owl's contemplative saucer eyes and masked face looked up to the saldrig sitting on its haunches. The wizened owl cocked its head to one side as if listening to some unseen advisor. Then, with an extended blink and a single flap of its silent wings, it rose into the sky, leaving behind a single ghostly feather.

Wilfred contemplated the feather as Osman had done with the stag's antler. Within it, he saw the entirety of the owl's life, absorbed its essence into himself, and now shared that wisdom with Osman.

Osman felt the mist owl's memory take its place next to the saldrig and the caribou stag in the landscape of his mind. Osman opened his eyes. Wilfred looked back at him, expression full of sorrowful pride, telegraphing the goodbye that was fast approaching.

"Lad, even if we're apart it doesn't mean we aren't still connected," Wilfred said sagely as Osman's eyes grew damp. "We have shared far too much for our souls not to remain entangled. I will be there for you if the need is great enough."

"I'm not sure where I need to go." Osman looked from Wilfred back to Alerese. "All I know is my father left the Argestian Inception with the crystal containing Richen and headed west." Osman added, "And he didn't return to Horizon's End until I was fourteen, almost seven years after he left in the middle of the night."

During Wilfred and Osman's reunion, Alerese had taken out their quill and a tiny canvas. They spoke without breaking the rhythm of their scratching away at their painting. "If the guardian cleansed the boy's soul for reincarnation, Tavi would next need to visit the Eurucian Inception to invoke the living fires of rebirth and the earthen foundations of a new life." Alerese glanced to the far horizon where Osman's enhanced sight could pick up a sliver of the shimmering sea. "Mornaserin is where your path lies."

"But how?" Osman looked around, spotting Grimspire far in the distance to the northeast. Realizing he was on the opposite end of Kyflenor, he stated, "Volgendeep is half a year's journey away on foot. Even as a saldrig, it would be Autumn before I arrived, and by then, there will be no boats for hire." Osman added, "And that's if I could even turn myself back to this form without your help."

"Osman, even as a child, you made the simple things difficult." Alerese chided. "Becoming is just a matter of seeing what you want to be." With a self-amused chuckle, they continued, "For you, that is just a bit more literal than most. Both in the seeing and the becoming." The quill paintbrush and canvas disappeared into one of Alerese's many pockets. "But you must remember all change comes with a cost. Sometimes just the food in your belly, other times something more."

"Regarding how you will get to Mornaserin, it is time to spread your wings, even if they are borrowed ones," Alerese added sagely.

The full implication of Wilfred's gift dawned on Osman. With an exuberance akin to his six-year-old self and qil-filled toes about to dance out of his boots, he exclaimed, "I can fly! I'm going to fly!"

"Calm yerself, lad," Wilfred said through a grin. "Ye won't have me there to guide ye, but the owl's instincts will be. She knows the skies like I know the sea. Let her be yer guide."

Osman's growing excitement to take to the air whisked away the sadness of his looming departure and leaving Wilfred behind. He looked to Alerese and asked, "Do you think I'm ready? I feel like there is so much more I should know about what I've become."

"I don't have your answers, just like I didn't have them at Horizon's End." They added prophetically, "None of us understand all we need to know about ourselves or what we are capable of when we start the journey. The only certainty of life is that it must be lived to discover all it can be."

Osman looked to the two timeless Uldani who had so changed his life. One setting his feet upon the path, the other guiding and nurturing him across Kyflenor to become the man he was now. The familiar qil of loneliness spread through Osman's back teeth even though Wilfred and Alerese were still in arms reach.

*I'm right here.* Wilfred mouthed silently, tapping his temple.

Alerese picked a palm-sized dark-eyed daisy and handed it to Osman along with a platinum coin. "For the Fatesinger's blessing and clothes when you get to Lumenaria. The rest is up to you."

Osman blushed, reminded of his near nakedness. He took a deep breath and, with eyes on Wilfred, drew forth the memory of the mist owl. Osman felt his soul inhale away from his Uldani flesh and flow into the foreign avian shape of the mist owl.

An airy lightness came over Osman as his bones became hollow and his arms lengthened into wings. Avian talons sprang from his feet, more wicked than saldrig claws. The mist owl's hearing and vision blasted Osman's mind with their overwhelming sensitivity. Osman tried to take a step forward but immediately stumbled.

Wilfred, bent only slightly to be eye to eye with Osman's stately mist owl form, advised, "Osman, let the owl take ye home. She's from Mornaserin. She knows the way."

Osman projected the concept of home to the mist owl and relaxed his mind to let the instincts of the owl take control. With a powerful stroke of her wings, they took to the air. Osman couldn't help but let out a whoop of delight as the owl circled over the two small figures in the field of yellow daisies and then headed west.

# PART II

## Fires and Foundations



*Year 883 PXF ~ Early Autumn*

Cerena threw the scrying orb against the dank stone wall shattering it, her fury destroying the fifth such orb in half as many weeks. Her hand reflexively went to her left eye, where the feedback from the broken spell made it too feel like it was shattering. Its orb bulged under her palm, swollen from the magic she had repeatedly channeled through it in the months since her brother's death.

Her immediate ire was her inability to locate the Vermillion Blade, or more accurately, she found it *everywhere*. Dozens upon dozens of scryings had yielded just as many possible locations, and each investigation, no matter how quickly she arrived, left her empty-handed. While her magical failures were a barb of frustration, she reserved the roaring inferno of her rage for Rabien himself.

Cerena had never liked her brother, dismissing him as a fool whose obsessive self-inflated ego skirted the edge of madness. However, the burning hatred she now felt had been born when the Vermillion Blade chose him after Talon's death. Through her machinations and magics, she was the one who had eroded Talon's binding brand upon the blade, releasing it from his control. Yet the ancestral glaive offered itself to Rabien as he cowered in a cave during the revolt's aftermath when all he had ever done was be soundly beaten by it.

Cerena ruefully swept one of her lab tables clean of all its contents, letting them crash to the cobblestone floor. She needed the sounds of destruction to drown out the constant beratings she flogged herself with. She should have killed Rabien the second she found him with the Vermillion Blade. All that stayed her hand were her memories of experiencing the damnable glaive in action when Talon had wielded it during their dueling match over Hearth's Rest.

It would have been so simple. Cerena had used her sight to track the blade to the southern coastal village near the encampment where she and her brother had prepared for the coup. Throughout the frigid winter, the villagers scorned Rabien while embracing Osman whenever he arrived twice a month like clockwork. Quick with a smile and always generous with his skills, Osman inspired loyalty, while Rabien demanded obedience.

Cerena found her brother lording over the town from the gore-soaked tavern. Always one to keep a grudge, Rabien had created a throne in the main room surrounded by the rotting heads of all who had dared to prefer Osman's kind geniality to his derogatory nobility. He was distracted, drug-addled, and overconfident from bullying unarmed civilians. Knowing all she knew now, Cerena was sure she could have ended him despite him being the wielder of the Vermillion Blade, but instead, she bent the knee.

Bowing to her brother but unable to set aside her pride, Cerena attempted to fill the role Toman played in Talon's life—controlling the cursed blade of her family's bloodline by puppeteering her brother. Disowned by their father, Eleryon in shambles, and the Cour-Vermane estate deserted and warded against intrusion while Toman faced trial, Rabien welcomed his little sister's guidance and especially her magic. It had all been going according to her plan until Toman reappeared with a reprieve from the Emperor.

Cerena paced around her lab restlessly. Her repeating path mirrored the circuit many of her experiments made within their cages, but currently, they all cowered as far from her pacing form as possible. Most had even quieted their incessant pitiful mewling, recognizing their captor's volatile and dangerous mood. Cerena realized too late that she had picked up a crystal vial as her rage splintered it into shards in her bare hand, the glass biting into her palm. She threw the bloody fragments through the bars of one of the dozens of enclosures in the room, eliciting a satisfying yelp and whimper from its occupant.

*"Where are you?!"* Cerena screamed, unable to hold in her frustration any longer. *"And where did you lose it, you worthless imbecile?!"*

Cerena knew yelling at her dead brother was of no use. His death was the only thing of which she was sure. Every Cour-Vermane was. They knew of his destruction the same as they learned of Talon's—from the screeching agony that vibrated through the black chains that tied them all together. When a natal chain shattered, the whole of the family felt it.

The mundane act of dying alone would never release a Cour-Vermane from their bonds to Darkness. To have destroyed her brother and Talon so utterly, Cerena and others knew it would take something extraordinary and powerful to succeed where so many had failed. For it to have happened twice in less than a decade begged the question, *were they now the hunted instead of the hunters?*

Cerena held no love for her uncle, especially since his iron grip on the family was weakening. After Talon's death, Cerena bore the brunt of Toman's ire. With every blow he landed on her, Toman had reminded Cerena that her one task had been to destroy his son's will through her manipulations of Osman. He cut his niece out of his inner circle and left her to fend for herself, instead focusing his attention on grooming Rabien.

A prideful smile sliced across Cerena's face as she reminded herself of her surroundings. Left to her own devices, she masterfully orchestrated the fall of Arnadore from within. It was the perfect place to harvest the corruption the Vermillion Blade had cultivated across the region to feed her predilection for evolutionary magic.

Rabien had also seemed to be drawn to her, carried by the currents of corruption that flowed into her clutches to feed her experiments. As his tentative hold on sanity weakened, Rabien continually ranted that he was being denied the full extent of the Vermillion Blade's power. He insisted that whoever or whatever killed Talon had captured a portion of it and was denying him what was rightfully his. Her magics confirmed his ravings were nothing more than a mind cracking under the weight of unearned power.

Cerena combed through her last memory of her brother for the hundredth time. Hours before his death, Rabien had come to Cerena in a manic hysteria. He had found the missing power of the Vermillion Blade and knew who had kept it from him—their cousin Talon was alive! Cerena did have to admit that there had been a strange vibration in the undercurrents of corruptive magic in Eleryon recently, but to hear her brother resurrect his lifetime of loathing Talon washed away all credence of his assertion. With little patience and in ill temper, Cerena had goaded Rabien to face this imaginary *Talon Cour-Vermane* in a one-on-one duel instead of with his horde of the Black Court. Hearing her condescension, Rabien stepped through the shadows in a huff without saying a word as to where he went to face this great foe.

And then he was dead.

Rage crept back into Cerena's countenance as she slammed her fist down onto the sturdy ironwood worktable before her, remembering the aftermath. When she had felt Rabien's natal chain break, she was sure the Vermillion Blade would be hers. When it hadn't appeared to her, and Toman teleported into her lab weeks later, leaving Cerena's arcane wards dissolving in tatters around him, she knew something was amiss.

To this day, she could still hear Toman's demand echoing through the room. "Find it. Draw on that abomination you bow to's eye if you must."

Cerena's scry was as efficient as it was powerful, yet it showed the blade was in thousands of places simultaneously. Toman read Cerena's failure on her face before she could speak it. He struck her across the mouth with a vicious backhand, knocking her to the floor. "Another useless bitch." He spat his words at her prone form and vanished.

Cerena could still feel the rush of satisfaction that came with that blow that left blood on her lip and spattered across her cheek. In the lab, her bloody hand absently went to the small amber capsule hanging around her neck. Within the translucent jewel was her most prized possession—three drops of Toman Cour-Vermane's blood.

After the abuses she had suffered at Toman's hand after Talon's death, she vowed never to allow him to take such liberty again without a price. Cerena had filed her teeth to near razor sharpness and hidden the fact with a glamor rune tattooed on the inside of her lip. The blood Toman had drawn at his last visit was his own, not hers. Toman was not one to be careless with his blood, but the slight healing properties she had arcanely evolved into her saliva would have covered her tracks within moments.

More to reassure herself that her deception remained undiscovered than from any pain it was causing, she spit into her wounded hand and watched as the lacerations slowly closed. Watching her flesh knit itself back together, an idea began to form. The Vermillion Blade had been bound to Talon's soul *and* flesh. Flesh that suffered decades of manipulation by Toman's hand. Ritual magic like that imprinted the will of the caster upon its target. Perhaps she should stop looking for the Vermillion Blade itself and start looking for any residual essence of Toman's magic that was passed on to the ancestral weapon through its bond with Talon. Magic that his blood could draw her gaze to.

The casting she chose was not complex but one she was uniquely attuned to excel at. Cerena prepared the shallow container leering over it impatiently as she waited for the liquid within to settle into a mirrorlike sheen. Cracking the amber jewel around her neck, the three drops of Toman's blood barely rippled the surface of the arcane fluid as it entered and tainted the view within.

The basin revealed Toman's arcane influence as it veined and seethed across Eleryon from horizon to horizon. Cerena turned her eyes away from the obscene display of Toman's overt and active corruption infecting the region. She sought something more subtle and out of character for him—spells not of destruction but the empowerment he had bestowed upon his son. The traces of rituals that were usually granted as acts of protection and love that Toman had twisted to his design.

Nearly hidden by the stain of the Vermillion Blade's appearance to Rabien years before in caves of the southern coast was the tiniest whisp of Toman's arcane influence flowing southward. She followed it out over the sea, manic glee rising inside her as she approached her quarry, perhaps a ship offshore. Just at the point where her spell's reach became blocked by the warded protections of the Uldani Isles, the trail split in two. The more substantial left fork continued south while the other tiny wisp veered westward.

Cerena's elation at finding her first clue as to where the Vermillion Blade might be blossomed into raging anger. Her concentration broke as she slammed her hands down into the stillness of the arcane fluid in the gazing basin. Jumping to her worst instinct at who the Vermillion Blade had gone to and the all-but-impenetrable elemental wards it hid behind, she screeched in frustration.

*"Osman!"*

# CHAPTER TWELVE



Osman loved flying. He could hardly help himself from letting out another cry of delight as the mist owl wings he soared upon carried him over the waves. He glided effortlessly on the prevailing winds that flowed over the strait of choppy sea that separated Kyflenor from the third of the Uldani Isles that had appeared over the horizon, Mornaserin. When taking to the air two days ago, Osman had submerged himself deep into the instincts of the avian form he wore to navigate the treacherous updrafts the cliff faces of Kyflenor stirred into the sky, but out here over the open ocean, he was in complete control.

While the flesh, blood, and bone were Osman's, its current form was shaped by the spirit of the mist owl whose memory he carried and was not something he could create without her. During the long flight, Osman had contemplated Alerese's words about there always being a cost to his soulchanneling. The full implications of having flesh able to be molded by the convergence of magic, fate, and the spirit memories he carried within him still eluded him. What would lie in store for him both as beasts and when he walked again on two legs?

Osman felt a responsibility to the imprint of the mist owl whose form he now wore. Its life, memories, and experience now lived on through him, and Osman felt honored and obligated by that burden. As he merged deeper into her memories, Osman began to think of the mist owl as the Matriarch. No hierarchy ordered her home colony perched above the fog-shrouded shores of Mornaserin, but the Matriarch had been hatching clutches in her rookery for decades. She had been an elder within its community longer than Osman had been alive—a feat of longevity surprising even to her. The Matriarch had lived a life worthy of respect, and Osman happily obliged her with that deference.

The recollection of the Matriarch's brood spanning fifty generations of coastal mist hunters inspired a preening pride in Osman. Children beyond number that brought a wary fear to any prey that ventured too far into the mists, regardless if they crawled the land or swam upon or under the waves.

As he soared upon the Matriarch's borrowed wings, Osman found it the most resonatingly natural thing to be a female owl. The memory of being courted by young males vying for the Matriarch's affection to mate, life growing within her body, caring for her eggs, feeding and raising her fledglings. While on his own two legs, prowling on four with Wilfred, or now soaring on the Matriarch's wings, Osman became aware how little one's flesh mattered to your intrinsic identity. Osman had not only seen the truth of the souls whose forms he now carried but also his own. Now that he had, he knew who he truly was and always would be.

Osman let out another cry of delight as he dove through a small cloud that passed beneath him. The Matriarch's instincts had gotten him off the ground and beyond the cliffs, but after the first few hours of uneventful soaring over the open sea, Osman had tentatively tested his skill and immediately fallen in love with the exhilaration of flight. It had been shaky at first, but the elongated wingspan of the mist owl evolved for open ocean soaring was thankfully forgiving enough that minor mistakes did not result in disaster. Survival would be unlikely if Osman crashed into the choppy surf below, so he kept his recklessness to a minimum and the Matriarch's instincts close at hand. Despite his antics, she guided Osman unfailingly westward, both of them secure in the knowledge that he would arrive at her home shores by moonrise.

The white foam of the crashing surf was the only delineation between the dark waters of the ocean and the black sand beaches of Mornaserin's southern coastline. The Matriarch's colony was still dozens of leagues away on the isle's northern shore, but in his exuberance for flight, Osman had expended far more energy than necessary on the traverse across the strait, and his avian body demanded sustenance. He would not reach the deep fog of the north shore this night. However, mist hunting was not the only skill the Matriarch had mastered, and Spring always created a prey-rich environment.

Osman heard an unfamiliar sound to his ears, but it rang like a dinner bell through the Matriarch's senses. A seal cub, grown out of its helplessness as a pup but not quite ready to commit to a life at sea, had let out an ill-fated yelp as it settled on the moonlit beach to sleep. Its black-speckled fur perfectly camouflaged it against the sparkling dark volcanic sand, but it mattered little as Osman was guided by the Matriarch's frighteningly sensitive hearing and a half-century of honed hunting skill.

Osman dove toward the cub, his soft feathers making not a whisper of sound. His momentum drove his talons deep into the seal cub's flesh, still fat with blubber from mother's milk. Claws closing around its spine, Osman lifted the seal, easily the size of a large suckling pig, into the air with a few beats of the Matriarch's powerful wings.

The cub squirmed in his claws, threatening to bite, at which point Osman sank into instinct, letting the Matriarch's experience take complete control. Correcting course slightly, the Matriarch gained altitude, heading toward a rocky outcropping. After two mighty wingbeats, her claws opened releasing the seal and letting it fall forty feet onto the rocks below. It hit with the delicious sound of an overripe melon splitting. Guided more by his stomach than skill, Osman dropped to the stone shelf where the cub's corpse lay splayed open and, with beak and talon, began to feast.

After satiating his hunger, gorging himself on nearly all of the seal's remains, Osman returned to the air, looking for a suitable roost. The volcanically active southern side of Mornaserin, devoid of vegetation, was rife with rocky towers of eroded lava cleaved by expanding ice from winter. The jagged spires offered many sites for inaccessible and safe places to perch; leaving the choice to the Matriarch, Osman eventually found one acceptable to her wary sense for potential danger. Closing his eyes and ruffling his feathers to capture the last warmth of early evening, Osman settled in for the night.

Even though three days had passed since he and Wilfred parted, this was Osman's first chance to sleep. While he had drifted into an almost hypnotic daze through the days of flying from Kyflenor, he had never truly slept. Now, perched in the darkness amidst the stark obsidian towers, a deep loneliness crept over him.

While Wilfred had not been as actively present in his consciousness the past few years, Osman had always felt his presence in his mind. Now there was just an emptiness. The Matriarch and the other spirits he held were a presence within him, but they couldn't replace Wilfred. For a decade, he had never been truly alone. Even in his healing sleeps, Osman had known Wilfred was close by.

Osman longed to retreat to his mindscape and familiar room as he became lost in the depth of his solitude. He wanted to disappear and trust the Matriarch's instincts to keep him safe, so he didn't have to face the long dark night alone. But the thought of all the memories he shared with Wilfred awaiting him made him physically wince. Osman ruffled the Matriarch's feathers again and willed himself to sleep, allowing exhaustion to overtake him. He dreamed of flying in a grey void of mist and fog, his solitary cry echoing over the sound of wind and surf. His lonely cry was answered first by one, then dozens of mist owls echoing in his ears, calling to him with offers of safety, community, and belonging.

Osman rode a morning updraft over the steaming ranks of newly forming foothills and ridges that flowed like stone glaciers down from the curving rim of the ancient caldera that had once been a part of Grimspire's parent mountain. The dull haze that wafted up from the alien landscape below him glowed pale orange where lava drooled from still-active vents birthing more land for the ever-growing isle of Mornaserin.

The ridge of the caldera Osman needed to cross was not nearly as high as the peaks of the Shieldwall Spine on Kyflenor; however, its width and volcanic nature would make foot travel across it at best treacherous, if not impossible. For leagues, the charred slopes of stone rippled like icing on an over-frosted nameday cake. Pockmarked across the landscape were chasms and deep pools where lava still languorously bubbled and burped, expelling globs of flaming liquid rock. From his perspective as he approached from the air, the landscape looked like the mountain had slowly melted in the sun and flowed like molasses to the sea.

As Osman passed over the leading edge of the slow-flowing rock, the Matriarch's instincts snatched control of Osman's lazy ascent. She banked him hard to the right, wings almost vertical, narrowly avoiding a towering geyser that erupted below them. With the column of boiling steam and water came a blast of heated air the Matriarch's skills deftly utilized to carry him hundreds of feet higher into the sky. Osman belatedly realized flying over land, especially thermally active land, was not the relaxed soaring of his ocean passage, so he relented control of his form to the Matriarch's innate expertise.

The air around Osman grew oppressively warm and thick the further inland he traveled. The constant winds off of Icefel pushed the heat and steam from the newly formed land before it, carrying the moist blanket of air higher and higher up the southern slopes of Mornaserin. Convection, thermal winds, and the rising ground channeling it upward accelerated the ocean of air even further. With the Matriarch's experience guiding him, Osman rode the turbulent wave of air like a piece of flotsam on a tsunami.

The Matriarch folded his wings closer to his body to throttle his speed and better navigate the rushing current of accelerating air around him. So powerful were the roaring winds and heated updrafts that to Osman, it felt more like he was diving for prey rather than rushing up the steep incline to what seemed like the lip of the world. The blanket of humid air became hotter and heavier upon his wings as Osman shot forward up the slope. Every moment the oppressive atmosphere felt thicker and more likely to smother him or soak his wings, causing him to crash into the earth like the seal cub he dropped on the rocks the night before. Unable to risk a single beat of his wings to gain altitude lest his feathers be torn from his skin, Osman had to dodge around spires of stone racing toward him. It took every bit of the Matriarch's instincts to avoid certain death.

The lip of the caldera was less than five-hundred yards away, but it felt like miles. A prominent ridge of rock ahead blocked his path with no way around it. With his current trajectory and speed, crashing into it was inevitable. The Matriarch instinctively extended Osman's talons high out in front of him to brace for impact. Every triumph and regret of Osman's life flashed through his mind. At the last second, the Matriarch reached Osman's claws high above his head, nearly flipping him upside down to do so. Talons scrambled on the leading edge of the ridge, their hooked shape immediately finding purchase. His claw's elastic muscles were pulled taut by his momentum and then launched him back up into the rushing current of air right as his tailfeathers began to crush against the sheer face of the ridge.

Wings pulled in tightly to his sides in a falcon's stoop, Osman's flying was more akin to that of a stone thrown from a catapult than a bird on the wing. Osman shot over the lip of the Mornaserin caldera missing it by less than a yard. The raging wave of air that had propelled him up the slope at breakneck speed became less than a breeze as the ground dropped out from under him. The Matriarch slammed out his wings like a parachute, leaving him floating seven thousand feet over a vast evergreen canopy of ironwood trees far below.

The legendary forests of Mornaserin spread out below Osman like a vast green carpet. Behind him, the warm wet air that had all but thrown him up the island's southern slopes curled into eddies created in the lee of the caldera rim. There they condensed into clouds and drifted out from the towering inner face of the caldera showering the trees and all the life sheltered in their boughs with their warm rains.

The ironwood trees were just the tip of the incredible forest Osman drifted over. Anson, decades before at Horizon's End, had called the ironwood he carved his sculpture from a mere sapling. Osman had listened with his mouth agape as Anson told him how a proper ironwood tree would have a trunk larger than the entirety of the grounds of Horizon's End. Anson spun tales of how, beneath and upon their boughs, whole ecosystems of fantastic plants and animals lived that existed nowhere else in the world. And at the center of it all was Arbor Lumenari, the world tree, and in its boughs the city of Lumenaria.

The Matriarch's instinct pulled Osman toward the fog-shrouded north shore where the vast forest met the sea, but instead, he made a wide descending circle over the sprawling forest below him. From the height he had arrived at, the massive scale of the ironwood forest was not readily apparent. Osman even mused that Anson preyed upon his impressionable six-year-old mind with his tall tales, but as he descended, Osman realized, if anything, his young mind had underestimated what Anson had tried to describe.

As Osman passed below the treetops, a multi-level terraced landscape unfolded below him, dozens of layers deep. He had expected to see a single small tree living on a branch of an ironwood, but he found whole glades. Crystal-clear ponds of rainwater cascaded from the higher levels down to the lower ones. Vines and curtains of moss spanned between boughs to form cradles that gave anchor for all manner of life that reached for the sun and gentle rains.

As Osman descended deeper into the ironwoods, isolated glades expanded to small forests in their own right. Hundreds, if not thousands, of these islands of life comprised the landscape, stacked and suspended among the branches of the ironwoods. It was not like anything Osman had ever experienced. The complexity of it all surrounding him overwhelmed him. Even hundreds of feet in the air, he felt like he was dozens of stories below the ground, and Osman began feeling like he was once again trapped deep in the maze of cells below the Hall of Judgment.

His mind retreated into the sanctuary of the Matriarch's calm instincts. Unbidden by his will, his beak let out a series of quick shrill screeches. Within his avian mind, the returning echoes of those cries painted a three-dimensional map of the towering ironwoods and the suspended terraced landscapes around him. On the Matriarch's wings, he navigated the living maze around him and broke free of the ironwoods climbing above the treetops into the clear sky.

Osman's mind calmed, but he was not ready to trust his own skills to fly again. The Matriarch began winging toward the mist owl colony on the coast, but Osman pressed a different destination into the Matriarch's instincts: Lumenaria.

# CHAPTER THIRTEEN



*Year 884* PXF *~ Spring*

Osman banked gracefully northward up the coast, skirting the blanket of fog that had begun to stack into a grey wall half as tall as the ironwoods just offshore. His silent wings surfed along the waves of warm air flowing out to sea before they cooled into the impenetrable mist. A contagious familiar elation filled the Matriarch's spirit as he glided over his home waters.

To Osman's left, waves crashed into the massive roots of the ironwood trees arching higher than a three-story inn. On his right, within the grey bank of icy fog, he could hear the voices of the mist owl colony filled with dozens of generations of his brood. The Matriarch dipped Osman lower to skim just above the rolling surf, gliding through the tube made by a crashing wave, a maneuver he would never have attempted on his own.

Cowering in wide-eyed amazement within the Matriarch's instincts, he snatched a small fish from the crest of one of the swells and devoured it in three bites without missing a wing beat. Osman let out a cry of appreciation as he smiled inwardly. The Matriarch was testing this new young flesh she inhabited and, Osman felt, was showing off to the youngster just what she could do in her prime.

Ahead of Osman, a stand of juvenile ironwoods blocked his path, like soldiers marching out into the sea and deep into the fog. Their upper branches peeked out of the top of the thick clouds like ghostly giants rising from the sea to guard the isle at their back. A dozen wing beats lifted Osman above the tangled domes of their exposed roots, where he could easily weave between their towering trunks. A quick slalom around their ranks brought him back out over the sea on the other side of the spit of land they anchored themselves to and into the unchecked ostentatious majesty of Lumenaria.

The city sat deep in the protective bay that lay on the other side of the sentinel ironwoods Osman had passed through. Shooting out hundreds of feet from the curving wall of domed roots that marked the shore was an ancient fallen ironwood tree. Long since petrified by the actions of sun and surf on the minerals in its wood, the felled tree now acted as the port of Lumenaria with births for ships notched out of its trunk. Only a single upper branch remained from its canopy. The towering spire held a globe of arcane coldfire at its pinnacle, acting as a beacon for ships traversing the ever-present fog enveloping the north side of the Isle of Mornaserin.

Osman glided on his silent wings over two Cinderfall schooners docked along the jetty, discharging several dozen exuberant Uldani just arrived from Mael Esari. A deep longing welled inside Osman upon seeing the group of older teens from the capital just on the cusp of adulthood but still entrenched in the wiles of their youth. This was everything he missed. Everything he had stolen from himself in the turmoil of his youth—the turmoil he now recognized as self-imposed and unjustified. Osman was not going to miss this experience again now that he had a second chance to have it. He swung wide around to the seaside rail of the schooner and landed.

Now for the moment of truth. Osman visualized everything he had become, everything he had learned about himself. Good and bad, scars and all, and willed himself to manifest it into being. He felt an airy fluttering shift within his flesh, and where once a mist owl was perched on the ship's rail, now sat an Uldani man.

Osman felt the cold metal of the platinum coin Alerese had given him resting in his palm. He expected to see the daisy as well, but when he opened his hand, it wasn't there. Looking down at his hand, though, and seeing his bare forearms and the raised silvery slashes of the scars there, he remembered what the coin was for and that he was practically naked with just his enchanted boots and the tattered remains of his old pants.

Osman was alone on deck, but the knot of passengers from Mael Esari was just over the opposite rail from him on the pier. They could look his way any moment, so he quickly dove through an open hatch into the hold. Osman nearly knocked himself unconscious on the low ceiling standing up, still not used to his new height. Around him, the mismatched trunks and crates that filled the ship's hold certainly were the privileged Mael Esari passengers' belongings.

Osman ducked behind a stack of cargo out of view of any crew who might come down to begin unloading. After quickly scanning the nearby trunks, he picked one likely to contain clothing and inspected the latches. Finding them locked, Osman was relieved to discover Talon's iron dagger had returned to his hip, still pushed through his worn belt. He drew it to begin work on the locks. As he began, Osman paused. The blade was no longer the frost-covered jagged icy blade he had felt against his skin in the field with Alerese and Wilfred, but a ghostly grey, long stiletto seeming almost incorporeal in substance. It was a mystery that would have to wait for another time. First – clothes.

Osman hoped the locks were more ornate than functional as he had neither the tools nor skill to do more than force them open. To his surprise, the ghostly stiletto's blade slipped effortlessly into even the smallest gaps between latch and lid, giving him the leverage to pop the locks with nary a sound. The first trunk was full of elegant dresses, which were far too tailored to their owner for him to attempt to wear. Luckily the second held an assortment of leathers, tunics, and jerkins that he felt he could make work.

The tunics were crafted for someone of slimmer build than even Osman had been when in the Arnadore guard. However, he found a magenta one constructed with generous extra fabric, a lace-up collar, and removable sleeves. By leaving the sleeves unattached and collar open, Osman hoped to squeeze himself into it without tearing the fabric.

As Osman went to pull the tunic over his head, he discovered where the daisy Alerese had given him as a token of the Fatesinger's blessing had gone. At first, Osman thought it had just become plastered to the skin near the bottom edge of his ribcage under his left arm, but he quickly realized it was an incredibly realistic tattoo. Another mystery for later that would have to wait. Although the fit was far from what was intended and pulled across his back, the tunic would have to do for now.

Osman discovered pants to be much harder to find. As much as he would have preferred them, Osman couldn't fit into any of the leathers he found in the pilfered trunk. Even after multiple attempts, and no matter how he tried, he just could *not* wiggle them over his more muscular thighs and past his fuller buttocks. Osman mused that perhaps years as a saldrig hunting big game had indeed manifested a downside when it came to his backside. Disappointed, he finally settled on some loose dun-colored cotton work britches.

Eyeing his clothes, Osman felt the familiar qil of self-consciousness rise between his eyebrows on the bridge of his nose, like a swelling pimple needing popping. Banished along with most of his childhood emotions, it had been decades since last he felt that specific emotion's tactile sensation manifest so clearly. It felt more substantial than Osman remembered, so much so his fingers longed to travel to his face and squeeze out the offending abscess.

Whether from its long absence or his new physiology he was still trying to understand fully, Osman became jubilant in the qil's returned presence. He dove into the awkwardness of his situation and clothes and, while completely unnecessary, even further tousled the mop of unkempt, unruly curls his hair had become to complete his immersion in the ungainly emotion.

With clumsy aplomb, Osman strode back onto the schooner's deck, across the gangway, and out onto the jetty formed by the fallen ironwood where the ship docked. The two groups of raucous *temptarai*, the Uldani term for teens of their age who had yet to tame their emotions, had merged and moved away from the schooners. They were about twenty yards ahead of Osman and moving down the center of the ironwood trunk where, over the centuries, foot and cart traffic had leveled the surface into a wide path.

Osman's keen eyes focused on some of the individuals to try to get a read of the group dynamic and a possible way to integrate himself with them. Scanning the faces, it struck him how *young* they all looked. His trials on Kyflenor had aged Osman more than the same amount of time should have with his Uldani heritage, but even the eldest looking among the group ahead looked over half a decade younger than himself as humans measured their years.

Osman then had to shift into an Uldani mindset as he watched the group's behavior. At that young age, the older you looked, the *less* mature you were with your emotional control. Since an Uldani's physical aging was tied to their emotions, it was highly variable from person to person during adolescence. The first decade of physical development was near the same rapid pace as humans, but as Uldani moved through their early teens and became less volatile in their emotions, that aging slowed.

Most temptarai traveled (or were sent by their parents) to Mornaserin in late adolescence, usually in their mid to late teens, once they had some control of their emotions but before they fully physically matured. The purpose of the exodus was for Uldani youths to burn through the myriad of passions that overwhelmed their control so they could reenter society no longer at the mercy of their unbridled qil.

Those who arrived at Lumenaria looking older—eighteen, nineteen, or even brushing against twenty—had been, or still were, the most volatile in their emotional development. The dichotomy made for an interesting adolescence for all Uldani—the most immature leap ahead in physical development while the more controlled and reserved's aging would slow.

Osman had seen both sides of that coin. He had been the smallest for his age before his father's first return. With that shock, Anson's departure, and then Tavi leaving him again, Osman's swirling emotions ignited a growth spurt in him, quickly outpacing any children who visited Horizon's End with their parents over the next several years.

Osman knew it was not unheard of for Uldani to return to Lumenaria to rediscover themselves or wrangle newfound passions or emotions they discovered later in life. Many after the war did precisely that. But knowing that he wouldn't have the experience of a young temptarai discovering life on his own for the first time did steal some of his excitement. Osman realized he couldn't just slip in with the group of laughing temptarai before him and recapture what he had missed.

The realization, and perhaps walking again on two legs, brought his purpose for being here back to the front of his thoughts. He was here to find out the fate of Richen and fulfill his Qat'malorn. Osman no longer considered that debt one he needed to repay to Talon. Certainly, Talon was the beneficiary, and the Qat'malorn had been invoked by Veronic, but the person Osman had truly betrayed was himself. Osman looked down at the scars on his forearms, his soul may have healed, but healing and forgiveness are not the same.

Osman had been so focused on the temptarai and lost in thought he had not fully registered the brazen grandeur of Lumenaria that had begun to envelop him. The fallen ironwood tree rapidly grew wider as they approached its roots. The center two-thirds had been carved out into a set of monumental stairs and ramps leading down through the bark and into the heartwood. Along its length and width, interspersed with the complex array of stairs and ramps, were landings as large as the central square of the Trellis Market back in Arnadore. At the bottom of the stairs was a breathtaking lagoon the color of the warm, clear waters of Jadenpool.

Flanking the central stairs on each side, the original root dome remained, but they had been carved and bonded into staircases arching into the boughs of smaller ironwoods on the shore. From his perspective on the fallen ironwood's main trunk, Osman could see now that the lagoon's surface was well below sea level. Upon falling centuries ago, the rest of the ironwood's root dome must have crushed together, creating a natural levee that kept the sea from encroaching on the socket left behind when the tree first fell and eventually became the lagoon.

The familiar tickle of wonder played around Osman's toes and spread to the arches of his feet as he took in all the intricacies before him. An overly wide grin overtook Osman's face at the return of one of his favorite and most nostalgic qil. As powerful and joyful as it was, a different emotion quickly overwhelmed it.

Perhaps it was the scale that had made it invisible to him or that his mind just could not process the enormity of what his eyes were seeing. As he raised his eyes from looking down on the lagoon, he realized the vast mottled brown and green backdrop to the scene in front of him was not the forest but a single ironwood—Arbor Lumenari, the world tree.

The tickling wonder of his toes fell to the background in the presence of the vibrating chill of awe. Its qil raced up Osman's spine from tailbone to the base of his skull, finally settling as a crackling spark between his shoulder blades. Then something unexpected happened, a sensation Osman had never felt before when experiencing awe's qil. The crackling spark between his shoulder blades began to expand, lifting off his back. It spread wider and wider until the sparking chill of awe felt like it was infecting two enormous mist owl wings sprouting from his back.

Panic's qil erupted behind his eyes, causing them to feel like they were inflating and about to burst, dulling the sensation filling the wings but not erasing their presence. Spinning in circles, Osman manically checked with both hands and aching eyes to see if the Matriarch's wings had actually manifested, but they found nothing. Relief washed away panic, and awe burst back to the forefront, not only for the world tree but also for this new expression of awe's qil. Arching his back, Osman threw his arms out to his sides, turned his face to the sky, and released a loud *"ya whoop"* of excitement.

The first giggle made Osman realize he was not alone. He had caught up with the temptarai group, who had also paused to take in the sight of the world tree and were now all staring at him. The numb throbbing of a zit sitting between his eyebrows surged back into existence. Maybe Osman could pass as a temptarai after all.

# CHAPTER FOURTEEN



One of the older-looking temptarai threw his arms in the air and let out his own excited *whoop* to match Osman's.

"Aw yeah! Right? Can you believe this?!" The bulky, pale-skinned Mael Esari youth called out enthusiastically. Then, in one continuous motion, he ran over, crouched down, threw his arms around Osman's waist, lifted him into the air, and began spinning around. Face turned to the side but still pressed up against Osman's midsection muffling his words, he continued, "Finally! Someone who isn't pretending that this isn't *amazing!*"

Osman was so startled by the motion of being lifted off the ground he didn't have time to protest. Once lifted and being spun around, air flowing through the awe-filled chill of his phantom qil wings made the sensation almost euphoric. His feet redoubled the tickling wonder dancing across his toes and up his arches. Osman reached even wider with his arms and spread the ghostly wings to their limit. He reared his head back and let out a laughing primal roar.

The temptarai holding him aloft stopped spinning him and looked up, his chin driving uncomfortably into Osman's abdominals. "Damn! What was *that?*"

Osman looked down and saw a tinge of uncertainty, maybe even fear, in the teen's dark eyes. He realized the sound he had just made was not something his Uldani vocal cords should have been able to produce. Osman replied with the biggest conspiratorial smile he could conjure, "Just a trick I picked up. I'll teach you how to do it!"

The uncertainty in the temptarai's eyes jumped to excitement. He dropped Osman back onto his feet and said, "I'm gonna hold you to that! Now it's my turn, big guy!" Throwing his arms out to his sides, mimicking Osman, he waited for Osman to lift him into the air.

While the two were equally broad of build, Osman was several inches taller than the gregarious Uldani who had picked him up. Still awash in his excitement and not wanting to be outdone, Osman squatted low and wrapped his arms around his new companion's calves right at the knees. Osman stood to his full height, lifting the teen high into the air with surprising ease. As he began to spin in place, Osman, with the side of his face pressed against his companion's thighs, called up, "Okay, let's hear it! Before you roar, you gotta howl!" Osman demonstrated by letting out a very humanoid-sounding "*Arooooooooooo!*"

A tentative but enthusiastic "A-a-arooo..." sounded above him.

Osman began to spin faster and jostle the temptarai he held aloft, "C'mon, you can do better!"

"*Aarrrooooooooooo!*" echoed out with vigor and conviction from above him.

Osman crouched and set his companion's feet back on the ground. The temptarai was all frothy excitement when they were face to face again.

"That. Was. Incredible!" he exclaimed. "I'm Yanri, by the way. Who're you?"

"You can call me Osman," He replied enthusiastically, infected by Yanri's personality and his own emotions.

"Well, bring it in, Osman. Gimme that face!" Yanri reached his hands up to place them on Osman's face.

Osman almost recoiled out of habit, but he was so caught up in his excitement and Yanri's jubilant demeanor that he lifted his hands. With wide eyes and infectious smiles, the two read and shared their faces with one another. Yanri was all but a blank slate, his face etched with a privileged and carefree, albeit mildly rebellious, adolescence in Mael Esari. While the sharing wasn't as deep as the one with Alerese or accompanied by visions of his past like with Wilfred, there was no hiding (nor desire to hide) his scars from Yanri. Osman watched some of the exuberance drain out of his eyes. The young Uldani lifted his hands off Osman's face.

"Aw man, I'm sorry." The words were as pure and heartfelt as most any Osman had ever heard from another living Uldani.

"Thank you." Osman replied, then added with a questioning smile, "We good?"

"Better than good!" Yanri replied, then turned back to the audacious grandeur of Lumenaria spread before them. "Let's go burn bright and *live*! That's why we're here, yeah?" Yanri gave a dismissive glance to all the other temptarai who were willfully ignoring the spectacle the two had made of themselves and started walking down the massive set of stairs that led to the lagoon below.

"Yeah!" Osman exclaimed, following in Yanri's wake. However, Yanri's words echoed in his mind. *Better than good.* How many times had he said those exact words to Talon? A tinge of guilt lodged like a peach pit at the top of his throat—his reason for being here was not at all the same as Yanri's.

Yanri stopped and threw his arm around Osman's shoulders, giving them a rough squeeze. "Hey, Osman. Buddy. Just one thing, we have *got* to get you some new clothes!"

Osman laughed, "You have no idea how badly."

The staircase carved through the ironwood trunk, with its many interconnecting landings and platforms, acted more as an open-air amphitheater than its architectural function to transition from the higher elevation of the port down to the lagoon level. As the two descended, Yanri would excitedly point out the young Uldani who gathered in small and large social groups to participate in various activities he recognized. The warm spring morning had drawn out hundreds of these groups, which had settled in almost every cozy nook or preferred area they had claimed their own.

Osman was more amazed by the planters of deciduous trees interspersed along their path than the gathered temptarai. While most had just begun to don their verdant spring foliage, he still could spot many tropical specimens that he knew from his time in Jadenpool with Cerena should not have been able to survive the climate of the Uldani Isles.

Pointing out a fig tree, Osman asked Yanri, "How do you think they keep it alive in the Winter?"

Yanri looked at him, astonished. "You're kidding, right? This *is* Winter, or so my parents told me. I didn't even bring my sweaters or coats, and I'm a thin-blooded bloke from Mael Esari, where we never even see snow." Yanri caught himself before continuing his jibing. He laid his hand on Osman's shoulder, giving it a hearty squeeze.

"Hey, I'm sorry. I keep forgetting you are as new here as me and from..." Yanri paused, finding the right words, "different circumstances." He then continued like a versed teacher. "The warm air from the volcanoes on the other side of the island keeps this side warm year-round." He then added in a lower voice, "At least that is the official story." Yanri made air quotes with his fingers around the word 'official.'

"Do I even want to ask?" Osman questioned.

"Not until we find a spice house, clothes, and food." Releasing his comforting grip on Osman's shoulder and closing his fist to give it a good punch, Yanri added with a grin, "Not necessarily in that order. You're hideous!" as he charged down a winding ramp leading to the lagoon's edge.

Osman followed, catching up with Yanri and effortlessly passing him, even spinning around and running backward in front of him to show off his ferally-enhanced athletic prowess. The amphitheater stairs' hard, petrified ironwood surface transitioned to soft golden sand as they arrived at their base. The fine sand was a perfect match to the color of the heartwood of the giant ironwood that made up the port. Reaching down and digging his fingers into it, Osman realized the sand was more akin to sawdust. The beach was the remains of what had been carved out of the fallen ironwood to make the entry stairs and amphitheater behind him.

Yanri had plopped down beside him catching his breath and began immediately unlacing his calf-high boots. He yanked them off once he got them loose enough and pulled off a pair of grey stockings to expose his broad feet and hairy toes.

"Real sand! Can you believe it? Not the pebbly tripe that passes for the shore on Invanora," Yanri exclaimed as he dug his feet into the sand. He added wistfully, "Man, I wish I had gotten wonder in my toes. I got it behind my knees, like the rest of my family." He looked up at Osman, who was still standing as he said the last with an almost mournful expression.

Osman had never talked with other Uldani about his qil, much less considered that there were known commonalities and that people might desire one more than another. Yanri must have seen the surprise and contemplation on Osman's face.

"Aw man, are you kidding me? Well, get over here Wondertoes, and tell me how it feels!" Yanri grabbed one of Osman's booted feet and yanked it out from under him, causing Osman to tumble in a heap beside him. Yanri pulled the boot he was holding off Osman's foot.

"How are your feet not chafed to shreds wearing boots with no socks?" Yanri exclaimed in his usual fashion. "Are these enchanted?"

Quick as a mongoose, Yanri grabbed Osman's other boot and had it off in a wink. For a second, he thought the young temptarai might intend to try them on or maybe even steal them, but Yanri set them aside. Instead, he grabbed one of Osman's ankles in each hand and pushed his feet into the sand.

"Okay, what's your wonder qil feel like? Tell me everything!" Yanri looked like an extremely overgrown ten-year-old full to the brim of youthful curiosity as he demanded all the details from Osman.

"Um, well..." Osman stammered, "I'm kinda more freaked out than feeling wonder right now."

Osman watched Yanri take stock of the position they both were in. Osman reclining propped up on his elbows, knees bent in front of him, with Yanri beside him holding his ankles and pressing his feet deep into the sand. Yanri began to laugh, and Osman couldn't help himself from laughing as well.

Yanri released Osman's ankles as soon as they stopped laughing and caught their breath. He twisted around and put an arm across Osman's bent knees and placed his head on it like a giant puppy. Yanri then sheepishly explained, "I get over-excited sometimes. My parents are older, and I didn't have many friends my age, so I didn't get to have a lot of the experiences other kids had."

Osman ruffled Yanri's auburn hair, which looked like it had been recently cut into its current style of loose waves that hung just below his ears.

"I understand, I..." Osman paused and gathered his thoughts. "It's a long story. Suffice it to say, until this moment I hadn't thought much about it at all." Now curious, Osman asked, "You feel the qil for wonder in the back of your knees?"

Yanri sighed forlornly. "It sucks. It makes you feel like you can't trust your legs to hold you up. I had a great-aunt who fell from hers and broke a hip during the last Helsparian venting ceremony. In all the great sagas the bards tell, the hero, or the maiden, or the funny sidekick everyone loves feels their qil for wonder in their toes." Yanri focused his dark brown eyes back on Osman's, "And I have always wondered what it *actually* feels like."

"Well, sand doesn't inspire much wonder in me." Osman almost mentioned his time on Jadenpool beaches with Cerena but thought better of it. He continued, motioning with his hand to the diverse and colorful buildings arrayed upon its golden shore. "But this absolutely does."

Osman focused on an area a quarter way around the lagoon from where they sat, where a spillover in the root levee allowed water to cascade down into a winding channel lined with mangrove trees. Bright pavilions with painted ironwood walls and vibrant canopies lined the flowing water as people ate and drank on the open patios. Osman let his eyes travel further around the lagoon, and the wonder of it all began to build in him.

Yanri whispered, "Tell me when it happens."

Osman had never really paid acute attention to a building qil and had to find the words as it happened. "Well, the qil begins as a ring that tickles its way around my big toes." Osman began almost reverently, trying to mimic Alerese's tone as they told the tale of his father and the Fatesinger, then continued, "And then it weaves in and out between my other toes like a wiggling eel." He glanced at Yanri with a bright smile and tried to make his face as expressive as possible. Yanri looked back, fully enraptured with his description. "Then it moves up to the arch of my foot where it builds into a fizzy ball and feels like someone is tickling the skin there with a handful of goose feathers." He added, "That part usually makes me have to stifle a giggle," which he was trying to do now with little success.

Yanri rolled his head and arm off Osman's knees in a melodramatic swoon and flopped on his back to lie beside Osman in the sand.

"Ugh! I'm so jealous! It's just like the songs say." Yanri said to the sky, rolling his eyes back and tilting his head to look up at Osman.

"You, my friend, are easily impressed."

Yanri propped himself up on one elbow and looked at Osman earnestly, "You mean it?"

"That you're easily impressed?" Osman asked. "Yeah, I mean it. You were swooning from me talking about—what did you call them? My 'wonder toes.'"

"No, not that," Yanri replied. "That we're friends."

Osman quickly dropped his kidding demeanor. Yanri was serious. Osman recalled his face sharing with Yanri and realized his new friend wasn't a blank slate emotionally, but rather an empty one. He was without any significant connections to anyone, good or bad.

Osman answered sincerely, "Yes. Of course, we're friends." He added lightheartedly, "That also means we're stuck with each other, y'know?"

"That works fine with me!" Yanri answered with his usual exuberance. "Oh, and it's not that you have 'wonder toes.' I called you Wondertoes. Just you wait. I'm gonna make that nickname stick." He then shifted around on the sand and laid his head on Osman's stomach with unexpected familiarity. Osman tensed initially but then relaxed as Yanri began to jabber about his trip here from Mael Esari. Osman's loneliness from the night before seemed a distant memory as he savored having a connection with someone of flesh and blood again.

# CHAPTER FIFTEEN

*Year 884* PXF *~ Spring*

"Hey! You hungry?" Yanri asked leadingly

The question seemed far away and almost dreamlike to Osman, who had drifted off into a light doze listening to Yanri's moment-by-moment retelling of his preparation and journey to Mornaserin. His stomach responded for him, letting out a loud growl. Yanri laughed and rolled his head to the side, placing his ear on Osman's belly, pretending to listen intently.

"Is that where you were hiding that saldrig?" Yanri asked playfully.

At the mention of a saldrig, Osman's consciousness sprang to awareness. "What? No. There's not a saldrig in me. Why would you say that?" Osman answered defensively.

Yanri sat up and looked at Osman questioningly. "The roar earlier? It sounds like it's right *here*!" Yanri playfully and over-enthusiastically slapped Osman's stomach hard, knocking the breath out of him and eliciting a loud *oomph* from Osman.

"Oh, right!" Osman played along, sitting up and slamming the heels of his hands into Yanri's shoulders, pushing him back down into the sand. Rolling to his feet in a single fluid motion, Osman offered his hand to Yanri as he scanned the buildings along the lagoon promenade. "Where do you think we can find food?" he asked. Slyly he added, "That is if you are willing to be seen with someone dressed as hideous as me."

Yanri grabbed Osman's offered hand, pulling harder than necessary in an attempt to topple him as he got to his feet, but Osman stood sturdy as an ironwood. "Oh, I have no intention to sit at a table with you. We'll get something we can eat while we walk to find you clothes." Yanri eyed Osman's mismatched outfit, "Are these even *yours*?"

"That's another long story," Osman replied as they walked barefoot down the beach carrying their boots in hand.

Osman caught the smell of meat pies frying nearby, and his stomach let out another loud groan. Yanri laughed and teased, "We'll make it, big guy! When was the last time you ate?"

At the question, Osman was surprised by the realization that he was so famished. He had eaten the Matriarch's weight in blubbery seal flesh the night before, which should have satiated him for days. Alerese's words revisited him regarding his soulchanneling transformations, "*You must remember all change comes with a cost. Sometimes just the food in your belly, other times something more.*" Osman didn't want to contemplate *something more* if shifting from mist owl back to himself ate up over fifteen pounds of seal flesh along with the fish the Matriarch had grabbed as a snack just a few hours earlier.

Osman spotted the stand selling the savory-smelling pastries from over a hundred yards away and made a beeline for them. His anticipation and hunger grew into voracious desire. With the emotion, an unknown qil began to manifest with it. Osman felt his canine teeth grow into the long saber fangs of his saldrig form. A feeling similar to the qil of his awe becoming giant versions of the Matriarch's wings. Knowing the saldrig fangs he felt couldn't possibly fit in his current mouth and would extend nearly down to his chest if they did, the new qil didn't drive Osman to check his teeth with his hands, instead only running his tongue across them to be sure.

Osman stopped dead in his tracks, Yanri slamming into his back with the sudden arrest in his forward momentum.

"What the Hells, man?" Yanri asked accusingly.

Osman stood frozen, looking away from Yanri. Panic began to inflate his eyeballs, and the feeling of the throbbing zit reappeared on the bridge of his nose. Osman probed his canine teeth with his tongue again, making sure he wasn't imagining things. Nope, what he was feeling was real. His canine teeth were longer. And sharper. Not saldrig sized and not nearly as large as his desire for food made them feel, but these were not the same teeth he had even just moments ago. Osman's mind raced for an excuse why he stopped and to answer Yanri.

"Uh... oh!" Osman shoved his hand in the pocket of the cotton britches he wore. "I only have this platinum. Do you think they will have change?" Osman held the coin over his shoulder, still facing away from Yanri.

"Is that it? I've got you covered!" Yanri shoved Osman forward and wrapped his arm around Osman's shoulders to guide him toward the pie stand. Once there, Yanri took charge as Osman tried to look natural with an awkward, closed-lipped smile. Yanri purchased a bag of a half-dozen of the delicious-smelling meat pies and handed them to Osman as he paid with a few silver. Hoping that satiating his hunger would get his teeth back to normal, Osman quickly shoved a whole pie in his mouth before Yanri could turn around.

"Woah, there, big guy! You planning on saving any for me?" Yanri playfully accused.

Osman grabbed another pie while holding the first one in his mouth and handed over the bag. The savory meat pie was just as delicious as it smelled, with just the right amount of peppery spices to make his tongue burn. After devouring the first pie, Osman could feel the qil of the ghostly saldrig fangs begin to fade. With a swipe of his tongue, he confirmed his actual canine teeth had started to recede as well, beginning to return to their normal shape. Just to be sure, Osman shoved the second pie into his mouth immediately after the first.

Yanri looked at Osman speculatively. He felt Yanri's gaze feeding a story to fit his mismatched, ill-fitting clothes; his unkempt, overlong curls; the single platinum coin; and now the ravenous hunger. Not one able to mask his emotions, Yanri's face flashed with what Osman read as jovial friendship, to pity, then to resolve, and back to its original camaraderie as Osman watched.

"Now for clothes!" Yanri exclaimed with his usual exuberance and then shoved a pie in his mouth to match Osman.

Osman's teeth thankfully returned fully to normal after his third pie, but it didn't stop him from having a fourth when Yanri begged off after his second one. Further down the beach, the two found a brightly colored shopping district with various shops selling all kinds of wares. Around the shops, the sand transitioned to sidewalks paved with thin cross-sections of ironwood branches as large as tabletops polished to showcase their mineral-laden sparkling growth rings.

Osman tried in vain to get a moment apart from Yanri to purchase some light armor suitable for venturing into the deep forests of Mornaserin. Eventually, he would need to begin his search for the Eurucian Inception to discover his father's and Richen's fate, but Yanri had no intention of letting them have a second apart. Working with one of the dismissive vendors who eyed his boots suspiciously, Osman was worried that even with the platinum coin, he could only afford a single set of clothes suited only for around the city. However, after Yanri produced a writ of credit from his family in Mael Esari, suddenly Osman's single platinum was plenty enough to purchase multiple tunics, jerkins, and leathers.

From the goofball bundle of emotions at the dock and on the beach, Yanri transformed into a shrewd bargainer and savvy buyer in the shops. Osman didn't follow their back and forth, but when all was said and done, Yanri handed back four gold and a couple of silvers as his change from the transaction.

"Thanks for the help," Osman said gratefully.

"I got you, buddy! Remember? We're stuck with each other." Yanri replied affably. After Osman had changed into some of his newly purchased items and left behind their purchases that needed to be tailored and picked up later, Yanri added, "Let's see what the rest of Feldtree has to offer with what's left of the day, and then we can head up to 'Bough Town' tomorrow."

"Feldtree? Bough Town?" Osman asked, confused.

"According to one of the know-it-alls on the ship, this is Feldtree Lagoon, and most temptarai call Upper Lumenaria 'Bough Town.'" Yanri pointed a finger up as he said the latter. Osman looked up. From this angle, he saw that the massive branches of the world tree overhanging the far end of the lagoon held aloft exotic and elegant buildings of all shapes and sizes. Osman could see the buildings had multiple floors and intricate architecture, but against the scale of the world tree, they seemed no larger than birdhouses.

"Wow," Osman said, awestruck. He pulled his eyes away before he was once again afflicted with the qil of the Matriarch's phantom wings but couldn't help but be amazed.

The two spent the rest of the afternoon circumnavigating Feldtree Lagoon. Yanri suggested they find a spice house to while away a few hours, but Osman talked him out of it. He wasn't sure how the mildly narcotic drug that similarly affected Uldani as alcohol affected humans would sit with his new and unfamiliar physiology. The last thing he needed was to grow antlers or a tail unexpectedly.

After a full day of exploring, eating, and drinking, the two arrived back at the shopping district where they had started. The moon had risen bright overhead, and both were afflicted with tired feet, aching bellies, and exhausted legs.

"Well, I am heading to the Windward Star, where I have boarding arranged. Where are you staying?" Yanri asked as he plopped down on a bench. Osman hadn't thought that far ahead. He had planned to find an inn and use some of his remaining coin to grab the cheapest room he could find.

After a slight pause, Osman replied, "I'm just gonna grab a room. I'm good."

Yanri picked up on the pause and asked, "You know new temptarai have flooded the city, right? Rooms won't be easy to come by for several months." Osman didn't have an answer. In their whole circuit of the lagoon, while he hadn't really been looking, Osman also hadn't seen any inns that he could return to, just taverns and shops.

"Let's see what mine looks like, and if we can make it work, you can stay there tonight," Yanri suggested. "And we *can* make it work. I am not letting my only friend sleep outside on your first night here."

The Windward Star was an upscale boarding house with a stuffy older woman who ran the foyer receiving lobby like a military operation. Yanri presented a sealed letter, and after taking both of their names, she handed Yanri two keys. She gave quick directions to the room and pointed to the stairs.

The room was on the fifth floor and well-appointed. It was a bit larger than Osman's old room in the Sojourn's Rest, and in addition to the large double bed and basic furniture, the main feature was a small balcony. Osman crossed the room and stepped through its open doors, relishing the cool breeze that flowed into the room. Out on the balcony, there was a stunning view of the Lagoon, the moonlit sea beyond, and the wall of fog shrouding the island. From inside, he heard Yanri's voice.

"Great! It's a double. We'll share the bed tonight and see if we can find you something tomorrow," said Yanri. "Or if we decide we want to be roommates, we will see if the old crone downstairs has something bigger for the both of us."

When Osman reentered the room, Yanri was stripped down to his underbritches and sprawled out on the bed. Osman hesitated a bit, unsure of how this would play out. Osman had been with men before, but with Yanri as his only contact in Lumenaria, and if this were leading to something, this would be his first relationship since Cerena. Osman really didn't need any other complications right now.

"I'm just looking to sleep, big guy," Yanri assured Osman, sensing his hesitation. "But I do cuddle, so be aware," he laughed.

Osman tried to set aside his reservations and similarly stripped down to his underbritches. He laid down on his back, arms to his sides beside Yanri, stiffly keeping to his side of the bed.

Yanri rolled onto his side, looking at Osman. "Hey, Wondertoes, you're making it weird."

Osman turned his head to look back at Yanri, trying to look innocent.

"Kiss me," Yanri stated matter-of-factly.

"What?" Osman questioned, not sure if he had heard correctly. Before he could say another word, Yanri pressed his lips into Osman's. He was initially startled, but having been without human contact and affection for so long, he reflexively returned the kiss. Yanri was the first to pull away.

"So you get any qil out of that? Love knots? Lust burn? Anything?" Yanri's eyes scanned Osman's face as he asked. Osman did a quick self-check. No emotions had manifested as qil anywhere across his body. The kiss held nothing more than just feeling nice on his lips.

"Good. Me neither. If it changes, let me know," Yanri stated plainly. "Now relax and get some sleep." Yanri threw his arm over Osman's chest and snuggled in tightly against him. Osman smiled and lifted his arm, wrapping it around Yanri. With the ocean breeze blowing across them, Osman slept better than he had in decades.

# CHAPTER SIXTEEN

Year 884 PXF ~ Late Spring

It had taken the better part of two weeks, but Osman finally felt he had his bearings around Lumenaria. The districts around Feldtree Lagoon were reasonably easy to navigate as most residents treated it like a giant clock face when it came to directions, with Arbor Lumenari in the top center position. However, Bough Town and the Sidetree districts were a completely different story; that is where he was headed back to again today, undoubtedly with Yanri in tow.

Even though Osman had fallen asleep alone in his and Yanri's room, where they still shared the same bed from the first night, he was not surprised to find Yanri cuddled at his side come morning.

"So, how was it?" Osman asked.

"She was... adventurous," Yanri replied. "Perhaps too adventurous." Yanri rolled his shoulder forward to display long red welts on his back and lifted his wrists, which looked like they had rope burn. "I think I can safely extinguish that flame from my passion pyre."

"Looks like you needed a safer way to extinguish things from what I'm seeing," Osman observed jokingly.

Yanri groaned, swung his pillow into Osman's face, and climbed out of bed. As usual, Yanri was rearing to start their day once his eyes opened. Osman had tried to convince him multiple times that he could get his own day started and leave Osman to his schedule, but to no avail.

"So, back up to Bough Town today?" Yanri asked as he pulled on his go-to pair of dark teal leathers, matching it with a heather grey tunic and black sleeveless jerkin. His auburn hair, not to be outmatched by the scruff peppering his jaw and cheeks, had also grown out over the last fortnight-and-a-half and was already beginning to brush his shoulders.

Having just thrown his legs over the side of the bed and sat up with a stretch and yawn, Osman replied, "You don't have to come if you don't want to." While Yanri's company was welcome, Osman had not shared his true purpose for being in Mornaserin with Yanri other than vague statements about wanting to explore outside the city limits eventually. Osman continued, "I don't know when or if I am going to find what I am looking for, but I feel it can be found up there."

"Hey, we have all the time in the world!" Yanri stated, adding playfully, "Well, me more than you, but still *plenty* of it."

Osman was still getting used to the older face that greeted him in the mirror each morning. When his body was healing in the chrysalis, he had seen the age that the serpent's breath and accompanying flood of qil had etched upon it, but he had only worn the face full-time as himself for just under a month. In many ways, Osman still actualized himself as the 'young Uldani companion of Talon Cour-Vermane.' However, when exploring Lumenaria, he was now viewed as Yanri's older companion.

Yanri's usual incessant chatter had paused, "So how *old* are you anyway?" he asked in a tone that spoke volumes about how long he had waited to pose the question.

"I'll be thirty-six." Osman replied, then continued after a moment's thought. "This month, in fact."

"Gods! Really? You look like you're fifty!" Yanri exclaimed indelicately, then realizing his words, quickly crossed to Osman and sat next to him on the edge of the bed. He put an arm over his shoulder, drawing him close. "Hey, I'm sorry. Wow, life really did a number on you, huh?" he asked gently. "I didn't understand but a sliver of what I could read in your face when we met, but if you ever want to tell me more..." Yanri let the words hang.

Osman wrapped his arm around Yanri's waist and gave a squeeze but remained silent.

Yanri then confessed, "I just turned twenty-one, by the way." Osman turned his head and looked at Yanri. He easily looked nineteen, perhaps on the edge of twenty in human years. If Yanri had only just turned twenty-one, his aging couldn't have slowed to any discernable degree during his life so far. Osman began to wonder about his heritage, but Yanri cut him off before he could voice the thought.

"Nope, full-blooded Uldani," Yanri answered Osman's unasked question. "I am much better now, but—well, you can see." He added, motioning to himself, his ears turning red with shame, "I only got enough control to even come here less than a year ago. But I think my parents would've put me on the boat regardless because of what an embarrassment I had become to them."

Osman squeezed Yanri tighter and looked across the room, catching their faces in the reflection of the glass-paneled balcony doors. By human standards, a nineteen-year-old and a twenty-five-year-old looked back, but for Uldani, they both were far more than what their faces conveyed.

Osman grabbed Yanri's forehead in one hand and the back of his head with the other, kissing the side of his friend's noggin with a loud *mwah*. He pulled them both to their feet. "No more of that. We have our new lives and passions to discover!" He then lightheartedly added as he examined the dubious rope burns on Yanri's wrists, "And maybe some minor healing to find."

Osman quickly sniffed the clothes he had thrown over a chair the night before and decided they could survive another day before being cleaned. Consisting of a functional off-white long tunic, faded grey leathers, and deep green jerkin, Osman felt his outfit would be acceptable for Bough Town. While his wardrobe was not as extensive or impressive as Yanri's, his few well-made items served him well in almost all situations.

Yanri was already waiting with the door to the room pulled open for their departure as Osman tried to get his freshly cut hair into some semblance of a style. Unlike Yanri, Osman visited a barber regularly to tame his neglected chestnut curls and indulge in a twice-weekly shave. Osman had never previously needed a barber's regular service, but now it was practically a necessity. Even the barber, a congenial old bloke whose services were included with Yanri's board, had commented on the thickness of Osman's hair and compared it to a bear's coat preparing for Winter. After receiving the comment, Osman had diligently checked daily to ensure he wasn't sprouting fur on the rest of his body as part of his new physiology, but thankfully his newfound hirsuteness was isolated to his scalp and face.

"Get a move on, Wondertoes. It is a long hike to get to Bough Town." Yanri chided as he impatiently beckoned Osman toward the door with his hand.

"Yeah, yeah. Let's grab fish rolls or something on the way," Osman replied as he slid the long grey stiletto that had been Talon's iron dagger into his boot and mock-scurried out the door.

The two descended the stairs with more joking and jibing, making a general ruckus and usual nuisance of themselves to the more reserved residents of the Windward Star. Lumenaria, in general, was the most genuine example of learning to judge people by their actions, not their appearance, and Osman and Yanri proved the point daily. Once outside the Windward Star, they sprinted, tripped each other, and wrestled their way to the juice stand where Osman got his morning beverage each day. Osman forced his way in front of Yanri at the last second and, with his arms spread wide, holding his roommate back, greeted Jaque, who stood behind the counter.

"Eye makeup looks great this morning, Jaque, and Nine Hells if you aren't gonna be bigger than me with all those workouts." Osman complemented, adding an impressed whistle. "What're the specials and your pronouns today?"

Jaque smiled and replied, "She/they and mango." Jaque looked to be about sixteen in human years but had confided to them that they were twenty-three. In an effort to speed up their physical aging, she was one of the few Uldani who were at Lumenaria to try and stoke all their emotions to burn as hotly as possible, having clamped down on them at a precocious age. It was a group Osman could have easily fallen into had his life gone differently.

Yanri stood on his toes and put his chin on Osman's shoulder. "You coming tonight? We're hitting Bough Town but should be back down well before sunset."

"Wouldn't miss it!" she replied, handing over two cups of mango juice and refusing payment from Yanri.

Jaque had spotted Yanri and Osman and their antics on the morning after they had arrived in Lumenaria. Thinking themselves hidden in the deep fog that rolled into the city in the early morning hours, they had stripped down and gone skinny-dipping in Feldtree Lagoon on a dare that got out of hand. Neither realized how quickly the inner city fog burned off once the sun rose, leaving them with nearly one hundred morning coffee drinkers as an audience to their exit from the water to retrieve their clothes.

As the two embraced the embarrassment and turned it into an impromptu burlesque, Jaque had called them over with free fresh-squeezed as a reward for the show. While they held their clothes in front of them to cover their indecency, Jaque introduced himself – as that was how he was identifying that morning – and said, "I need the kind of help only the two of you can offer." With a totally unnecessary but appreciated bribe of free juice every morning, Jaque had joined Osman and Yanri in whatever the two got up to whenever they could.

"See you there!" Yanri replied over his shoulder as they walked away.

"What's tonight?" Osman asked.

"You'll see," Yanri replied mysteriously.

Osman rolled his eyes and sighed, "Gods help us."

The fact that the allure of the upper district to many of the longer-time residents of Lumenaria was their relative difficulty to access was not lost on Osman as he and Yanri made the trek to them once again. After following the lagoon promenade to the port, they climbed the amphitheater stairs to the jetty level. The two paused to grab some spiced raw fish rolls sold in the market that appeared every morning, selling the overnight catch fresh out of the nets.

The two sat on a stack of fish traps and nets, enjoying their breakfast and resting before the next part of their hike to the upper districts. Osman longingly watched the mist owls darting in and out of the fog as it retreated out to sea. He had not shared with Yanri his ability to soulchannel or how he came to be able to do so, and it was starting to weigh on his conscience. Yanri had been forthright and open with him, but Osman had withheld that part of himself from his friend.

The night Yanri had drawn his finger across his forearm and the scars there, Osman did not even flinch at telling him their origin. However, he did not give the details on how they had healed and how it had changed him. His soul still felt raw and exposed from that experience, like it hadn't completely settled into place yet. While he didn't mind sharing the parts he felt were behind him, Osman wasn't ready to fully share what and who he was now.

Yanri snapped his fingers in front of Osman's eyes, which were focused out to sea, "Hey, we better get moving. Still a long way to Bough Town." Once he had Osman's attention, he asked, "So, Runt or Rail?"

The Sidetree districts were located amongst the branches of two smaller ironwood trees growing just outside the embrace of the levee roots of Feldtree Lagoon, and through them was the only way to access Upper Lumenaria. Much to the consternation of their inhabitants and proprietors located there, the two Sidetree districts had come to be known as Runt and Rail. What had started centuries ago as a temptarai play on their real names of Runevail and Ryleri had stuck like glue. Now, even the most esteemed Shaman Councilmembers could be caught in unguarded moments referring to them by their temptarai monikers of Runt and Rail.

"Let's go through Rail. We always go through Runt." Osman replied.

"But Rail is *taller*." Yanri drew out the last word with a pleading whine.

"I'm just trying to be helpful," Osman replied playfully. "You could use the extra exercise!" He slapped his open hand on Yanri's belly, which could hardly be called a belly anymore. While always strong and heavily built,

Yanri had shed the layer of baby fat he arrived with due to his constant daytime activity with Osman and nighttime extracurriculars with others.

"Oh yeah, old man? You just see who makes it to the top first!" Yanri took off in a sprint and started up the arching stairs formed by the remaining upper roots of Port Feldtree that led to Rail.

Braggadocio was all well and good until it came time to pay the piper. Osman finally overtook Yanri, but it took far longer than he expected. Even with his enhanced stamina inherited from years of channeling his saldrig form and the links of life energy that still flowed into him from his father's sacrifice for Talon, Yanri didn't make it easy to catch him. Both, panting and out of breath, struggled for every additional step as they side-by-side made it to the crest of the arched winding staircases leading to Rail.

It didn't surprise Osman to find a group of temptarai armed with colorful fans and driftglide potions when they arrived at the landing that marked the apex of the stairs. He and Yanri had encountered the same on the Runt side stairs all the times they had gone that way to Bough Town.

While this point was only three-quarters of the way to Rail, this was the highest point driftgliders could launch from short of going up to Bough Town. Osman watched as three temptarai, who looked to be no more than fifteen, drank the sparkling pink potions, leapt off the root pathway, and began to drift, light as a feather, down to the lagoon below.

They snapped their oversized fans open as they fell to guide their descent, making them look like giant flower blossoms floating on the breeze. Osman and Yanri would descend in a similar but more rapid fashion later that day when they would take the Friend's Last Walk in Bough Town to return to the lagoon.

Osman pulled on Yanri's shoulder and said, "Almost there," pointing to the downward arch of the stairs that led onto the outer branches of Rail.

"Down is the worst! If we had gone through Runt, we would be there already! See?" Yanri pointed across to the stairs and path running along the roots on the far side of the lagoon, which, indeed, had already joined with Runt's branches.

"But think of the adventure! Seeing a new part of the city for the first time!" Osman spoke as he guided Yanri toward the stairs. "There might be a new spice house we could try..." Osman said leadingly.

"Oh, yay. A new part of the city. You get to be all Mister Sparkly Wondertoes while I get weak in the knees," Yanri said dejectedly but couldn't hide his smile.

Osman pinched Yanri's cheek like the elder Uldani used to do when he was growing up at Horizon's End. "Aww, if you swoon, little guy, don't you worry. Your buddy, big ole Osman, will catch you."

Yanri playfully slapped away his hand. "Don't kid about that! My legs are already shaking, and *you'll be sorry* if I fall to my death off the side of a thoroughfare." He delivered the last bit as melodramatically as a chided child while wagging his finger under Osman's nose.

The full trip to Rail took a little over two and a half hours, including their stop for breakfast and a slower pace as they descended the stairs from the landing where the driftgliders were. Osman was actually thankful for the pace Yanri set. While he had no intention of letting Yanri know, the back of Osman's legs burned painfully by the time they arrived in Rail's entry district.

Rail showcased the typical cultivated architecture of the other tree districts. However, Rail presented an elongated elegance to its structures instead of the sturdy solidity of Runt or the opulence of Bough Town. Like all the upper districts, the streets of Rail ran along the overlapping branches of the ironwood tree it inhabited. The builders of Rail had expanded many of the natural forks and intersections of the tree's structure with living mats of dense vines, moss, and lichen to form solid ground on which to create courtyards, open gardens, and parks. The open spaces accentuated the height, flowing curves, and beautiful intricate carvings decorating the woven building structures, reminiscent of tales of hidden cities of their elven ancestors.

Osman took a moment to catch his breath and take in the calming aesthetic of his surroundings. Turning to speak to Yanri and urge that they continue onward, he found his companion had wandered off. Osman spotted Yanri staggering over to an external window counter in a beautifully carved building perched on the courtyard's edge across from the stairs that had deposited them onto Rail's outer branches. After a few moments, he returned, handing a restoration elixir to Osman.

"Shut up and drink it," Yanri said before Osman could protest. "I saw the grimace you were trying to hold in for the last twenty minutes." He downed his small vial of green liquid before continuing with a refreshed smile, "And I still expect you to be my hero if I swoon." Yanri batted his eyes like a damsel in a bard's play. "Oh, and I grabbed these for later." Yanri handed Osman a pink driftglide potion.

Osman nudged him with his elbow and said, "Thanks," as he quaffed the restoration vial. Relief was immediate, but with the throbbing in his legs eased, he immediately realized how hungry he was.

"Food." The two said simultaneously, anticipating each other's need.

In a familiar ritual, they both sniffed the air like ravenous wolves. While Osman was unsure if Yanri picked up the scent, he immediately caught a whiff of bacon in the air and turned his head to track the delicious smell. As soon as Osman's head snapped toward a direction, Yanri let out a loud "Arwooooo!" to which Osman immediately added his voice.

While the courtyard was far from crowded, those nearby shook their heads disapprovingly. Osman's sensitive ears also picked up a few exasperated sighs and murmurs of "temptarai."

With stomachs filled to not insubstantial discomfort with rashers of bacon, dozens of eggs, and multiple loaves of hearty dark bread smothered in crock-fulls of butter, Osman and Yanri waddled back into the streets of Rail. After releasing a thunderous burp, Yanri asked, "Where to, boss?" He then added in the sing-song tone of the shaman life guides that seemed to appear whenever temptarai least needed direction, "In which direction are your passions guiding you today?"

"I'm not quite sure," Osman replied, slowly turning in a circle. "But there is something here, I think."

"Here, here? Or in Bough Town? I can see the levtrails if we want to start heading that way," Yanri proffered.

"I don't know. It's almost something familiar. I can't place it." Osman searched his senses to figure out what was itching in the back of his mind but couldn't identify. It was so insistent he wished he could shift into his saldrig form and use the senses it offered to find out what it was. Instead, he just began to wander aimlessly down the nearest street.

"Osman? Hey, Osman, you okay?" Yanri called from behind him.

Osman continued until he reached a small, unmarked building. Most likely a residence. It had a quaint and welcoming feel to it. Shamanistic magic had shaped its main structure from the surrounding burls and branches of Rail's ironwood tree and an elegant porch wrapped around its entire perimeter. Along the porch's columns, beams, and rails were intricate carvings that seemed almost to hypnotize Osman. He followed them around the side of the home, running his fingers in the perfectly sanded and beautifully finished grooves carved in the wood. As he rounded to the back of the house, Osman came to a standstill.

"Anson?" fell from his lips as though the name was a piece of dropped crockery.

# CHAPTER SEVENTEEN

*Year 884* PXF ~ *Late Spring*

"Anson, is that really you?" Osman repeated.

The man sitting in the chair of the same style as the ones they sat in beneath the stars at Horizon's End had only changed in the slightest of ways from Osman's childhood memories. A bit more silver in his grey hair, an added crease at the corner of his smiling eyes. Anson stood slowly, the steaming mug in his hand trembling slightly with emotion.

"Osman?" Anson's voice caught in his throat. "You did come."

Osman vaulted over the porch railing, not bothering with the stairs that entered from the back garden. He leaped into a bear hug of the only caregiver he ever gave a damn about.

"Anson," Osman whispered as tears began to fall.

"Gods, you've grown! You were such a small thing," Anson observed.

"There is so much. So much." Osman said shakily, releasing his crushing embrace on Anson, grabbing his wrists, and bringing Anson's hands to his face. He laid his hands gently on Anson's as he opened himself completely for Anson to read his life. Osman knew his eyes must be wide with trepidation as its qil bloomed as a trembling stitch in his side. Osman's eyes brimmed with tears as he watched the reactions to his life's story play across Anson's face as he discovered them. Osman dreaded but also yearned for whatever judgment or acceptance might come.

Tears began to fall from Anson's eyes. "I am so sorry. I am so sorry. So... So very sorry." Anson wrapped his arms around Osman, embracing him as tightly as Osman had embraced him moments before. He moved a hand to the back of Osman's head to pull it tighter. Relief and joy mixed with thirty years of pain and sorrow all poured out of Osman onto Anson's shoulder. Anson stroked Osman's head as he wept, fingers tangling in his mop of curls. His sobs began to fade, but he wasn't ready to relinquish the comfort of Anson's embrace. Anson then quietly started to speak.

"He said it would be terrible. All the things you would have to endure to make it this far. But I never imagined–" Anson swallowed down the emotion that had choked his words and continued, "it would be so horrific."

The words Anson spoke and had spoken earlier began to sink through the shock and swirl of Osman's emotions. "What?" Osman asked as he pulled away from Anson.

"I didn't want to leave, Osman. Gods, please believe me. I wanted to stay." Anson's words tumbled out of him pleadingly as he grabbed Osman's upper arms with his calloused sculptor's hands. "I would have raised you as my own. Either here or at Horizon's End. Wherever you wanted, I begged Tavi to let me."

Osman's confusion manifested as a dozen different qil blooming and fading across his body as Anson continued.

"Tavi refused me and demanded that I abandon you. I told him I couldn't. Then he showed me–" Anson's face twisted into an expression between pity and disgust. "He showed me that poor twisted soul in the crystal and the thing feeding on it. He said that its fate is what awaited us all if you didn't become–" Anson's eyes lifted to meet Osman's, filled with sorrow but also pride, "didn't become *you*."

It was all too much. How many people would this web of fate entangle? How many lives would it twist to its purpose? At that thought, Osman remembered Yanri. He spun around and saw Yanri patiently standing at the side of the house, allowing him privacy for his reunion with Anson. Yanri's face held questions, but all Osman could see was its open innocence—an empty slate that Osman's life would despoil with pain, corruption, and blood. Osman marched across the porch, keeping the rail between him and Yanri as though it would somehow protect his friend from becoming spattered with the detritus of his fate.

"Yanri, you need to leave," Osman said pointedly. "Now."

Yanri looked up at Osman and squared his shoulders, his face becoming more severe than Osman had ever seen in their time together. "No," Yanri said flatly.

"You can't be near me," Osman reiterated as though Yanri misunderstood.

"Or what?" Yanri replied almost flippantly. "Is this because you're a werewolf?" He asked. "You think I don't already know? That's at least a quarter of the reason why I like hanging out with you so much!"

Osman was stunned into silence.

Yanri, scratching the back of his head, continued speaking to fill the awkward pause, "Just don't bite me, okay?" he said uncertainly. He quickly overcorrected by adding, "Not that there is anything wrong with being a werewolf." Now stammering, he said, "I'm just not sure if it's what I want for me," finally adding a delayed, "Well... yet."

Osman hadn't had time to plan in his rashness on how his dismissal of Yanri would go, but this surprised him to the extent he had to respond to it.

"You thought I was a *werewolf?*" Osman asked incredulously.

"Well, yeah," Yanri replied in the matter-of-fact tone of a student who believes they have outsmarted their professor. "Your teeth do that thing when you're hungry. You showed up the first day in clothes that weren't yours because you must have ripped out of all your old ones during your last transformation. And I am betting that platinum coin was minted from an arrowhead someone shot you with to try and kill you." Yanri counted off each piece of evidence on his fingers as he recited them. "Oh, and your hair is *definitely* not normal Uldani hair. You are double-coated like our dog back in Mael Esari."

Osman placed his palm over his face, rubbing his temples. "Yanri, I'm *not* a werewolf." He sighed. "And it's silver, not platinum." Yanri opened his mouth to protest, but Osman beat him to it. "But you're right. I'm not exactly *normal* either." His voice trailed off.

This time, Yanri interjected before Osman could continue. "Fine. Whatever. I am *not* leaving. We're stuck with each other, remember? You said so." Yanri walked around the corner of the porch and ascended the steps with hand outstretched to Anson. "Sir, I'm Yanri, and I'm Osman's friend. Whatever's going on, I'm sticking with him come Hells or Icefel."

Anson shook Yanri's hand. "I'm Anson. I'm–"

"Anson's my dad," Osman said, turning to the two of them with a half-smile.

Yanri dropped the handshake and immediately pulled Anson into a warm hug, pinning his arms to the side. "It's nice to meet you, sir!"

Anson's eyes wildly searched for Osman's.

"He does that. You'll get used to it." Osman explained. "Well, I guess we should get all the cards on the table. Is it okay to talk out here?" He asked Anson.

Yanri looked over his shoulder as he still hugged Anson, "So I can stay?" he asked Osman.

"Do I have a choice?" Osman intoned blithely.

Yanri looked at Anson, "So, are *you* the werewolf then?"

Anson disentangled himself from Yanri as he answered Osman, "We shouldn't be disturbed. I have a few apprentices and students who drop by occasionally, but that's usually in the evenings. If people are looking for me, they usually find me at my studio in Warpwood Gnarl."

"And..." Yanri asked leadingly.

"And no, I'm not a werewolf," Anson replied. "I need to grab something from inside to help explain my part of things. Make yourself at home."

Yanri flopped down in one of the low-reclining wooden slat chairs. Osman sat down beside him. "So does this mean you *can't* bite me and make me into a whatever-you-are, too?" The disappointment in Yanri's voice was palpable.

"Yanri... no." sighed Osman.

"No, you can't? Or no, you won't?" Yanri probed.

"Seriously?" Annoyance began to creep into Osman's voice. "No, I can't. That's not how it works. Anyway, you just said you didn't want me to bite you a second ago."

"But that was when I still thought you could," Yanri said dejectedly.

Osman couldn't stifle the laugh that crept up from a place deep inside that cherished Yanri for demanding to stay and being exactly who he was no matter the situation. Yanri's laughter joined his own as Osman looked out off the porch to the area behind Anson's home.

Osman had been so focused on Anson and then Yanri that he had failed to register what lay beyond the porch. The area behind the house was filled with statues. Anson had carved them from living ironwood roots carefully grafted onto interwoven smaller branches extending from the huge one his home sat upon. The twisting natural arches the roots naturally formed reached now for the sky instead of the earth, giving them a haunting familiarity.

In some places, Anson had enhanced the root's inherent rough beauty by sanding and polishing them to a glossy finish. In others, he had only selectively pruned and trained them as they grew into the intertwining shapes he desired for them. The true highlight, however, was the fully realized carved figures and creatures that emerged and disappeared into the thick knots and intersections of the ironwood roots. Osman remembered Anson's childhood lesson about sculpture being about perspective. These sculptures were the epitome of that—the foundations of their very city yearning for the freedom of the sky.

In each far corner stood a masterwork rendered in full-scale. The left sculpture depicted Anson in ironwood with a hammer and wood chisel working on an unfinished sculpture behind him. On the right was the finished sculpture the carved Anson had been working on. It featured a young Uldani boy reclining high on one of the roots, feet reaching toward the sky. The tips of the branches above him had been polished down to their mineralized age rings, so they sparkled like stars.

Osman rose to his feet, blinking back tears. He began drifting down the stairs to get a closer look when the door behind him opened, and Anson returned to the porch. Anson laid his hand on Osman's opposite shoulder and stood close beside him. "I never forgot you."

Osman laid his hand on top of Anson's, unable to find words to express his feelings. He turned, holding Anson's hand in place on his shoulder, and returned to the chairs. The three sat in a loose triangle around a central table.

Yanri leaned forward and gave a light punch to Osman's upper arm. He motioned to the statue of the little boy. "You were a cute little guy. Sucks that you grew out of it." Yanri bit his tongue between his front teeth to emphasize the joke. Osman rolled his eyes, and Anson cleared his throat.

He laid his hand on an intricately carved box he had retrieved from inside. Anson suggested, "Perhaps you should catch us both up with what has happened with you so far, and then I can fill in whatever gaps I can."

Osman took a deep breath and told them everything that had happened. From his leaving the Isles at eighteen, his time with Talon and Cerena, his treason against the Empire and imprisonment, to Wilfred, the Guardian, and his becoming a soulchanneler. It took him two hours to tell it all, trying his best not to miss any crucial details.

Osman finished, motioning to Yanri, "And the rest you mostly know, I have been trying to find out any information about the Eurucian Inception, reincarnation, or where my father went."

"I don't know how much more I can add," Anson admitted. "Your father banished me from Horizon's End to return here to my home. A year and a half later, he appeared here having removed that thing feeding on the boy's soul." Anson continued sorrowfully, "As you said, it was now feeding on him."

"Your father was weak and saving his magic for whatever test he needed to face. He required my assistance to traverse the forest, but I refused unless he told me more of what dark path he had set us all upon." Anson looked up at Osman. "He extorted my help with the promise that you and I would meet again. He could not say when, but it would be within this life."

"I could see in his eyes it was a lie, in as much as it was only his hope and not written in stone." Anson smiled and added, "So at least part of his scheming has borne fruit."

"We arrived at a portal of root and stone on the far side of Arbor Lumenari. I wanted to enter with him, but he forbade it. I truly thought he would strike me if I tried." Anson sighed, "He bade me to return to my home and wait, so I did." He looked first to Yanri and Osman before continuing, "I waited five years, instructing students and taking on apprentices. I wondered if Tavi had survived, and then this appeared." All their eyes settled on the beautifully carved wooden box.

"It is my work, without a doubt. And, from what you have just shared, it is meant for you." A saldrig, a mist owl, and a caribou were carved upon the lid.

"But I have no recollection of ever carving it."

Osman picked up the box, turning it over in his hands. He could find no seam, latch, or other indication of how to open it or that it even could be opened.

"How does it work?" Osman asked Anson.

"I don't know." Anson took the box from Osman. He pointed at the small details between the figures and hash marks of the bas-relief's shadowing.

"This is my artisan's cipher, another confirmation that it is indeed my work. It forms a message. *When the time is nigh, your choice will come. Let years, nor fate, nor lifetimes sway you. All are meaningless where earth meets flame.*"

"I can only assume that 'where earth meets flame' is the Eurucian Inception." Osman surmised. "But the rest, I can only guess."

Anson and Osman sat in silence, pondering the message.

Yanri, after having been quiet for longer than Osman could ever remember him being, finally spoke, "Anson, can you take us to this portal?"

Osman hoped the shock didn't show on his face. It was as good an idea as any. They certainly weren't getting anywhere sitting here on Anson's porch.

Anson thought about it for a moment. "I think I can get us back there. It is doubtful that we can follow the same path Tavi guided me on, but I know the general area where it is." Anson stood up. "Let me gather a few things. We will need to spend the night in the forest, whether we leave now or in the morning, so we might as well get started. I have a few packs and travel cloaks you can borrow. That way, you don't have to head back to Feldtree just to come back up here again tomorrow."

Anson returned and left the door open so Osman and Yanri could follow. Osman got up and drifted through the open door with Yanri close behind. Inside revealed Anson's home to be a small one-room cottage. The thick walls were formed from living ironwood, with only a few deep-set windows providing only a dim light. It even took a moment for Osman's saldrig-enhanced eyes to adjust after stepping in from the bright early-afternoon light that bathed the porch.

Osman could hear the sounds of Anson's rummaging for supplies drifting down from an open loft area overhead and spotted an elegant carved spiral staircase he must have used to access it. The rest of the house was one large open room with no additional walls except for a tiny privy in the corner. Everything within the home was tidy with a welcoming, lived-in feel. The large bed on the far wall was freshly made, and everything in the kitchen nook was in its proper place. A worktable next to the largest window had an assortment of woodworking tools strewn upon its surface, and as Osman's eyes lingered over the many sculptures displayed on tables and shelves, he could see that the fine powder of sawdust gathered around some of their bases.

The home was so profoundly and distinctly Anson that Osman felt the qil of serenity tickle his cheeks and nose as though a cloud of freshly blown dandelion seeds had skirted across them. Yanri had crossed over to a small seating area to the left of the door and was examining a highly detailed statue of a long-legged bird that stood nearly three feet tall. Anson came down from the loft area carrying one large pack that seemed already loaded for an excursion and two smaller ones that appeared empty.

Osman walked toward Anson as he held out the packs. "They aren't great but will do for an overnighter." Osman took one for himself, slinging it over his shoulder, and saved the other for Yanri.

"Uh, Anson, sir. I think you have a customer?" Yanri said from behind Osman.

Osman could feel the saldrig's hackles rise to something he couldn't perceive. He turned and saw a figure in a heavy black cloak had come up onto the porch from the back garden. From beneath a deep hood, he saw the visage of a sallow-faced human. While the man had no particular features that stood out, his grey skin was striking in its own right and not from a region Osman was familiar with. The man opened his mouth to speak, revealing teeth that were black with rot.

A gurgling, hollow voice dribbled from his lips. "Return what you have stolen. The Vermillion Blade belongs to my Mistress by blood and right. You have no claim to wield it."

The saldrig's voice growled accusingly in Osman's mind.

*You have allowed the she-serpent to stalk you unawares again. This creature is not what it seems.*

The stiletto from his boot was in Osman's hand instantly as he stepped forward to confront the strange messenger. Before Osman could speak or rebuke the accusation, the man lunged toward him, his grey hands outstretched toward his throat. Osman's stiletto plunged deep into the man's chest, clear to the hilt. He could feel the man's rotten breath on his face as he crumpled over his outstretched arm. Thick, clotted blood, barely lukewarm, flowed over Osman's hand. He yanked the stiletto out of the man as he collapsed to the floor. The body lay motionless, wholly covered and obscured by the black cloak.

A chill ran up Osman's spine as he looked over the body sprawled on the floor. Yanri had picked up the bird statue he had been admiring like a club. With a glance over his shoulder, Osman saw that Anson had moved toward his worktable, where a hand axe was hung on pegs beside the window.

"What in the Nine Hells?" Yanri exclaimed, still holding the bird statue at the ready.

"I honestly don't–" Osman began, but the saldrig's growling voice cut him off.

*This isn't done, boy.*

The black cape began to flap like it was being blown by a brisk breeze, and the hood flipped back off the fallen man's head. From within the hood, two glowing orange eyes peered out at Osman. The cloak began to peel off the prone body revealing a grey underbelly and two parallel rows of short, curved fangs that retracted into slits like gills. The human's back was a tortured nightmare of puncture wounds, dissolved flesh, and exposed bone. Once detached, the cloak, far thicker and fleshier than it appeared when draped over the human, flapped its body like one of the rays that lay in the shallows of the Feldtree Lagoon and lifted into the air.

The bottom of the hood beneath the creature's eyes opened into a maw filled with rows of needle-sharp teeth and shrieked at Osman. As Osman lifted his dagger to defend himself from this new monstrosity, the bird statue wielded by Yanri slammed down on the cloak creature, driving it back to the ground.

Quickly assessing the situation, Osman recalled one of Talon's favorite adages when telling stories of his exploits across the continent: *The best way to win a fight is to avoid it.*

"Get outside! We'll trap it in here." Osman called to Yanri and Anson. Yanri, who was closest to the door, darted out, keeping the bird statue gripped in one hand as he went. Anson had already grabbed the hand axe from his workbench and leaped over the counter separating the kitchen nook from the rest of the room, following Yanri. The creature was looking up at Osman as it began to rise off the floor again, and that is when Osman saw the faceted obsidian talisman filled with reflected eyes embedded in the creature's forehead. Eyes that matched Cerena's.

Osman was going to scream at her that he didn't have the damned Vermillion Blade to try and diffuse the attack but held his tongue, reconsidering.

"I'll do everything in my power to ensure you never get Talon's blade," he yelled at the eyes focusing on him from within the crystal facets.

If Cerena didn't know where the Vermillion Blade was and somehow thought Osman had it, deceiving her might help protect Talon from her ire. He vaulted over the creature, his weight pushing it back toward the floor. He dove out the door to expedite his escape, rolling on his shoulder, spinning around, and springing to his feet as Yanri slammed the door behind him.

"We need to get out of here and fast." Osman scanned the surroundings as he spoke. His eyes fell on a gap in the short garden wall between the two large statues of himself and Anson to the open sky beyond. Osman reached into his waist pouch and handed Anson his driftglide potion.

He then looked to Yanri. "Show him how we do it. Get as far down as you can before you drink it. Remember, this isn't over the lagoon, so don't hit any branches on the way down."

"You two think you are the first to take the Friend's Last Walk? In my day, we practically got our toes wet before drinking our potion." Anson scoffed and began running toward the back of the garden and the opening in the wall.

Yanri started to dart after Anson, then pulled up short and asked, "What about you?"

"I got my own wings, remember? Now go!" Osman slapped Yanri on the back to get him moving. A loud crash came from the other side of the door, emphasizing his urgency.

Osman watched Yanri run across the garden, never slowing down as he and Anson leaped over the edge. Osman grabbed the carved wooden box still sitting on the outside patio table and shoved it into the pack Anson had handed him. Closing his eyes, Osman took a deep breath and called forth the essence of the Matriarch. He felt the airy burst of fluttering magic as his soul flowed into its new flesh.

From the side of the house, Osman heard the crash of glass as the cloak-ray-thing burst through the window above Anson's worktable. As its flapping form swung into the back garden, the creature's orange eyes and Cerena's reflected ones in the crystal looked directly at Osman and passed over him, the Matriarch's form triggering no hint of recognition.

Osman heard Cerena's slithering arcane command through the Matriarch's arcane-attuned ears as the cloak ray whirled around the back garden.

*There! Over the side! Find them!*

Osman could hear the strain and distortion in Cerena's voice, as though she was trying to speak through clenched teeth over the howling winds of a wildfire. He was hearing the wards of Mael Esari powered by the harnessed Helsparian Inception trying to break her connection to the creature. That meant she was not on the Isles but instead controlling the cloak ray from afar.

The cloak ray dove over the garden's edge and would spot Anson and Yanri easily, even if they had yet to drink their potions. Osman launched on the Matriarch's wings into the sky, her instincts guiding his action. In the air, as on land, the higher ground always had the advantage. Osman gained altitude and then dove toward his target below. The cloak ray's wings were not jointed like a bird, so its dive toward Anson and Yanri did not have the aerodynamic edge of the Matriarch's stoop.

Osman's talons raked across the cloak ray's black leathery skin as the Matriarch's body slammed into it. Osman sprung off the creature's back like he had the ridge at the caldera's rim and launched himself high above any retaliatory strike that might come from the cloak ray's jaws or its barbed serrated tail.

The cloak ray wheeled on Osman, its orange eyes alight with fury. Osman heard Cerena's voice again.

*Forget the pet. Get the two who were with your prey.*
*Kill them!*

Her voice cracked like a whip to regain control of the creature, the strain from before escalating to an active struggle against the invoked agony of the Isles' protective wards. The cloak ray wheeled and plummeted toward its targets. No longer trying to control its dive, it had relaxed its body to its cloak-like form, falling like a piece of fabric wrapped around a large stone. Osman could see it had folded its tail underneath itself like a harpoon aimed directly at the now-floating Yanri.

There was no way the Matriarch could catch up to the creature as it fell. Osman pleaded to the Matriarch to do something, to have some other trick within her experience. In desperation, she opened their beak and shrieked a continuous cry in the pitch she had used to map the path out of the ironwood canopy Osman had become lost in.

Osman heard Cerena's voice cry out in a tortured scream in his head. His consciousness traveled like a lightning bolt back along the arcane tether between the creature and his old lover. There was a blinding flash as the connection broke, leaving the afterimage of Cerena's face, eye alight with burning elemental fire. Free of its leash, the cloak ray spun from its original target and extended its wings, stopping its dive instantly.

Osman had no time to react. Unable to slow his descent, the barbed tail struck the Matriarch and impaled him through her shoulder. The cloak ray ripped through flesh and feathers with a wicked yank of its tail, nearly amputating Osman's wing. Osman dug his claws into the cloak ray's wing, shredding its edge as he fell from the sky. If he were going to die, he would take Cerena's abomination with him.

Owl and cloak ray remained locked together as they tumbled from their domain of the air toward the unforgiving ground. The ray found its bearings and caught enough wind beneath its damaged wing to slow its fall. Osman's tenuous hold on the creature failed in the sudden arrest of its descent.

Osman's head swiveled around, trying to find Yanri and Anson below him. The Matriarch's keen eyes caught their movements as they ran under the cover of the Ironwood trees. The Matriarch's destroyed wing was useless. The vertigo of freefall did not last long.

The Matriarch hit the ground with a sickening crunch as her delicate bones shattered upon the rocky shores of Mornaserin.

# CHAPTER EIGHTEEN



Osman felt nothing. There was only an unfamiliar voice regal like the clarion call of a horn.

*Your herd has entered my domain. Allow me to protect them as is my duty.*

A weak, unspoken "yes" was all Osman could muster. He felt his body fracture and crumble like ancient stone, seemingly turning to dust. Osman's soul stretched and grew to fill unfamiliar flesh. Long legs stretched beneath him, and a heavy crown of antlers weighed down his head. He leaped to his feet from the rocky beach and began to run at a breakneck pace. Osman's vision came into focus as he jumped over the giant roots of the ironwood forest and swerved around their trunks. Osman's senses fell into the rhythm of his motion. Not a run, but a gallop. His consciousness merged into the spirit of the caribou Prince of the Forest whose flesh he now inhabited.

Osman could hear the crashing in the branches above him. Even without Cerena guiding it, the cloak ray continued its hunt for Anson and Yanri. Osman conveyed only one request to the Prince. "Find them, protect them," he asked as he let the Prince's instincts and skill do the rest. Osman began dashing even faster through the dense woods by lowering his head and using his antlers as a shield. His ears swiveled to track the cloak ray falling further behind him when he spotted Anson and Yanri ahead.

With a deftness Osman could never have mustered, the Prince plucked first Anson and then Yanri off the ground with his antlers, depositing them on his back.

"Osman? This has to be you, right?" Anson asked.

Osman trumpeted in reply as they charged forward, hoping Anson would take that as an affirmation of his identity. The act of picking up his two passengers and their added weight had slowed Osman down, and he could hear that the cloak ray was now upon them.

Anson, who sat in front of Yanri, grabbed one of the backward-facing points of Osman's antlers, "I'll guide you to the portal. Just run!" Concern filled his words.

Anson pulled the Prince's head to the left by the antler, and Osman had to assure the Prince internally to follow his lead. As they veered to the left, the cloak ray crashed through the branches beside them. The Prince deftly twisted out of the creature's maw as its needle-sharp teeth snapped shut where Osman's haunches had just been—a rear hoof kicking into the cloak ray's forehead in retaliation.

The Prince navigated the treacherous forest floor without stumble or pause, hooves never faltering in their placement. Osman could only follow the desperate combat that Yanri and Anson were engaged in by their shifting weight and sounds of their struggle.

The cloak ray banked tightly, recovering from its near miss, swerving under a high arching root and darting in for another attack. Yanri twisted around on Osman's back, swinging his makeshift club wildly to try and keep the creature at bay.

"On your right!" Yanri called out.

Osman heard the cloak ray crashing through the towering underbrush to his right, then silence. Osman charged forward and leaped off a high root to clear a chasm in the forest floor. Suddenly, the cloak ray was passing under him, flying in the shadows of the gully below. Serrated tail held high, its barbs raked across the Prince's vulnerable belly. The ray arched up out of the darkness to arc over Osman's head. Osman could feel Anson rise, all but climbing the Prince's antlers, and heard the loud *THUNK* of Anson's hand axe burying itself in the cloak ray's thick hide. The power of the blow caused the creature's wing to scrape upon the tips of the Prince's antlers. Osman felt the cloak ray's cold blood splash down upon his head and muzzle as the beast shrieked in pain and anger.

The cloak ray momentarily disappeared as it wheeled around for another attack.

"We better be close. We can't take much more of this," Yanri exclaimed with panic rising in his voice. "It got my leg in that last pass with that damned tail."

"The portal should be in the gap between the next two roots of the world tree," Anson replied less confidently than Osman would have liked. Osman could feel the wound in the Prince's belly throbbing with an unnatural creeping pain. *Poison,* Osman thought to himself, but almost as soon as he identified it, he felt the burning of the venom lessen. A strange fizzing tingle filled the wound, and soon, whatever toxin had infected it was neutralized by the Prince's physiology.

Osman pushed forward toward the enormous root of the world tree, rising like a cliff before him. The Prince sharing Osman's thoughts never slowed as he navigated the footholds of the craggy ironwood bark like one of the goats climbing the fjords of Kyflenor. Their route and the challenges of keeping his two heavy passengers mounted slowed their ascent drastically.

Osman knew the cloak ray would be on them any second. As though reading his mind, Osman felt Yanri spin on his back to face backward, preparing himself for the next onslaught.

As they crested the root, the cloak ray's attack came from above. It crashed through the low foliage above them and slammed its full weight into Osman's side. Had Yanri not diverted some of its impact with a two-handed swing of his ironwood bird sculpture club, the creature would have succeeded in throwing them off the root to fall to the forest floor far below. The Prince's quick reflexes redirected the rest of the force of the cloak ray's blow to his advantage. Added to his own momentum, he launched them down the other side of the root. Osman's mind could only process their downward path from his acrobatic experience. This was not a descent as much as redirecting their free-fall with each leap from foothold to foothold.

Osman heard the cloak ray's screech above them as it recovered from the daze of Yanri's blow and resumed its pursuit of the trio.

"There!" Anson yelled. "Between the stones embedded in the bark of the world tree!"

Osman could see the portal ahead of him. Two carved granite monoliths flanked a shimmering membrane held between them. Arbor Lumenari's bark had nearly engulfed the stones entirely, but Osman could make out the similarities of the carvings to the ones on the rock he and Wilfred had passed beyond to get to the Argestian Inception. Osman lowered his crown of antlers and dashed forward with everything he and the Prince had left. The Prince's ears swiveled backward, and Osman could hear the wind whistle around the cloak ray's wings just seconds behind them.

With a bounding leap, Osman crossed the threshold of the portal. The transition was not kind. Osman felt like the head and shoulders of the Prince's body slammed into a wall of gelled sugar. His spine and haunches felt like they were crashing into his front half, like they were traveling at the speed of a holiday rocket. The Prince's instinctive reflexes braced his large, powerful legs and body against the strange forces working on him. He arrested his forward momentum, but even once free from the portal, Osman skidded forward two dozen feet before coming to a halt.

In a flash of insight, Osman yanked control of his caribou form from the Prince and wheeled around, throwing Anson and Yanri from his back in the process. He lunged back toward the portal, antlers lowered with their tips barely breaking the surface. Not two seconds later, Osman felt the impact of the cloak ray as it impaled itself on all eighteen points of his deadly antlers. The force pushed him and the cloak ray, shrieking in its death throws, backward down the trail his skidding stop had made just moments before.

The elation Osman felt seeing the cloak ray hanging limp from his antlers eclipsed everything else until he heard Yanri's scream.

"No! Osman!"

Only then did Osman register the throb of pain in his chest. He looked down and saw that the cloak ray's tail had swung forward in its abrupt stop from hitting Osman's antlers and had plunged deep into the Prince's chest –dangerously close to his heart. Osman felt the impact of the ground before he ever felt himself falling. As his eyes closed, he saw Yanri limping over to him in a mad scramble, blood and ichor pouring from a wicked slice in his leg, and pressing his hands onto the wound in the Prince's chest.

"Hang on, Osman! Anson is seeing what he has in his pack."

Just.

Hang.

On.

# CHAPTER NINETEEN

*Year 884* PXF *~ Late Spring*

The echo of Cerena's shriek of pain reverberated off the stone walls of her lab and haunted its way through the cells that extended outward into darkness. The burns around her eye still glowed with an elemental fire whose garish orange glow reflected off the facets of the Obsidian column she stood before. A malicious smile split the lower half of Cerena's face despite the searing discomfort raking across it.

She had found it.

Cerena diverted her minions tracking the second wispy trail of Toman's magic and sent them to Mornaserin. She had her target. She gave her creatures a singular directive: kill Osman. Leave none around him alive. She scanned the dozens of locked cells that contained her growing brood. One way or another, she would have the Vermillion Blade.

"Osman?"

"Osman, wake up."

The shaking on Osman's shoulder roused him from his deep slumber. Instead of opening his eyes, he rolled away from the voice onto his side, pulled the quilt around his shoulders up over his head, and nested further into the comfort and warmth of his bed. Another round of insistent shaking rattled his prone form. Exasperated, Osman sighed and opened his eyes to the familiar wall of his room at the Sojourn's Rest.

Everything hit Osman with the subtlety of a thunderclap, and he sat bolt upright and exclaimed, "You can't be here!" as he looked at Yanri.

"Where is here?" Yanri asked, startled and holding his hands up, showing he meant no harm as he still kneeled on the floor beside Osman's bed.

"No, no, no. This can't be right." Osman stuttered as he looked around the room, verifying where they were. "We're in my mind."

Osman looked at Yanri and watched the expression on his face turn from one of concern to one of disgust, then horror. Yanri recoiled and began scurrying backward, crab-walking on all fours away from Osman, eyes locked on his face. At first, Osman thought it was from his words, but he then glanced down at his arms and realized the illusion of his corporeal self was fading, revealing his fully healed but horribly scarred soul and face.

"Yanri... It's okay. It's me. What you are seeing is the real me—my soul." Osman slowly got up from his bed and approached Yanri like one would approach a frightened animal. Osman was dressed as he had been during his convalescence, wearing only the comfortable cotton breeches he slept in so the scars on his chest and forearms were on full display along with his face. "Remember? I told you about these. I'm not ashamed of them. I survived them. They are a part of me and always will be." Osman reached out his hand to Yanri.

Yanri's gaze bore deep into Osman's eyes, and the fear drained away. He leapt to his feet and grabbed Osman in one of his signature hugs, pinning his arms to his sides. "Gods. I thought I understood, but–" Yanri pulled away and let his eyes take in the entirety of the visage of Osman's soul. His hand instinctively lifted to touch Osman's scarred face. Yanri paused in his motion and asked gently, "Will you share *this* face with me?"

Osman's initial reaction was a defensive tensing of his body, but it quickly melted in the earnestness of the request. Osman nodded, and Yanri lifted his hands to read Osman's soul. There was no hiding or subterfuge when two souls were in direct contact. As Yanri read his face, Osman could sense him standing beside him in every moment of his life: through his childhood, in Arnadore with Talon, his darkest hours below the Halls of Judgement, his journey across Kyflenor, and even the moments that included Yanri in Lumenaria.

Yanri's right hand drifted off Osman's face and down toward the scars on Osman's arm. There was still one place Osman had guarded from him. A single tear of shame fell from Osman's eye, and Yanri questioned with a look if it was still okay for him to continue. Osman nodded and took Yanri's left hand that had remained on his face in his own. He guided it down to the scar on his chest. Yanri's right hand alighted on Osman's forearm as gently as a butterfly. There was no hiding when a soul touched a soul, even from the places you dared not tread alone.

*18 Years Earlier ~ 866*PXF *~ Late Winter*

Osman kneeled on the rocky beach and looked at the bloodblade in his hand. Such an easy thing it had been to conjure. He had learned the incantation when he was just a boy. It was not some dark, horrific weapon whose mysteries were guarded by the Uldan people, although some historical etchings portraying Uldani berserkers would make you think so. To Uldani, it was a tool; like any tool, the wielder's intent defined it.

A bloodblade is a fragile thing, a poor weapon to wield against most any foe. Its ability to hurt someone relied entirely upon their willingness to be wounded by it. It was mainly used in ancient rituals of binding Uldani tribes and houses together to confirm the intent of all parties involved. But Osman had not spilled his blood for the blade he now held to bind a house together. His blood was shed to sever one apart.

Osman wished it was just hate he had for his father. Hate was something many Uldani dealt with. He could manage hate; its qil burning like a wreath of embers behind his ears and around the back of his skull. Many great war heroes told stories of how their hate for Xallia drove them to victory after victory. But when it came to his home and his father, Osman also felt the qil of abandonment, betrayal, disappointment, frustration, and with this last homecoming, the last grain of his hope had soured to despair. He was in constant pain. Osman knew he should be able to balance painful qil with positive ones, but his father had stolen every joy his home had once brought him.

Osman ruefully invoked his father's name, Farseer Architavia Therandus—Painter of Hope, who had utterly destroyed all hope in his only son. How ironic was it that Osman's only relief from the agony of his raging qil was when he looked at the bloodblade in his hand and thought of what he was about to do?

Osman had said the words and conjured the bloodblade with a quick slash across each of his palms. To bolster its strength and his resolve, he used its wavering edge to make eighteen more cuts, nine on each forearm—one for every caregiver that had broken his spirit since his father sent Anson away. The bloodblade fed on the rivulets of blood flowing from the slashes in his arms, pulling the lifeforce of Osman's pain into itself and growing from little more than a pocket dirk to a thick-bladed hunting knife. Osman held the bloodblade out before him, blade pointed toward his chest. His only desire, his only need, was for the pain to stop.

Osman plunged the blade deep into his heart.

He screamed, but there was no splatter of blood. Osman's flesh was unharmed. He had cried out in relief as that part of his soul withered and died.

Present Time ~ Unknown

Osman was still clasping Yanri's open hand to his chest as he raised his lowered eyes to meet Yanri's gaze. Tears streamed down Yanri's face as the illusion of his corporeal self disappeared, revealing the unblemished soul within. Osman stifled a gasp at the beauty of his friend's true self, its purity and glowing vitality so unlike his own. Yanri grabbed Osman and pulled him to himself, holding him in an aggressively protective embrace. In the physical world, Yanri was shorter than Osman, but in this moment, Osman laid his head on Yanri's chest—Yanri's soul now a full head taller than himself.

"I am so sorry," Yanri began. "Sorry that you ever felt that way. That what you did was your only way out." He stroked the back of Osman's head as Osman began to sob. "You are not alone anymore. I know you have Wilfred, Anson, and your Krolh'dran, but now you also have me." Osman looked up at Yanri, who continued barely above a whisper, "I have seen every part of you and never doubt you are still loved. Scars and all."

"Thank you," was all Osman could choke out as he turned back into the embrace, laying his head on Yanri's chest. "You are loved as well, my friend." Yanri's vitality and warmth flowed into Osman as he lingered in his arms. Osman's eyes snapped open as he recognized what he was feeling and shoved Yanri away from him.

"Oh, no," Osman said, his mind spinning. "This is bad. I think this is really bad." Osman spun and looked at the end of his bed and the chrysalis there. It was not the same shape as the one his body had occupied. It was smaller and more round than oblong as his had been. Osman could barely see a trail of glowing golden energy flowing around his shoulder from Yanri into the chrysalis. He ran over to it and within was the Matriarch.

Looking through the translucent lid at the mist owl, Osman explained, "I am feeding off you." With a flick of concentration toward the real world, Osman confirmed what he suspected. He looked to Yanri, who was still standing in the same spot across the room, staring at Osman. "We are in the saldrig, and I need to hunt."

"Wait, are you saying your saldrig is eating my body?" Yanri asked, concern making his voice squeak.

"No, the saldrig isn't eating anything. That's the problem. I think your body is in here somewhere, and my body and the wounded spirits here are absorbing its vitality." Osman was trying to make sense of it all himself. "I am new to this too, remember?"

"But first, I love you and all, man, but you have *got* to imagine some pants."

# CHAPTER TWENTY



"Oh! Sorry!" Yanri apologized as he looked down and realized his nakedness. "Woah! What the–"

"Yeah, we will chat about your high opinion of yourself some other time," Osman interrupted teasingly. "For now, pants. Just imagine something familiar and comfortable. Keep it simple."

"*Okaaay*," Osman sighed as he saw what materialized to gird Yanri's loins. "I guess that will work." Yanri was wearing a pair of saldrig print flannel sleeping pants with attached slippers that had stuffed felt claws on the toes.

Yanri smiled joyously, "These were my favorite when I was a kid, but I outgrew them!" He flexed his feet, making the slipper claws move up and down. "*And* it's a saldrig! How awesome is that!"

As Yanri joined Osman at the chrysalis containing the Matriarch, Osman noticed Yanri had returned to his normal height. If anything, now Yanri was of a slighter build than his actual body and looked a bit younger.

"Hey, I'm not bigger than you anymore," Yanri observed.

"Things are a bit fluid in here until you get used to it or have a more defined sense of yourself. I figure you are still discovering yourself, and your soul reflects that as you try on different aspects of all the things that make up who you are," Osman said.

Yanri looked down at the Matriarch. "She's hurt really bad, huh?"

"Yes, she is." Osman placed his hand lovingly on the chrysalis. "I think you are part of what's keeping her alive." Osman looked across his rooms to where the boreal forest merged with the far wall. "Perhaps the Prince as well."

"Is that the reindeer?" Yanri asked.

"Yeah, that's him." Osman added, "At least he isn't in stasis like the Matriarch is." Osman nodded his head to the mist owl. "We shouldn't waste any more time. We need to get your life force off the dinner menu." Osman continued, "Time is like a dream here, so it hasn't been as long as it seems, but with two creatures plus your wounds drawing off your life force to heal everyone, every moment counts. I'll explain more once we get moving."

Osman reached out his hand to Yanri, "Trust me and just go with the current." Osman willed them both into the saldrig's body. Osman heard Yanri's *WAHOO* as they were incorporated into the saldrig's senses and flesh. There was no sense of panic coming from Yanri's consciousness, only a frenetic excitement.

Osman felt annoyance from the saldrig, similar to when blood flies harried them in the height of summer. Osman projected a thought at Yanri, understanding what was probably happening from his own experience. "You don't have an actual mouth, so you have to project your words to me directly. Otherwise, you are just yelling at the saldrig, which he does not appreciate."

Yanri dumped his stream of consciousness into Osman's head. *"OhMyGods!ThisIsSoAmazing!GodsIFeelSoStrong!DoYouSmellAllThat? AndSeeWhatIamSeeing?IsThatAnson'sHeartBeat?HeSmellsReallyGood! AreWeHungryForAnson?AreWeGoingToEatAnson?"*

Osman involuntary extended the saldrig's claws at the onslaught of Yanri's thoughts.

*"WoahAreThoseOurClaws?ThoseAreMurderous!DoIGetToKillSometing WithOurClawsOsman?"*

"Yanri. Slow down. Yes, I sense everything you do. No, we are not going to eat Anson. We need to be efficient and quick, so no killing for you this time."

"Aw, man!" Yanri pouted. "Wait, *this* time? So you are saying maybe *next* time?"

With Yanri calmed down, Osman got to take in their situation. They were in the small clearing just on the other side of the portal. Anson was staring at Osman oddly, pack in hand and mouth slightly agape.

"Well, something is going on in there. Osman, are you back with us? Or Yanri, even? I saw the caribou and Yanri surrounded by a flurry of ice and snow, and then the saldrig was there. You have been as still as one of my statues until just now." Anson reached his hand forward in a calming, concerned way, "Are you okay? Both of you? Either of you? Is this like it was with your wilicho friend Wilfred?"

Osman stepped forward and licked Anson's face with his big saldrig tongue and placed a heavy paw on his shoulder.

"Okay, okay, I will take that as a general yes, and not to worry," Anson said as he dumped Osman's paw off his shoulder and stepped back.

Osman snickered at Anson's silver hair, which now stood in a tall peak from the swipe he had received from his saldrig tongue's lick. Osman didn't know how to convey that they needed to hunt, so he walked deeper into the forest and looked back, trying to communicate to Anson that he needed to follow.

While slipping into his saldrig form was like sliding on a well-worn pair of shoes, their surroundings were unfamiliar to the saldrig's senses and Osman's small bit of knowledge about the ironwood forest as well. Back on Kyflenor, the stones had marked a boundary around the inception, but the portal here seemed to have been a gateway to another place entirely. A feeling of primal possibility coursed through the dense landscape teeming with life. The world tree that had loomed over them like a mountain was nowhere in sight, nor any other evidence of the forest they had traversed to get here.

"Where are we?" Yanri questioned tentatively in Osman's mind.

A low growl filled with tension and uncertainty roiled in Osman's chest, not from himself but the saldrig, to hush Yanri.

"You're awfully judgy," Yanri chided the saldrig. "What's his name anyway? You have the Matriarch and the Prince. Who is this?"

"You know, I never really thought about it. Wilfred bonded with him long before I did as I healed and passed on the skills he learned to me," Osman answered. "I'm not sure how much he approves of me, actually."

"Like I said, judgy." Yanri, hit with inspiration, asked, "How about the Judge?"

Before Osman could answer, a haughty purr rumbled in the saldrig's throat.

"Well, I guess that settles that," Osman proclaimed. "The Judge it is. Now, can we get back to hunting if the two of you are done?" Osman blinked the Judge's vision over to veilsight, and the intensity of what he saw nearly blinded him. Every rock, leaf, bush, and branch glowed like a sleeping ember in a banked forge. However, they contained not heat but the flicker of raw life energy. As Osman gazed at the spectacle, he could discern a pulsing flow to the power around him that originated from a central point ahead of them.

More importantly, Osman saw the tracks of something large and full of vitality glowing white hot, crossing their path ahead of them. Osman continued forward to examine the trail more carefully. The creature's smell and prints were alien to Osman's and the Judge's experience, but one thing was sure—it was a predator. With the Judge's veilsight, Osman tracked the trail of prints through the underbrush. The predator had swung wide and curved back around to follow Osman and Anson. They were now the hunted. Anson laid his hand on the Judge's shoulder, almost even in height to his own.

"I see," Anson said flatly.

Anson left his hand on Osman's shoulder as they continued through the thick brush filled with overgrown ferns and plants with leaves the size of banquet tables. They came to a large clearing where a dense mat of roots from the surrounding trees had kept the underbrush from getting a foothold. Osman stopped and turned his head to Anson, staring deep into his eyes. He pressed his forehead into Anson's chest and gave a slight nudge. Anson looked at him and pulled his hand axe from where it hung on his belt.

"I understand. I trust you," Anson said with a nod.

Osman walked away, leaving Anson alone in the clearing.

"What are you doing? Why are we leaving Anson behind? Whatever is following us will get him!" Yanri was in a panic. "Are you using Anson as bait? We can't use your dad as bait!"

"Now is not the time for sentiment. We must face whatever it is on our terms, not its terms." Osman answered in a cold and deadly tone. "Anson has been in the forest before. He just has to not die in the first few seconds of the attack." Offering Yanri no chance to reply, Osman silently got into position.

Anson stood alone in the clearing. Hand axe raised with eyes scanning the dense underbrush in the direction they had just come from. The creature following them was not subtle. Its size and mass most likely making things such as stealth unnecessary, if not impossible. Even from his new position, Osman could feel its steps through the pads of his paws. The creature paused upon seeing or sensing Anson, the weaker and easier meal, alone and unguarded. Without pause or consideration of subterfuge, it charged forward toward its prey.

Even without the help of feral senses, it was apparent that Anson heard the beast's charge, and he readied himself for whatever would emerge into the clearing. The creature that leaped toward Anson was enormous, nearly three times the size of the Judge. It was the shape of a bear but so perfectly camouflaged that it would be hard to spot even in direct sight. Instead of a pelt of fur, its hide consisted of moss and roots that grew from its flesh and encased it in living armor.

Anson dove out of the way as Osman impacted the bear midair, dropping in ambush from the tree branch above. A knotted mass of roots protected the bear's neck from the Judge's saber fangs, deflecting them harmlessly away. However, Osman's front and rear claws dug deep into the beast's flesh, the roots and vines making perfect catch points for their razor-like edges. The bear roared and threw Osman off his back, wheeling on him and standing on its hind legs. Osman swiped wide at the bear's exposed belly without connecting, knowing better than to get under the creature's front claws where it could drop upon him and pin the Judge to the ground.

Having not goaded Osman into its ploy and only able to move awkwardly when on its back legs, the bear dropped back down to all fours. Osman slunk low to the ground, circling the creature as it roared in challenging defiance. Osman saw the spinning axe out of the corner of his eye just before it embedded itself deep in the side of the bear's skull above its eye. The bear roared in pain and spun toward Anson, who was waving his arms and shouting. That was all Osman needed. The neck was not the only place where critical arteries flowed. Osman pounced and spun in the air, sliding under the bear on his back. His claws dug into the bear's sides, and Osman drove the Judge's saber fangs into the soft flesh between the bear's armpit and ribcage.

Osman felt warm, wet air whoosh out of the bear's collapsing lung. Locking his jaws with saber fangs still embedded deep beneath the beast's ribcage, Osman kicked the bear off him with his powerful legs. The bear heaved into the air, leaving most of its ribcage and vital organs behind, still locked in Osman's jaws.

"*Fuuuck.*" Yanri drew the word out in awe.

Osman rolled off his back and got the Judge's paws back under himself. He gave a nod to Anson and then turned his attention to the bear. The bear's vitality burned like a pyre in the Judge's veilsight.

"If you want to wait in my room so you don't have to be a part of this, I understand," Osman offered to Yanri.

"Are you kidding me? Eating the bear-plant-thing that was hunting us, that we just killed by cracking it open like a keg of ale. With. Our. Teeth! No experience in Lumenaria could hold a candle to this!" Yanri exclaimed.

Yanri's excitement almost wrested control of the Judge from Osman. Osman held fast, but then, surprisingly, Osman felt an instinctual nudge from the Judge himself to relent, so Osman acquiesced and faded into the background.

"Are you kidding me? Are you freaking kidding me?!" Yanri's elation was palpable. "This is how it feels. I mean, riding along was great, but holy gods!" Yanri paced around the clearing and leaped almost kittenishly into the air, pouncing disturbingly on the bear's ribcage.

Osman heard Anson's voice, "Okay, now I know Yanri's in there, and you just gave him the reins." Anson's lighthearted tone dropped, "We probably should get a move on, though."

Osman momentarily took back control from Yanri and pointedly looked at the dead bear.

"Oh. Okay. Um, I'm going to stay close but let you take care of that on your own," Anson replied uneasily.

"Okay, you wanted to experience this. Now eat that so we aren't feeding off you anymore." Osman gave control back to Yanri, who dug into the bear's carcass enthusiastically.

Just as he had done when Wilfred consumed the Prince, Osman looked to see if a spirit of the bear lingered nearby. Not all spirits of creatures he hunted made themselves known to him, so the bear not being present wasn't unexpected. What was different was the glowing energy of the roots and vines that had formed the bear's natural armor coalesced into a seed. Yanri, fully engrossed in his primal feeding frenzy, did not even notice as the seed merged with them, but Osman felt it become a part of him, not alongside the other spirits within him, but in a place all its own.

After about half an hour, Yanri finally began to slow his feasting and regain some semblance of higher intelligence. Between mouthfuls, he asked, "How can I be this hungry?" Yanri then scanned the Judge's eyes across the massive bear's corpse. "The Judge is big and all, but where is all this going? I still don't feel full, maybe just like I had a light snack."

"I don't completely understand it," Osman admitted, "but see how the bright life-fire that was roaring in its body has dimmed a little? We aren't just eating meat but that life force as well. It is what is hopefully healing the Matriarch, the Prince, and your leg as well." He continued, "Also, it will let me shift again. Changing forms always has a price, and I hope my three soulchannels so close together didn't extract that cost from you."

"So, everything I have been eating off this bear would have come from me instead?" Yanri gulped nervously at the realization. He turned back to the bear and resumed eating with new vigor.

"Whatever happens, we'll deal with it," Osman said comfortingly.

"No talk. Busy eating," Yanri replied. He mumbled his words as though his mouth was full, even though that was metaphysically impossible.

It took several more hours, but Yanri finally declared with a groan, "I can't. Eat. Another. Bite."

Osman and even the Judge groaned in sympathy. Osman had never felt so bloated and stuffed after a hunt. Even distanced from the Judge's senses, Osman felt like his stomach would burst. A content lethargy filled him from the Judge's primal mind as the great hunter mewled softly, wanting rest. Osman examined the remains of the bear. There was hardly anything left, and all the vitality had gone dark.

"Okay, well, that's all we can do," Osman said to Yanri. He sank his mind out of the Judge's, pulling Yanri with him down into his room within the mindscape. Osman materialized back at the end of the bed beside the Matriarch's chrysalis, but instead of beside him, as he expected, Yanri reappeared lying on the couch. He gently rubbed his comically distended stomach, his expression dancing between dazed, contented, and slightly nauseous. Thankfully, he still wore his saldrig pajamas, but now the paws and claws on his feet looked far more realistic and no longer seemed to be made of felt and flannel.

"I can't believe I ate the whole thing," Yanri moaned.

"You did great, Yanri, truly," Osman stated thankfully.

Osman noted that the Matriarch's chrysalis now glowed with its own burning vitality, and there was no trace of it pulling life from Yanri. Her flesh was also no longer the distorted form it had been, with bones protruding from her skin at all angles. On the far side of the room, the Prince stood tall and proud at the edge of the boreal forest. There were still telltale stains on his fur from the wound in his chest, but he looked hale and hearty otherwise. It actually amazed Osman and was somewhat disconcerting to him how quickly their healing had happened compared to his own.

"I bet you didn't picture this is how your day would go when we left brunch this morning," Osman said nonchalantly over his shoulder to Yanri, knowing it would pull a vivid picture of the two of them to the front of Yanri's mind. Feeling the image take hold, Osman willed them both back into their bodies.

Osman felt his soul flow back into his Uldani flesh and the physical presence of Yanri beside him. They were sitting in the middle of the clearing away from the bloody remains of the bear and less than twenty yards from Anson, who was reclining against the trunk of the tree Osman had launched his ambush from.

"You're back. Good. We need to get moving for no reason other than to put some distance between us and the scavengers who are bound to show up soon," Anson stated matter-of-factly as he stood up. Osman noticed that Anson swayed on his feet as though he had been sitting far longer than just the few hours they had been eating.

Osman stood and pulled Yanri to his feet, examining him physically and assessing his condition as he did. Yanri's clothes, which he always had tailored to fit his bulky frame like a glove, hung more loosely on him, no longer accentuating his broad shoulders and full chest. His face also looked leaner, revealing the contour of cheekbones that weren't usually visible.

"How do you feel?" Osman asked guiltily, adding, "You've lost some weight."

"A little fatigued, if I'm honest, but how do I feel? Are you kidding? I feel amazing! That was *incredible*!" Yanri exclaimed even more exuberantly than usual. Yanri ran to Anson, "Did you see how we jumped down on that bear and slid under it, and *rawr*!" Yanri made a clawing motion with his hands and bared his teeth as he recounted the story.

"I was right here," Anson said blithely.

"Oh, right, and you did the axe thing! Oh wait, that was before the slide and the *rawr*!" Yanri paused to get his story in order. Then, he excitedly grabbed Anson by the shoulders, continuing, "And you were totally right! That was me! Osman let me drive, well, I guess the Judge did too, that's the saldrig, and then I ate and ate and ate until I thought I would burst so Osman would stop eating me."

"Wait, what?" Anson asked, looking at Osman, who had crossed over to them.

"I'll explain as we go," Osman replied. "How are you doing? You seem a little wobbly on your feet." Osman asked. Then, pointing to a bright red fox curled up beside Anson's pack, he questioned, "And who is this?"

"I don't rightly know," Anson answered. "Little thing showed up while you were eating. I made the mistake of throwing her some jerky, and she led me on quite a chase around the tree when she nicked the whole bag. Had me spinning in circles and so dizzy the whole world seemed to fold around me before she decided to make herself comfortable." Anson gently shook his pack to wake the fox. "Wake up, c'mon now. Time to go. We don't want scavengers finding you either."

The fox made a whole production of coyly uncurling herself, yawning, and stretching deep into her front legs. She then looked up, cocking her head to the side while eying each of the three of them in turn. Seemingly satisfied, the fox got up and began walking in the direction they had been initially traveling.

"Well, I'm certainly not one to argue with an animal guiding the way." Osman casually stated as he turned to follow the fox deeper into the strange forest.

# CHAPTER TWENTY-ONE



The fox was more than just a fox, if it indeed was a fox at all. At first, Osman thought the strange flickering of its coloration was the play of the light and shadow through the trees across its scarlet and gold fur. He had even convinced himself it was just a visual illusion by comparing it to Yanri's amber hair, which also seemed alight with an inner fire. But, the longer he watched, even when the fox was still, which was not often, her coat shimmered like heat above a bed of coals.

That was not the only thing about the fox, though. Osman could have his eyes locked on the fox walking on the trail just a few feet in front of him and catch a glint of light out of the corner of his eye hundreds of feet ahead. As soon as his eyes would dart instinctively to the flash, the fox would be where his eyes landed, grinning at Osman and no longer on the path directly ahead of him. It was as though cause and effect had no power over the creature, and the rules of the physical world were just a game it could choose to play or not.

Osman knew full well that the fox understood the frustration it was causing him. What began as a taunting 'try to catch me in the act' amusement for the first hour of their hike turned into the fox blatantly defying all logic with its antics during the next hour. It would flash from walking on the trail to strolling up the side of a tree as though gravity was pulling at right angles to its usual direction to being in two places at once—both sitting on Anson's shoulder and curled on top of Yanri's head like a hat simultaneously.

Yanri, of course, found it hilarious, narrating every impossible thing she did.

"Oop, now she's sitting on the bottom of the tree limb, grooming herself."

"She's off again. Oh, nope, there she is! Would you look at that? Her tail is on one side of the trail, and her head on the other!"

"Anson, I think she is in your jerky again. She *is* a clever one!"

Their line came to a halt once again as Anson fished the frisky fox out of his pack for the third time. He playfully booped the fox on the nose, saying, "You are gonna give yourself a tummy ache, little one," playfully chiding it.

Osman didn't want to waste any of the vitality they consumed from their hunt to soulchannel himself into the saldrig but, tired of the fox's antics and delays, blurted out, "Maybe I should just turn into the Judge to guide us." Before he uttered the first word, the fox was on Osman's shoulder, sitting with a rigid back and moving its mouth, mocking his words. Osman turned his head to the fox, ready to scold it, but stopped when she placed her forehead on his and looked deep into his eyes.

Reflected in her pupils was the image of his father.

She disengaged her stare and looked up the trail, giving a slight nod.

"You've seen my father? Up ahead? That's where you're taking us?" Osman asked.

In answer, the fox leaped off his shoulder and began walking up the trail as any creature of the physical world would. Yanri came up on one side of Osman and Anson on the other, each laying a hand on his shoulder.

Anson was the one to speak. "Well, let's see what she wants to show us."

Osman led the way with the two close behind. Their destination wasn't far. Oddly, it was literally around the next bend in the trail. Even though there was no indication that something lay ahead until suddenly there it was.

They entered a large open glade that posed many more questions than the one it answered. At its center was an ironwood tree. Although it was nearly forty feet tall with a trunk wider than Osman could reach, it was evident that it was newly sprouted, its massive seed hull still visible, half buried in the soil at its base. It wasn't just any ironwood tree. It was Arbor Lumenari.

Understanding hit Osman like a wave. This forest wasn't somewhere else. It was some*when* else. Their whole journey once through the portal had been within the footprint of the world tree as it existed in their time, but at the time when it was first born.

"I see my friend found you," said a gravelly voice as Tavi stepped into view from the far side of the world tree.

Tavi looked the same as Osman's last memory of his father. He was haggard, gaunt, and broken, with robes unkempt and leaning heavily on a gnarled walking stick. Yellow-orange motes of light flickered across him occasionally like the sparks kicked up from a fire when poked with a stick. The rippling illumination was familiar to Osman.

"You aren't him," Osman observed. "You're' a wilicho, aren't you?"

"A bit more sentient than a wilicho and more intentional, but that is a close enough assessment of what I am," the echo of Tavi replied.

Yanri whispered in Osman's ear, "Like Wilfred, right?"

Osman gave a slight nod, then continued addressing Tavi, "Why are you here?"

"Your father left me here, of course," Tavi replied with the same grating tone of superiority that so annoyed Osman in life. "I am here to help you complete what I could not."

"How can I possibly do something that the great Architavia Therandus could not?" Osman asked, stating Tavi's formal name mockingly. Osman now knew so much more about his father and himself, but seeing this echo of him and speaking to him slammed him right back into all his old feelings about his father.

"Because you were always meant to achieve far more extraordinary things in your life than I ever did in mine." Tavi's confession was heartfelt and sincere, deflating Osman's hostility somewhat. Tavi continued, "I failed. Spectacularly so. In more ways than I can count, but most tragically, I failed you." Tavi sighed. "In trying to make my own journey, and then your journey, easier, I laid you upon the worst possible path to achieve what fate required."

The echo of Tavi crossed to Osman, hand outstretched as though to lay it on his chest, but Osman stepped back, not allowing Tavi to touch him. The echo spoke sincerely to Osman, "I knew you couldn't stay on the Isles, but I never intended or wanted you to harm yourself."

Yanri stepped between Osman and Tavi. "That is all well and good, but I saw what you did to him. I felt what he felt. I was there." Yanri's voice was quavering on the edge of rage.

"It's okay, Yanri," Osman said, gently laying a hand on Yanri's shoulder.

"It is *not* okay." Yanri rolled his shoulder out from under Osman's hand. "You stole everything from him, from your own son, and let him run away in pain, writhing in the anguish of his qil without even going after him." Tears were streaming down Yanri's face, and Osman realized he was no longer just talking about what he had experienced when they shared souls. Yanri continued, "You trapped him in that prison you called a home when you told him he couldn't leave. That he was too much of a disappointment. Too much of a failure."

Osman forcibly turned Yanri to face him and hugged him with all his might. "It's okay, Yanri. It's okay. *We* survived. We moved on from them." Osman cradled Yanri's head to his shoulder, "We found each other. We found our family." Osman pulled Anson, whose eyes were also brimming, into the hug. When they had collected themselves, the three turned together to Tavi, who had drifted a respectable distance away.

"What do *we* need to do?" Osman asked.

Tavi made no further attempts at reconciliation but got straight to the point. "Did you bring the box?"

Osman swung his pack off his back and retrieved the carved box.

"Good." Tavi continued, "As you have probably surmised, time is different here. It does not march forward like in the real world but moves however the primal forces of the arcane necessitate. So, while we are existing here together, for me, it is four months after your father left me here. While for you, judging by your age alone, it has been over twenty years since he was here."

Osman testily replied, tired of the twisted knots woven by his father. "You still haven't told us what we have to do."

"As I said, you have to complete the task at which I failed." The box popped open in Osman's hands, revealing a crystal shard glowing with silver light.

"You have to reincarnate Richen."

# CHAPTER TWENTY-TWO



"I *what?*" Osman demanded. "This whole journey, following in your footsteps to see what happened to Richen. To pay my Qat'malorn to Talon, and you *failed*?" Osman threw his hands up in exasperation. "And now it is on *me* to bring back the person who ruined my life! Gods! You are everything I knew you were."

Tavi didn't even have the decency to look abashed at Osman's outburst. He looked Osman in the eyes and said, "I did everything wrong. I came here with ulterior motives and was deemed unworthy."

Tavi explained, "In my continued hubris, I was going to make things right with you. I would return home with your newly reincarnated baby brother—buy your forgiveness by giving you someone to love and care for the way you never were. Let our relationship heal, and when Richen was old enough, I would send you with him to Talon to fulfill the vision the Fatesinger showed me." Tavi paused. "I was trying to game fate, and she did not appreciate my folly. So now the choice and the future of the Fatesinger's plan falls to you."

"Damn you! Damn you to the Nine Hells!" Osman screamed at Tavi. "Choice? You talk of choice, but what choice do I have?" Osman's voice took on a haughty tone mimicking Tavi's as he addressed him, hand held high above his head, "Do fate's bidding, or the world ends!" Osman looked red-faced back to Tavi, "That's not a choice. It's extortion!"

Infuriatingly, Tavi responded calmly. "Fate did not burden you with this, so it is not yours to pick up. The Fatesinger will choose another to bring her purpose to fruition. You can simply release Richen's soul to the veil and be freed from fate's grasp."

The echo of Tavi continued. "Our meeting not only brought you to my time but also me to yours. A time when Tavi is dead, and as his echo, I inherited all his memories, but there are two sets. In one, I return from Lyria Bay, having never received reincarnated Richen as an infant from my echo I left here. I destroy the parasite feeding on me and regain my strength. We eventually reconcile, and you have the father you deserved, albeit a bit delayed in his arrival." Tavi paused, "The other is much as I assume you remember it."

"When I was fourteen, you told me you were going to Lyria Bay. Is that after this? Is that *when* you are?" Osman asked. "What is so important about Lyria Bay?"

"That is *'when I am,'* as you say. Lyria Bay is adjacent to a rift in our world. While not the same as this place, it is similar enough that if you choose to reincarnate Richen, I can take him directly from here to Tavi without alerting Toman to his resurrection. Between his reincarnation and the rift's energies, Richen will be shrouded from detection unless something leads Toman's gaze there."

Osman voiced his internal conflict, "If I just walk away, all the pain, all the loneliness, all the rejection just goes away?" Osman looked down at his forearms, running his fingers over the scars there, and longingly whispered, "*All this*, just disappears?"

"This will all fade like a dream. Fourteen-year-old you will wake in your bed to the news that your father is returning home, this time to stay."

The clearing fell silent.

Osman finally spoke, "It all disappears." His voice was soft but carried through the silence. "But so do Talon and Wilfred." Osman reached out his hand to grab Anson's, "and finding you again." Osman then turned to Yanri, "And so do you." He shared a long smile with Yanri, the person to whom he had just bared his whole soul.

"When I arrived on the Isles, I very well might have chosen differently, but now the choice is easy." Osman grabbed Yanri's hand and turned to Tavi while still hand in hand with Anson. "It might come with pain and heartbreak, but this is who I am. I'm not proud of my scars, but they're a part of all the things that are *me*. Erasing them would be the same as erasing myself. So, I'll do it." Looking to Yanri and Anson for confirmation and getting a nod from each. "We'll do it. We'll reincarnate Richen."

Tavi's expression wore a rueful, self-effacing smile, "The only thing I ever did right was to trust you, but I couldn't even manage that until after I lost you."

"How do we do this?" Osman asked.

"It is practically already done," Tavi replied, leading them to the far side of the world tree. There, a polished depression was carved into the seed pod that formed the tree's base. With the scale of the tree, it was near chest height and covered with runes. "The only part of the ritual remaining will come from you." Tavi looked to the three of them, "All of you."

"Every reborn soul needs Fire—the passion to re-ignite the soul's will to live, and Earth—a foundation upon which to build its new life." Tavi's words had taken on a ritualistic cadence. Tavi's echo looked to Osman,

"Place the soul crystal in the basin. Your father's power that flows into you from his sacrifice will guide your hand."

Osman looked first to Yanri and then to Anson. "Are you okay with this? I know I spoke for us earlier, but you don't have to do this if you don't want to."

"I abandoned you once, Osman. I will not do it again. Whatever you need, I am here." Anson replied.

"Do you really have to ask?" Yanri said with a smile.

Placing the shining crystal in the basin, Osman smiled at the people who were his foundation and fire that would soon become Richen's. "Well then, let's fulfill destiny's ends, whatever they ultimately may be."

Feeling his father's influence and magic flowing through him and intermingling with his soulchanneling, Osman looked to his thumb and willed the nail to grow into one of the Matriarch's talons. Saying the words he had once intoned in despair, he now invoked them with hope. He sliced his palm with the Matriarch's talon and allowed the blood to form a bloodblade in his hand.

He looked to Yanri and couldn't help but smile as the needed words formed in his mind, "You are the fire bright enough to reignite an extinguished soul." Yanri held his hand over the soul crystal in the basin. The bloodblade cut true and deep as Osman drew it across Yanri's palm. As Yanri's blood hit the crystal, it burst into a vibrant dancing flame.

Osman then looked to Anson, eyes brimming with tears as he said, "You are the stone, solid and true, the foundation upon which all this new life's troubles are weathered and triumphs celebrated." As Anson's blood fell, it joined the fire, turning to molten rock, engulfing the shard and filling the basin.

The surface of the lava filling the bowl expanded like rising dough into a dome as it turned grey and cooled. Everything was still for a breathless moment. Then, the stone crumbled into a fine cloud of glowing embers that drifted skyward. Within the basin, an infant lay where the soul crystal had one laid.

A boy with stormcloud eyes reborn to a new life, looking up at the man who had endured so much to ensure his return.

Osman reached down and lifted the tiny babe in his arms. Anson had already fetched a fresh cotton shirt from his pack, and when Osman seemed unsure of how to proceed, Anson expertly swaddled the child in the soft fabric. Yanri stared at the infant in Osman's arms in abject awe, having one of his rare moments of speechlessness.

"Hello, Richen," Osman said in a gentle voice.

A tiny hand reached up and grabbed Yanri's pinky finger. Yanri's face beamed brighter than the sun.

"A new life will need a new name," Tavi stated sagely. "Names can be powerful things, and the identity of this soul must remain hidden from powerful eyes. What will you have him named?"

Osman looked to Anson and Yanri for help only to find them looking just as expectantly back at him. Osman closed his eyes and sank into the new qil manifesting within him as he cherished the comforting weight of the baby in his arms. It was a tiny sensation, but it encompassed his entire world—a second heartbeat nestled deep in his chest, beating in perfect rhythm with his own. A dozen other qil that would typically overwhelm his senses blossomed across his body, but none could eclipse that tiny pulsing beat nestled against his heart.

"Quentin," Osman said as he opened his eyes, meeting Anson and Yanri's.

"Quentin," Anson repeated approvingly with a nod.

"Quentin," Yanri choked out through tears. "It's perfect." He looked to Anson and Osman, placing his hand on his chest, "Do you feel it?" He patted his chest, "Here. Like he is right here."

Osman nodded.

"I do," Anson said as he looked at Osman and put his arm around his shoulders. "But I have felt it before for another child I held in my arms."

Osman smiled at the two men to whom he was now bound to by blood and love through Quentin. He looked at Tavi and stated sorrowfully, "We have to let him go now, don't we?"

"I am afraid so. I need to deliver him to your father in my time." Tavi replied. "Tavi has chosen someone wonderful there to raise him. Your father will remain only on the child's periphery to ensure that Quentin isn't found, leaving before he is old enough to remember him." The echo of Tavi added forlornly, "Until, in four years' time, your father returns to Horizon's End and drives you away to Arnadore."

Osman only nodded and stepped forward toward the shimmering echo of his father. The apparition reached out, and as his hand made contact with Quentin, they both vanished. Yanri and Anson stepped forward, and the three huddled in an embrace, heads pressed together, overwhelmed by the moment.

Whether they stood there for hours or days, Osman could not tell. Their stasis was finally broken by a thick mucus-filled and snuffled inhale from Yanri.

"So," Yanri wiped his nose on his sleeve, then asked Osman, "You were fourteen, and now you are thirty-six. That means Quentin is twenty-two, right?"

Osman quickly confirmed the math in his head. "Yeah, that makes sense."

"So let's go get him!" Yanri exclaimed.

In usual fashion, Yanri had distilled any discussion of "what now?" down to the most simple and direct course of action. Osman looked to Anson for any objection and, seeing none, was about to endorse the plan when he remembered the cloak ray and Cerena.

"You're right, but remember what the echo told us: Quentin must remain hidden. That cloak creature almost killed us, and I'm sure Cerena sent it." Osman replied thoughtfully.

"Shit. We are going to need a plan." Yanri said dejectedly.

Osman countered, "But you are right about one thing. We need to get moving and out of this place."

As if on command, the fox reappeared at their feet. Anson knelt, his bag of jerky all but magically appearing in his hand.

"Hello, little one. Can you lead us back to the portal?" Anson asked as he offered the shimmering fox a piece of dried meat. The fox darted around in a circle and then zig-zagged between their legs. She landed on Anson's shoulder with a single leap and grinned teasingly at Osman with a mischievous twinkle in her eye.

The entire forest shifted around them while they remained standing still. Trees whirled by. Ferns bent out of their path. Gullies and grottos were bridged before them, only to reopen after they passed. With a shudder and a lurch, they stood back at the portal as if they had never left. The fox chirped with a burst of strange, barking laughter.

"Okay, that was impressive. Nauseating, but impressive." Osman replied to the fox's smug grin she flashed at him from Anson's shoulder. Osman noticed a quizzical look on Anson's face and that he didn't seem nearly as affected by the fox's strange form of transportation.

Before he could inquire about it, Yanri began poking the cloak ray's corpse with a stick, a grim reminder of the danger they still faced. Osman went over to it and drew his dagger from his boot. It had returned to the shape of the iron dagger, with a shimmering coating of frost covering the blade. A theory began to form in Osman's mind regarding the dagger, but there wasn't time to explore it now. He went to the creature's head and cut out the obsidian crystal, which was now dark with no sign of Cerena's reflected eye.

Careful not to touch it with his bare hand, Osman cut a scrap of leather off the cuff of his pants, wrapped it around the talisman, and then placed it in his pack. He was unsure if it would be of any use, but anything that was once connected to Cerena could potentially be of help.

Osman turned to the fox and said, "We got off on the wrong foot, but you have been a great help. Thank you." Looking to his companions and then back to the fox, he added, "It's time for us to go."

The fox leaped onto Osman's shoulder in the way of a reply.

Osman looked at it and said, "I'm not sure you can come with us." The fox remained resolute in its position perched on Osman's shoulder.

"Okay, I know better than to argue with you." Osman stepped through the portal with Yanri and Anson close behind.

There was a lurch of the portal and then the familiar burning flash of heat that accompanied using a returning stone attuned to a hearth.

A moment of timelessness hit Osman. The fox playfully danced before his eyes, its red tail burning like a torch. As it burned, the sparks it unleashed swirled around the fox until it disappeared. An onslaught of memories flooded Osman's mind—his father's memories. He saw Tavi as a child playing on the cliffs of Horizon's End long before he laid the first foundations. Even at this young age, Osman could see his father's affinity for the elements. He frolicked among the trees and waterfalls with a familiar fox conjured from the fires of the thermal forces deep below the location where his sanctuary and home would soon stand.

Tavi's life unfurled before Osman: his pain, his love, his journey, and his loss. All the things left unsaid. The vision ended with a hunched figure sitting before a canvas in the moonlight, painting a shattered stained glass window as he longed to share one more moment with his son. Osman saw a pulse of pain ripple through his father, and his paintbrush dropped to the floor. Osman felt the familiar qil of shards of glass cutting across his palms as he watched the Last Friend reach into his father's chest and pull out Toman's parasite, crushing it in their palm. Tavi had carried it and all the pain it brought for decades to give his son this chance. The Last Friend then took Tavi's hand to escort him on his final journey.

Osman felt the fox's spirit settle into his mind alongside the Matriarch, the Prince, and the Judge. He knew her name without a moment of thought: the Trickster.

# CHAPTER TWENTY-THREE



*Year 884* PXF *~ Late Spring*

Osman awoke lying on the ground in front of a hearth. Yanri and Anson were leaning over him with concerned looks on their faces. Osman sat up and looked around the dim room lit with only a single glowing lantern. The room was in chaotic disarray, but he recognized it as the inside of Anson's home.

Yanri pulled Osman to his feet. "Somehow, we ended up here." Yanri offered, "I thought the portal felt like a returning stone, but I wasn't expecting this."

Osman was still getting his bearings. "It was the fox." He said as though it explained everything. Anson and Yanri looked at him expectantly, waiting for further details. "It's a lot. The fox was also an agent of my father, and now she is up here with the rest." Osman tapped his head. Osman looked around. A helpful neighbor must have removed the human's body and boarded up the window the cloak ray had broken through. Between the gaps, he could see only darkness.

"It's late. Anson, is there somewhere we can sleep?" Osman asked.

"There is a double bed in the loft if you don't mind sharing," Anson answered.

"That'll be great," Yanri answered, guiding Osman toward the stairs.

Osman was still reeling from the revelations of his father's life now swimming in his head. He allowed Yanri to get him upstairs, strip him down to his underbritches, and put him under the covers. Yanri soon joined him and cuddled up under his arm.

Seeing him without his shirt, Osman could not ignore the amount of mass Yanri had lost during his time in the saldrig with him. Osman ran his hand along Yanri's upper arm, the remaining muscle in stark relief under paper-thin skin.

"I am so sorry," Osman whispered.

Yanri pulled away, looking Osman in the eye. "I'm not," Yanri replied. "I would have happily given up an arm or a leg for all you have shown and given me." Yanri tenderly ran the back of his fingers along Osman's face. "I got to experience a small part of your life in all its heart-wrenching terrible beauty. I might have known you before, but now I understand who you truly are. You've shared the truth of *You* with me."

Osman's eyes brimmed with emotion as the qil of gratitude warmed his torso like a gentle sunbeam falling across his chest on a chilly morning.

Yanri flopped over onto his back and laid his forearm across his forehead. "I have a son," he stated, seemingly amazed at his proclamation. "I mean sort of, right? I'm not his dad or anything, but he is a part of me. I can feel his tiny heart next to mine when I think of him."

"A soul and the life forces of two people came together and resulted in a person. It doesn't matter if it was by magic in this case. And while you aren't a dad to Quentin now, you have a lifetime to become one." Osman added with a hopeful uplift in his voice.

"Three people," Yanri corrected. "You were a part of this too. Your bloodblade, your inherited magic," Yanri grasped Osman's hand and looked into Osman's eyes. "It means we can all stay together and share a life with each other."

Osman didn't let the sad smile he felt in his heart reach his lips. Yanri was so young. Osman didn't doubt Yanri's earnest belief that his words could become real. That life could be a big, hopeful adventure followed by a happy ending and enduring love.

Osman had seen Yanri's soul just as Yanri had seen his. Love had yet to touch his young friend's heart. To be someone's first love in Uldani culture was considered one of the most sacred honors and responsibilities because it undoubtedly meant you would be their first heartbreak as well. Whether Yanri was feeling its qil yet, Osman couldn't be sure, but he could see a reflection of himself looking at Cerena for the first time, coloring his hopeful gaze into Osman's eyes.

"Kiss me," Osman said.

Yanri leaned in and kissed Osman deeply. The warmth of Osman's gratitude for having someone like Yanri as a part of his life who also wanted him to be in their life as well coalesced into a gentle knot deep in his stomach. The knot tightened as the kiss lingered. The qil of love bloomed within Osman for only the second time in his life.

Yanri broke the kiss and leaned back. "You too?" Yanri smiled.

"Yeah." Osman nodded back. Yanri explored Osman's face with his lips, brushing the stubble of his cheek against Osman's smooth jaw as he went. Yanri's kisses found every place on Osman's face where a hidden scar marked his soul and gently laid his lips upon each, finally finding Osman's mouth again. The kind affirmation of his true self had ignited the Judge's hunger, and in response, Osman's canine teeth had already fully formed into fangs to meet Yanri's lips as they pressed into his.

Yanri ran his tongue along Osman's pointed teeth and said between kisses, "Someone's hungry."

Osman paused in their kissing and looked at Yanri with serious eyes. "First love is dangerous, Yanri." He said tenderly. "I wasn't sure I would survive or if I could ever love again after mine. It never ends well."

"I know," Yanri said a bit sadly, "But when it gets messy– if it gets messy– I want it to be with you."

Lust ignited a burning fire at the nape of Osman's neck, both at hearing those words and with the added fuel of the intensity of their shared experience over the last day. Osman bared his fanged teeth and began to kiss Yanri's mouth again in earnest.

Yanri accepted his savage kisses, then slowed, wearing a sly smile Osman couldn't decipher. Yanri pulled himself closer and threw a leg over Osman's hips.

"What the Hells?" Osman exclaimed, looking under the sheets.

"It wasn't on purpose. I swear," Yanri's sly smile turned positively wicked.

"Huh," was the only reply Osman could muster as his fangs grew even more ferocious.

Morning dawned with Osman for once cuddled under Yanri's arm. He yawned and slowly stretched, trying not to disturb Yanri as he rolled onto his back, but to no avail. Yanri's eyes fluttered open, and he rolled over to snuggle into Osman's chest.

"Can we stay here just a little longer before it all comes crashing down on us again?" Yanri asked.

Osman stroked Yanri's hair in consolation, but Anson's voice drifted up from downstairs before he could answer, "Coffee's ready." Anson continued, "You boys should get back down to the Lagoon and pack for travel. Whatever our plan, it probably involves a boat." As an afterthought, Anson asked, "Where are you staying? I can meet you there once I bring some order to this mess."

"We're at the Windward Star," Yanri called down as he quickly rolled out of his bed, onto his feet, and began to put back on his clothes from the day before. Osman again wished he had Yanri's ability to go from sleeping to out the door in a handful of heartbeats.

Yanri was already downstairs with a mug of coffee when Osman joined them, rubbing his bleary eyes and fussing with the bird's nest of curls his hair had opted to create this morning. Anson offered him a steaming mug, but Osman declined.

"I'll just grab some juice down below," Osman said as he ran his tongue across scummy teeth, now returned to usual size.

Anson placed two driftglide potions on the counter. "I always keep a couple around in case I get a yen to scavenge for driftwood."

"Thanks," Yanri said, then gave Anson a big hug. He pulled back, and the two clasped each other's forearms. In a sincere but lighthearted voice, Yanri continued, "In a way, we're Quentin's parents, ya know, even though our son is technically a year older than me." He then smiled gratefully, "It seems we've only known each other for less than a blink, but I can't imagine a better person to have shared this with—and depending on how this all works out, more of my life with."

Yanri moved aside to make room for Osman, who hugged Anson fiercely. He gently pounded Anson on his back with his fist. "Don't ever leave, Dad."

Anson, with choked breath, replied, "Never again, Son. Never again." Anson pulled away and said, "Okay, you two take care of each other, and I will see you this afternoon."

"We will." Osman and Yanri replied in unison as they walked out the door.

Since they were headed to the lagoon, Osman and Yanri couldn't jump from Anson's garden. They instead retraced their steps back to the entry district of Rail to take the stairs back to the landing at the apex of the arching root stairs, as from there, it would be close to a vertical drop down to the Windward Star. Along the way, they passed multiple members of the Shaman Council walking the street. Osman and Yanri gave them a nod as they passed them and assumed there must be some gathering in Bough Town to bring so many out this early in the day.

The driftglider platform was deserted at this hour as those coming up from below wouldn't arrive until mid-morning. With a quick kiss, Osman and Yanri leaped out into the open sky. Having had enough excitement from the day before, the two only waited until they were three-quarters of the way to the ground before giving each other a nod and quaffing their potions. They instantly decelerated into a slow drift and glided down to the promenade.

They landed a hundred yards away from Jaque's juice stand, but apparently, Jaque wasn't working this morning as the silhouette of a statuesque figure with broad shoulders and a tight bob of well-coifed hair occupied the space behind the counter. As they approached, the figure turned to them and immediately dropped their drink from their manicured hand.

"Yanri? Osman? We thought you were dead!" the figure exclaimed.

"Jaque?!" Osman and Yanri exclaimed in unison.

Jaque looked to be at least twenty years old if not twenty-one. Only a single word came to Osman's mind to encompass Jaque, which he shared immediately.

"You are magnificent! But what in the Nine Hells is going on?" Osman couldn't keep a hint of panic out of his voice but shakily remembered his manners. "What's the special and your pronouns for the day."

"They/Them and passionfruit guava," Jaque replied by rote, then ran around the counter on shoes that could be more aptly classified as weapons to hug the two of them. "Where have you been? Everyone said you died in the first attack." A creeping dread began to rise in Osman as his mind tried to grasp what was happening.

Yanri was the first to recover his reasoning, "Jaque, how long ago was that?"

"Over five years ago," Jaque replied without a hint of deception.

*Year 889 PXF ~ Late Summer*

Osman reeled as understanding hit him—the price. This was the price of his shifting forms. Of choosing to deceive Cerena and fight instead of telling her he didn't have the Vermillion Blade. Osman knew the scales hadn't balanced evenly. Yanri had lost perhaps fifteen pounds, but Osman had soulchanneled three times in a handful of minutes, and then the Matriarch's dramatic healing in the chrysalis, along with Yanri and the Prince's wounds being all but erased. It had taken his body a decade to pull itself back together with Wilfred's constant ministrations. He suddenly realized—it hadn't been hours in that clearing as Yanri ate the pyre of vitality that had been the bear. It had been years. The price was *time*.

Yanri was snapping his fingers in front of Osman's eyes. "Come back to us, Wondertoes. We need you, big guy."

Osman grabbed Yanri like he was drowning, "This is the price. It's my fault. We lost five years. Cerena has had five years–" Osman's head snapped around to look at Jaque. "You said the first attack. What's been going on?"

"Let's just all sit and calm down." Jaque circled the counter, grabbing three specials, and guided them to a small high-top table. Handing Osman one of the tankards of pink fruit juice, they said. "Drink this, you've gone pale, and we don't need you swooning on us." Jaque leaned in and began to tell the tale.

"After the first attack up at Rail, there were three more. People said the creatures had snuck in on boats disguised as people's luggage, and one was rumored to be *inside* some poor guy." Jaque leaned back from the table, "Well, the Shaman Council was going to have *none* of that, so they closed down the whole damned port while implementing security measures." Jaque waved their hand in front of their face. "It was a mess. We had to live off what we had or what they could teleport in and bring down from Bough Town for three months." Jaque paused, gauging the interest of their audience.

"Then what?" Yanri asked, engrossed.

Jaque threw one arm behind their chair and continued, "It was quiet for a bit, then a year and a half later, something big went down at the port. The Shaman Council burned two ships out of Eleryon down to the waterline and sunk them in the harbor. Witnesses say they saw dozens of nightmare creatures diving off the ships trying to escape the flames."

Yanri dutifully exclaimed, "No!" to Jaque's pause for emphasis.

"Yes." Jaque nodded. "They say Mael Esari was ready to declare war on the Empire again, but the Emperor of Xallia disavowed any involvement with Eleryon or the creature attacks on our shores. As an offer of good faith, they offered the Shaman Council stations aboard their ships to patrol the waters between the continent's southern coast and the Isles."

Osman sat stunned, trying to process what it all meant. Had Cerena and possibly Toman been so desperate and misled that they would risk restarting the war with the Uldani Isles? Cerena perhaps, but Toman?

Jaque, catching Osman woolgathering in the middle of their story, snapped their fingers in front of Osman's eyes. "Stay with me, Twinkletoes."

"Wondertoes." Yanri corrected.

Jaque shot Yanri a withering look, then sighed and continued. "It's been quiet since then, but rumors began to flow with the new cooperation with Xallia. It is all jumbled about what happened when, but here is what they say." Jaque cleared their throat. "Remember that uprising fifteen years ago across the channel? The knight that went rogue? They say he came back."

Osman and Yanri glanced at each other. "Talon"

"Yeah, Talon Hyphen-noble-name-something," Jaque confirmed. "Well, he tore the whole place up again. Pillaging and terrorizing everyone who was left. Meanwhile, up in that city of theirs, the place is being overrun with–get this–the *same* type of creatures that showed up here."

Osman and Yanri looked at each other again.

Jaque, realizing they were losing their audience, fluttered their fingers and finished with, "And there is some crazy cursed sword or some such that everyone is looking for or something."

Osman calmly asked, "And there have been no attacks for the last three years."

"Not that I've heard of, and I hear everything," Jaque replied.

Osman took a deep breath and grabbed Yanri's wrist. "We need to go." They got up from the table and started to leave when Osman asked over his shoulder, "Do you think the Winward Star will have rooms?"

"Are you kidding? The place is deserted compared to the old days," Jaque replied. "Heck, they probably still have *your* room. When I tried to gather your stuff when you died, the crone at the desk wouldn't let me in because *his* parents paid some outrageous amount for a whole decade up front." Jaque waved a manicured finger at Yanri.

"Thanks, Jaque!" Yanri called and blew them a kiss as they ran toward the Winward Star.

Their room was much as they had left it, albeit freshly dusted, the bed made up, and clothes that had been on the floor five years ago folded neatly on the bureau due to the weekly cleaning service that came with board. Osman began pacing the room as Yanri settled on the bed.

Both were speechless, processing all the implications of losing five years. Yanri spoke first.

"So I'm twenty-six now?" He then repeated almost gleefully, "I'm twenty-six, now!" He ran to the small mirror over the dresser, seeing that his face was unchanged from how it looked when he last was in this room. "I'm twenty-six, and I look my age! I'm not some overgrown teen embarrassment anymore."

Osman smiled as Yanri relished his new 'maturity' and considered what it meant for himself. There was a slight knock at the door. Osman opened the door to find Anson. His face was etched with grief.

"Five years. My studio," Anson began, "It's' gone."

Osman gently guided Anson into the room and sat him on the bed.

Anson continued speaking in a hollow voice, looking back and forth between Osman and Yanri like a man looking for someone to wake him up from a bad dream. "My studio in Warpwood Burl, my gallery, the statuary garden—all are gone. Sold and liquidated. My apprentices didn't know where I was and were forced into it by the council." Anson's confused look soured into anger. "The council is using it to train security forces in combat magic!" His voice turned icy cold. "They were using some of my statues of people as targets."

"I demanded answers from a council member patrolling the street. 'How can this be?' I yelled." Anson put his head in his hands. "She said, 'They attacked our children, our haven for them to explore life.'" Anson looked directly at Osman. "The war chanters are gathering in Mael Esari and Cinderfall. The Isles are readying for war."

Osman walked out onto the balcony silently as Yanri caught Anson up with all Jaque had told them. Osman returned inside when silence fell over the room. "What do they know that we don't know? If there have been no recent attacks, why are they still preparing for war." Osman continued. "I know Cerena. She didn't just give up, so she either figured out I don't have the Vermillion Blade or has found Talon."

"Are you sure he is still alive?" Yanri asked.

"I have to trust what I saw in the Solenfel. I heard his heartbeat and saw the chains binding him shatter." Osman explained as best he could, "The links of those chains now flow into me." Opening his palms out to Yanri and Anson, still showing the wounds of the bloodblade, he said, "It was his energy and yours that let Quentin be born."

Anson calmly asked, "Okay, so what do we do."

Osman closed his eyes and painfully stated, "You two need to go find Quentin without me." Before they could protest, Osman explained, "Cerena was looking for me and possibly still is. It's too risky for me to go anywhere near Quentin. Hopefully, he is just living a quiet life in Lyria Bay, and the two of you going there will not draw an ounce of attention to him."

"We should come with you then. Quentin has been fine for twenty-two," Yanri paused to correct himself, "twenty-seven years. You're going to need our help."

"But what if he has not been fine?" Osman asked. "Hopefully, he isn't in danger, but if destiny has made his life as strange as mine, he probably needs friends." Osman smiled lovingly, "Or maybe even his Dads."

"But what about the brewing war?" Anson asked.

"I don't have it all put together, but I have little doubt that Toman Cour-Vermane is behind whatever is going on to pull the Isles into his plans," Osman replied. "He's Talon's father, was my father's rival, and he murdered Richen. He's connected to too many people bound by fate not to be entangled in all this. If he knows about Quentin..."

Anson stood and grasped Osman's forearm, "I don't like us splitting up, but I agree." Anson reached out his arm to Yanri, who reluctantly grabbed his forearm and completed the triangle by grabbing Osman's other arm. Osman looked deep into Yanri's eyes and mouthed, "I love you."

Yanri swallowed hard and just nodded.

"Where are you going?" Yanri asked, his voice cracking with emotion.

"I'm going to find Talon."

# PART III

## Loss and Found

Year 889 PXF ~ Late Autumn

Harvest time was always a time of change at Milgran's Orchard. Dozens of people looking for work or simply a basket of apples for their homestead trickled in and out of Gwen's property daily. Most were trying to bring a bit of purpose and meaning to the meager life they had pieced together in the still-recovering remnants of Eleryon. It had been six years since Rabien's death, but the land and people still suffered the scars and echoes of the terror he and his Black Court sowed across the region.

The handful of permanent residents of the orchard tried to wrangle the influx of new faces and guide them to where they could work the harvest or find a bed and a hot meal. Rarely did those seeking shelter or kindness bring strife to the orchard. If ever there was trouble, Gwen's reputation with her ever-present rifle quelled it quickly.

Thorn placed three apples in his pack and hoisted the full basket onto his shoulder, but not before letting his eyes linger on the largest tree in the center of Milgran's Orchard. No hint divulged that the Vermillion Blade lay embedded deep within its trunk. Even the circle of blighted ground made by Rabien had all but disappeared. Apple trees twice the size they should have been for their age filled the space, erasing all but its memory. The legacy of Talon Cour-Vermane was slowly fading from the land, even if it still lingered with the person he had become.

Thorn briskly returned from the grove and headed to the sorting tables near the barn. Lunch break had ended, and a small group of workers had gathered for afternoon assignments. Thorn's shoulders tensed as he spotted two familiar faces in the crowd.

Jenkins and Lander had worked on the orchard during the last two harvests; however, labeling their contribution as 'work' was generous at best. They labored far harder consuming their daily ration of free cider Gwen offered at the end of the season than getting the last apples from trees into picking baskets. Once they spotted Thorn, they didn't waste a moment to begin causing trouble.

"Aie, lookie, lookie, lookie," Lander called out to the gathered group, "the hedgeborn stray is still faffing about like he's worth a squirt."

"Oi," Jenkins leaned forward, squinted his eyes, and pointed at Thorn, "I think I see hair on the twat's chin finally!" Jenkins smacked the back of his hand against Lander's chest, "wonder if the first one's sprouted between his legs yet!" he shouted as he grabbed his crotch.

The rest of the crowd drifted away from the two, but whispers began to pass among the new faces who had joined the harvest for the first time this year.

"I thought he was Gwen's son." An older man whispered to his wife.

"I bet he is part elf. They're always leaving mixed-bloods on the side of the road." A teenage boy said louder than he intended to two younger boys beside him.

Thorn sighed. The hedgeborn rumor had started a handful of years back when it became apparent that he was not aging at a typical human rate from harvest to harvest. Luckily, three years ago, his age had stabilized at what Balanon had determined was the equivalent of nineteen years old and had not regressed further. Regarding Lander's comment, even Talon had never been able to grow a beard, and the rest was none of his business.

Placing his basket of apples on the ground, Thorn began giving afternoon work details. "You three head to the west quarter," Thorn told the three gossiping boys. "You two," pointing to the married couple, "They need some help bringing in the morning baskets over by the pond. Lander, Jenkins–"

"Well, well, well, now he's giving the orders all high and mighty," Lander mocked. "I know you ain't Gwen's son, so I reckon I know what's put you in charge. Old bird must like 'em young and tender in her sunset years," Lander said luridly.

"Her husband must be spinnin–" Jenkin's began.

*CRACK*

Thorn's fist landed squarely on Jenkins' jaw, knocking him unconscious before he even hit the ground.

"Don't ever let me hear you utter one word out of either of your filthy mouths to tarnish his memory," Thorn spoke to the unconscious form of Jenkins, but his eyes were burning like daggers into Lander. "We clear?" Lander gave a weak nod. "Then get over to the north quarter, and don't come back empty-handed at sunset."

Thorn knew there was a fifty-fifty chance they wouldn't return at all. The north quarter was closest to the makeshift road that serviced the orchard and would make for an easy exit for them to skulk off. Thorn wasn't a fan of violence, but there were too many people in need to let those two spoil things.

Despite the gossip, Thorn was thankful for even the most challenging days in the apple groves. He enjoyed a simple farmer's life not marred by a noble name or the frenetic pace of a vast city. Even Lander and Jenkins were silly annoyances with easy solutions compared to his past challenges. He deposited his basket of apples at the sorting tables and headed to the cidery.

Gwen was at the bar when he arrived, arranging tankards and pulling a small keg from among the larger barrels for the workers' evening allotment. Thorn looked to make sure the room was clear before speaking.

"Well, I might've given the rumor I was your son some more fire," Thorn said apologetically as he joined Gwen behind the bar.

"Lander and Jenkins?" Gwen asked prophetically. Seeing Thorn's questioning look, she continued, "They swaggered in all stink and spite as soon as the fog lifted."

"We'll see if their thirst for free cider overcomes their pride come sunset." Thorn postulated. "I don't *think* I broke Jenkins' jaw."

"If he got you that full of piss and vinegar, he should count his blessings I wasn't there. Landers would be digging a six-foot hole this evening instead of picking apples and sipping cider." Gwen stated deadly serious.

When he heard the cidery door open, Thorn instinctively turned away and faced the barrels stacked against the back wall, making himself look busy. Visitors this early in the day were a rare and unusual occurrence. When a familiar Uldani accent colored the stranger's words, and Thorn heard the snap of a gold coin against the counter, he realized how unusual it was.

Thorn missed what the stranger said as his thoughts swirled but came to his senses when Gwen tapped him on his shoulder, indicating him to pour the visitor's drink.

"I am looking for someone. An old rumor came to my homeland regarding the last Knight Captain of Arnadore," The Uldani said. Thorn's throat constricted, and his heart pounded so loudly in his ears that he could hardly hear. Gwen waved the Uldani off with the standard epitaphs branded upon the traitor Duke and his guards, covering for Thorn and his former identity. When he turned around to hand the filled mug to Gwen, Thorn dared to glance at who his heart knew must be there.

It was Osman, changed but still recognizable. His brother from another life that Thorn had feared he would never see again. Thorn stood frozen when Osman's eyes fell upon him, locked in place by equal parts fear and hope, but Osman's gaze slid off Thorn just as quickly as it landed without a hint of recognition. Thorn handed the cider to Gwen and spun back to the barrels, hands shaking.

Both relief and disappointment washed over Thorn at the lack of recognition. If someone as close to Talon as Osman had been could no longer identify him, then no one would. Still, an undeniable stab of pain also passed through Thorn's chest. Looking into the eyes of someone he still held so much love for, and there being no glimmer of connection, no spark of the closeness they once had, was unexpectedly devastating. So much so that he almost missed Osman's last words.

"If he is alive and you see him, tell him his little brother is looking for him and that he found Richen."

Thorn and Gwen stood frozen after Osman, heeding her dismissal, left the cidery. Waiting a few more moments after the unexpected visitor's exit, Gwen spoke to the empty room instead of turning around to address Thorn.

"I won't stop you." She paused thoughtfully, "unless you want me to."

Turning from the stacked barrels, Thorn recovered enough from his shock to give Gwen an answer, "He won't go far. The Osman I knew would have picked up that there was more to learn here."

Gwen finally turned to face Thorn and leaned back against the bar, looking at him sternly.

"Osman will abide your wishes that he move along for the night," Thorn assured Gwen, "but will make himself easy to find for anyone who might seek him out."

Thorn waited to leave until sunset when the orchard's community gathered in the barn for supper and cider. As he expected, Osman did not make his trail hard to follow. By the time he reached the main road, Thorn had found two pieces of twine and some straw tied into Uldani knots and 'carelessly' dropped along his route. Thorn spotted a telltale column of campfire smoke with only the quickest of scans of the horizon—a carelessness only skilled fighters or reckless bandits would make.

An icy wariness took root in Thorn's chest. This was almost too easy. He and Gwen had lived their lives with a remarkable level of peace, experiencing no retaliation from the powers they had thwarted six years ago. Whether that was from Caspharian or the bound power of the Vermillion Blade resting in the orchard, Thorn could not say. Perhaps today was the day when that all would end. The allure of seeing Osman and his news about Richen had lured him alone into the night with only his small enchanted hammer for defense. Thorn slowed his pace and decided to exhibit some caution.

Thorn did not often venture far from the orchard. Only occasional hunting took him away from his daily routines in the grove. But he still knew the surrounding countryside well enough, paired with his intuition, to guess the approximate location of Osman's camp and how to approach it undetected. Thorn left the road and skirted around the rolling hills, marking the beginnings of the uplands to the north of the orchard. Less than twenty minutes of travel later, on high ground within a natural depression in the hilltops, he found Osman's camp. Thorn crept through the tall scrub grass turned brittle by Autumn's end and peeked over the edge of one of the low rises sheltering where his once-brother had settled for the night.

A large unbanked fire sent embers and dark smoke into the sky. Beside it was a pack and a bedroll laid out for sleep, but there was no sign of Osman. Talon's old instincts screamed that this was a trap. Thorn swept his eyes around the periphery of the campfire's light, trying to spot unseen adversaries, but he saw nothing but the crackling fire.

Thorn began to creep further forward, his curiosity getting the best of him. He had moved no more than a few inches when the largest owl Thorn had ever seen swooped silently down out of the sky and dropped a freshly killed rabbit next to the fire. The owl seemed to look directly at Thorn before spreading its wings and disappearing into the night.

Thorn had spent enough time with Naz to know everything was not as it seemed with this campsite and the owl. No more than two minutes later, the person claiming to be Osman strolled into the firelight, sat down on the bedroll, and began to skin the rabbit with a wicked stiletto pulled from his boot.

# CHAPTER TWENTY-FOUR



Osman's would-be stalker had shrunk back down into the tall grass at the ridge of the hill and was currently out of sight.

"I'm hoping that waterskin on your hip holds more of that fine cider from earlier." Osman pulled a rough-hewn pewter mug out of his pack and placed it on the ground beside him, ready to be filled. "I'm happy to share some rabbit in trade if you are interested."

Osman continued preparing the rabbit, letting his offer simmer. After a few minutes without response, Osman kept talking, "I saw you behind the bar at the cidery earlier, yes? Maybe you know something of the people I spoke about?" After getting the rabbit affixed on a spit and banking the fire low for cooking, there was still no answer from behind the hill.

"Maybe you are just curious about an Uldani visiting your orchard? Perhaps when you were just a boy, you saw an Uldani dueling in the streets of Arnadore with the Knight Captain I spoke of?" Osman was running out of ideas and began to wonder if his visitor actually knew anything at all about Talon.

"His name was Osman." The voice came from a different direction than where Osman had spotted the teen spying on his camp as the Matriarch. Whoever this kid was, he had skills to move quietly enough that Osman's heightened senses had not tracked it.

"Indeed it was," Osman answered cautiously. For the boy to know his name, he must have been more than just a one-time observer of their Hearth's Rest duels, perhaps the son of a tavernkeep or merchant. Maybe even one of the orphans he and Talon made a point of including in their antics.

"How can I convince you to join me at my fire?" Osman asked. "Ask me something about the last Knight Captain of Arnadore that would prove I mean him no harm."

There was a long silence, and then the question came. "Where did you dine before becoming the companion of the Knight Captain?"

The question was not at all what Osman was expecting. Perhaps this was the son of one of the alleymen he used to visit. Osman warily answered, "Many places, but mostly in the alleys near the brothels. Old Man Fredrick's alley stew was a staple of mine, even though it tasted as awful as it sounds."

The teen emerged from over the hill and walked resolutely into the firelight toward Osman. There was something hauntingly familiar about the way he moved. "If it were anyone else, I would think you were his son, but I know that can't be the case," Osman pondered aloud to the approaching figure. "Who are you?"

The young man walked straight up to Osman and hugged him tightly. After a moment, he stepped back, grabbed Osman by the shoulders, and said, "The man I was, you called your Krolh'dran, and this man I became called you his. Neither would have survived without you as a part of their lives."

"I don't understand," Osman said.

"Talon Cour-Vermane died, but the part of him that was your Krolh'dran lives on in me. I am Thorn."

The earnestness of Thorn's proclamation as he looked up at Osman erased any of Osman's wariness, but it could not assuage all his doubts. "You better open that cider," Osman said as he sat down on the bedroll. "And I thought I was going to have a hard time explaining things," he added with a smirk.

Thorn began to tell Osman the tale of all that had happened in his life since they last saw one another. Osman listened intently to Thorn's descriptions of Oldstone and his dragonborn brother, Nazge. Thorn's details about the curse and his physical changes lent added clarity to what Osman had seen in the Solenfel.

Thorn paused the recounting of his life and asked, "What is it? You still wear your emotions on your face, and I can see something is troubling you."

Looking into the fire, Osman said, "I had an encounter with one of the primordial guardians of the Isles during my exile. It showed me things written upon the memory of the world." He turned to Thorn, continuing, "Hidden things about Talon, his father, and mine. The stuff of nightmares perhaps better left unknown."

Osman could see Thorn was digesting his words. He probably should have waited, but the glow of gratitude was like a sunrise in his chest, so he started to speak again. "I saw the chains that bound you on the day of the revolt." Osman's eyes welled with the memory of what he saw. "Thousands of chains surrounding you, binding your limbs and ripping you apart to try and force your hand. Every one of them wanted you to murder me." Osman's tears began to fall from his wide eyes, looking into Thorn's. "And you saved me even after I betrayed you, leaving you to face your fate alone."

Osman could not decipher the fleeting expressions that played upon Thorn's face as he said, "Honestly, sometimes I wonder how Talon resisted the will of the chains and if I would be strong enough to do the same." Thorn continued, voice filled with the love he still felt for his little brother, "But with every part of my being, I would try to do the same."

Osman reached out and squeezed Thorn's hand. It felt small compared to how Talon's hand used to engulf his own, but even with the physical change, their hands still seemed to fit together like a key in a lock. He said earnestly, "I owe you my life as well as all I have become. I recognize how miraculous it was that you didn't kill me that day. Not a miracle of the Gods, but one of your own making."

Thorn cleared his throat exactly as Talon used to when his emotions began to well up inside of him. "You *saw* the Vermillion Blade's chains?" Thorn said, amazement filling his voice. "They are the very essence of its power that I only ever revealed to one other person. For you to even know of their existence makes me believe whatever hidden things you saw were grounded in truth."

Osman heard the trepidation in Thorn's statement, so he added, "The Vermillion Blade's chains were not all that bound you. Another vile black chain, grown out of your soul's core, tethered you to some source beneath your father's estate." Thorn's face showed horror and shame, but he slowly nodded in affirmation. Osman squeezed Thorn's hand harder, "but they were not the worst that I saw." Osman paused, giving Thorn one last chance to halt his words.

When no objection came, he finished. "Your father wove the last chains from Richen's love, a chain that crawled through your veins and infected your body. He used it to violate and mold your flesh into the twisted image of what he wanted you to become."

Thorn swallowed the information down like a bitter drought. "I had begun to suspect as much." Thorn dropped Osman's hand from his own and began pacing around the fire. "The beast that attacked Richen—the bite, it was more than just an infection, wasn't it?"

"It was a magical parasite. It fed on Richen's life force, and when my father tried to banish it, the parasite killed Richen and fed on his soul." There was no way for Osman to soften the blow of the words.

Thorn fell to the ground, his knees buckling under him. "He's dead? All these years, I assured myself I would have felt it had he died. How long?" When Osman didn't immediately answer, Thorn demanded, "*How Long!*"

"Thirty-five years," Osman said as gently as he could. "But it's more complicated than that."

Thorn leapt back to his feet, "Complicated?" He thundered at Osman, "*Complicated?* For thirty-five years, I have chased a phantom. I have been manipulated endlessly by people and Gods and forces beyond my understanding. All with the hope and promise that we would find each other again, even for one single day, and he's been dead all along?" Thorn sat hard on the ground across the campfire from Osman, placing his head in his hands. Osman barely discerned him whisper, "A whole life wasted on a lie."

Osman got up and crossed to Thorn to sit beside him. Thorn knocked Osman's arm away the first few times he tried to lay it across his shoulders to comfort him, but eventually, he relented. When he finally did, Thorn threw his arms around Osman, all but crawling into his lap like a child, and wept.

"Thorn, listen," Osman said once he felt Thorn was capable of hearing his words. "You never felt Richen's absence because he never made his final journey with the Last Friend. My father cared for his soul until it could be reborn." Thorn lifted his head off Osman's shoulder, eyes filled with hope. "And that is what my friends and I have done. What I have done for you, Krolh'dran. Twenty-seven years ago, Richen was reborn and taken to a place where he would be safe from your father's gaze and hells-born schemes."

"Reborn?" Thorn asked. "Twenty-seven years ago? I don't understand." Thorn climbed out of Osman's embrace and sat beside him.

"You are not the only one who has had a strange journey, brother," Osman said with a slight smile. "But before we get too far into the rest, you should know what my father did for you. For us." It still felt strange to Osman to think of his father with kindness, but there was no denying what he sacrificed for them both. "To keep your father unaware that he had cleansed Richen's soul, my father transferred the parasite to himself. Once transferred, it was the energy of my father's soul that Toman infused into you up until the time of his death." Osman licked his lips and proceeded carefully, "When Talon died, and all the chains binding him were shattered, that energy from my father began flowing out of you and was drawn back to its source. Or, more aptly, the next closest thing—me."

Thorn took Osman's larger hand in his own, comparing the two. Concern marred his expression. "Is that why you have grown? Have I passed the violation of my flesh onto you?" Thorn shook his head in dismay and self-disgust.

"No. No, it isn't like that." Osman considered a moment, "Not directly, at least. Too many higher powers were at work for it to be that easy. I think a component of what I have become came from Toman's arcane intent to mold your flesh. But this," Osman motioned to himself, "was not of his design or intent."

"What have you become then?" Thorn asked.

"It is probably easier to show you, but it means you won't have any rabbit for dinner, and I might need to step away and hunt," Osman replied.

"While I always enjoy fresh rabbit, I brought more than cider. I have some fresh-picked apples and turnovers Gwen made. I won't starve." Thorn quipped.

Osman took the half-cooked rabbit off the fire and laid it on the ground, noting Thorn's questioning looks. He then closed his eyes and channeled the spirit of the Judge. Osman felt the familiar flurry of ice surround him, and his flesh and soul expanded into his saldrig form.

"Woah," Thorn said wide-eyed as he took a step back.

As Osman's senses fully merged with the Judge, there was an instant recognition of Thorn's scent. It was nearly the same as his own. Both Osman and Thorn now contained the echoes of the power their fathers had infused into Talon's soul. The Judge knew them to be soul-bound together as brothers in more than name or title.

Thorn moved slowly and put out his hands in a non-threatening way. "Osman? How much of you is in there?"

Osman let a deep purr rumble in his chest and rubbed his head and muzzle against Thorn's side, nearly lifting him off the ground.

"Okay, okay. I get it." Thorn said playfully as Osman pressed the Judge's forehead against Thorn's chest. Thorn's arms could barely reach around the Judge's head to scratch under his jaw. The two leaned into the strange embrace, which seemed somehow more profound than their hug from earlier.

It had felt strange listening to Thorn speak about his life and Talon in the third person. A disorientation in seeing the physical shape of Thorn but having the emotional history and connection to Talon. Osman had begun to sense it before, but now, through the Judge's eyes, it was so obvious. His bond with Talon was never due to his hulking size, position as Knight Captain, or martial skills. Osman's connection was with the part of Talon that he hid from the world, the part Osman had coaxed out of his stoic exterior. His love had been for the man he saw inside. Thorn *was* the part of Talon that had always been his Krolh'dran.

"There is so much I want to know and understand about your life," Thorn said with genuine interest and care. "However, I assume the comment about the rabbit is because a change like that must pull vast amounts of energy from somewhere if it is anything like the magics I studied with Naz." Thorn looked to the rabbit and then back to Osman, "But brother, you are *huge*. I've seen smaller horses, and that rabbit will be barely a mouthful for you." Osman saw a twinkle in Thorn's eye. "You mentioned hunting..." Thorn let the statement hang before adding, "And since you are nearly the size of a horse and I am–"

Osman was surprised at the Judge's upwelling of kittenish deference and need for approval in his attitude toward Thorn. Before Osman could even think, the Judge lunged forward, forcing his muzzle between Thorn's legs, and tossed him over his head and onto his back. Osman felt Thorn scramble to turn himself around and get a secure hold on the ruff of the Judge's neck. Osman looked over his shoulder to make sure Thorn was ready. His brother sat with a smile beaming upon his face, an open and honest joy Osman had never seen expressed by Talon, but he always knew was there.

The same profound joy filled Osman. He could feel the resonating truth that he was seeing his Krolh'dran in the flesh for the first time. He let out a roar, the likes of which were utterly unknown upon the shores of Eleryon. It echoed across the hills and lowlands, stirring the breeze and chilling it with the echoes of Kyflenor. Osman had found his brother once more.

Osman and Thorn leaped into the night, the moonlight igniting the Judge's fur into a ghostly luminescence as the evening fog spread its tendrils across the land. Osman's powerful strides and leaps carried them as fast as any horse, and he quickly latched onto the scent of boar. Osman didn't even slow, pouncing into the small glade where his prey slumbered, dispatching it before it could squeal. Osman apologetically looked over his shoulder at Thorn as he tore into the boar's viscera.

"Doesn't bother me," Thorn replied. His hair had come loose from the leather thong that had secured it, forming a wild mane framing his head. "You want me to hop down while you eat? I guess that's probably easier." By the time Thorn had dismounted and pulled an apple out of his pack, the boar was gone.

Osman glanced over at Thorn, who had sat down and leaned against a small wild plum tree to eat his apple. Nostalgia hit Osman like a blow, seeing Thorn sit in such a familiar pose, but there was something else. The apple was more than it seemed. Osman blinked his saldrig eyes over to veilsight, but it revealed nothing. The apple appeared as nothing more than it should. A sly feminine voice he had never heard before entered his mind.

*A treasure hidden in plain sight*

The Trickster.

Osman padded over to Thorn and sniffed at the apple.

"You want one?" Thorn offered, pulling another from his pack and holding it out to Osman.

Osman delved into whatever insight the instincts of the spirits within him could give: the Judge, who was always wary of hidden danger, the Matriarch in all her experience and attunement to magic, the Prince, with his resistance to poisons, and the Trickster's initial reaction. With no objection and a swipe of his massive tongue, he swept the offered apple into his maw and ate it.

The effect was immediate. Osman felt as though he tapped into the life energy of every living thing for miles around him. It flowed into the Judge like a torrent with its blinding radiance. Osman felt every part of himself and the spirits within him filled to overflowing with divine light.

With a shimmer of arcane incandescence, Osman channeled back into his Uldani form. He grabbed Thorn's hand and asked reverently, "Where did you get that? What is it?"

Thorn looked at Osman as he finished his own apple, looking more perplexed than when Osman had turned into eight hundred pounds of sabertoothed predator before his eyes. "It's an apple. I picked it from the orchard this morning." He answered.

"That's not just an apple," Osman stated.

Thorn looked at the remaining core in his hand and then wondered out loud, "Maybe it's not." He looked at Osman, "How did you–?"

Osman answered before Thorn could finish his question, "Its connection to the land is indescribable in its scale—a well of energy beyond anything I've experienced. You feel nothing?"

"No, and I have eaten hundreds of these over the last five years. I have an idea of what it could be, and what you describe makes sense if what I suspect is true, but," Thorn glanced at the surrounding countryside, taking in their surroundings and marking their location, "perhaps we shouldn't talk about it here."

Osman looked around and, after a few moments, recognized where they were—less than a league from the Cour-Vermane estate. "Perhaps not," he replied.

Thorn looked at Osman and the bloody stain on the ground where the boar had been, "Does this mean we're going to have to walk."

"Actually, the opposite. The apple is like nothing I have ever felt before. I usually need to eat after each time I soulchannel, change forms," Osman clarified for Thorn, "or there is a cost. But the apple is something different. It is like every part of me is overflowing with vitality. Like a took a sip from every living entity for miles around."

"So, saldrig again? You were a saldrig, right?" Thorn asked, "Talon read about them as a boy."

"Yes," Osman confirmed. "Oh, and he likes you. A lot. We call him the Judge, and he only tolerates most people, but you," Osman paused, "He knows you're his big bother." Osman scratched the back of his head awkwardly, "Our souls have the same scent."

Thorn grabbed each of Osman's upper arms in his own and, with an earnest look, said, "I would have it no other way, and that makes a lot of sense, considering."

Osman's smile beamed at Thorn, "Fair warning, he is like a kitten around you. A very large, very playful kitten. I can hold him back, but if you're up for it, he *really* wants to have some playtime with his big brother."

"Can't say I have ever sparred with a saldrig, but I'm here for it! Also, remind me to tell you about the mining machine Naz and I fought in Oldstone." Thorn replied.

Osman flurried into the Judge's flesh, and Thorn leaped upon his back. By the time they got back to Osman's camp, the moon was low, the fog was rising, and any scant warmth the late Autumn day had offered had turned into the frosty chill of night.

Thorn slid off Osman's back and stoked the fire's last embers. "I wasn't thinking ahead when I came," Thorn said, breath fogging as he looked at the single bedroll Osman had laid out.

Osman gave Thorn a playful bat with his huge saldrig paw and flopped down beside the bedroll. Thorn took the message immediately, laid on the bedroll, and put his head against the Judge's chest, who began to purr peacefully.

"Good night, brother," Thorn said, looking up into Osman's feline eyes.

*Good night, Krolh'dran,* Osman said internally, and before he could intervene, the judge gave Thorn a mighty lick with his tongue.

"Good night, Judge," Thorn replied, scratching the sensitive spot between the Judge's forelegs.

Sleep found them all as the moon set and the stars overhead arced through the firmament.

# CHAPTER TWENTY-FIVE

*Year 889* PXF *~ Late Autumn*

Osman awoke as the Judge with Thorn nestled into the warmth of his saldrig body like a kitten. The overwhelming feeling of protectiveness for Thorn was more significant than anything the Judge's instincts might inspire. It eclipsed even his feelings for his Krolh'dran. Within his chest, next to the Judge's mighty heart, he could feel the tiny matching beat of his qil for Quentin and that this human snoring gently next to him was that little heartbeat's true love.

Osman's shuddering intake of breath at the thought shook Thorn awake. He rolled over with a yawn and a stretch, giving the Judge's belly a rub in the process.

"Sleeping next to you is like curling up with a furry furnace, big guy. As much as I appreciate the warmth, we probably should talk. There's still a lot we need to discuss." Thorn said as he stood up, breath visible in the chill morning air. He ventured to the edge of their camp, the higher ground between the hills left blessedly free of the thick fog smothering the rest of the lowlands around them, and surveyed the dawn.

By the time he turned around, Osman had regained his natural form and was sitting on the bedroll.

Thorn looked over his shoulder as though he sensed the change. "How are the reserves holding out?" Thorn asked immediately, checking on Osman's well-being.

"Great. With the boar and the apple, at least two more channels, if not more, depending on what we are tasked with doing." Osman replied, adding with a smile, "Good morning, brother," Letting the words linger in his heart. The sight of Thorn looking out from the campsite lit by the morning sun transported Osman to a morning long ago in Kyflenor.

"Thorn, I would like to share something with you if you are willing," Osman said, continuing with a bit of formality. "It is how my people share themselves, both in simple greetings and when forging a deeper bond with those they care for."

"I would like that," Thorn replied. "What do I do?"

"Come sit," Osman said, motioning to the place across from himself. "For humans, it can be underwhelming, but for Uldani with deep connections, it can also be intense. For us, with our shared souls? Who's to say? So sitting down is probably for the best."

Osman continued, reciting all he remembered from when Anson taught him to read other people's faces. "My people believe that all emotions are etched upon our faces and that you can read them if both people open themselves to sharing them." Osman gave Thorn a nod to see if he was following. Thorn nodded back. "Just place your fingertips upon my face and let your feelings guide them to where they need to go."

Thorn tentatively placed his fingertips across Osman's forehead arrayed over his brow. Osman mirrored the configuration on Thorn's face and then opened his qil to being read.

A searing pain ripped through Osman as the sky turned blood red, and the earth cracked and blackened like a festering scab around them. He was no longer sitting, and Thorn stood beside him as the rising sun turned to an unblinking eye—Cerena's eye. It scanned the despoiled countryside in a manic search.

*Where are you, Osman? Those fools said an Uldani was skulking about. You can't hide from me.*

Thorn grabbed Osman's hand with one hand and yanked a necklace from around his neck with the other. He bound their hands together with the necklace's vinelike links adorned with what looked like a silver acorn. "This will hide us," He said with urgency. "Is this normal? It reeks of Cour-Vermane blood magic," he added, looking around at the haunting scene.

Osman replied, "No. Even qil visions don't feel like this." He scanned their surroundings, trying to discern how to break the connection that held them in this reality. To Osman's side was the spirit presence of the Matriarch, her form shimmering with the light of the Solenfel and eyes filled with burnished golden fire. Cerena's voice echoed across the scene before them.

*I feel you spying on me, Osman.*

The gaze of the solitary eye continued to roam over the landscape, now more slowly.

*Funny how in all your weepy pillow talk, you never mentioned that your father had another son.*

Osman squeezed Thorn's hand tighter, wondering if Cerena had somehow spotted them, mistaking Thorn's identity for some unknown brother. At the thought of the question, the Trickster appeared on

Thorn's shoulder and shook her head in the negative, confirming their shroud still held. Cerena was speaking of someone else.

*He did well to hide him near the Lyrian Rift.*

A wave of dread hit Osman. Its qil like a sinking galleon in his gut. Cold sweat broke out on his brow as he fought to remain still and silent, eyes locked on Thorn to draw strength. Cerena continued in a slithering lilt.

*They say the two most potent forces of the arcane are Blood and Love,
and while Talon's silly, deluded heart might have sent you what was
rightfully mine,
your own Blood will be what betrays his bond to you.*

*Bring me the Vermillion Blade or Quentin dies.*

An image of Arnadore Keep assaulted Osman's mind as the scene of the desiccated landscape shattered around him. Just as quickly as it had begun, Osman found himself in his original position, sitting across from Thorn with hands on one another's faces. Both their eyes wide with what they had just experienced.

"We shouldn't speak until we are back at the orchard," Thorn whispered urgently, his hand going to the silver acorn still hanging around his neck, unaffected by his actions within the vision.

Osman nodded, his thoughts spinning. Cerena had found Quentin. She referred to him as "his father's son" and not Richen or any in any way that connected him to Talon or Thorn. Was it possible that she didn't know that Quentin was actually Richen reborn? Would she care?

First things first. Thorn said they needed to get to Milgran's Orchard as quickly as possible. Osman felt his body dissolve into embers and reform as the Trickster. Osman did not fully understand the Trickster but knew some of what she could do. He leaped onto Thorn's shoulder and sank into her instincts with a single thought– *'the cidery.'*

Osman felt Thorn's body lurch in reaction to the dizzying and disconcerting sensation of the world seeming to fold around them while they stood still. Immovable objects leapt out of their way or distorted in strange, unnatural ways to allow their passage. After less than a handful of breaths, they arrived inside the cidery, standing near the shrouded night lantern that still cast its warm glow in the early morning hours.

Thorn folded over, only catching himself from falling by placing his hands on his knees. Osman deftly leapt off his back and returned to his humanoid form, patting his brother on his back while scanning the room for a rubbish barrel in case Thorn's stomach decided to completely turn over.

"Efficient, but not terribly pleasant, I'll admit." Osman consoled. "But far more useful than a returning stone. From what little I have tested, an open flame only needs to be present at your destination, and she can't cross open water."

"Gods! A warning would have been appreciated, brother." Thorn said, choking back bile. "The safest place to speak openly is in the orchard near the largest tree in the center." Thorn weakly stated as he righted himself, still wobbling on his heels.

Osman and Thorn stepped out of the cidery into the deep fog blanketing Milgran's Orchard. Osman almost grabbed the night lantern, seeing the impenetrable shroud of gray, but Thorn waved him off. Of course, he would know the way. Osman followed Thorn into the grove of apple trees that looked like regiments of ghostly sentinels standing at the ready.

If similar to the rest of his travel across Eleryon, Osman knew it could be hours before the sun's rays would burn through and chase away the rime frost that sugar-coated the smaller branches and few remaining apples on the trees. A shiver danced like an ice fairy up Osman's spine, the qil of déjà vu separating him from his body and making it seem like he was seeing through a second set of eyes just an instant behind himself. The deep fog and the orchard's crystalized foliage were playing tricks on Osman's senses, twisting the tress into the recalled memory of the bodies frozen in the guardian's grove.

As they progressed, the ranks of lesser trees seemed to part and gave homage to the looming presence of the grand central tree of the grove. Compared to the other trees in the orchard, it was like an oak among saplings. At nearly double the height and twice the breadth, it drifted imposingly out of the fog as they approached. Osman followed Thorn and ducked under the tree's low-hanging boughs, the first thick branch hanging barely above his head.

"Hopefully, this is safe from Cerena's magics. If it weren't, she wouldn't still be looking for the blade." Thorn stated as he laid a reverent hand on the scar where the Vermillion Blade was embedded in the tree's trunk.

"It's here?" Osman asked. "Practically in her backyard? And she never came for it? How?" he continued, bewildered.

Thorn told Osman about Caspharian, the sickle, and all the details of his battle against Rabian. "I think this is as close to hallowed ground as possible outside Caspharian's sacred groves and the spring I've encountered. If I've learned anything about my enigmatic conjoined patron and their nature, it's that balance is integral to their workings."

"The evil of the Vermillion Blade balanced with the blessing of the orchard." Osman pondered aloud.

"Exactly," Thorn confirmed. "This is the tree the apple came from."

Osman scanned the branches, which were bare of the remarkable fruit. "Are there no more?" he asked.

"He reached into his pack. I have only this one I know is from the tree. I picked the last ones remaining on its branches this morning, and they will be long sorted in with the rest of the harvest by now. Do you think you can spot them among all the others?" Thorn asked, a voice full of hope.

"I'm not sure. It was just a hunch that the apple was special, and that was when there were no others around. Perhaps, but certainly not easily." Osman reasoned, "I assume that is why the tree hasn't drawn any magical attention. If the apple's power were apparent, the tree would shine like a divine beacon to any who looked."

Thorn turned back to the tree, placing his hand again on the scar. He bowed his head and dejectedly sighed, saying, "I can't give it to her, Osman. Even to save your brother's life."

Osman crossed to Thorn and laid a hand on his back. "I know. We can't let her or your father ever possess the Vermillion Blade again." Osman paused, "But Quentin is not my brother. That's the name we gave Richen when he was reborn to hide his identity."

"What?" Thorn demanded. "Quentin is Richen?" Thorn spun as he dropped to sit on the ground, back against the tree beside the scar. He drew his knees up, supporting his head with hands at his forehead. "I nearly died in this exact spot to bind the blade, ready to trade my life to rid the world of its evil. Now, I must choose between Richen, whom I have loved for a lifetime, and unleashing the blade once again?" Thorn's voice sounded utterly hopeless.

"A friend of mine would say we should look at all the blessings we have in our boat and stop chasing the dream that got away," Osman said sagely, then adding, "But not this time. We are getting him back, *and* we'll keep the Vermillion Blade out of Cerena's hands."

Osman sat beside Thorn, putting his arm around his shoulders, and pulled him in tight as they leaned against the tree. "We just need a plan."

Thorn drifted out of his hopelessness and stated, "Talon worked in the keep for fifteen years, from lowly guard to Knight Captain. I know its layout and passages like the back of my hand."

Osman squeezed Thorn's shoulders, "There we go." He added his insight to their assets. "From my experience with one of her creatures, Cerena can't detect me when I'm in my soulchanneled forms. So we potentially could have the element of surprise."

Thorn mused thoughtfully, "Naz has been working on something for me. It wouldn't fool her for long, if at all, but perhaps it could distract her long enough to be useful if she was already startled."

"In every situation," Osman cleared his throat with a hint of embarrassment, "Cerena always demanded to be in control. Once we take that away from her, she gets flustered." He clarified, "She enters everything she does assuming she has thought of all possibilities and planned for them. The more we can keep her off balance, the better."

"We are going to need time," Thorn said. "We can't rush into this. One mistake could doom all of us and deliver the Vermillion Blade into her hands."

"I'm not sure how we can get her a message without giving away any of our advantages," Osman stated.

"Oh, I have an idea of who 'those fools' she mentioned most likely were," Thorn said, rolling his eyes.

# CHAPTER TWENTY-SIX



Osman trotted around the apple trees as the Trickster, his coat soaking up the late morning sun that had finally broken through the fog. Each drop of melted frost hitting the ground released a cornucopia of smells, chief among them the pungent aroma of forgotten apples left to ferment. The Trickster had no doubt that where there were ripening odors, mice would never be far behind. While not as dramatic as the Judge's hunting, the Trickster outsmarting orchard rats and their plethora of escape routes both into the trees and under the ground offered Osman its own form of exhilaration.

Thorn assured Osman before leaving him for his daily duties that Gwen wouldn't be taking potshots at him. She knew the benefits of a predator in the grove come Fall, and all who worked the fields of Eleryon knew it as well. Rodent populations exploded every harvest and were the far larger threat if not culled before Winter. Lucky for all, with the effects of the apple wearing off and wanting to save their last one for whatever plan they hatched, Osman had a saldrig-sized appetite even when channeling the Trickster's body.

Half sunk into the Trickster's instincts, Osman found the quick and efficient hunting of the orchard's mice a balm for the chaotic disorder of his thoughts about a plan to outsmart Cerena. The Trickster's hunting tactics began to form a structure to the disjointed pieces of information circling in his mind. But the real breakthrough came when he encountered a rat viper stalking a fat mouse half drunk on fermented apples. So intent on its quarry and overconfident in its fangs and poison, the snake never realized it was being preyed upon until Osman had it in his jaws and snapped its neck with a quick shake of the Trickster's head.

The key to success would be to lure Cerena into a trap they set, not to foil hers.

"A nice ginger tabby cat would be a heck of a lot more convenient to explain being in the storehouse than a fox if we got caught," Gwen said pointedly to Osman as she stood with one hip cocked to the side and her ever-present rifle cradled under her arm. The three stood under the apple tree at the center of the orchard. A silence had hung between them until Gwen had broken the tension with her comment about Osman becoming a farmhouse cat.

"Unfortunately, that's not how it works," Osman explained. "Trust me, the cat I can become would be *much* harder to explain."

"Right. The saldrig. See, I reckoned giant long-toothed cats were just a myth to keep people away from that frozen island of yours." Gwen said, giving Osman a nod to acknowledge his Uldani heritage, "But, Thorn here assures me you two were gallivanting around in the moonlight like an imp riding a wicker hog on the Drowned Moon."

Gwen's straightforward, outspoken manner had won Osman over even while he was still in the Trickster's form when she met them at the barn after darkness fell to look for apples from the central tree. To Osman's disappointment, none of the empowered apples jumped out to the Trickster's senses from the towering stacks of crates and barrels in the storage stalls. There were indeed some in the mix, but finding them would be all but impossible. It would be like looking for a diamond in the snow. Realizing a greater need to solidify a plan, Osman had leaped onto Thorn's shoulder and nudged him to head for the orchard.

Gwen seemed thoroughly unimpressed with Osman's return to his Uldani form, only noting. "I kinda thought you were gonna be naked." Her tone suggested that Osman had accrued an unpaid debt that he would owe at a future date, which made Osman appreciate her even more.

"I think we can hold off Cerena for a few days, but no more before she becomes impatient. That gives us until Hearth's Rest, at best." Osman offered.

"So we have four days." Thorn stated flatly, "We'll need to gather all the assets we have at our disposal and figure out how we can use them to our best advantage." He continued, "If the plan includes going to the keep, we can utilize Balanon's sanctuary under the ruins of the Sojourn's Rest. We'll still have to contend with the creatures inside the walls of Arnadore, but with the returning stone Balanon gave me, that gets us half way to the keep."

"In order to upend whatever she's planning, we will have to fool not only Cerena but her magic as well," Osman postulated. "From my experience and the things I saw she was capable of while we were together," Osman held his eyes on Thorn, keeping them from darting to Gwen, not knowing how much she knew of his involvement in the coup attempt, "Her magic is sight-based. Without a doubt, she will spot magical illusions and enchanted objects of any kind from leagues away. Maybe we can use that to our advantage?"

"I think I have that covered," said Thorn. "But retrieving Quentin and getting back out again is going to require a heck of a trick."

"There's no way she's giving y'all what you want," Gwen said, butting into the exchange. "A snake is always a snake, and she has too big a prize just to give it away if she can end up with both. Whoever she offers you in trade for that thing," Gwen motioned with her head toward the tree, "won't be Richen." Gwen stated flatly. "Or Quentin or the person you think it is," she added, trying to cover all her bases. "You boys and your names," she sighed with mock exasperation.

The three plotted deep into the night until the fog settled in, and Thorn and Gwen's teeth began to chatter.

Gwen looked to Osman, rubbing her hands together to make some warmth, "I'd invite you into the house, but there's five of us sharing it right now, and no matter how careful you are, if an Uldani is spotted in the main house, word will get around. You sure you can't become a tabby cat?"

"It's fine," Osman offered. "I need to figure a few things out about this before I change back to the Trickster for the day," Osman said. He drew the dagger, which had changed again, out from where it was tucked through his belt. The blade now glowed with a dim orange heat. Sapphires ornamented the ends of the cross guard, their blue depths seeming to wink conspiratorially in the moonlight. White leather wrapped the hilt's grip, giving the totality of the weapon the coloration of the Trickster's tail.

Thorn looked at it for a moment before, even with all the changes, recognition hit him. "Is that Talon's dagger? The one he stabbed you with at the keep?"

"It is," Osman answered. Osman's eyes that had been on the dagger found Thorn's. "Talon's mother gave it to me when she set me on my Qat'malorn to repay my debt for betraying Talon. For betraying you." His eyes went back to the dagger. "It's changed a lot since then. We both have."

Osman caught a pained look in Thorn's eyes before he looked away. But it wasn't at the mention of the betrayal. It seemed to be more in empathy for Osman's guilt. His voice drifted to Osman gently, "Love is a force as strong as the tides; it can change a person's life as easily as a storm reshapes the shore. When wielded as a weapon, even the foundations of who we hope we are become vulnerable to its power." Thorn laid a hand on Osman's shoulder. "I forgave you long ago, brother. It's time for you to forgive yourself."

Thorn nodded in assurance before turning and walking into the darkness, following Gwen, who had drifted away during their exchange. Osman stood alone under the apple tree, the gathering fog beginning to pool around his ankles and his breath rising like a ghost in the moonlight from the chill night air.

Osman looked past the moon and into the night. Far to the south, Yanri and Anson were searching for Quentin in Lyria Bay. He had no way to get them a message and wasn't sure he would send one if he could. Not until Quentin was safe. At least they were far from Cerena and out of harm's way.

Osman examined the dagger in his hand. The blade had changed aspects each time he channeled a different spirit he carried, reflecting the forms he took. This ornamental aspect always appeared after the Trickster. Previously, Osman had witnessed the dagger as an icy cold raw iron blade all but identical to its original form after channeling the Judge and the misty stiletto after the Matriarch. He had yet to see what the dagger would become after the Prince, but until necessary, he didn't want to use the resources it would take to soulchannel into the Prince's form while restricted to only a diet of mice.

Osman recognized the elemental pattern to the dagger's aspects but, other than their appearance, had not tested any unique enchantment each aspect might carry. Osman tentatively touched the glowing ornamental blade, testing it for internal heat correlating to its fiery origin; however, he found it cool to the touch. Osman even drove the dagger into a fallen dry branch to see if perhaps his target would burst into flames but to no effect. It wasn't until, in mild frustration and recognition of its perfect balance, he threw the dagger into a nearby apple tree that he unlocked its secret.

With but the thought of retrieving the dagger, the world folded around Osman, and he was transported to the dagger's location, finding his hand firmly on the hilt. He threw the blade again, and, like before, Osman found himself where the weapon was embedded after experiencing the same disorienting translocation as the Trickster's ability. Again and again, Osman tested the dagger's range and limitations until his guts were heaving from the repeated translocations.

Osman sat on the ground to regain his balance and composure. He quickly assessed his well-being, specifically trying to determine if using the dagger had exhausted some or all of his internal reserves of life energy that empowered his soulchanneling. As far as Osman could surmise, whatever powered the dagger's ability was separate from what enabled him to change forms.

The fog was getting thicker as morning approached, and Osman spent the rest of the night trying to get more accustomed to the dizzying sensation of the Trickster's dagger. Osman drove himself through the old training Talon had drilled into him in the days with the Arnadore Guard, adding translocations into the mix of maneuvers. The ever-deepening fog made for an exciting challenge, and Osman realized that the unique power of the Trickster's blade did not rely on sight, just will. It gave him an idea that he would pose to the group when they met again.

Dawn brought a ruddy glow to the deep mists surrounding Osman. It also brought a rumble to his stomach, and he felt his teeth elongating and sharpening as the qil of hunger filled him. With the qil, Osman felt the chill of cold iron in his hand and realized he was no longer holding the Trickster's ornamental dagger but the Judge's frost-covered blade.

Osman raised his free hand to his teeth, feeling their feral shape. Was his qil the connection to controlling the blade's aspect? Osman closed his eyes and relived the moment he first saw Lumenaria. The qil of awe burst from his spine as the Matriarch's ghostly wings and the dagger transformed from the Judge's iron blade to the Matriarch's shimmering gray stiletto. Osman's excitement at the discovery was short-lived as his stomach reasserted its demands, dispelling his awe and returning the dagger to the Judge's cold iron. Osman noted he would have to work on controlling his emotions to master the dagger's aspects and realized he had yet to feel a qil associated with the Trickster or the Prince. But that would have to wait for tomorrow.

The sounds of the orchard waking for the day began to drift through the fog, heralding the end of Osman's time in his Uldani form. He channeled into the Trickster and spent the next few hours greeting the rodents of the orchard by inviting them to be his breakfast. Belly full and head swimming in ideas, Osman then spent the rest of the day napping in sunbeams on the low roof above the barrel storage shed attached to the cidery.

# CHAPTER TWENTY-SEVEN

*Year 889* PXF *~ Late Autumn*

Osman had already donned his Uldani from when Thorn arrived with the fall of twilight across the orchard. He held in his hand what appeared to be an empty quiver devoid of the arrows it would typically carry. After a quick embrace in greeting, Thorn spoke.

"Naz's contribution to our efforts has arrived," he said, lifting the quiver.

"I'm a horrible shot if our plan hinges on arrows, and my impression of Gwen is that she only shoots bullets," Osman remarked.

"There are two rules to artifice and enchantment: items should convey precisely what they are and do, or they should never be what they seem." Thorn recited in a strange accent Osman could not place. "Or so Naz always says."

Thorn reached into the quiver and withdrew its contents, eliciting a gasp of astonishment from Osman. Thorn had drawn the full ten-foot length of the Vermillion Blade from out of the standard-sized quiver.

"Naz has been working on this replica for several years in case anyone came to the orchard investigating the disappearance of Rabian and the Vermillion Blade. From my descriptions and his knowledge of my curse, even its magical aura *should* fool most anyone," Thorn said. "Of course, Cerena isn't just anyone."

Osman let out a low whistle. "It certainly looks as I remember it. But won't she realize it is a fake as soon as she tries to wield it?"

"That's both the intent and the challenge," Thorn explained. "It's cursed. Naz and I always assumed it would be Toman or another magic user who could track the Vermillion Blade to this location. So, we made the curse especially devastating to those who delve in the realms of the arcane. Undoing the curse to release their magic instead of breaking it directly will take time." Thorn continued, "The trick is to distract her enough that her zeal for the blade erases any caution she might typically have before taking hold of it."

"That's going to be a challenge," Osman agreed. "Me walking in the gate with the Vermillion Blade to trade for Quentin is giving her exactly what she wants. As well as she knows me, my willingness to trade or risk the Vermillion Blade will immediately raise her suspicions."

The two looked at each other in silence, neither having a suggestion on how to overcome this new hurdle. "We'll work on it. Maybe Gwen will have an idea when she arrives." Osman said when he finally broke the silence. "In the meantime, I discovered something while working with the dagger last night." Osman threw the dagger, currently in its Trickster form, at a nearby apple tree and translocated to its new location.

The movement startled Thorn in its suddenness, and Osman could swear his complexion turned a little green in memory of his travels with the trickster, but he admitted, "Okay, *that* could definitely be helpful."

"And I don't have to see the dagger to travel to it." Osman closed his eyes, threw the dagger into a different tree, and transported himself to it just as easily. "Which gave me an idea. If you can get that message to Cerena, we could meet for the exchange at dawn while the fog is still thick. Between the dagger and the Matriarch being at home in the mists of Mornaserin, that's two advantages for us she won't be expecting."

"Well, the fog won't block any magical detection, but anything that obscures the line of sight of the naked eye will undoubtedly help," Thorn said.

"Oh, and if I can call upon your training as an artificer, there is also this," Osman imagined Lolly's table in the kitchens of the Sojourn's Rest loaded with all his favorites, eliciting a pang of hunger in his belly and the growth of his teeth into saldrig fangs. The blade in his hand morphed into the cold iron of the Judge's dagger. "Each of the spirits I hold has an associated emotion that manifests as a unique qil, and that qil draws out an aspect of the dagger."

Osman, pointing out the differences to the iron dagger in his hand, waited for a response from Thorn, then realized Thorn's attention was not on the weapon at all. Osman met his wide eyes.

"Are those fangs? Did you just grow fangs?" Thorn asked cautiously.

"Oh yeah," Osman replied proudly, smiling wide to fully display his longer, sharper teeth and long, pointed canines. "They freaked me out the first time, too," he added casually. Caught up in the moment, as though showing off a gifted toy at New Dawn's Beginning and not reading Thorn's trepidation. "They can get even bigger, too!" Osman pulled the image of Yanri lying in bed at Anson's home into his mind and felt another wave of hunger overcome him. His upper canines grew even longer, and the lower ones that had only sharpened before now thrust up from his gums menacingly.

Thorn stepped back away from Osman, a mixture of horror and curiosity on his face.

Osman put up both hands non-threateningly. "Still just me, brother." He said gently through his toothy maw. "This is just your friend, the Judge, manifesting to my emotions. In this case, hunger."

Thorn's eyes widened further at hearing the word 'hunger.'

"Seriously?" Osman exclaimed, "Not for you, for food!" Osman said exasperated, then added under his breath, "And for someone else." Directing his words back at Thorn. "You jump on the Judge's back without a single qualm, but your brother sporting saldrig teeth is where you draw the line?"

"It's just—wait, 'Someone else?'" Thorn looked at Osman with a wry, teasing smile, all trepidation and fear erased from his face. "Little brother, have you found someone?"

Osman felt the blush rise to his cheeks and the gentle knot of love twist in his stomach. "His name is Yanri." Osman scratched the back of his head as he replied, unable to contain the even larger smile that came to his lips.

Thorn rushed Osman playfully, punching at his stomach teasingly. "Are those big ole fangs for him, then? You said hunger, right?" Thorn stepped back and mockingly looked at Osman's pants, "Oh, I can see that now."

"Thorn!" Osman said animatedly, covering his crotch with his hands only partially jokingly. "Shouldn't we get back to planning?"

"Not an instant before you tell me all about Yanri." Thorn admonished, sitting down under the tree and patting the ground beside him. "That is if you can sit with all that going on," Thorn added with a laugh.

Osman crossed his arms in exasperation and remained standing where he was.

"I am still your elder even if I don't look it," Thorn said. "If I have learned anything in this life, it is that nothing is more important than this moment right now. It doesn't matter what the moment is; just don't let any of them slip away worrying about the future. Tomorrow can wait."

Osman acquiesced and, with an embarrassed minor adjustment, sat next to Thorn.

"So, tell me about him," Thorn said.

Osman gazed out into the orchard. "He's too young, and too innocent, and so naïve," Osman said dejectedly and then added with dreamy wistfulness in his voice, "and so utterly perfect." Osman looked to Thorn, unsure of what to expect, but saw on his face a beaming smile.

"Sounds like someone I know," Thorn said. "I am so happy for you. You deserve every joy he brings you."

Osman let out a breath he didn't realize he was holding. "Thank you, brother." He tried to hide his mouth full of fangs as he smiled.

"No, no. Let me see them," Thorn said.

Osman set free the smile he had been restraining.

"Wow. They really are miniatures of the Judge's, aren't they?" Thorn observed. Osman could almost hear the change in Thorn's thoughts as he tapped into Talon's tactical experience. "You know, in a pinch, these could save your life." In an analytical tone, Thorn asked, "Do you mind?" as a small arcane ball of light appeared between them, and his hand was inches away from Osman's mouth.

"Um, I guess not," He answered.

"Well, they certainly are sharp," Thorn commented, testing the edge of a longer upper canine with his finger. His face was now inches from Osman's as he examined his fanged teeth. "But they are almost too long to be really useful at this size," Thorn added.

Osman opened his mouth further—far more than any humanoid should be able to. A double-hinged jaw inherited from the Judge, along with the teeth, allowed his chin to drop nearly to his throat. Osman felt his face turn beet red as he recalled when he discovered this particular inheritance.

"Well, then, I stand corrected," Thorn stated. He pulled away and sat back where he was. "We should add that to our tricks if the need arises." Getting back on track, Thorn asked, "So what were you saying about needing my skills as an artificer before I got sidetracked by your teeth and your boyfriend?"

Osman grinned again even more sheepishly, hearing Thorn referring to Yanri as his boyfriend, then presented Thorn the Judge's dagger, saying, "I don't know what enchantment manifests with this aspect. It's from the Judge, so perhaps cold or ice? Can your training help figure out what it does exactly?"

Thorn traced a few simple arcane runes in the air with his fingers. "Interesting. You are correct about ice, but not necessarily cold. More of a minor stasis." Thorn stated. "Not terribly powerful. Most could shake it off eventually, but it would slow them down momentarily."

"And I have one more that I can manifest," Osman said. "Don't worry. It isn't as dramatic as the fangs." Osman fell into the memory of seeing the world tree for the first time and the awe it inspired in him. He felt his fangs disappear and jaw snap back into place as the Matriarch's phantom wings sprang from his back. Osman held the Matriarch's stiletto out to Thorn so he could once again trace the runes to identify what enchantment it held.

Thorn looked Osman over, "So nothing?" Thorn asked.

"Well, it feels like I have giant wings on my back," Osman replied. "And before you ask, no, I can't fly." He added sardonically, seeing the question race to Thorn's lips. "I checked."

"You know, it begs the question, though—why not?" Thorn stated. "If the fangs become real, why not the wings? It's something to think about." He then traced the runes over the blade and, after a moment's contemplation, said, "It's a phase blade. Not exactly how someone like Naz could make it, but it's the same idea. It can slide through even the smallest gaps in armor or the tiniest cracks in almost anything. It only partially exists on the material plane."

Osman looked at the blade and said, "That makes sense. I pried open a lock way too quickly and easily when I was stealing clothes in Lumenaria."

Thorn looked at Osman with a questioning eyebrow raised. "You care to explain why you were stealing clothes?"

"Well, I was basically naked and wanted to blend in with all the temptarai arriving at Lumenaria. Oh! And I didn't know him yet, but Yanri was there." Osman explained badly.

"Unless you have more surprises or some grand plan you have invented connecting all the eggs we have in the air that soundly defeats Cerena, I think you need to tell me all about it," Thorn said, wrapping his arm over Osman's shoulder.

Just before midnight, Gwen joined them under the apple tree, having made excuses for Thorn's absence all evening and making sure no prying eyes ventured into the Orchard. They caught her up on the replica Vermillion Blade, the different forms of Osman's dagger, and Thorn's plan for a meeting at dawn on Hearth's Rest.

"No doubt it was Jenkins and Lander who told Cerena that an Uldani had visited the Orchard," Thorn explained. "It's been a couple of days without any activity or word, so Cerena or their own curiosity will have them sniffing around here again soon. I figure we just write Cerena a note of where and when the exchange can happen."

"And how do you reckon they won't just take a torch to the whole place?" Gwen asked.

"Well, you are about as close to a neutral party as one can get in these parts, and that has value. Even to someone like Cerena." Thorn said. Gwen acquiesced to his logic and nodded her approval.

"So tell me more about this fake Vermillion Blade. How's it work, and are there any more fancy things it can do?" Gwen asked.

"Well, other than the curse, which activates with a rune on its shaft, it can hold a few simple spells. Naz included some scrolls we could choose from to read into it now that can be cast later," Thorn explained, listing off the scrolls Naz had sent with the blade. "And I have to feed it some of my blood."

"Wait, what?" Osman and Gwen asked simultaneously.

"Calm down. This is Naz we're talking about. I literally have entrusted my life to his magic." Thorn said calmly. "Without Cour-Vermane blood, its aura won't match the Vermillion Blade's. And Cerena has seen the Vermillion Blade multiple times, including up close in action when she dueled you and Talon in Elery Square." Thorn said, looking at Osman.

The three spent the next several hours debating what scrolls to imbue into the weapon, talking through every combination that might be helpful. But, even after settling on those, they still had yet to have a surefire way to get the cursed glaive into Cerena's hands without her suspecting something. With only a handful of hours before dawn, Thorn suggested, "Brother, why don't you sleep inside tonight."

Gwen immediately crossed her arms and said disapprovingly, "It was too risky last night, and it's still too risky tonight. I said what I said."

Thorn suggested, "For an Uldani, yes, but a fox is easier to hide, and with my room on the ground floor and my perchance of sleeping with the window open, Osman has a quick way out, and we could explain it if we had to in a pinch." He looked to Osman, "That also gets you ready for your day in the orchard tomorrow."

"Works for me," Osman said. "As long as you are okay with it, Gwen."

Gwen gave it a thought and then nodded. "I've had to explain stranger things than a fox finding a warm place to sleep."

Osman shimmered into the Trickster and leaped onto Thorn's shoulders, draping his body around his neck like a fur stole. The house was dark, the rest of the residents having already retired for the night after a hard day's labor. It gladdened Osman to see the genuine hospitality evident in the farmhouse's simple décor. He smiled inwardly at the ease and genuine affection with which Thorn hugged Gwen goodnight. She climbed the stairs, and he passed around them to a door tucked beneath the landing.

Thorn's room was far smaller than the suite of rooms Talon had inhabited at the Sojourn's Rest and not much larger than the room Osman had rented there after the gala. However, what it lacked in size it made up for in character.

A hand-crafted patchwork quilt covered the bed adjacent to a triple set of pane windows that looked out into the fog. If Osman had his bearings correct, the windows would offer an expansive picturesque view of the orchard come afternoon. A small rough-hewn wooden chest of drawers was on the wall opposite the bed, on top of which were several soft-bound books that looked like farmer's almanacs. Across from the door was a desk littered with journals, charcoal pencils, and loose pieces of parchment. A few sack-cloth tunics hung off the back of the desk's chair, one on top of the other.

Osman leaped off Thorn's shoulders and began to curl up in one of the corners. Thorn opened one of the windows next to the bed wide enough for a fox to pass through and said, "Not a chance, little brother, there is plenty of room on the bed. It's not like you're the Judge or even your new size. Heck, I'm not even my old size anymore." He added, "Besides, I owe you for not letting me freeze the other night."

Osman gave Thorn a bright, foxy smile.

"Hey, don't get all fangy on me. I know what that means now!" Thorn joked. He pulled off his work clothes and donned a long sleeping shirt as Osman leaped onto the bed. Thorn joined him and laid his head on one side of the oversized goose feather pillow. Osman curled up on the remaining portion, nose nuzzled into Thorn's mass of unruly hair.

Among all his brother's belongings and with the Trickster basking in his familiar scent, even Thorn's snoring couldn't keep Osman from being lulled instantly to sleep.

Osman stumbled upon the idea while drifting in the liminal space between awake and dreaming. The night before, even with every conceivable combination of scrolls, the three had been unable to overcome the most fundamental flaw in their plan—Osman bringing Cerena the Vermillion Blade. Whether he offered it willingly or challenged her to take it by force, she would have all the time she needed to examine the replica closely. Just a moment's caution could alert her to the curse Naz had laid upon it and undo their plan. The idea churning in his head might negate that caution.

During the night, Osman had dreamed of Talon and their days in Arnadore. The familiarity and comfort of Talon's presence washed over Osman, and he found that he too was the same as he had been in those days. Talon towered over him, a grim protector looming beside his smaller, lithe form as they traversed the taverns of Elery Square and the Trellis Market. The dream settled on a single night after flashing through a series of overlapping memories. It was the night of the gala, and Osman sat behind Talon, braiding his hair into the Uldani knots that marked him as his Krolh'dran—his big brother and life's guide. A deep resounding joy and contentment filled Osman as he laughed and Talon complained about the braiding.

In the back of Osman's mind, even in the dream, a pang of guilt intermingled with his happiness to see Talon. A part of him knew the person sitting before him in the dream was gone. Thorn was his brother now and, in many ways, always had been. At Osman's thought of Thorn, the dream lurched sideways, and suddenly, Thorn and Talon stood side by side before him. The juxtaposition of the two together thrust Osman out of his slumber so disorientingly that he couldn't recognize where he was or *what* he was for a moment that felt both instantaneous and eternal.

That was when the idea was born. The Trickster's instincts, which had also leapt to alertness from the dream, ready to fight or flee, considered the thought drifting through Osman's mind. Her voice came to him.

*It could work*

Osman asked internally, "But can we do it?" already knowing the answer. Somewhere deep inside, be it his own instincts, the wisdom of his father, or one of the other forces within him, he knew the answer was yes.

Osman crept off Thorn's pillow in the pre-dawn gloaming, and while the Trickster leaped through the farmhouse window, it was the Judge who disappeared into the thick fog. Osman needed to hunt more than just mice this day.

Osman presented the plan to Thorn and Gwen that night. Thorn's eyes grew wide with dismay and then disgust as Osman laid out his idea. The color drained from Thorn's face and Osman heard his breath turn into shallow gasps as though he were a fish gasping upon the shore. Before Osman fully finished, Thorn spun away from the group and staggered away into the darkness.

"Thorn!" Osman called after him, following him.

Catching his breath Thorn found his voice, "No. Just No. I can't. I can't even think about it." He spun to face Osman. "Why? How could you conceive of this?" voice shaking with emotion.

"It's okay. We'll think of something else. We don't have to do it." Osman placed his hand on Thorn's shoulder.

"No! Gods damn it!" Thorn said through clenched teeth, knocking Osman's hand away. He squeezed his eyes shut, releasing tears that he hadn't shed. "That's the problem. You're right. It *will* work." He said just above a whisper. "But, I am not okay with this, and don't you dare make me be a part of it." Osman tried to reach out to Thorn, but he put his hands up, refusing the gesture. Thorn turned his back on Osman and walked away.

Still reeling from Thorn's rebuff, Osman returned to Gwen, who did not attempt to hide her displeasure. "You don't have a clue what you've just forced on him, do you?" she accused. "Give me proof you can do it, and I will bring him around if only to end all this for him."

Osman tried to explain himself but Gwen silenced him with a raised hand.

"I hope it's worth it. He may never forgive you. Now show me." Gwen said flatly.

Osman nodded, calmed his nerves, and remorsefully showed Gwen how he would once again betray his Krolh'dran.

# CHAPTER TWENTY-EIGHT

*Year 889* PXF *~ Late Autumn*

Cerena smiled graciously at the two commoners from the orchard who had arrived in her 'parlor' via the returning stone she had provided them.

"Oi, we came here right like you said," the one called Landers proclaimed. "We didn't even get our free cider out of that old bag, Milgran, so I suppose you owe us."

"And, don't you go acting all poor and destitute or nothin'," the one called Jenkins added. "We reckon you're pretty well off and gots magic of your own 'cause ain't no one who just hands out a returning stone."

"Yeah, we coulda sold that for good coin, but out of the graciousness of our 'arts we done come back with this here note." Landers said with a lofty air. "Given us by the Lady Milgran herselfs." Landers placed the note on the table with an awkward flourish.

"Of course," Cerena practically purred at the two. "I am deeply indebted to your graciousness. Let me see what I can offer you two, fine gents." Cerena, wearing a glamor to make herself look like an eccentric commoner, made a great show of looking around the room that she had likewise cloaked in illusions. It currently appeared to be the small hovel outside the walls of Arnadore where she typically received informants from around the region. With a far more polished flourish than Landers had displayed with the note, she turned around with an object in each hand. "As you so cleverly surmised, I do indeed have a bit of magic, and while I have little use for coin, I have plenty of enchanted items to trade."

Cerena placed the two items on the table, "One for each of you, but you will have to choose who gets what." She continued, motioning to the vial of swirling liquid she had placed on the table before them, "This is an elixir of perpetual good health. You will never get ill or suffer from pestilence, and most injuries will heal practically overnight." She then motioned to the silver ring beside the potion, "And this is a silver tongue ring. No matter how bold the lie, people will believe what you say is true."

The two looked covetously at the items before them, but she could see the telltale workings of a devious mind behind Jenkins' eyes.

"Oi, I'll take the ring," Jenkins said, "cause you get that cough come every winter, and you can finally get rid of those scabies you're always itching at."

"That's mighty thoughtful of you," Landers said, offering his hand for a shake. "I do hate them little buggers always irritating me." The two shook hands with a smile and gentlemanly nod.

Jenkins snatched the ring quick as a viper and placed it on his finger. "Landers, that vial is poison. Don't you drink it no matter what she says." He said in a calm voice. "She's trying to kill you. You should run."

Landers looked with horror at the vial and then Cerena before bolting for the illusionary door. Cerena remained silent, watching the scene unfold before her. Jenkins immediately grabbed the vial and chugged it down. Landers said with rising panic as he fumbled with the doorknob, "Hey, the door's locked." He looked over his shoulder as Cerena allowed all the illusions cloaking the cell they occupied fade away and dropped the glamor she had wrapped herself in.

Lander's screams of terror were only matched by Jenkins' gurgling screech of agony as his flesh began to writhe and twist under his skin as the 'potion' began its grim work.

Cerena calmly read and pocketed the note. Turning from her two visitors, she strode from the cell, locking it behind her. Two days would be plenty of time to prepare. Traversing the rest of the cells filled with her creations, she arrived where she had secured her other guest and looked in on him. Quentin's eyes blazed with unmasked hatred as Cerena peered through the small window in his prison's door. He strained against the chains binding him to the wall, clenching his teeth in frustration and fury. The black runes carved into the stones of his cell flashed sickly green at his rising anger until he lowered his eyes and slumped back to the ground.

Everything was working out perfectly. Soon, the Vermillion Blade would be hers, and she would free herself from Toman Cour-Vermane.

Time had not been kind to Cerena. Three years ago, when her attempts to retrieve the Vermillion Blade from the Uldani Isles failed disastrously, Toman paid her a visit. Her uncle did not tolerate disobedience. It was bad enough that she had attempted to reclaim the blade without his consent or knowledge, but her failure in such a public manner while implicating Eleryon was intolerable.

The reprimand he administered to Cerena had been cruel, brutal, and unending. He had violated her mind, flesh, and soul within her own home for months before his anger was sated. When Toman had finally left her for dead, Cerena had been reduced to something lesser than even one of her mutated creations held captive in the dungeons. However, her magic had protected the one part of her that was truly her own—an undetected and unscathed white-hot need to kill Toman Cour-Vermane.

After Toman's admonishments, Cerena had licked her wounds, freed all the creatures she was working on to roam Arnadore, and abandoned Eleryon. If she were ever to have a chance at killing Toman, she must possess the Vermillion Blade. She might have been thwarted in her attempts to reach Osman on the Uldani Isles, but she had never forgotten that strange second path she detected with Toman's blood leading away from the Isles to the west.

Cerena looked again at the slumping form of Quentin. He had been at the end of that trail of blood magic, and now he was delivering Cerena her salvation.

Osman, wearing the Trickster's form, was dozing on the barrel storage roof when Thorn found him. It had not been a peaceful rest. The guilt plaguing Osman's mind had disallowed sleep, and he had long since finished his morning hunt for rodents.

"We're leaving for Balanon's within the hour. I'll meet you by the central tree." Thorn's delivery was brusk and cold. Osman slunk through the grove; the Trickster's head and tail hung low to wait by the tree for Thorn's arrival. Half an hour later, he arrived laden with packs and the strange quiver that held the fake Vermillion Blade.

With no more than a nod of acknowledgment to Osman, Thorn said, "Well, here we go." He lifted Balanon's returning stone to activate it, leaving Osman barely any time to leap on his shoulder before they disappeared. Upon their arrival, Thorn unceremoniously shrugged Osman off his tense form, saying, "Balanon has warded this place against magical scrying, so you can show yourself."

Osman shimmered to his Uldani form in a sparking of embers as Thorn turned and walked away. Osman looked around the dim chamber lit by the soft buzzing glow of arcane light. He could pick out the familiar details that revealed it to be the baths below the Sojourn's Rest, but it was devastating to see them so changed from how he remembered them.

A half-elf with a shaved head came up the steps out of the drained central pool. "*Valhanari*, cousin," he said, offering the traditional greeting between elves and Uldani. "I am Balanon and you must be Osman. We've never met, but I have heard stories of your time with Talon."

"*Valhanari*," Osman replied with a bow of respect. "Thank you for your hospitality. We honor the opening of your home to us and offer deference to our elders." Osman recited the formal words unused by him for decades, adding his own commentary, "However, we are perhaps not the most gracious company right now."

Balanon looked across the dark chamber to where Osman could see Thorn near a row of cots sorting items from pack to pack. He said, "While Talon was known for his bouts of pique as a child, I must admit I have never known Thorn to have them." The half-elf looked back at Osman, "But if you are to have any hope of success tomorrow, you should not carry this animosity between you any further. If you cannot forgive one another, at least find a balance between you." Balanon drifted away back to his work.

*Balance.* There was that word again. Thorn had spoken about his conjoined god of nature. His own journey had taken him to the inception points between paired elements. The Vermillion Blade and the orchard, the past and the future—all felt like they were balanced precariously on the fulcrum of now.

Three months ago, in time as he knew it, Osman was holding Quentin in his arms as a newborn infant, but that was twenty-seven years ago to the man now held captive in the keep. Osman felt the qil of his connection to

Quentin beating in rhythm beside his heart. His eyes then found Thorn, now sitting on a small cot across the room, shoulders slumped, head in hands with hair cascading like a curtain shrouding his downturned face. A wave of tenacious resolve washed over Osman—to protect his brother, to protect Quentin, and to protect a love that had endured nearly forty years. Osman's back straightened as the qil of his responsibility to them reinforced his spine, and then he felt them—the Prince's massive antlers weighing upon his brow.

Osman drew the dagger from his belt. It had become a wicked curved bone knife with a hilt of raw antler. As he held it, Osman felt a strange tightness in his skin as though it was made of tanned leather. On a hunch, Osman drew the blade across his palm. It left nary a trace nor cut. He tested the edge with his thumb and felt its razor sharpness. Osman tried it again on his palm using far more pressure than should be required, and this time, it did bite into the flesh, but just barely.

Osman wanted to abide by Thorn's wishes and respect his space, but knowing the full extent of the Prince's blade could be critical. Osman crossed the room to Thorn, walking between the drained central pool and the roiling surface of the heated pool that Balanon seemed to now use for sterilization. He stood a short distance from Thorn, waiting to be noticed and invited closer. Thorn did not change his position, speaking to him with his head still down, words addressing the floor, "You can use one the cots at the end of the row."

"Thorn, I've unlocked the Prince's dagger," Osman said softly. "It's protective somehow, but I don't know to what extent."

Thorn released a heavy sigh and lifted his head, looking to Osman's face, a rueful retort on his lips. Before he could say anything, his eyes crinkled in amusement and said, "Those are new."

"What?" Osman asked, bewildered. Thorn's eyes were on Osman's forehead. "Oh, gods!" Osman's free hand snapped to his temple. It never occurred to him they could be real. The qil of the antlers resting on his brow would be far too large to fit on his head without scraping the low ceilings of the baths. The Prince's antlers were a fearsome array of dagger-like spikes as tall as a broadsword.

What Osman's hand encountered wasn't even remotely like what his qil felt. He instead discovered a tiny little velvet-covered two-pointed antler smaller than a child's outstretched hand. Osman's mouth hung open as he explored their diminutive profile, feeling the qil of a phantom zit sprout on his nose.

"I... I–" Osman began to stammer.

"Aw, aren't you just the most adorable reindeer in the New Dawn parade?" Thorn mocked brotherly.

"It feels like they're ridiculous. Are they ridiculous?" Osman asked frantically. "Their qil is as large as the Prince's rack of antlers. A dozen and a half points each as large as a sword."

"We can discuss your inflated opinion of yourself another time." Thorn teased.

Thorn's words instantly transported Osman to the similar words he had used with Yanri, and his slack-jawed embarrassment turned to laughter. Thorn smiled and let out a slight chuckle that faded quickly as the surprise of Osman's antlers faded.

"So, the dagger?" Thorn asked, his voice now an even monotone. Osman presented it to him, hand still unconsciously drawn to the nubby antlers sprouted from his temples. After a moment and a quick casting, Thorn handed it back, "Protective is correct and not insubstantial. It will help you resist most damage, both physical and magical. It could be a big help if things go badly and you have to confront Cerena directly."

*You.* Osman's mind hung on the word. It was the plan, of course. There was no denying that was what they had agreed upon and discussed, but it felt so lonely to hear it. Thorn was going to get in and get Quentin, while Osman distracted Cerena and hopefully trapped her with the cursed replica of the Vermillion Blade. Osman would channel the Trickster, translocating himself to them in the dungeons. Then, utilizing the returning stone Naz had given Thorn years ago, they would escape to Oldstone. If anything went wrong, Thorn and Quentin should leave without him. That was the plan.

Thorn had turned his attention back to the packs, pulling out the tight-fitting tunic and leathers Gwen had dyed black for him. A dark pair of artificer goggles lay beside them.

Thorn handed Osman the quiver holding the false Vermillion Blade and the single apple. Without further acknowledgment, he said, "You'll need these."

"Thorn," Osman began, but the words caught in his throat as he saw his brother freeze in place and tense up. He wanted to say so much but could tell Thorn didn't want to hear it. "I'm sorry," Osman said and walked to the far end of the row of cots. He took out the Prince's dagger and looked at it. His hand went to his temple, but the little antlers had melded back into his flesh, his confidence no longer as indefatigable as it had been.

This didn't feel like balance. Maybe balance wasn't possible when it came to such moments. One side or the other would prevail, light or darkness. Good or evil.

Family or Fate.

# CHAPTER TWENTY-NINE

Year 889 pxf ~ Late Autumn

Osman awoke well over an hour before dawn. He saw Thorn's empty cot and looked to Balanon, who confirmed what Osman already knew— Thorn had left the sanctuary early to fulfill his part of the plan. Osman knew the unmended rift between him and Thorn potentially doomed them to failure, but he hoped the gambit that had so estranged them would be worth it and that he could at least at least save Thorn and Quentin, if not himself.

Osman ate the apple and soulchanneled his first form of the plan, eliciting a gasp from Balanon as he passed through the door into the streets of Arnadore.

As she awaited her prey, Cerena peered through the mist and darkness that had yet to disgorge Arnadore Keep into the light of dawn. She had flung the main gates wide and taken her position opposite them upon the battlements overlooking the courtyard, surveying her preparations. With a rueful smile on her lips, she mused that the Osman she faced today was not the sniveling besotted boy she had bedded fifteen years ago. That boy would have charged the keep, swords brandished heroically, to save his half-brother like a bards-tale hero as soon as she had thrown down the gauntlet. No doubt he was planning something equally doomed to failure, but at least this might offer her a little fun. Who knows, if Osman impressed her enough, she might chain him to a wall somewhere for her personal pleasure when this was all over with.

It still vexed Cerena that her eye could not penetrate whatever magics he was using to shroud his movements. Even in such close proximity, unprotected by the wards of the Uldani Isles, she had only been able to intuit his eavesdropping on her search for him and not truly detect him. Since then, so impenetrable was his cloak that if not for the two fools from the Orchard delivering his message, she would be completely unaware of his whereabouts.

The timing he had requested was interesting. Darkness was Cerena's domain, and the fog an ally. To meet here at dawn would mean he would have to traverse the city's streets in the pre-dawn darkness, where the creatures she had abandoned three years ago now ruled. Cerena smirked. Even years later, her feral creations cowed to her will and the command not to kill him outright; she needed Osman inside the gates.

While the full density of the fog blanketing Arnadore had not penetrated the keep's courtyard, enough piled along the walls, corners, and still places between the ruined outbuildings to serve her purpose. Her plan hinged on one single variable she couldn't control but was sure of nonetheless— Osman's altruism. Her patron's power, knowledge of the Vermillion Blade, and planning were unyielding facts in her favor, immune to anything Osman did. He only needed to bring the blade into the courtyard, and she could claim the only thing in existence able to exact the full vengeance she had planned for Toman Cour-Vermane.

Cerena looked over her shoulder to where she had bound Quentin to a post leaning precariously over the battlements. Below him were a dozen sharpened stakes. She could release his bonds with but a thought, letting him plummet to excruciating death by impalement. Quentin recoiled at her glance as though he could see through the glamor making her appear as she did when Osman loved her.

She barred her teeth and whispered, "Play your part, fool, and you will be rewarded. Disappoint me, and what happened to your friend will seem like a blessing." With a portion of the precious higher magic her patron miserly rationed to her, Cerena had empowered the illusion making the cretin called Lander appear to be Quentin. She hated to use her precious spells this way, but Osman had to be utterly convinced this was Quentin and that his half-brother was not still secured in a cell below the keep. As an extra measure, she had retrieved the silver tongue ring from Jenkins and placed it on Lander's finger in case he had to speak. Everything was in position; the final piece would soon fall into place, and then retribution would be hers.

Cerena could hear the sounds of her creatures harrying Osman outside the gates. A smug smile curled her lips at the thought of Osman stumbling out of the fog bloodied and exhausted before her, whimpering like a kicked pup. Cerena peered intently through the threshold of the keep, searching the miasma beyond. Slowly approaching, just entering the range of her innate arcane sight, she beheld the blinding magical signature of the Vermillion Blade. It arced through the thick gray mist, dispatching her minions with practiced swift efficiency. The fog still obscured Osman to both her naked and arcane eye, but the blade burned like a beacon.

Cerena couldn't help but lock her gaze upon the weapon she had coveted and needed so desperately getting closer step by step. She could feel the Cour-Vermane blood that had varnished its heartwood shaft for centuries calling out to her. *Just a little further, lover. Bring it to me,* kept repeating in her head. Cerena was poised to strike with fifteen years of hate and loathing as the shadowy figure wielding the Vermillion Blade stepped out of the fog, and just as quickly, all her plans shattered around her.

"*Impossible!*" Cerena shrieked as something ruptured disconcertingly deep behind her eye in the depths of her mind.

"You want the Vermillion Blade? Come and take it from its true master!" boomed out the voice of Talon Cour-Vermane as his imposing form stepped into the courtyard, clad in his full Knight Captain's plate armor with the gleaming Vermillion Blade held at the ready.

There was neither an illusion nor transmutative magic upon the figure that strode confidently to the courtyard's center. Cerena knew her eye could inherently detect even the most powerful of arcane subterfuge. Talon Cour-Vermane stood before her in the flesh.

"You're dead. We felt you die!" she screamed at her cousin.

"Not dead! Only free from the chains of our family." Talon paced confidently forward. "I never considered you a bigger fool than your brother, Cerena. Yet, here we are. Release Quentin!" commanded Talon, pointing the Vermillion Blade at her chest.

Cerena's mind scrambled to piece some semblance of a plan back together. Talon had won the blade in accordance with the ancient rites twice now. It was not as simple as ripping it away from someone not of Cour-Vermane blood with her patron's pact, as she had planned. However, as evidenced by his wielding it against her, Talon had again bent the weapon against its nature and will. Cerena had broken the blade free of his influence once before. She could do it again.

"Kill Him!" she screeched. Half a dozen of her more recent and deadliest creatures prowled out of the pockets of fog around the courtyard as the keep's gates slammed shut behind Talon. "You will not only die yourself, cousin. You've killed your precious Osman's brother as well." With a dramatic look and malicious smile, Cerena released 'Quentin's' bonds with a wave of her hand. His body fell with a sickening wet thunk onto the sharpened stakes below.

"No!" Talon screamed.

Assured that Talon had seen the result of her actions, Cerena touched a smoky gray gem on her wrist, flooding the courtyard with a bank of magical fog further bolstered by the environment around them.

Cerena knew she had to break Talon's will or at least weaken his concentration enough for the pact with her patron to rip the Vermillion Blade from his grasp. The boy's death would start that process, and her creations could hopefully overwhelm him sufficiently for her to strip the weapon from his control. She watched the brilliant crimson glow of the Vermillion Blade dance through the fog, all else obscured to the naked eye. As much as she wanted to see the full extent of the battle below, she needed to save her remaining higher magics for wresting the blade from Talon when the chance presented itself.

Cerena blindly shot bolts of energy into the fog at her best estimation of Talon's location based on the dancing Vermillion Blade but to no avail. Then she saw her opening, a slight stutter in the swinging arcs of the blade. Something had thrown Talon off balance. She reached out for her family's blood, for her birthright, for what she was due after all of her suffering under Toman's hand. She channeled the power of her higher magic into her call, beckoning the Vermillion Blade to come to her hand. She flooded the summons with her magical reserves, opening herself to her connection to her family's blood within the blade. Cerena ignored another disturbing pop behind her eye, this time accompanied by a sickening movement of internal structures where she knew no movement should be felt, and redoubled her efforts to bend her family's bond with the Vermillion Blade to her will.

The Vermillion Blade shuddered momentarily, then flew like an arrow loosed from a bow to her hand. Cerena snatched the glaive out of the air with a cry of triumph as the weapon welded itself firmly in her grasp.

As Thorn crept through the damp, narrow passage under Arnadore Keep, his mind kept returning to a single place. Somewhere above him, Talon Cour-Vermane was walking the earth once more. The flesh that was the culmination of Toman's heinous design, whose creation had begun with the death of Richen. A body that his father had groomed into a perverted version of the man Thorn was meant to be by gorging it on the life force of his beloved and Osman's father. And now, his soul brother was wearing the corpse of the life Thorn had left behind.

The plan would work. Cerena would never see it coming, and the subterfuge would be undetectable because the form Osman wore was Talon's flesh for all intents and purposes. But emotionally, Thorn couldn't overcome how violated he felt. Even if they did succeed and he finally was reunited with Richen, how would he ever look at Osman the same way again? Had he regained his true love only to lose his brother in the process?

Thorn came to the hidden door that gave access to the dungeons. He put his eye to the peephole but only saw darkness beyond. He closed his hooded lantern to the narrowest of slits and pulled the lever to release the hidden panel that concealed the passageway he had traversed.

Thorn slid back the panel. The acrid smell of chemicals, decay, urine, and feces assaulted his nose, making his eyes water. Thorn slipped out of the passage and into what should have been the guard's common area but was now fitted out for a different function. The room looked like a mix between an alchemy lab, a surgery, and one of Naz's arcane workrooms.

Thorn was thankful the dim light of his lantern did not illuminate more of the horrors that filled the myriad of containers or the blood and viscera-soaked tables menacingly fitted with manacles.

Looking down the hallway of cells he sought, Thorn could see the eyeshine of the juvenile creatures within staring back at him. He couldn't decide what was more unnerving, the sheer number of eyes or that none of the twisted animals behind their barred confines made even the slightest sound at his intrusion. Thorn crept forward and down the hallway of cells. The pitiful distorted creatures behind the bars cowering as he passed, some daring to let out only the tiniest of hopeless whimpers as his light moved by them.

Thorn hoped his hunch was correct that Cerena would put Quentin in the fully enclosed cell at the end of the hallway, barred by a heavy wooden door. As he crept closer, the sliver of light from his lantern caught the eyeshine of a pair of eyes at the end of the hallway nearly at the level of his own.

"Well, if it innit my old friend, the hedgeborn orchard twat," Jenkins said in a slurred voice.

Thorn could hear the sticky sound of wet flesh being pulled apart as the eyes in front of him began to rise higher and higher over his head. Far higher than Jenkins was tall. With the sound of bone against metal, something swiped the lantern out of Thorn's hand. It slammed into the floor with a clang, extinguishing the only open flame in sight and leaving him in total darkness.

Osman, channeling Talon's flesh, braced himself and stood ready in the courtyard as the fog engulfed him, his cry of "No!" still echoing off the courtyard walls. Osman kept reassuring himself. *It wasn't Quentin. It wasn't Quentin.* Osman had barely had time to look at the man who fell onto the spikes. In a strange twist of irony, he had to trust Cerena that the person she killed even *looked* like Quentin, as he had only seen him as an infant. Gwen had to be right. She *had* to be. Cerena wouldn't throw away her best bargaining chip so quickly. Osman just had to execute the plan.

The gray wall of fog that engulfed Osman must be from something Cerena had cast because it wasn't his. Just to be sure, he unleashed the similar spell they had stored in the replica of the Vermillion Blade before activating the curse rune. Tracing out the combination of patterns etched in the shaft, the curse and accompanying enchantment came to life. As planned, the weapon began to animate of its own accord. Osman leaped into action before any hidden predators Cerena summoned could close around him. Leaving the blade to do its work, Osman shimmered into the form of the Trickster, willing his destination into her instincts - *Thorn.*

Osman braced his innards against the onslaught of the world folding around him, but nothing happened. Osman tried another destination – *the dungeons.* Still nothing. Cerena's creatures were almost upon him, and Osman couldn't risk confronting any of them in the Trickster's fragile form. He blindly scrambled through the fog cloud, hoping they would attack the floating weapon that harried them instead of the live prey that was zig-zagging its way to cover.

Crackling magical explosions began to fill the courtyard around Osman as his borrowed instincts guided him. He dove under collapsed wagons and weaved through the ruins of the courtyard outbuildings. Snarling shadows leapt over him, and jaws snapped at his bushy tail as the animated weapon slashed and parried at its attackers from above. Osman's mind, still racing, tried to understand why the Trickster's ability couldn't reach Thorn inside the keep. Perhaps Cerena had magics strong enough to thwart them or, more likely, there were no open flames in the lower levels. If that was the case, what had happened to Thorn and his lantern? Something had gone wrong.

Behind him, Osman heard the clack of tooth on metal as one of the creature's jaws clamped down on the Vermillion Blade. His fur bristled and stood on end as arcane possibility built up throughout the fog around him like lightning about to strike. He heard the whoosh of the blade flying overhead and across the courtyard. A cry of triumph punctuated the resounding clap of the haft of the Vermillion Blade hitting Cerena's hand. Osman knew he had no time left. He had to find Thorn. Between one leap and the next, the Trickster became the Matriarch who was no stranger to hunting within blinding mists.

As he flew skyward, careful to remain in the densest part of the fog, Osman didn't need the Matriarch's sensitive ears to hear Cerena's call of triumph turn into a howl of fury. With a rapid succession of high-pitched screeches, his echolocation revealed the scene unfolding below.

Cerena was staring in rage at the weapon welded to her hand. Osman could hear through arcane attuned ears the curse stripping away the spells surrounding Cerena and spooling what remained of her more powerful magics out of her and binding it into a knotted skein. Cerena broke her concentrated stare at the cursed weapon and focused on the courtyard below. She leaped off the battlements and ran to the remains of the courtyard's old smithy in a limping sprint.

Osman knew he should flee and try to locate Thorn, but he couldn't pull himself away. He circled once on silent wings and let out another series of high-pitched calls, unable to leave without knowing Cerena's fate. His senses revealed Cerena as she tied a scrap of leather thong around her forearm, cinching it tight with a practiced skill. Cerena's form, as he knew it, was slowly dissolving as the curse continued to eat away at her magic. She picked up a rusty axe, laid the wrist of the hand welded to the false Vermillion Blade on the pitted anvil, and swung.

*Flee now!*

The Matriarch's gravelly command in his head pulled him out of the horror of what he was watching as much as the clang of axe blade on metal did. Cerena's head snapped to his location as though she also heard the Matriarch. Her face was a sick grotesquery of what it once had been. Osman heard her voice slither around him as the false Vermillion Blade clanged to the ground, her hand still attached.

*This isn't over, lover.*

# CHAPTER THIRTY



Thorn heard Jenkins' voice rattle in the darkness as it swallowed him, "Lil' hedgeborn all alone in the dark, with no gun guarding over him." A bony fist slammed into Thorn's side with enough force to knock him against the bars of the cages lining the hallway with a loud clang. As he slid to the floor, he heard the cell's occupants scurry away, along with the sound of a water trough being upended and its contents spilling across the floor as they fled.

Thorn was unable to see in the inky blackness. While he could easily create light magically, he knew even the simplest spell within Cerena's lair would be like a fly disturbing a spider's web, alerting her to his presence. It was also apparent that Jenkins could see perfectly through the darkness. Thorn was only lightly armed as he had stripped himself of all but the most mundane of arcane items to avoid Cerena's sight, leaving him only his enchanted hammer and the returning stone, but luckily, not all an artificer's tricks were magical.

Thorn leaped to his feet and ran up the hall, pulling his nearly opaque artificer's goggles over his eyes. Reaching a gloved hand into a small pouch at his waist, he scooped out a handful of metallic pellets and threw them in a wide arc toward the cell whose bars he had impacted. As they tinked against the metal bars and across the floor, when they came in contact with the spilled water, they ignited in strobes of blinding white flame.

Jenkins roared in pain at the flashing light cutting through the darkness, and Thorn got his first look at what he had become through his shaded goggles. Jenkins looked as though his skeleton had been stretched to twice its length without the consent of the surrounding flesh. Huge open rents marred his skin where it hadn't fallen away entirely. Sinew tight as bowstrings pulled oddly at bloated limbs hugely swollen with muscle as he tried to shield his eyes and staggered backward. The restrained movements of his twisted form combined with the strobing flashes from the burning metal made Jenkins look like a marionette with hopelessly tangled strings.

"I'll kill you, you hedgeborn shite," Jenkins spat, still covering his eyes with one distorted hand while swinging wildly with the other.

Thorn knew he didn't have long, but seeing Jenkins' sorry state, he almost hated to use the other item he had brought. His resolve began to falter as he pulled the sloshing bladder out of his pouch, feeling the weight in his hand.

"Hello? Is someone there? Help me, please!" a voice pleaded from through the closed door behind Jenkins. The voice was unmistakable. Every second he had spent with Richen all those years ago flashed before Thorn's eyes, and his hand moved of its own volition.

The bladder burst on Jenkins' chest with an evil hiss, the acid within finding every open wound and seeping deep into the exposed tissues. The rancor of Jenkins' rage transformed into pleading cries of anguish. The acid, which could strip a hundred years of rust off a mining mill in minutes, found little of notable resistance in Jenkins' body. Liquified flesh began to pour out of Jenkins' every orifice as acrid smoke and the sickly sweet aroma of burnt sugar and talc filled the corridor. The monstrosity that had been Jenkins fell to the floor, spasming in a puddle of his liquified remains.

The strobing flashes of the burning metal died out, and Thorn lifted his goggles. He stood still for a moment, listening to the darkness for signs of other threats. It felt like the world was holding its breath as Thorn struck a flame with his tinder and recovered his lantern. He walked forward like he was in a dream, the rest of the world disappearing around him, unbelieving of what possibly lay ahead. Thorn lifted the lantern and looked through the small barred window high in the door.

It was as though he had been hit by lightning. Features he never thought he would see again in this life looked up at him pulling every bit of air out of his lungs. Stormcloud eyes and raven-dark hair burned away every bit of darkness and gloom that surrounded him.

"Richen." The name escaped Thorn's lips before he could stop them.

The young man in the cell strained against manacles that chained him to the wall, a pleading look on his face. Osman had said he would be twenty-seven years old, but the person before Thorn was the twin of Richen as he last remembered him at the spring when they were celebrating Talon's seventeenth birthday and Richen was barely nineteen. A creeping unease began to fill Thorn. Was this person another of Cerena's deceptions? Thorn looked closer at the prisoner and saw his ears' subtle elven sculpted shape, revealing an Uldani heritage. That was not something Cerena would have conjured in an illusion had she known her prisoner's true identity. All caution thrown to the wind, a loud arcane knock echoed through the dungeon as the wooden door before him burst its locks and swung open.

"There're symbols on the walls," the reborn twin of his lost love said.

Thorn quickly looked and saw the cold black etchings on the stonework. Naz had always said he was better at breaking runes than making them, and speed was now the critical factor. Thorn brought up his small hammer and activated the enchantment, giving it the power of a maul. He swung it at the connection between the first rune and the second, shattering the etchings and stone along with it. He watched as the now unbalanced magic of the first two runes unraveled and overloaded the rest.

"We need to get you out of here," Thorn said as he used two more arcane knocks to break the locks on the manacles. Thorn moved to the door, shining the shrouded lantern down the hallway to see if it was still empty.

"You called me Richen. My mother always told me that was a secret name I should never tell anyone. Only one person knows that name —the Falcon Knight who exists only in my dreams," the prisoner said, suspicion marring his expression.

Thorn crossed back to where his first and only love stood. "I may not seem it, but I am your Falcon Knight, and I promised the Gods themselves that I would find you. Always."

"*Always,*" Richen echoed back to Thorn, hand going to his lips as though he was surprised that he had said it.

"You are right, though. We should call you Quentin. That's your name, right? We can't let anyone discover your other name." Thorn said as he grabbed Quentin's wrist and pulled him through the door. They were halfway up the hallway when the dim light of his lantern revealed a shadowy figure as it turned the corner out of the makeshift laboratory and began limping down the hallway of cells toward them.

"Well, now what do we have here," echoed Cerena's voice, clenched in anger. "A little bird has come to steal my worm." With a wave of her hand, all the torches in the dungeon burst to life, revealing her true face.

Thorn couldn't hold back the gasp when he saw the ruined visage of his once beautiful cousin. Her cascading curls now fell as dead-hangs of lank graying straw. A smile that had lit up rooms was but a cruel slash filled with sharpened shark's teeth. Most disturbing was her lidless left eye that eclipsed the whole side of her face like an overripe pumpkin of the Drowned Moon rife with the veins of spreading rot. The ruptured socket and raw burn-scarred skin surrounding the obscenity of her eye barely held in its bulbous weight. The malevolent eye scanned the room of its own accord, independent of her right eye, which stayed locked on Thorn and Quentin.

"Cerena, you don't have to–" Thorn began, but his words evaporated as a long amphibian-like tongue stretched out of Cerena's mouth to lick and moisten the vulgarity of her swollen eye.

"You have no right to say what I *have* to do," Cerena snapped as the tongue slipped back into her mouth. "What I've already done, what I've sacrificed and endured, is beyond anything you can comprehend, *boy*." Thorn now saw the dripping, ragged stump of Cerena's right arm and fully noted the odd twist of her gait. It was as though her hips had been broken repeatedly at some point in the past and poorly set to heal. Her left arm lifted, and she pointed a single finger at Thorn and began to chant. Her swollen eye spun from its roving to lock on its target and began to glow with an otherworldly green light from the depths of its murky orb.

Even her distance from him could not dull the signature of the powerful magic Thorn felt coalescing around Cerena. Thorn scrambled backward, pushing Quentin in front of him, trying to reach the cover of Quentin's cell. Thorn kept his eyes on Cerena, only daring to glance at their destination as they ran, knowing they would never make it in time. The skin around her bulging eye stretched and distended like something beneath was trying to push through. Cerena's chant slowed and became labored screams as she worked to complete the spell.

For a moment, Thorn thought Cerena had sprouted wings from her ears as the giant mist owl slammed into the back of her head and tumbled talons over beak through the air down the hallway towards them. The somersaulting mass of gray feathers transformed into arms, legs, and a set of tiny velvet antlers as Osman landed in a three-point stance between Thorn and Cerena, bone dagger drawn just as the spell she was casting finished.

# CHAPTER THIRTY-ONE



The crackling green ray of energy leaped from Cerena's finger, arcing down the hallway to where Osman had interposed himself between it and its target. The beam burned through the bone dagger, notching its blade, but its trajectory was deflected just enough to pierce Osman's right shoulder instead of hitting him in the chest. The beam left a gaping hole where the flesh it contacted had disintegrated entirely.

"No!" Cerena shrieked. She limped down the hallway, remaining hand extended in a claw. Osman heard her muttering under her breath as she drew closer, her oversized eye glowing brighter as she spoke. "Give me more. I must kill them. The blade will be mine. I *need* it!"

Osman turned and harried Thorn and Quentin into the cell, slamming the door on them as he yelled, "Go! Get him out of here. *Now*!" Osman spun to face Cerena, whose progress toward him had halted. Her remaining hand now clutched the side of her bloated eyeball.

"What are you doing?" Cerena demanded. "No! Not this! You promised me! You promised!" Her words did not seem to be directed at Osman as she writhed in place, hand and stump roaming across her face, leaving a trail of blood. Her disturbing dance suddenly froze. Cerena's arms dropped to her sides as her normal eye focused on Osman.

"Osman, save me," she pleaded as she lurched forward, falling to her knees and stretching her remaining hand out to him.

Osman looked at the pitiful corrupted creature his first love had become, his joints feeling like they were rusting in place as the qil of his pity swelled within him. Cerena's plea knotted in his stomach as the ghost of their love rose from its grave to haunt him. His hand instinctively reached out towards hers even though the distance was too far for them actually to touch. As she looked up at him pleading for help, Osman could almost see the beauty of her face that once entranced him. Then he heard the sickening rip of tearing flesh.

A tentacle wormed its way out of her left temple, followed by another. Cerena's teeth shifted under her flesh away from her mouth to the cracking of bone. From out of her nostril, another tentacle emerged. The three writhing stalks pointed at Osman, their ends splitting open, revealing the eyes hidden within. Cerena let out a mouthless scream from deep in her throat that faded and gurgled into silence, her remaining human eye dulling to lifelessness.

Osman stumbled backward, choking back bile as three more eye stalks joined the others. As though being birthed, Cerena's bloated eye pulled free from its ruined socket and floated into the air, bringing her teeth and jaw with it. The tentacle eye stalks spread out like a halo around the central eye, focusing on Osman. Right arm limp at his side from the wound in his shoulder, Osman faced the monstrosity before him. He held the bone dagger before him as the qil of glass slicing into his palms manifested in his hands—death was near.

The creature's eye flashed deep green, and Osman watched in horror as the bone dagger in his hand reverted to a plain iron dagger, the same as it had been when gifted to him by Lady Cour-Vermane. He then tried to channel the Judge's form and found his flesh was no longer malleable and locked in its current form. All magic seemed to drain out of him as the swollen eye peered in his direction. The creature's strange mouth constructed from pieces of Cerena's jaw seemed to smile at Osman in the same way a cat grins at a trapped mouse.

With nowhere else to go, Osman dove under the floating eye and rolled on his good shoulder to his feet, spinning to face the creature. Once out of the creature's eyeline, Osman felt the iron blade in his hand revert back to the bone knife, but no sooner than it had, the creature swung around on its axis. He was again caught in its gaze, leaving him drained of any arcane ability and his dagger no longer enchanted.

Osman dropped to the ground as a ray of freezing energy blasted over his head from one of the smaller writhing eyestalks. The edge of his left palm landed in a slimy puddle of goo, and he felt the bite of acid into his flesh. Osman scraped the iron dagger through the puddle and flung a wad of the caustic slime at the creature's central eye. The floating eye spun to avoid the attack, shifting away its nullifying gaze. Osman summoned his hunger, feeling the iron in his hand turn cold, and his teeth elongate into sharpened fangs.

Osman lunged up and forward, the Judges dagger in his outstretched hand before him, teeth barred. He was surprised when the blade scraped across the bony underside of the eye instead of plunging into soft flesh, but his open jaws connected with one of the eyestalks. Osman bit down hard, his sharpened fangs sliced through the rubbery tissue, severing it cleanly off the creature's bloated form. Oily ichor filled his mouth as it drained from the severed eye stalk.

The creature's silent scream ripped through Osman's mind as it spun to capture him in its gaze. However, Osman could see its motion was more sluggish than before, the Judge's dagger having bit deep enough to impart its slowing stasis on the floating eye. Osman jumped into the air, using the bars of the cell behind him to leapfrog around the eye. Two of the creature's eyestalks followed his motion, now wary of Osman's antics. Although he had escaped the central eye's gaze, the two smaller eyes attacked with their beams of arcane energy.

He avoided one beam as it flew by him like a battering ram, slamming into the cell door where Quentin had been kept. Unfortunately, his dodge put him in the path of the other, which struck his incapacitated right arm. Osman felt the arm hit by the beam grow heavier and watched in dismay as it greyed and turned to stone.

Shards of a seven-dimensional language sliced through Osman's mind, filled with covetous need. The desire was not directly for the Vermillion Blade, but for the twisted fates it left in its wake. Destinies like Osman's that it had consumed then excreted as a corrupted parody of its original path. This aberrant creature fed on the kinetic power of disrupted and shattered lives.

A loud bang echoed down the hallway as the heavy door of Quentin's cell that the eye beam had hit fell off its hinges. Osman felt like his heart dropped out of his chest as the dust settled. There stood Thorn and Quentin pressed up against the cell's far wall. Seeing Quentin there, the second tiny heartbeat that beat next to his own, the qil of fatherhood, grew to take the place of his own heart that had fallen low. In his hand, the icy cold of the Judge's dagger turned to the soft glow of the Trickster's.

In the space between one heartbeat and the next, Osman threw the ornamental dagger toward the ceiling, ricocheting it off the stone there. Before it even finished its flight, Osman willed himself to it, just as the gaze of the floating eye would have landed upon him. The world folded around him, and Osman was then floating over the creature. He slammed the dagger into the top of the eye and channeled the Judge's soul into his body.

Osman's form erupted into the massive form of the Judge, and he drove his saber fangs into the bloated, bloodshot central eye. They plummeted to the floor, Osman's claws ripping eyestalks from the creature's body as they fell. With the sickening squelch of a popped boil, the Judge's mass flattened the monstrosity, smearing its remains further across the stones with his heavy paws.

Osman blinked his eyes over to veilsight to confirm no living essence remained of the creature. Its corpse was a black stain upon the background of natural life that thrived in dark places. Looking at the cells, he also saw the perverted life forces of Cerena's experiments cowering in the corners. Osman lamented their plight but couldn't let them become the focus of his concern. He shimmered back into himself in a flurry of ice. His petrified arm hung heavy in its socket. Out of habit, his good hand searched his belt and found the comforting frosty presence of the Judge's dagger.

Osman walked weakly past the corpse of Cerena, averting his eyes, and into the cell where Thorn and Quentin waited.

"Why didn't you go?" Osman asked.

"It didn't look like she had much fight left in her," Thorn replied. "So we waited for you. We were watching through the bars when that thing showed up, and when it looked at us, the returning stone went dead." Thorn held up the rune-covered stone, which had gone dark. "It's like the charge has been drained out of it."

Osman reached out his functional arm toward them to usher them out of the cell. Quentin surprised him by springing forward and grabbing him around his chest in a powerful hug. Osman, stunned, wrapped his good arm around Quentin, and the thumping qil of a second heartbeat, now nearly a match for his own, beat deep in his chest.

"Thank you," Quentin said breathlessly. "Who are you? Why did you save us?"

Osman looked to Thorn, his voice catching in his throat. "Just Osman. Let's get you out of here."

They climbed out of the bowels of Arnadore Keep and back up toward the courtyard. Ahead of them, the fog, both magical and mundane, had cleared from inside the walls, but Osman could see in the distance it had yet to burn off entirely outside the gates. Just as they crossed under the threshold of the portcullis separating the inner keep from the courtyard, Quentin came to a stop.

Osman turned to check on him, finding Quentin's body trembling violently, feet seemingly frozen to the ground, the whites of his eyes showing clearly around his stormy irises. His gaze was locked on the ruined smithy across the cobblestones from them. Osman drew his dagger and readied himself awkwardly, unaccustomed to the dead weight of his petrified right arm. Simultaneously beside him, Thorn prepared himself in a crouch, armed with his hammer, but Osman could see a slight tremor afflicted his weapon hand.

That is when it became clear the reeking smell hitting Osman's heightened senses emanated from a single source, not just random scents on the wind—sulfur, brimstone, and rot. A terrifying canine head with burning red eyes rose from behind the rusted anvil of the smithy, seemingly carved from solid shadow. It locked eyes with each of the three of them individually, marking them with its gaze, but displayed no immediate signs of aggression toward them—It already had its prize. For within its jaws was the replica of the Vermillion Blade.

"No! Don't let it get away!" Thorn screamed. The hellish canine turned and dashed toward the gate at the sound of Thorn's voice. Its form dissolved into smoke and shadow along with the weapon it carried before even reaching the outer gate.

"What? I don't understand," Osman asked, confused. "It's just the fake one. What does it matter if that thing has it?" Looking at both Thorn's and Quentin's faces drained of color, he added, "And we are in no condition to fight."

Thorn ignored him and ran over to the smithy. Osman followed as quickly as he could, sheathing his dagger and supporting the weight of his stone arm with his opposite hand.

When Osman arrived, Thorn was looking around frantically as though his search might disprove what they all had just seen. "Gods, please no," Thorn said as his knees gave out, leaving him sitting on the low wall of the open forge.

Osman drifted up beside him with Quentin close behind. Quentin was the first to speak. "What was that thing? I have never felt so terrified in my life. It was like every part of my being was screaming." Quentin asked.

As he looked up, Thorn's nineteen-year-old face looked like it carried the full weight of the half-century he had actually lived. He paused like he was trying to correctly formulate a response and then gave up in exhaustion, "A creature like that is what killed you," he replied to Quentin. "My father sent it. Why now? Only the Nine Hells know, but–" Thorn closed his eyes in abject defeat, "Now he has my blood. Shed freshly less than two days ago."

Thorn met first Quentin's and then Osman's eyes, "Toman is about to know his son is alive." Thorn's eyes remained glued to Osman, and Osman could see the thoughts churning in Thorn's head. Slowly, Thorn's expression slid from resignation to a rueful disdain that he inexorably linked to Osman.

Startled by the venom in Thorn's gaze, Osman still managed to shake off the tension between them. It would have to be dealt with later. Osman urgently stated, "We need to go. Now!" He reached out with his good hand to pull Thorn from his seated position, but Thorn refused it. Rebuffed, Osman sighed. The weight of his guilt and regret forced his gaze to the ground as he turned to leave, following Thorn. A slight sparkle near the anvil caught his eye as he went.

Cerena's severed hand lay on the ground, a familiar charm bracelet still wrapped around her wrist. Osman couldn't help but notice the perfectly manicured nails decorating Cerena's fingers. Despite the horror she had become, this part of her was still as he remembered. Osman couldn't help but wonder if Cerena saw them the same way. He could almost picture her elegant fingers wrapped around a wine glass at the Blossom Gala where they first met.

Osman looked up, realizing he had fallen behind Thorn and Quentin, and they were almost out the keep's gate. With the petrified arm weighing him down and now pulling painfully on his torso, Osman would be hard-pressed to catch up. He considered channeling one of the spirits within him and taking its form, but he most likely had only one channeling remaining without a cost to himself or his companions. Not knowing what tomorrow might bring and feeling the need for communication later could be paramount, he opted to save it unless it was a dire need.

It was Quentin who turned and slowed to come to assist him. Thorn's mind was so far away even Quentin leaving his side did not break him out of his tormented thoughts. With Quentin's help, the two caught up with Thorn, and the three continued on in silence.

Thankfully, the creatures that had harried Osman on the way to the keep and within its walls kept their distance as they navigated back to Balanon's sanctuary. Osman could feel them lurking on their periphery, but by luck or some greater force at work, they did not attack.

The fog had entirely burned off when they arrived at the ruins of Elery Square, revealing a blue Autumn sky the likes of which bards could sing about, but none of them lifted their eyes to witness it.

# CHAPTER THIRTY-TWO



Balanon, seeing their condition, immediately went to work on their cuts, bruises, and, in Thorn's case, broken ribs. The half-elven surgeon worked efficiently and quickly, Osman demanding that he treat Quentin and Thorn before addressing his own wounds.

Osman's mind replayed the last few days as he waited—everything that had led them here and everything he could have done differently to have it not end like this. No matter his intent or action, it felt as though destiny planned to see him betray those he cared about most. Everything he had learned through his journey about his father and Talon confirmed the truth of it. They both had been doing everything they could to avoid hurting him, and he repaid them by making their sacrifices harder.

Osman could see that he brought only strife and pain wherever he went, even to Yanri and Thorn when it was the last thing he intended to do. They were to be a new start at happiness and a chance at the life denied to him in his youth. He had almost gotten Yanri killed, and the wounds he inflicted on Thorn were far more indelible than any creature or poison could deliver.

Osman even questioned if he had betrayed Cerena. Not only in those final moments when she begged him to save her but much earlier as well, when she began her plummet into darkness. His first real love had become just as twisted and corrupted as he had made his own fate.

The memory of the creature touching his mind returned to Osman. How it hungered for the misery the Vermillion Blade left in its wake. Was he so different from that cursed weapon? A voice interrupted Osman's train of thought.

"Unfortunately, *that* is beyond my current capabilities," Balanon repeated, motioning to his petrified arm.

Shaking off his self-loathing Osman replied, "I thought as much. I believe the plan is to still head to Oldstone if the returning stone recovers its charge. Or we'll find other means. Hopefully, the dwarves or Thorn's friend Nazge can revert it, if it's possible at all."

Balanon tended Osman's other wounds, stitching them shut and treating them to ward off infection. As he worked, Osman looked across the open room to the row of cots where Thorn and Quentin sat across from each other on separate beds. There was an awkwardness between them. Still shaken by the shadow hound and what it meant, Thorn kept frantically trying to connect with Quentin as though he were Richen. When Quentin would rebuff him, Osman heard Thorn repeat another variation of "You don't understand."

Osman could see Thorn desperately needed the comfort of Richen in this moment. He was as shaken as he had ever seen, but that wasn't an excuse to ignore Quentin's words or refuse to accept that he was *not* Richen.

Quentin finally got up and walked away. He descended into the drained pool where Balanon was working on Osman to see how he was.

"How are you doing?" Quentin asked.

"I'll live, and I've had worse," Osman said, nodding his head at the hard, smooth stone of his right arm between them. He looked at Quentin, who leaned against the high treatment table where Osman was sitting with his legs dangling, opposite where Balanon was still working on his acid-burned palm. It was the first time Osman really had a chance to get a good look at Quentin.

His human soul shone through his visage brightly, but Osman spotted the signs of his other lineage even beyond the subtle hint of an Uldani curve to his ears. The slight uplift to the corner of his eyes was from Anson, and the shape of his upper lip was identical to Yanri's. He thought the familiar shape of the bridge of Quentin's nose reminded him of his father but then recognized it as his own. Quentin caught him in his examination.

"What is it?" Quentin asked.

"Nothing," Osman said, trying to play it off lightly, but the concern about his influence tainting another life is what truly held his tongue.

"No, that was definitely something," Quentin observed. "Do you recognize me? Not the way he does," Quentin's eyes darted over to where Thorn was, "but some other way?" He continued, "I don't look like my mom, I don't look like a Lyrian, I don't fully look like an Uldani or elf. Thorn says I'm Richen, but that 'me' is a dream, not the real world," Quentin said with confusion and frustration, leaning against Osman's stone arm and then recoiling like he had hurt him.

"It's okay," Osman said, "it doesn't hurt, and it's plenty sturdy. At least this means it's good for something." Quentin leaned back over on Osman's statue-like arm. His presence was a balm and perhaps a chance to do things right this time.

"Look, I don't have all the answers, but I will tell you everything I know. Even the parts that are hard to hear. But it's a long story, and we all need some rest first." Osman gently added, "Thorn is in a really bad place right now. I saw what his father did to him, how he used him. Violated him. And all of it, everything that he thought was behind him, is now back. Parts of it in this very room. He lost Richen due to his father's plans, and now he's afraid he will lose you." Osman added, "He's been trying to find you again for his whole life."

Feeling Quentin tense up beside him, Osman interjected, "That doesn't mean you owe him anything. You don't even have to hear his side of things if you don't want to. I'll stand beside you if that's your choice. But here's something I've learned, but wish I had known sooner." Osman paused until Quentin raised his eyes to his own. Thinking of Anson, he said, "Life is not a painting; it's a sculpture. You'll never understand it completely unless you change your perspective and see things from all the different angles. Even the difficult ones."

Balanon finished wrapping Osman's hand, and Osman reached across his body to pat Quentin's head comfortingly, noting as he leaned on his stony shoulder that even as Quentin, he kept his raven dark hair short in the dagger-cut locks of a blacksmith.

"I'll try," Quentin said. "But no promises," sounding younger than his years. He sat up and looked at Osman. "You know you are pretty good at this." The beating qil of fatherhood bloomed in Osman's chest and was not dispelled when Quentin added quickly and awkwardly, "You know, this whole rescue thing."

Quentin hopped off the table and walked back over to Thorn, who was hunched over on the cot, holding his head in his hands. Quentin laid his hand on Thorn's shoulder and sat down beside him.

"It is only fitting that you see him as family. He is your child after all." Balanon said to Osman. Osman started at the statement as Balanon continued, "I've practiced medicine for six centuries, and there is no hiding that your blood flows in his veins. It doesn't matter how it got there, but he's yours." Balanon laid his hand on Osman's shoulder, "Be there for him." Osman opened his mouth to speak, but Balanon allayed his protests before Osman said them. "On whatever terms the two of you choose."

Osman had slept fitfully, skipping like a stone on a pond between sleep and wakefulness. A tentative shake on his shoulder pulled Osman out of his doze. Instantly alert, he sat up and felt the weight of his petrified arm pull harshly on the flesh it attached to. Thorn was hovering over him in the dim light of the sanctuary. Further away, Osman could hear the rhythmic breathing of Quentin a few cots over.

"I need to talk to you, brother," Thorn whispered, saying the last word as though he was questioning if he could still use that term.

"Of course," Osman whispered back.

Thorn motioned with his head to the far side of the sanctuary where one of the private alcoves of the old baths still remained. They padded in silence across the room, Thorn leading the way. Within an instant of arriving, Thorn turned and began to speak.

"I'm sorry. I've been–" Thorn stumbled to find his next word.

"Thorn," Osman interrupted, "No, I should be apologizing to you. I didn't consider all you have been through to be here—to be *you*. Even before the hound, what it would mean, bringing Talon back."

Thorn nodded in acceptance of Osman's words, then spoke. "I have to know," Thorn swallowed hard before he continued, "was it *all* of him when you brought him back? Was it like the Judge? Was a soul there?" Thorn's voice quavered as he asked, as though he feared the answer.

"No," Osman replied truthfully. "Just his body. That's why I knew I could do it. After he died and the chains shattered, you shed the augmented flesh of Talon Cour-Vermane that your father had burdened you with. Through the connection with my father, it flowed into me. I just called it forth. It was only me in that body." Osman tentatively put his still-usable hand on Thorn's shoulder and said, "You've only ever had one soul—Thorn's."

Thorn sighed in relief and said, "You didn't let me finish before. I was wrong to be mad at you. You're not responsible for what my father did to me or the choices your father made that brought Talon's form to you." Osman began to cut him off, but he continued, "I was the one who added my blood to Naz's trap. That my father has it now is on me, not you." Thorn looked across the room to the sleeping form of Quentin, "Everything you have done has been to help me get him back. But I need to ask for one thing more."

Thorn looked at Osman and took a deep breath, his body trembling. "I need to see him." Thorn's eyes were full of trepidation but also resolute in the request. "I want to see Talon. Through my eyes, not in a mirror's reflection through his."

Seeing how hard this was for Thorn, Osman didn't ask for a second confirmation or think twice about the cost. He closed his eyes and felt chains wrapping around him and choking off his breath as he channeled the flesh of Talon Cour-Vermane. Osman opened his eyes and looked down on the relatively diminutive form of Thorn standing before him.

Thorn reached up and touched Talon's face. His hand lingered in the hair that was so like his own. Thorn's eyes drifted down to the breastplate of the Knight Captain of Arnadore. His fingers traced the embossed crest of Eleryon and found familiar dents and scratches as he became lost in memory. Osman stayed silent, standing stoically in the borrowed flesh of the man he once knew.

Thorn looked up into Osman's eyes, seeing only Talon, and said, "I don't even recognize you anymore as who I was. You truly are a dead part of me. I don't fear you somehow rising within me and eclipsing who I truly am. I'm not you. I never was." Thorn let out a sharp exhale, and relief danced across his face.

"Osman, don't ever bring him back again."

Osman dropped the channel instantly, face marred with guilt, still in the stoic stance he had assumed while channeling Talon. Thorn stepped into Osman, surrounding him with his arms, his breath pumping like a bellows and body still trembling. Osman slowly returned the hug with his one functioning arm and then surrendered to it with a stuttered exhale of the breath he had been holding.

Thorn gently pulled out of the embrace and studied Osman's face, then said, "You've been defining yourself as a betrayer for so long, brother. To your heritage, your father, to me, and all those around you." Thorn's eyes searched deep into Osman's. "We all cause pain, sometimes. Even when we don't mean to. But the joy and happiness you give so freely and bring to all those around you is the reason why you are loved, Osman." Thorn laid his hand on Osman's heart.

"You're not a betrayer, Krolh'dran. You're family. We all are. And you are forgiven."


THE END

# EPILOGUE



*Year 889* PXF *~ Early Winter*

Toman Cour-Vermane walked through the ruin of his niece's lab below Arnadore Keep. The stench was unbearable, but it did not affect Toman in the slightest as he strode down the hallway, looking for what had drawn him here. The creatures that remained alive in their cells cried out to Toman, their desperation overcoming—or perhaps attracted to—the fear they would typically have in his presence.

With a blink, Toman obliged their cries and snuffed out their lives, inhaling their corrupted spirits into himself. He walked past the ruptured remains of the bloated aberration of the tentacled eye with the smug disdain one would hold for a tick feeding off a corpse in a ditch. Toman then arrived at what he came for.

He looked down at the corpse of Cerena and thrust his hand through the veil, clasping her natal chain. He let unlife flow from his hand, down the chain links, and into her flesh. He waited for a gasping inhale to fill her lungs before brutally kicking her in the ribs, eliciting a satisfying crack of breaking bone.

"Get up," Toman commanded. "Your vow to return my son back to me and house Cour-Vermane is not yet fulfilled." He turned and walked back up the hallway from whence he came as the corpse rose to its feet. A single bloody tear fell from the corpse's remaining eye as Cerena shambled behind her master.

*To be continued in*

*Book III of the A Time of Falcons and Roses Series:*

*Oath of the Unbroken Storm*

# ACKNOWLEDGEMENTS

My deepest heartfelt thanks to my family, friends, and readers who have supported me as I chase this dream. I could not have done this without each and every one of you.